Fawcett Crest Books
by Helen MacInnes:

MESSAGE FROM MALAGA

Helen MacInnes

FAWCETT CREST • NEW YORK

A Fawcett Crest Book
Published by Ballantine Books
Copyright © 1971 by Helen MacInnes

Library of Congress Catalog Card Number: 79-160406

ISBN 0-449-20398-0

This edition published by arrangement with
Harcourt Brace Jovanovich

Alternate Selection of the Book of the Month Club,
February 1972

Selection of the Doubleday Mystery Guild, August 1972
Selection of the Bargain Book Club, August 1972

Manufactured in the United States of America

First Fawcett Crest Edition: September 1972
First Ballantine Books Edition: September 1983

For my friend Julian
a man who has never given up the ship

The characters in this novel, and their actions, are purely imaginary. Their names and experiences have no relation to those of actual people, living or dead, except by coincidence. But much of the background of the story is based on fact. And Department Thirteen does exist.

HELEN MAC INNES

Message
from
Málaga

1

So this, thought Ferrier, was El Fenicio, an open courtyard behind a wineshop, a rectangle of hard-packed earth on which rows of small wooden tables and chairs had been set out to face a bare platform of a stage. Its four walls were the sides and backs of two-storied houses, old, faceless except for a few windows, tightly shuttered, and a single balcony, dark, withdrawn. Lights were sparse and haphazard, a few bare bulbs attached high on the walls, as coldly white as the moon overhead, but softened by the clusters of leaves and flowers that cascaded from the vines and ramblers climbing over the worn plaster. There was the lingering scent of roses still heavy with the heat of day. There was the smell of jasmine as ripe as sun-warmed peaches, fluctuating, tantalizing. And there was the music of a solitary guitar, music that poured over the listeners at the tables, surged up the faded walls, escaped into the silence of night and a brilliance of stars. It seemed, Ferrier imagined, as if the perfume of the flowers suited its mood to the ebb and flow of sound, weakening or strengthening when the guitar's chords diminished or soared. His touch of fancy amused him: he had come a long way from the tensions and overwork of Houston, a longer way than the thousands of miles that lay between Texas and Andalusia. He hadn't felt so happily unthinking, so blissfully irresponsible in months. He lifted his glass of Spanish brandy in Jeff Reid's direction to give his host a silent thanks—not for the brandy, it was too sweet for Ferrier's taste, but for this beginning to what promised to be a perfect night.

It was all the more perfect because he hadn't quite expected anything like El Fenicio. "Some flamenco now?" Reid had asked at the end of a late and long dinner. "The real stuff. None of those twice-nightly performances for the tourist trade, along the Torremolinos strip. I know a little place down by the harbor. Friday is good there. It will be packed by one o'clock. We'd better drop in around twelve-thirty and make sure of my favorite table. You like flamenco, don't you?" Ferrier nodded, pleased by the fact that Jeff had remembered his taste in music, but a bit doubtful, too. He was thinking of the little places down by the harbor that he had seen in Barcelona, in Palma. What difference would there be in another seaport town, like Málaga? The little place meant a small dark box, a hundred degrees in temperature and unventilated, with an aging tenor in a bulging black jacket, puffy white hands clasped before him in supplication to an unseen mistress, his thick neck straining to bring out the high notes of the Moorish-sounding scales but only producing a sad cracked wail. The little place meant a nervous guitarist disguising mistakes in a flourish of sound. It meant one dancer, elderly, thickset, trying to compensate for lost technique by the height she twitched her flounced skirt up over a naked thigh. It meant three or four fat women dressed in screaming pink or virulent green, the shiny satin of their tight dresses as artificial as their purple smiles, as furrowed as their tired faces, as hard as the jagged mascara around hopeless eyes, who sat together at a table near the staircase (there was always a narrow staircase climbing up one wall of the room) and measured the rough mixture of foreign seamen and nervous tourists who imagined they were seeing a bit of authentic Spain. The little place was too often a sad place, of failures and might-have-beens, of vanished hope and flourishing despair. But Ferrier had kept his doubts to himself, and thank God for that, although he had made a feeble try to sidetrack Jeff: "There's no need to make an effort to entertain me. I'm perfectly happy—" Reid had cut in with his warm smile, "Well—just to please me—will you come? I haven't yet missed a Friday night at El Fenicio." So Ferrier retreated with a joke. "What?" he asked. "No wonder you never find time to get back to the States for a visit. Is this part of your job?" Reid looked at him sharply, then laughed. "Oh, a businessman has to have some compensations."

And now, as Ian Ferrier listened to the guitar—no microphones here, no electronic jangle—and wondered what the music was (perhaps an original composition based on a *malagueña*?) and then decided it didn't matter—all that mattered was the sound that caught one's heartbeat, sent one's pulse quickening—he had a strange attack of conscience. He glanced at Reid, lost in his own thoughts like all the silent listeners in the crowded courtyard, and realized that if anyone had changed in these last eight years, since Reid and he had met, it was not Jeff; it was he who had altered most. At thirty-seven, you've become a self-centered bastard, he told himself: you want everything your own way, don't you? And if he blamed this moment of truth on the combination of guitar, scent of flowers, night sky glittering above him, he had only to remember the way he had almost ruined the journey to Málaga with his reservations and doubts and afterthoughts. Those damned afterthoughts . . . At one point, he had almost canceled this whole trip.

That afternoon, he had driven across the mountains, leaving fabulous Granada behind him, and headed dutifully for the Mediterranean. (Dutifully? That was the word. He wasn't bound for a lazy beach and blue water, or a picturesque fishing village.) His emotions had been not only mixed but also definitely roiled. He was having an attack of second thoughts, and they were always an irritation, especially when it was too late to do anything about them. He had only himself to blame, of course: this was what he got for imagining he could snatch a visit to Granada in between a week of professional business (and how did that creep into his vacation time, anyway?) and a couple of days with an old friend. It had seemed a good idea, back in Houston, to write Jeff Reid that he was coming to Europe, that part of his time would be spent in Spain, that naturally of course most definitely he'd make a point of dropping in on Málaga—if that suited Jeff. It did. Jeff had replied that eight years had been far too long since their last meeting, and the exact date was set. Perhaps that was what depressed him now: he had quite enough of exact dates and deadlines in his present job with the Space Agency. Or perhaps it was just that a glimpse of Granada was too damned unsettling. He kept feeling—well, not exactly cheated. Frustrated? It was like being passionately kissed by a beautiful woman who slipped out of your arms and vanished.

He had routed that attack of gloom by concentrating on some high-speed driving over a winding, narrow, but well-made road that cut along the top of hillsides. (Okay, okay, forget that Málaga was listed in the guidebook as a bustling, modernized town; just remember you wanted to see Jeff Reid again.) The Spaniards, wise birds, were having their long siesta in this intense heat of day; the road was empty for twenty miles at a stretch, the village streets were as deserted as if plague had struck them, the vast stretches of fields and olive groves that sloped into great valleys lay abandoned to the sun. He had Spain to himself. And as a backdrop, there were the jagged Sierra Nevada peaks, crowned with snow even in June, sawing into one of Spain's best blue skies. Then he came down from the hills and the pine trees to an abrupt edge of coastline, where terraced vineyards ended in cliffs

that dropped steeply into sea. He liked that. He liked the sugar-
cane fields, too, and a couple of ruined Moorish castles and the
fishing villages. Until he began to see some high-rise hotels and
French restaurants. Progress, progress . . . His depression returned full whack as he drove into Málaga and found himself—
siesta time now being over—in the same thick syrupy congestion
of city traffic that he could enjoy anywhere in America. Was this
what he was traveling abroad for?

Reid had sent him a rough sketch of the district where he
lived. "You'll find me easily," he had written. "An old Air Intelligence type like you doesn't need instructions how to get anywhere." So the directions, if concise and clear, were minimal.
The crisscross of smaller streets, no doubt an unnecessary complication to an old Air Reconnaissance type like Jefferson Reid,
was left unmarked. At last, almost an hour later than he had
hoped, Ferrier found the place. He stared at the large house, retreating behind palm trees and flowering shrubs, a replica of its
neighbors in their equally lush gardens along this placid street.
A villa, no less. And there must be servants to go with it. Good
God, had Jeff Reid changed as much as all this? Was he really a
settled businessman, with a position to keep up, living abroad,
avoiding some taxes and all the headaches of present-day America? It certainly looked as if the sherry business was thriving—
Reid was head of the Spanish branch of an American wine-
importing firm. Well, thought Ferrier, as long as Jeff hasn't
changed into a complacent fat cat, all the more power to him.
But he found he was climbing slowly out of his rented car, taking his time in picking up his jacket and bag. He felt his sodden
summer shirt clinging to his back muscles, his trousers sticking
to his buttocks. The truth was—and at the last minute he was
admitting it fully—the truth was that old friendships could
atrophy. That had been the core of his depression all the way
here. People changed. And all the irritations and annoyances
that had almost ruined the journey for him were simply excuses
to cover his real doubts.

But there had been no need to worry. Reid's welcome was no
pretense, no sentimentalized fake. The changes were superficial.
His dark hair had grown thinner on top and gray at the temples.
He had put on ten pounds (his height carried them well, even
needed them), and developed a permanent tan. He had adopted
the snow-white shirt and narrow black tie of a Spanish businessman along with his precise tailoring, and looked so smooth that
Ferrier might easily have passed him by if he had been sitting at
a café table over a small cup of ink-black coffee. But the hand-

shake was strong, the eyes sympathetic as they studied Ferrier's tired face, the voice both casual and warm. "You look like a man who needs a long cool drink, a cold shower, and part of the siesta you wouldn't take. In that order. When did you get to bed last night? By the dawn's early light? Actually, I laid a bet with myself that I'd never pry you loose from Granada. Glad I lost, though. What about dinner at ten? See you down here then. Okay?" Very much okay, Ferrier thought, accepting the tall drink with the admirably clinking ice that Reid held out to him, and followed the middle-aged woman who had already carried his bag halfway upstairs. This was Jeff Reid, all right. They might have seen each other only last week, and not eight years ago. Yes, it had been worth the trip to Málaga, if only to find that old friendships could take up where they had let off.

In the courtyard, the music quickened. The guitarist brought the last surge of rippling notes into a falling diminuendo of one, listening to its last sigh as intently as the people sitting before him. The note faded slowly into nothing. There was a long moment of silence, all eyes watching the stage—a giant table, almost twelve foot square and a hand span thick, with four massive barrel legs—that was backed against the end wall of the courtyard. The applause broke out, crisp, brief, critically measured. It pleased the guitarist enough, though. He inclined his head gravely, his gaunt face relaxed a little, intense dark eyes lingering only briefly on his audience as if they scarcely existed. He was good, and they knew it, and that was sufficient. He lifted his narrow-backed chair in one hand, swung it lightly into place at the end of a row of six others before the bare plaster wall.

"No encore?" Ferrier asked. "Or didn't we clap loudly enough?"

"He has plenty to do later on." Reid glanced at his watch, then back at the stage, where the guitarist had sat down again and was concentrating on some silent fingering. Reid looked at the open doorway near them, a narrow space without any light tacked overhead, shadowed still more by a cascade of bougainvillaea. There was no sound of women's voices, no movement from inside the door, no one gathering there to join the guitarist on the stage.

"One o'clock," Ferrier verified from his watch. "Isn't that when the show really gets moving?"

Reid said lightly, "Oh, you don't keep account of time in Spain. Ten minutes here, half an hour there, what does it mat-

ter if you are with friends?" And delays happened: dancers'
dressing rooms had more than their share of tantrums and
temperament. But, Reid wondered, was this the beginning of a
natural wait? Or was it being carefully engineered by Tavita to
last precisely fourteen minutes? If so, then it was no ordinary
delay, but a warning signal from Tavita—one that only Reid
in all that crowded courtyard could understand and act upon.
(It had been Tavita's idea of how to preserve security—one
that had amused him at first, even embarrassed him, but he had
let her have her way. She had confidence in it. And it had been
successful. No one had ever noticed. What more did he want?)
Well, he thought as he controlled his rising tension, if this is
the beginning of an alert, I'll know in exactly fourteen minutes.
And what do I do then, with Ian Ferrier sitting beside me? Just
as I usually do, I suppose: wait until the dancing starts and all
eyes are riveted on the stage and I can slip away. And Ian? My
God, it would have to be tonight that an emergency happened.
. . . All right, all right—let's wait and see if this turns out to be
a signal. Just wait and see. Meanwhile, talk. "We're in luck," he
told Ferrier. "Usually there are six chairs on that stage. Tonight,
seven. So Tavita is dancing. For my money, she is one of the
best in Spain, but it is only at the weekend that we can get
her down from Granada. That's where she lives."

"Oh?" Ferrier was definitely interested.

"Not in a cave with the gypsies," Reid added. "She has a
house on top of a hillside, not far from the Alhambra. An artist
left it to her when he died—his paintings of her are all over the
place. Yes, she's quite a girl."

"Nice going; lives in Granada, dances here. But why not in
Granada?"

"Since the tourists get taken by the hundreds in the gypsy section of town? No, not for Tavita. She's a purist. Flamenco is
something she really believes in. She dances in Seville, mostly.
On Fridays, she dances here."

"But why?" In Málaga? And was I just another gullible tourist in Granada? Ferrier wondered. He supposed that idea was
good for controlling his ego, but he didn't enjoy it.

"Out of sentiment. Also—" a smile spread over Reid's face
—"she owns El Fenicio."

"Nice going. I placed *him* as the owner." Ferrier nodded discreetly in the direction of the middle-aged man with a thin and
furrowed face, thick black hair, large dark eyes, who stood near
the main entrance. He had greeted Reid with a handshake and
Ferrier with a restrained bow.

"Esteban? He manages El Fenicio for Tavita—he's one of her old bullfighter friends. Tavita got her start as a dancer here when she was fourteen. It was a wineshop with a staircase down to a small cellar in those days. She never forgets it, though."

"And they don't forget her?" Ferrier looked around him. There were only a few women, quietly dressed, obviously married, well guarded by a phalanx of males. And the men? A mixed crowd, in age and appearance, but whether their clothes were cheap or expensive their appearance was well brushed and washed, either as a compliment to El Fenicio or as a matter of self-respect. The contrast between them and a group of four young men who had just arrived in bedraggled shirts and stained trousers was so marked that the newcomers might just as well have entered shrieking.

"All dressed for a hard day's work in the fields," Reid said, and looked away from the group. They were being led to the last free table in a back corner, and didn't think much of it. Their protest didn't have much effect on Esteban: take it or leave it, his impassive stare said; preferably leave it. "They'd have to be American," Reid added with a touch of bitterness, as he listened to their voices. "Just hope those two tables of dockworkers down front don't decide to move back and have some fun. They're allergic to people who make a mockery out of poverty. That's how they see the fancy dress. If these kids were poor and starving, they'd give them sympathy, even help. But the poor don't travel abroad; the poor can't afford cafés and night clubs; the poor don't have checks from home in their pockets."

"Kids?" Ferrier asked with a grin. The one with the beard might be in his teens, but two others—one white, one black—were certainly in their twenties and the fourth, who wore his dark glasses even in moonlight, might be closer to thirty. "You know, I think I've seen one of them before." Thin beard, young unhappy face, drooped shoulders and all. But where? Today . . . Not in Granada. Here in Málaga, when I was driving around searching for numbers on a street: Reid's street, in fact. Almost at Reid's gate, that's where I saw him. "No importance," he said. "He was just like me—another lost American." But he's still lost, Ferrier thought, lost in all directions. Then his attention was switched away from the back-corner table to the doorway beside him. Another guitarist had emerged to make his way slowly to the stage. He was followed by a white-faced man, middle-aged, plump, whose frilled shirt was cut low at the collar to free the heavy column of his neck. The singer, of

course. A young man came next, one of the dancers, tall and
thin, with elegantly tight trousers over high-heeled boots and
a jacket cut short. He disdained the three rough steps that led up
to the stage, but mounted it in one light leap without even a
footfall sounding. Control and grace, admitted Ferrier, but how
the hell does he manage to look like a real man even with a
twenty-inch waist? Strange ways we have of making a living.
My own included. Who among all these Spaniards would guess
what I do? And here I am, the most computerized man among
them, yet less formal than most of them in dress and certainly
less controlled. No one else was showing any impatience. The
two guitarists had started a low duet, a private test of improvisation between them; the dancer, standing behind them along with
the singer, was tapping one heel at full speed, quietly, neatly, as
if limbering up; the singer looked at nothing, at no one, perhaps concentrating on a new variation in tonight's *cante jondo;*
the tables continued their quiet buzz of talk, a few men rose
to talk with friends or make their way to the lavatory, and all
Reid had done was to glance casually at his watch. Ferrier concentrated on the Spaniards around him. "Who are they? Longshoremen and who else?"

Eight minutes to go—if this was an alert. Reid's attention
swung away from the questions in his mind and came back to
the courtyard. "Well, of the regulars here, I can pick out fishermen, a lawyer, a couple of bullfighters, some businessmen, an
organist, several artists, workers from the factories across the
river, shopkeepers, and students. And a policeman." He dropped
his voice judiciously. "That's him, the man in the light-gray suit
at the table just in front of our four fellow-citizens."

"State Security?"

Reid nodded.

Ferrier, sitting sideways at the table, could glance briefly toward the back corner of the courtyard without swerving his head
around. He saw a man in his mid-thirties, small, compact, cheerful, with dark complexion and curling hair. He seemed to be
concentrating on his companions, who were talking volubly.
"Who are the two men with him?"

"A journalist, and a captain of a freighter that docked this
morning. From Cuba."

"And where's that?" They exchanged smiles, remembering the
missile crisis, a tricky situation indeed, that had brought them
together in a strange way. Reid had been one of the flyers who

had volunteered to take photographs, at a low and dangerous level, of Khrushchev's rocket installations in Cuba. Ferrier had been one of the intelligence group who had analyzed the original photographs taken at high altitude, discovered the area that seemed to deserve closer attention, called for some low-altitude shots, and found the sure proof. "We ought to work together more often," Ferrier said.

"We certainly called Papa Khrushchev's bluff that time."

"Do you do any flying nowadays?" Ferrier's question was purposefully casual. He wondered for a moment if he'd ask Jeff outright why he had resigned from the Air Force. Sure, he had had a bad smashup, still flying too low, still taking dangerous chances for a more closely detailed photograph. At the time, he had said he didn't want to be pushed into a desk job, and with his injuries that was certainly where he was heading; but what was a businessman except someone attached to a desk? That separation from his wife had something to do with it. He had moved abroad soon after, which was one way of definitely putting distance between himself and Washington where Janet Reid lived. But I can't ask him about that, either. Not directly. Several of Jeff's friends had lost him completely, trying to nose into that puzzle. And now Jeff wasn't even answering his question except with a shake of his head. So Ferrier backed off tactfully, tried another angle. "Interesting town, Málaga. I begin to see how you enjoy it. Plenty of action, movement in and out."

Reid looked at him sharply, then relaxed. "Oh, we get a bit of everything wandering through here, from honest tourists to strayed beatniks and traveling salesmen."

"Not to mention all those freighters along your docks, packed like cigars in a box. Stowaways and narcotics and smuggling in general?"

"All the headaches of civilization. But at least there has been peace and growing prosperity. I'll take that, headaches and all, over war any day."

"And civil war, at that," Ferrier said quietly. He was looking at the packed courtyard, a mass of faces waiting expectantly as they talked and laughed and listened to the guitars' improvisation. Incredible, he was thinking, how people can look so damned normal as they do, when they've been through so much. Sure, it was thirty-odd years ago, another generation, and yet . . . He shook his head and added, "I keep remembering what you told me about it, on our way here—"

"If you must talk about that, keep your voice down."

"It's down. We are both mumbling like a couple of conspirators."

"And that," Reid said, trying to look amused, "is not too good, either."

What's wrong? Ferrier wondered. Jeff is suddenly on edge. And that's the third time he has glanced at his watch. What's worrying him? Does he think that Tavita may decide not to dance, after all, and the whole evening becomes a letdown? Not just for me. These quiet faces around me—how would they react? "Okay," he said. "Voices back to normal. No more questions about their civil war. I asked you enough of them, anyway."

"It wouldn't be the old Ian if you didn't," Reid said, but he made sure of changing the subject by starting some talk on the history of this courtyard. Its name, El Fenicio, was a reminder of the Phoenicians who had founded Málaga, long before the Romans had even got here.

Ferrier listened, but his own thoughts were wandering. His mind kept coming back to Jeff's answers to his questions this evening as they had driven down through the city toward the wineshop.

Ferrier had looked at the busy streets through which they were traveling slowly, at the bright lights, the crowded cafés, the masses of people on the sidewalks. "They've forgotten," he had said. "Or didn't the Civil War touch them much?"

Reid had stared at him. "They haven't forgotten. That would be difficult," he had added grimly.

"Was it as bad as that here? In Málaga?"

Reid had nodded. "That's why they don't talk much about it. Not to me, not to—"

"But you've lived here for almost eight years."

"I'm still *el norteamericano* when it comes to politics; let's not kid ourselves about that. There's such a thing as an experience gap, you know. We didn't go through what they suffered."

"Some foreigners did."

"Only for a couple of years. They weren't here before the war started, or after it ended. They didn't live through twenty years of misery."

"Twenty?" Ferrier had been disbelieving.

"I'm not even including the years when grudges and hate were built up, long before the violence really started."

"And when did it?"

"In Málaga? 1931. Forty-three churches and convents burned in two days. A pretty définite start, don't you think?"

Ferrier had been puzzled. (As someone who had been brought up on Hemingway and graduated to Orwell, he thought he knew something about Spain.) "Have you got your dates right?" he asked half-jokingly. "There was an elected government in power then. Newly elected, too. It didn't have to burn and terrorize. It had the votes."

"And couldn't control its anarchists. Not in Málaga, certainly. Those burnings took place just one month after the Republic was declared."

"But that doesn't make sense!" Anarchists and communists had been on the side of the Republic. "Unless, of course," Ferrier said thoughtfully, "it was some kind of power grab."

"It was just that. The Republic was never given a fair chance. The anarchists had their ideas of how to dominate the scene; the communists had their own plans for coming out on top—anything that created a revolutionary situation was all right with them. So things went wild. Burning, looting, kidnapping, killing. Málaga had five years of that before the Civil War really got going. And you think no one remembers? Look—they have only to walk down their most important street—the one we have just passed through, all modern buildings and plate-glass windows. When you looked at it, what did you think all that newness meant?"

"I didn't think. I just assumed. Natural growth of an active city." Experience gap, thought Ferrier. He was being given a sharp lesson in the meaning of that phrase. But he had asked for it.

"Once, it had historical buildings, some fine architecture; a kind of show place. It also had rich families and art objects—an unhappy combination when anarchists are taking revenge. In 1936, it became a stretch of burned-out rubble." Reid's tone was quiet, dispassionate. In the same even way, he continued. "A couple of months later, the Civil War started. You know what that meant. Bravery on both sides; and cruelty, and hate, and vengeance. At one point, the communists thought they were going to win, and that's when they made sure the anarchists wouldn't give them any future trouble. So it was 'Up against the wall, comrade anarchist!' Literally. In Barcelona—but you know about that?"

"I've read my Orwell. The anarchists were shot by the hundreds, even thousands, weren't they?"

"Just after they had come out of the front-line trenches. Their rest period." Reid shook his head. "I don't know why that seems so particularly bloody in all that bloody mess. The right wing would call it poetic justice, I suppose. But I've never seen anything poetic in justice: it's too close to reality. And the realities went on, and on, long after that war was over. Starvation and poverty—the outside world never heard the half of it. But what else do you expect from so much destruction? The food source was gone: cattle, fields, ranches, farms. And jails and executions for men who had jailed and executed others." Again he shook his head. "The innocent suffered too—on both sides. They always do. Whether you won or lost in that war, there was plenty of misery for everyone."

Civil war . . . "A lesson for all of us," Ferrier said. "Don't take anarchists or communists as your political bedfellows unless you want to wake up castrated." The twentieth-century experience, he thought. "But the radicals never learn, do they?"

"Nor do some nationalists," Reid said bitterly. "If trouble breaks out here again—" He didn't finish that thought. "The hell with all extremists," he said shortly. "Their price is too high."

Ferrier's thoughts came back to the courtyard. Around him, the tables were buzzing with talk; expectations were rising—you could hear it in the gradually increasing volume of sound. Everyone was out to enjoy himself. Ferrier looked at Reid. "Sorry. My mind drifted. You were saying the Phoenicians—?"

"Not important. Just a footnote." Only a brief remark to keep Ian from noticing this delay too much. It was ten minutes past one now. Four minutes to go. If this was an alert. "You know, Ian, you're a lucky man. You have a job that's worth doing, a job you like. You can keep your eyes fixed on the stars and not worry about politics." Because that's all I do now, Reid thought. I, too, have a job that's worth doing, but before I entered it I hadn't one idea of how much worry was needed over politics. The things that never get known, that can't be published unless you want to throw people into a panic; the things that stand in the shadows, waiting, threatening; the things that have to be faced by some of us, be neutralized or eliminated, to let others go on concentrating on their own lives.

"Not worry?" That had caught Ferrier's attention. "I wish I could keep my eyes on the stars instead of all that junk that's floating through space."

Reid studied his friend thoughtfully. "It's more than junk that's bothering you, isn't it?"

Ferrier nodded. "What about a nice big space station up

there? Not ours. What if a politically oriented country got it there first? One that doesn't hesitate using an advantage to back up its demands?"

"Another blackmail attempt, as in Cuba?"

"1962 all over again. Except, this time, the rocket installations would be complete with armed missiles or whatever improvements the scientists can dream up," Ferrier said bitterly. "And the whole damned package would be right above our heads, way out there." He looked up at the sky. "Not to mention various satellites that now have their orbits changed quite easily by remote control. God only knows what they contain." He tried to lighten his voice. "Well—one thing is certain. There is no future in being ignorant. Or in being depressed. You know what's at stake and you keep your cool. If you don't, you've had it." He finished his drink, didn't taste it any more.

Reid looked around for the waiter. "Where's Jaime? Oh, there he is—transfixed by our fellow-Americans." He clapped his hands to signal to the boy, small and thin, who had been standing against the rear wall.

Ferrier glanced briefly in Jaime's direction, caught a passing glimpse of the back-corner table. Four pairs of eyes had been leveled at him—or at Reid. Four pairs of eyes automatically veered away as he noticed them. It was a very brief encounter, and if there hadn't been that unified evasive action, Ferrier would have thought his imagination was playing tricks. "Ever seen these fellows before?"

"I've seen a thousand like them in the last three years." Reid was concentrating on Jaime, who was just arriving with expert speed. "Like to try the wine this time? It's local, out of a barrel, sweet but nourishing. There isn't much choice, actually. This is grape territory."

"I'll stick with the brandy. Sweet but less nourishing." And after Reid had given the brief order and Jaime, with a bright smile on his lips and in his eyes, had left them, Ferrier said, "I admire your Spanish. But doesn't he know English? He seemed to be listening to what I was saying."

"He's learning. And if I know Jaime, he's fascinated by your jacket. He's going to save up and get one just like it."

"One thing about Jaime—he could teach those fellows back at the corner table how to look cheerful."

"You should see the village he comes from, back in the hills. It was one of those that almost starved—"

From the doorway came the sound of women's voices, a burst of argument still going on, a quick command, silence. And then a rattle of castanets, light laughter. A clatter of heels came over the wooden threshold as four girls stepped into the open. There was a rustle of silk as wide ruffled skirts swept toward the stage in a mass of floating color. Smoothly brushed heads, each crowned by one large flower, were held high, long heavy hair caught into a thick knot at the nape of slender white necks. Three profiles were turned just enough to let the courtyard see a long curl pressed closely against a barely pink cheek, dark-red lips softly curving, an elaborate earring dangling. The fourth girl, lagging behind although she walked with equal poise and dignity, paid no attention to anyone, not even to the quick flurry of guitars reminding her, with a sardonic imitation of a grand fanfare, that she was later than late. The male dancer greeted her with a burst of hoarse Spanish that set the others laughing. She tossed her head, drew the small triangle of fringed silk that covered her shoulders more closely around her neck, sat down with her spine straight and a damn-you-all look at the front tables. The longshoremen roared.

"Constanza," Reid was whispering. "She's always in trouble. But her temper improves her dancing." He looked at his watch. Almost fourteen minutes. Tavita's exact timing never failed to amaze him.

To Ferrier's ear, there seemed to be some slight trouble at the rear of the courtyard, too: an American voice briefly raised in anger, a sharp hiss from the neighboring Spaniards that silenced it. He glanced back with annoyance, saw the youngest of the four—the bearded one—heading toward the wineshop, thought that this was a hell of a time to choose to go to the men's room, looked once more at the stage. The girls, a close cluster of bright colors, were settled in their seats, leaving the last chair free. The singer and the male dancer stood behind the guitarists at the other end of the row. The lamps around the courtyard walls went out. A softer glow, as amber as candlelight, focused on the stage. Suddenly he was aware that another woman had entered from the door beside their table. Silence fell on the courtyard.

Good God, thought Ferrier as he glimpsed her profile. She brushed past them, paying attention to no one. Reid was no longer looking at his watch. The silence intensified.

She was taller than the others, Ferrier noted, and moved with a grace that was notable even by the dim light. She reached the stage, mounted it, walked its length toward the empty chair with that same effortless stride. Around him, the silence broke into a storm of welcome. He could almost feel the excitement that filled the courtyard before it swept over him, too. She was worth waiting for, this Tavita. A small delay, it seemed now, not worth noticing; a little time lag that had served to stir the emotions and rouse expectations. She was unique, no doubt about that, although she was dressed like the others in the stylized costume of flamenco. And it wasn't her selection of colors that was so different—the others had made their choices, too, combining favorite contrasts to give variety. It was the way she wore the splendid clothes. She dominated them, made them part of her individuality.

She had reached her chair, sat down with her spine erect and head high, like all of them and yet like none of them, sweeping aside her wide skirt with a slender arm so that its rippling hem spread out on the wooden floor like an opened fan around her feet. The sleeveless top of her dress was black and unadorned. It molded her body, from low rounded neckline down over firm breasts and taut waist almost to the line of her hips. There, the many-tiered skirt, black lace over red silk, belled out in a cascade of ruffles that ended above her ankles, dipping slightly in back almost to the heavy high heels of her leather pumps. These were the practical note, the classical shoes of the flamenco dancer, which could beat out lightning rhythms like a riffle on a drum. The small red shawl, fringed in black, was practical too: it covered the bare back and shoulders against the cool touch of early-morning air. But the flower in her elaborately simple hair was completely exotic, large, softly frilling, startlingly pink. She wore long earrings to balance the curl over her cheek, but no necklace, no rings, no bracelets. The bones of her face were strong yet finely molded, cleverly emphasized by the skill of her make-up. Her large dark eyes were shining, her smile lingering. "Good God," Ferrier said again, aloud this time.

Suddenly, without any apparent signal, any noticeable exchange of glances, the four girls rose and swept into a round with the first bright chords of the *sevillana*, paired off, laced, separated, came together again, filling the little stage with a swirl of skirts, a flurry of heels struck hard, a crack of castanets from upraised hands. The guitars quickened, heightened, their rhythms marked by hard hand-clapping from the singer and dancer. From Tavita, too. Her eyes were watching the stamping feet with pleasure and excitement, her smile breaking into laughter. "Go! Go!" she called out to Constanza. *"Anda! Anda!"*

Reid was studying Ferrier's face. "This is just for openers, you know. The individual dancing comes later."

"They really enjoy themselves." And I along with them. "Why the hell don't I give up my job, move here, see this every night?"

Ferrier settled back in his chair. At this moment, he thought, I am a very very happy man.

Reid said softly, as Jaime came out of the darkness and placed their brandy before them, "Excuse me for a few minutes, will you? This is just as good a time as any—Pablo will have to dance, Miguel to sing, Constanza or Maruja to demonstrate an *alegría*, before we get Tavita's performance. Don't worry, I won't miss that. Hold the table. Some of the late-comers are ready to pounce on any free space."

Ferrier nodded, his eyes on the stage. But he was aware that Reid had moved, not toward the back of the courtyard, where others had previously sauntered out to the washroom, but through the door in the wall beside him. Special privilege, Ferrier thought, and was briefly entertained. And then he forgot about Reid as the climactic moments of the *sevillana*, with violent strumming and rapping on the guitars, wildly swinging skirts, rattling heels, lightning castanets, caught him up into the excitement of movement and color and sound, a frenzied crescendo that ended abruptly, completely, jolting everyone into a shout of applause.

2

Reid slipped out of the courtyard into a room that was dark and silent. And oppressive; the collected heat of the day had been trapped under its heavily timbered ceiling. It was mostly used for storage: at one end, adjoining the wineshop itself, were grouped barrels, crates, sacks and cartons, their shapes vaguely outlined in the deep shadows. Someone had tried to cool the place and opened two of the shutters on the wall opposite the courtyard entrance, but the effort was only partially successful. Between the doorway where he stood and the barred windows, which were glassless, there was a hint of cross-ventilation, but the minute he started climbing the wooden stairs on his right, he felt the warm air close around him. It smelled of wine and wood, of leather and dust, with a touch of carnations from the perfume the girls liked to use. Their dressing room was upstairs, part of a winding warren of little apartments. The men had their quarters on the ground floor, reached by a passage that began somewhere under the staircase; there, the smell of wine and wood and leather would be mixed with cigar smoke, hair oil, and lime cologne. To a stranger, the geography of this interior would be completely baffling. To Reid, it was a matter of fifteen wooden steps that hugged the wall all the way up to the landing, where there were two naked light bulbs, a venerable clock that had never yet failed in its timing, and two entrances. The one on the left led to the girls' side of the house; the one on the right to Tavita's own corridor. It was this doorway he chose.

It was a narrow hallway, with several small rooms branching from it. Tavita's receiving room, dressing room, bathroom, special sitting room were on one side, and naturally overlooked the courtyard. The other side of the corridor had a series of little square spaces no better than interior boxes, where clothes were made and stored and cleaned and pressed under old Magdalena's supervision. She would be there now, in the biggest of the boxes, a small skylight open above her gray head, a radio picking up some Algerian station and its soft wailing music, working alone, ironing out frills and ruffles on Tavita's change of costume, her shapeless black dress bent over bright colors, gnarled hands smoothing out fine silks with strange delicacy.

But as he passed her door, ready with a brief greeting and a friendly nod, he saw she was standing just inside the threshold, waiting. She put a finger to her lips, her other hand on his wrist, her eyes looking along the corridor as if she thought someone might be listening at its other end. So he took a step into the little room, carefully avoiding the wide hem of the white-and-yellow organza skirt that floated down from the ironing board, watching Magdalena's pale, heavy, peasant face, with its tight lips and intense frown. She spoke in a deep hoarse whisper. "Important, this one. Very important. Tavita says you must get him away from here at once. Tonight. That's what she says."

Reid looked at her in surprise. In the six years Tavita and he had been running this little operation, there had never been any request like this. There never had been any urgency. Secrecy, certainly; that was a necessary part of security. A refugee from Cuba, smuggled out of Havana into Málaga, needed a place where he could find safe shelter until he could continue his journey to other parts of the country. There, relatives or friends would help him. (They had been contacted quietly, weeks and sometimes months before, to make sure that they were able and willing.) But in Málaga there were Castro agents and informers watching for stowaways; and the first day of freedom for a penniless man, often hungry and sick, could be a perilous one. There had been cases of political refugees, barely off the docks, who had been shanghaied right back to where they had come from. Others had thought they'd be safe if they could reach a police station or some official bureau, ask for asylum, be willing to face detention until their case would be judged. But it seemed impossible to prevent publicity: the news would leak out. Within hours, there would be a request from Havana for the man's extradition: he was a murderer, an embezzler of union funds, a forger, a kidnapper and extortionist; full details of his crime— place, date, names of witnesses—to follow. And the details did follow, again within a few hours. "This man has to leave tonight?" Reid asked. "When did he arrive?"

"This morning."

"The usual way?" Reid had worked out a simple—and so far dependable—method of bringing a refugee into El Fenicio. The first of them, six years ago, had been Tavita's brother. El Fenicio had chosen itself, as it were, for the role of safe house.

"No. He did not come from the docks. He came from Algeciras."

"But how?"

Magdalena shook her head. She knew nothing. Tavita had given her the message for Señor Reid and she had passed it on. "He is dangerous, this one" was all she said. Her worst misgivings about helping any refugee had been fulfilled. She always had complained about the risks for Tavita. Not for *el norteamericano*; he could look after himself. So could Esteban. Even young Jaime. But Tavita? She could lose everything.

"Do you know this man?" Reid was watching her face closely.

She shook her head, pushed him out of her way as she reached over to switch on the iron. "Tavita knows of him," she said. "He was a friend of her brother's. That was many years ago. Here, in Málaga."

"What is his name?"

Magdalena shrugged, tested the iron, began pressing a ruffle. She knew little, wanted to know even less. Whoever this man is, Reid thought, he really silences her. He reached out, gave her bent shoulders a reassuring pat, and then stepped into the corridor. Quickly, he walked its length, taking out his key to the sitting-room door. It was kept locked on the nights it held any special visitor. How many times had he come along here, just like this, in the last six years? No more than thirty. Some might think that a small achievement indeed, but it had been successful. Thirty men who would never have been given permission to leave Cuba had found their way out. And after tonight? Possibly this could be the end of the whole operation: the man behind this door hadn't come here through regular channels, hadn't even been expected. Yet he must have known the right identifications, or else Esteban would have played stupid, turned him away when he had arrived this morning. I like this as little as Magdalena, Reid thought as he turned the key in the lock and then knocked three times before he opened the door.

The room was in darkness except for a vertical strip of subdued light where the tall shutters had been left ajar. Down in the courtyard, Pablo's heels were beating out a frenzied *zapateado*. The man who stood looking out at the balcony could not have heard Reid's knocking against the collected noise, but he had sensed the door opening. He swung round on his heels, stepping aside from the band of light, and faced Reid.

"Close the shutters. Draw the curtains," Reid said in Spanish. What kind of a fool am I dealing with? Had he actually been out there, on that balcony? Possibly it was safe enough, provided you moved slowly and kept well back in the shadows: it was partly recessed, and the iron railings and side pillars were thickly covered with climbing vines. Even so, there was a risk, and it irritated Reid.

"*You* close them," the man told him in English. He stepped farther away, merged completely with the darkness.

Reid moved quickly, wasting no time on argument. He pushed the shutters gently together, fastened them securely; the strumming guitars, the stamping feet, the clapping hands, the cries of "*Olé!*" faded into the background. He caught the heavy folds of the long curtains, drew them close until their edges overlapped; the last vestiges of grayed light were blacked out. Behind him, the small lamp on the central table was switched on. Reid turned toward it, but the man was no longer there. He was now standing some six feet away, his right arm held stiffly, his eyes watching Reid's hands. Reid kept his voice casual. "Were you out on that balcony?"

"It's a good place to see what is going on."

"It could be a foolish place, too." Reid chose the nearest chair, sat down, crossed his legs, made no attempt to reach for his cigarettes.

"Did *you* see me out there?" The man slipped his throwing knife back into the cuff of his tight sleeve.

Reid shook his head. And was I supposed not to notice that knife? "You know, if I had come up here to kill you, I would have entered with a revolver pointed. I would have peppered the room in the direction you moved. There's a good six-to-one chance that I would have got you."

"A noisy method."

"There are such things as silencers. Even without one of them, the noisy method might have seemed only part of the flamenco. Pablo's heels rattle like a machine gun."

The man sat down at the table. "Don't be so sure you would have got me," he said softly. "The light from the shutters reached the threshold of the door. I could see your feet—and your hands."

So this was a type who never apologized, and if he explained it would be to show how right he was. Certainly, he wasn't afraid of risks; but he calculated them. And his reflexes were remarkably quick. Physically, he was of medium height and weight, with even features, thick dark hair now graying, heavily tanned skin, pale lips, two deep furrows on either side of his mouth, expressionless brown eyes under heavy brows. He was dressed, surprisingly, in a neat summer suit of silver-gray, a cream silk shirt, a broadly knotted tie of almost the same color. He was totally unlike any refugee who had ever emerged from a packing case in the hold of a cargo ship.

"You were late," the man was saying, continuing his explanation.

"Two minutes."

"I saw you leave your table. Someone could have been waiting for you near the staircase. A matter of substitution, you understand."

"Quite," said Reid gravely. He repressed a smile. He had the feeling that this man might not appreciate any joke about conspiracy: he seemed to accept it as a natural way of life. Yes, Magdalena might have been right—this man could be trouble. "How did you know who I was?" He could risk taking out his cigarettes and lighter.

"Tavita pointed you out to me. Necessary, wouldn't you say?"

"Certainly cautious." Reid took a cigarette, was about to light it, remembered politeness, and rose to offer the pack. "Do you smoke?"

"I prefer cigars."

"But not here," Reid said quickly. "Tavita doesn't smoke cigars." He lit his own cigarette, sat down at the table with his hands well in view. The lighter was at his elbow. "The smell stays in a small room for days."

"Does she smoke this brand of cigarette?" The man reached across the table, lifted the pack, examined it briefly, tossed it back.

"As a matter of fact, she does," Reid said. "We are cautious, too, you see. I'm sorry we had to lock you in here, but that is also part of— Something wrong?" The stranger had stretched his arm across the table again, tapped Reid's left hand.

"Only your watch. I'm amazed that a careful man lets it run slow."

"I don't think so." If he's interested in this watch, then let's encourage him, Reid thought. Let's keep his curiosity away from the lighter. Reid unfastened the watch from his wrist, wound it a little. "It usually keeps perfect time. Are you sure it isn't your watch that is fast?"

"Perhaps. Certainly, it isn't as elegant as that one. So very thin."

"The newest fad. All face and no work. Like some people I know."

"No works?"

"Hardly any. See?" Reid displayed the watch with an owner's

usual pride, let the man examine it closely. "I don't suppose there are many of those for sale in Havana."

"The first I've seen."

Reid took the watch, strapped it back on his wrist. "Now, where were we? Oh, yes—caution. I was explaining why we had to keep you locked in here. But we don't want any stranger opening that door and—"

"There is need for caution," the coldly factual voice cut in. "I saw three men down in that courtyard, each of whom would have been quite capable of killing me. When I saw them, I thought that was why they had come here."

Reid's amusement ended. "If you've blown our little operation—"

"They may not have been following me. I doubt that. I have been excessively careful. They may only have been putting in time, spending it agreeably, normally; or they could have chosen to meet here where men of all types and nationalities can be found. We will watch them, of course—"

"Will we?"

"They are potentially dangerous, quite apart from me. They—"

"I'd prefer to hear about you. There are several questions. How did you get here, why did you come, who are you, where are you going, what relatives or friends have you in Spain?"

"Relatives? None. Friends? Tavita. Where am I going? To safety. Who am I, why did I come? The answer is the same: I am a defector."

Reid stared at the quiet face opposite.

"And how did I get here? I've planned the journey for months." He watched the American take off his jacket, throw it over a neighboring chair, loosen his tie and the collar button of his shirt. "Yes, it is warm," he said with his first smile, small and brief. But not for me, he seemed to be saying when he made no move to slip off his coat. Perhaps, thought Reid, he doesn't want to show the gun he is carrying.

"Where did you start the journey?" Reid asked. Was this man really a defector? He could be Spanish Security. He could be a Castro spy. "And we'll talk in Spanish now."

"It was planned in Cuba, and started in Mexico when I went there on a special mission last month. From Mexico to Venezuela and then to Morocco. From Morocco to Spain, by the port of Algeciras—as a tourist. I even took an excursion across the bay to have a look at Gibraltar. Yesterday, I joined the tourists to see the beauties of Andalusia. I did not come into Málaga on that bus. I had a headache, a feeling of slight fever, so I left it when we stopped to make a brief visit to Torremolinos. What changes there are in that place! I knew it as a fishing village. Now there are a hundred hotels—like Miami's. A stranger is not even noticed. And there are so many kinds of strangers, from the naked to the fully clothed. This morning, I came to Málaga by public bus—and then a short walk, and then a taxi; another stroll, another taxi. Oh, not to El Fenicio direct! Really, Señor Reid, you must understand that I *do* know this business. If you wonder how I arranged so many changes of clothing, passports, all I had to do was to have a small suitcase waiting for me in various cities. As I told you, I had plenty of time to arrange all that: six months of preparation, once I had decided on the plan. I used reputable hotels, American Express, Cook's, even an airport in one place."

"And if anyone had been curious and opened the suitcase stored with him?"

"Tragic for him. The locks could not be opened by any stranger without the case blowing up in his face."

"And who left these cases for you to collect?"

"Various agents, helped by some sympathizers. They are accustomed to leaving suitcases and parcels for someone else to pick up. My department has quite a lot of experience in these matters. Don't look so surprised. I have directed so many people to move between countries and continents that surely I know how to arrange my own travel." He paused, smiled slightly again. "Do you understand all I've been saying? Or shall we go back into English? You now know that my accent *is* Spanish, and not Cuban or Puerto Rican or any other variety. Isn't that so?"

That was so. But it was better to keep using Spanish; this man talked more freely in it. Reid ignored the smile. "You know," he said softly, "you're so damned smart, I don't think you need anyone's help to complete your escape." And if you hadn't dropped the word "defector," he thought as he stared at those unreadable eyes, I wouldn't have spent another two minutes on you; you aren't the kind of refugee who needs any aid or comfort. What are you—defector, or agent for Castro's Cuba? "In any case, there isn't much you can expect here, except a bed and food and new clothes. That's all Tavita ever provided, first to her brother, then to his friends, and then to friends of his friends. It has been mostly a family affair."

"I know that. Don't worry; I kept this 'family affair,' as you call it, out of our files. It seemed to me, when I first discovered it, that it could have its uses. Tavita does owe me her brother's life. But to be quite frank, I didn't come here to ask Tavita's help. I want yours."

"Mine?"

"You have an organization behind you. The CIA. That is what I need now. Fully organized help."

"You're being ridiculous." Reid stubbed out the cigarette that was almost singeing a fingernail, glanced at his watch. Pablo's dance was over. From the courtyard came a muted minor scale. Miguel and his song about blighted love seemed very far away. "I think I'd better return to my friend," Reid said, rising. "Tavita would like you to leave. Find someone else to help you. We can't."

The man hadn't moved. "Sit down," he said quietly. "Do you think I am here to spy on you? I tell you the truth. I am a defector."

"Then go to the American Embassy. Ask them for help. Come to think of it, why didn't you slip into the United States and defect right there?"

"Because I do not intend to live in the United States. I do not wish to spend the rest of my life evading exiled Cubans, or Castro's agents, or—" He paused, then ended, "Or the KGB."

Now, wondered Reid quickly, how had Soviet Intelligence come slipping in there? And which branch of it—internal security or foreign espionage? He sat down again. "Why not add some of Mao's boys to the list?"

"Your renegades, your black revolutionaries, your visiting students from friendly foreign countries? Yes, there are plenty of them around in your United States." He reached over the table suddenly, picked up Reid's lighter. "Always obedient, always helpful," he went on as he turned the lighter over in his hands. It was made of dark polished steel, with a small brass insigne on its smooth surface for sole decoration. "What's this?" he asked, examining it. "Oh, yes, Air Force. Of course." He glanced up quickly at Reid, but the American seemed to be little interested; he was still waiting for a direct answer to his question. "Yes, the Chinese communists would be curious, too. If they knew I was alive."

"Oh—so you're dead, are you?" Reid put a cigarette between his lips.

"Assassinated in Mexico."

Reid held out a hand for his lighter. "Now how did that happen?"

The man balanced the lighter in his hand, then tossed it back.

"The fishing boat on which I was meeting two Mexican comrades exploded and burned."

Reid lit his cigarette, dropped the lighter back on the table beside his pack. "Just five minutes after you timed your departure?"

The man studied Reid deliberately. For a moment, Reid wondered if he had pushed too far: obviously, if any acid comments were going to be handed out, this man would insist on dealing them. The man said coldly, "Ten minutes."

"And no questions asked?"

"Immediately? No, I think not. There was an attempt on my life last year. In Havana. I used that incident to make my death acceptable. Of course—once investigations are made and cannot uncover who ordered my execution—there could be serious doubts. Unless I accomplish what I mean to do: drop completely out of sight, stay out of sight, have no floating rumors attached to my name. Then my death will be accepted as accidental. Now you understand why I don't walk into your Embassy and ask for help? Or make contact with old friends who are left alive in Spain?"

"By 'friends' you mean communists?"

"The others were never my friends," the man said contemptuously.

"Then why did you make contact with Tavita?" And what worries me, Reid was thinking, is that this man has involved her in helping an enemy of the state; what worries me is that she may be in additional danger if any of his friends connect her with him.

"She never had any politics that mattered. She was only a child—seven or eight years old when I was last in Málaga. No one will connect me with Tavita. That is what worries you? I assure you, it is as much in my interest as it is in hers that we remain unconnected."

"But her brother—"

"Yes, I was a close friend of her brother. He was many years older than she was, the head of her family. I helped him to escape to Madrid in 1937 when Franco's troops took Málaga. I helped him to escape again in 1939. Then we followed different roads. I was sent to Moscow. He went to Mexico, then to Cuba. And there he changed. He was one of those socialists who like to feel they have been betrayed: it nourishes their sense of martyrdom."

Reid glanced at his watch. Outside, the song had ended. A

dance was beginning. "Did you have contact with him in Cuba?"

"No. I watched him closely. But we never met."

"When did you arrive in Cuba?"

"1963."

"Why?"

"In order to take charge of one of our departments there that had become—well, let us say it was careless, inept. It needed reorganization."

"You were an agent for the KGB?"

"I am a member of the KGB."

Reid noted the correction and was impressed. He also noted the use of the present tense, and was disturbed. In another session, he thought, I'll have that clarified. But now—he glanced again at his watch—now he must get the essentials. "Name?"

"Which of them?" The man was amused by the increased tempo. Perhaps he was taking it as proof that he was accepted. "To Tavita, I am Tomás Fuentes."

"Why was there an attempt on your life?"

"There have been procedural disagreements within the department. I lost the argument. Meanwhile."

Meanwhile . . . A revealing word, thought Reid, when spoken with such bitterness. Was this man a defector in the real sense? Or was he simply playing for time—some months, perhaps even a year—until he was proved right? If he actually hoped for some kind of reinstatement, then he would give nothing away that was of any importance. Let's keep talking, decided Reid, and see how much he is willing to tell. He asked, "Disagreements? Between orthodox and revisionist factions in your department?" And the answer to that would at least indicate just where this man stood.

Perhaps Fuentes guessed the reason for Reid's question. Or he welcomed a chance to cut the American down a little. "That is being much too simplistic. There are no revisionists in the department. There cannot be. Or it would cease to exist. And that's the reason that made my position extremely insecure: I was represented as revisionist. Not true. But my chief opponent was a Cuban, and we were, after all, in Cuba. Also, he had been most helpful to Moscow in the death of Che Guevara, while I had advised Guevara—privately, of course—not to go to Bolivia. Oh, I had no illusions about the man. He had veered far left, toward the Chinese faction; he did not believe that we could achieve our ends quickly enough by peaceful coexistence. He was too much of an anarchist, and therefore unreliable. But there were safer ways of dealing with him. So, I was against the Bolivian project. I insisted on the realities: it was not possible at that time to open another Vietnam. My mistake was that I over-estimated world opinion, Señor Reid. I had feared your news-papers would headline the lack of Bolivian communist support for the Guevara forces. No communist party disobeys its direc-tives; if they had been told to support Guevara, they would have done so. I also overestimated Guevara himself. I thought he would react violently once he discovered he had been sent on a lost mission." He paused. "When you contact Wash-ington—"

"First," Reid said, "I need some short but definite answers."

"But I've told you—"

"Not enough. You say you are Fuentes, a member of the KGB, sent to supervise some branch of your department that has been established in Cuba. You say you are afraid for your life, and you've given me a reason for your flight. But the Che Guevara incident, if true, is three years old. What is the reason for leaving Cuba now?"

Fuentes stared at him coldly. "Further disagreements. And because of the Guevara incident, my position has been weak-ened. The suggestions of my opponents have been favored in directives from Moscow. They are now in operation. I foresee great danger to the department. And when trouble comes, I do not intend to be held responsible for something I disapproved of."

Moral scruples? At least, thought Reid, this may be more pleasant to hear. "And that was?"

"The widening of our selection of recruits."

Reid's brief touch of sympathy faded. "You are afraid your standards will deteriorate?"

"Not that. Our training is of the best. No one is chosen un-less he has the necessary courage and determination. But once he graduates, he may give us unexpected trouble unless we are sure of him psychologically. With increasing numbers of graduat-ing students, that is not always possible. Some of them get tired of waiting. They may want action before we judge it is time for action. The younger they are, the more impatient. They want to prove how clever they are. In other words, they could become agents out of control." Fuentes was talking rapidly, the words pouring out as if he had declared them several times before, and from the irritation in his voice it was obvious that no one had listened to him. "That creates several problems. The greatest of these is adverse publicity."

"Surely your propaganda experts can come to the rescue," Reid said bitterly. "Blue is yellow, and purple is green. They know how to color the picture."

"A propaganda machine is only as effective as people are stupid. We cannot assume that we will always be saved by the simple-mindedness of our enemies. To attract *any* publicity is a fatal mistake for my department. We must not seem to exist."

"And what are you?"

"The Thirteenth Department of the Foreign Intelligence Directorate."

Reid froze. In spite of the heat of the room, he felt chilled. The beads of perspiration on his brow were cold. "So Department Thirteen is still active," he said, trying to speak casually, almost succeeding.

Fuentes was delighted with the effect he had produced. "Not even Khrushchev would interfere with it. Fortunately. There is more opportunity for it now than ever. So you see, Señor Reid, I am a defector of considerable value. You agree?"

Reid only stared at him. Department Thirteen had two divisions. One of them dealt with assassination. The other organized terror: bombs in cities, fires in warehouses and harbors, destruction of railways and bridges, sabotage of defense industries and installations, general violence and the creation of fear.

Fuentes was saying, "When you contact Washington, I would advise you not to trust your usual methods of communication. Messages can be intercepted. And codes can be broken easily and quickly by computers. I suggest a courier: yourself in fact. Señor Reid—are you listening to me?"

Sure I'm listening, Reid thought grimly. Department Thirteen . . . I'm out of my depth. This is far beyond me, and I know it. But I'll keep listening. And I'll keep you talking. "You mean I take three days away from the wine business? Fly to Washington and back?"

"Why not? It ensures complete security. And you must go direct to the top—or quite near the top. Robert O'Connor is the man you need. He thinks he is an expert on Department Thirteen. He has specialized on Cuba. He will certainly know me—as Carlos Vado. You will tell him that Vado can give him the names of certain agents, now placed and waiting in the United States. In exchange, he will arrange to get me secretly to Switzerland, supply me with money and necessary papers. And that is all. There is to be no surveillance once I reach Switzerland—I know exactly where I shall go, what identity I shall adopt. I need no further help."

"Which division was yours in Department Thirteen, by the way?" This time, Reid had managed to be completely casual. "Assassination or terror?"

"Assassination. I supervised the selection and training of recruits."

"And it is being expanded?" Reid went on quietly. "Why?"

"Both divisions are being expanded. Terror is of course a diversionary activity, but it does create the necessary—"

"Why?" Reid insisted. "Why expanded? What are they preparing for?"

"Just what *you* are preparing for. The year 1976. The two hundredth anniversary of the United States. An interesting target date." Fuentes almost smiled as he watched the American's face, tight with shock. "And there is a good chance of success, with the way the United States is going these days," he added in the same calm businesslike voice.

By God, thought Reid, he's enjoying this. "Civil war? Is that what you are planning for us?"

"Let us say: an end to your system of government. And frankly, we do not need to plan too much—not at this stage. Now, we only need to supervise, to guide and counsel and support."

Recruit and propagandize and train, thought Reid. And civil war it would be.

Fuentes was still watching the American's face. "You don't believe it can be done?"

"I don't know if I can believe *you*," Reid said, his anger breaking loose.

Fuentes was silent. Then he said, "I'll give you a demonstration of my credibility. And of my good faith. Come to the balcony." He rose, moved over to the curtains. "I told you that there were three men down in that courtyard who would be capable of killing me. I ought to know. Two of them attended our school in Cuba, went on to Moscow for final instruction. The third is a Lithuanian who has assumed a Swedish identity. He is a painter, with a studio at Fuengirola not far from here. Popular with foreign wanderers, most of them political innocents."

Reid said, rising to his feet, his left hand slipping into his trouser pocket and gripping the duplicate lighter, "Just a second! Open the curtains as I put out this lamp." He switched off the lamp on the table, heard the scrape of curtain rings as he exchanged lighters. Too bad he had to do that now, but there might not be another chance. He came quickly over to the window, seeing his way by the hint of light from the courtyard. Fuentes was unfastening the catch on the shutters. "Most of them political innocents? And the others?"

"They are his special charges. His mission is to superintend the safe arrivals and departures of our agents in transit through Málaga. He also makes a report on them. I had several of these in my files." Fuentes opened the shutters gently. "You'll see him at the back corner table with the two Americans."

Reid put out a hand, stopped the opening shutters. "No need," he said, dropping his voice. "I saw the men. But there were four of them in that corner." And then, for the first time in ten minutes, he was aware of the music. This was Tavita's dance. Constanza's *alegría* must be over, and he hadn't even noticed.

"One of them left—the young man with the beard. A quarrel, I think. I don't know him. Possibly a pickup, someone to lend an authentic touch." Then Fuentes stood listening to the music, too. His face was lost in memories. "So many years," he said softly. "So many, many years."

"I must leave." Reid pressed the shutters together, fastened them. It was difficult with the exchanged lighter in his right hand, but he hadn't dared risk slipping it into his pocket. "Turn on the light after I close the curtains," he warned. Behind him, the lamp was switched on as he drew the curtains roughly together. He came back to the center of the room, where Fuentes now stood looking down at the table. "Their names?" Reid asked. "The three men in the courtyard?"

Slight hesitation. Fuentes was debating whether he'd give this much information at this stage.

"Names," Reid repeated.

"Gustaf Torrens is the one with the Swedish passport. The Americans, according to *their* passports, are Edmund Pitt, black; Lee Laner, white."

"When do they arrive in the States? And where?"

"Later," Fuentes said. "We'll save these details for later. I'll give you them at our next meeting."

So, thought Reid, no more information at this session. To be continued . . . He frowned, took a few thoughtful paces around the room, his hands jammed into his pockets, his head bent. "All right," he said, accepting Fuentes' decision. "Now you get back to your own quarters. I'll see you there when the show is over." His hands came out of his pockets as he stepped briskly over to the door.

"And what about your friend who is now sitting at your table? How do you get away from him?"

"He will be delighted to spend a couple of hours with Tavita. Who wouldn't?"

"She tells me his visit has been long planned. True?"

"Yes." So he had actually questioned Tavita about Ian. But of course he would. Ian was the unexpected, the unknown factor.

"Is he connected with the CIA?"

"No."

"Tavita said something about your Space Agency. She was vague, of course. And our time together was brief. Ferrier—isn't that his name?—what is his job there?"

"Something to do with tracking."

"Tracking? You mean keeping an eye on the things that are flying overhead? What does he do—simply record them, or analyze?"

"It is none of your damned business. Come on, let's move. I'm late."

"So he is in some kind of space intelligence? In a way, it is my business. Such a man has a trained mind. The type who asks questions and—even more dangerous—finds answers."

"He isn't in your line of work," Reid said sharply. "Keep him out of this. And Tavita, too." And that, my friend, is why you are leaving El Fenicio tonight—before tomorrow, certainly.

"That would be difficult. I stay close to Tavita until you produce action from Washington. She is my insurance."

Blackmail? "I wouldn't threaten Tavita, if I were you. She won't be pushed."

"She wouldn't denounce me."

"You'd better not risk that. If she finds out you are a Soviet agent—"

"She won't. I am simply a communist who is traveling through Spain, and asks her for help. She will give it. She has to."

"Because of her brother?"

"She owes me two debts. One is her brother's life; the other is my silence about his past."

"But you said he was a changed man."

"He is changed. But what he did in Málaga in 1936 can never be changed. If the Spanish government knew the full facts, they would not have welcomed him home. They would have brought him to trial." Fuentes watched the younger man's face. "That comes as a shock, does it? You didn't know this when you helped Tavita's brother get established back here? Disconcerting."

And highly dangerous, if all this was true. And if Fuentes had no real damning facts, he could invent them. "You'll leave here before dawn," Reid said. "And don't worry about your safety. I shall make sure of that."

"You do not sound too happy about it." Fuentes was highly amused. "And it is I who decide when I leave El Fenicio."

Reid turned abruptly to the door, unlocked it, looked out into the corridor to make sure it was empty. "Why the hell did you have to choose Málaga?" he asked bitterly, and thought he had the last word.

But he was wrong. "Who would expect me to come back here?" Fuentes asked derisively. "Walk right into the arms of my oldest enemies?" He slipped past Reid, turned right, and vanished around the corner of the far end of the corridor.

Reid picked up his jacket, made a last check of the room. If any of Tavita's admirers came up here after the performance, they'd find everything as usual: pink lights softening white plaster walls decorated with clusters of photographs and bright artificial flowers, lush silk curtains, satin mats, a plethora of chairs. He went to the center table to pick up his cigarettes and lighter. The lighter was gone.

He drew a deep breath. The substitution had paid off. He had little fear of detection—the missing lighter was an exact duplicate, outwardly at least, of the one now safely in his pocket. But the whole thing had been so quick, so close, that he couldn't even enjoy this small sense of triumph. Next time, he wondered, will I be able to outmaneuver Fuentes? I had luck tonight. Tomorrow?

He left the placid room. Fuentes, by this time, would have skirted the courtyard, following the long narrow passage that ran on this level inside the blank wall behind the stage. The passage had no windows, no doors to other rooms. It was bleakly lit, bare of furniture except for a large wardrobe at its end. But inside the wardrobe was a concealed door. Once through that, Fuentes would be in the ancient warren of Esteban's house.

On impulse, Reid moved to the corner and made sure that Fuentes was not loitering. The passage was empty; the wardrobe was closed and innocent. Fuentes was safe on his own side of the courtyard, in a top-floor room where one small window looked out on a narrow street. It wasn't the most luxurious accommodation, but it was well insulated from the rest of the house. On the floors below, Esteban's usual guests were some not-too-successful bullfighter and his nondescript entourage. Esteban, like Tavita, was strong on old loyalties.

Reid retraced his steps, headed back down the corridor. Old Magdalena was now in Tavita's dressing room, the shutters

slightly ajar to let her hear the guitars and castanets and the delib-
erate rhythm of slow-moving heel beats. Her hands struck crisply
together in perfect timing. Once, she too had danced the *seguir-
iyas*. She looked at him as he stopped briefly at the door. "Tell
Tavita this one is important. Keep him safe. I'll get him away
from here by dawn." She nodded. As he hurried on his way, her
fingers began that sharp hard clapping again.

Reid increased his pace. His guess was that Tavita was almost
two thirds through the dance: he could hear Pablo's feet now,
stamping, dominating; then dominated in turn by Tavita's own
rattling heels. He'd have time yet to see the climax. Perhaps it
would inspire him a little, give him some idea of how to combine
the entertaining of Ian Ferrier with the necessary arrangements
for Tomás Fuentes. How much could he be believed, that fellow?
The hell was, one couldn't afford to disbelieve him.

Reid pulled on his jacket, straightened his tie, started down the
stairs at a light run. Halfway, he stopped abruptly. He stared at a
pile of wine barrels in the storage room below. A shadow had
formed, was moving, came into the half-light at the foot of the
staircase. It was the American called Lee Laner.

Laner put a foot on the bottom step, looked up at Reid with a
friendly face. He was slightly built, of ordinary height; a man in
his mid-twenties, with hollow chest and hunched narrow shoulders. A tangle of long lank hair, indeterminate blond, sun-
streaked, swept heavily across his brow and covered his ears. The
eyes were bright and intense, and watchful. The grin on the gaunt
face had widened, become even friendlier. The voice was friendly,
too. Gentle, hesitant, disarming. "Thought I'd look around, you
know. Take some notes. I'm a writer. This place, you know, is
weird, man. Really weird." He shook his head in disbelief. "I got
lost, you know—yes, got lost all over this place. Weird, man,
weird." He had mounted the first four steps, casually, as he
talked; he halted there, one foot splayed slackly on the next tread.
In one limp hand he held a small notebook; in the other, a heavy
fountain pen. Casual and relaxed, that was Laner. He stifled a
sneeze, exchanged the notebook for a crumpled handkerchief in
his hip pocket, blew his nose. "Must be a thousand years old. You
know. Beautiful, man, beautiful. And up there?" He gestured
vaguely with the pen toward the landing, his eyes looking past
Reid. Swiftly, as he swung his weight up one more step, his arm
straightened. The pen's direction shifted straight for Reid's face.

Reid moved, in the only direction there would be safety, swirling on the ball of his foot to vault sideways over the railing that

edged the staircase. He felt its weak supports quiver under his weight, and then he was plunging down onto the floor below. It was an ugly fall, off balance because of his desperate speed, and he landed with a leg crumpled under him. There was bad pain in his arm, too, and a jarring sensation throughout his whole body as if everything had been shaken loose. But that was nothing compared to what he had evaded. On the staircase where he had stood, there was a small cloud of vapor from Laner's spray gun. One mouthful of that, and he would have dropped dead. Of a heart attack, it would have been said.

He lay motionless, his face set in a grimace as he tried not to groan, not to call out. He wondered if the sickness he felt was caused by the agony of his leg—of course he would have to fall on the leg that had been smashed once before—and did this coldness, suddenly clamped to his body, come simply from shock? Or as he had turned aside, up there, face averted, breath held, eyes closed even before he made the leap, had he even then been a fraction of a moment too late? Obviously he hadn't caught much, if any, of the cyanide vapor or he wouldn't be alive. But he was sick and cold and pain-racked, losing consciousness. He thought he heard footsteps. He couldn't be sure. Perhaps someone had come down to stand over him, and then gone away. He couldn't be sure. He clamped his teeth tightly, lay there, as still as death.

3

In the courtyard, the dance was exploding into a swirl of sound and movement. No one had heard Reid's fall, far less Laner's own light jump, back down the staircase, to the threshold of the open door. He drew into its side, keeping out of view from the nearest table, uncovered his mouth and nose, slipped his handkerchief along with the spray gun and its spent ampoule into his trouser pocket. He drew a deep breath of fresh clean air.

Nothing to it, he thought. Nothing to it. I stood below the pig and fired upward. Couldn't get a whiff even if I hadn't had my face covered. He fell for it, he fell, all right. Sure it was a risk, but I'm here, and he's flat on this face. Better check?

Cautiously, Laner circled around the bottom stair, looked down at Reid but not too near. Reid might have carried some of that vapor with him. They said it disappeared at once; they said it left no trace. But they also said that before you fired that gun you had to take the antidote, a day before. A day before. As if you could always plan these things in advance, as if you were clairvoyant or something . . . Laner moved cautiously back to the door. You grab the chance, that's what you do. It comes, and you grab it. That's what I did. No pill in advance. And I'm feeling fine.

But as an afterthought, he took the handkerchief out of his pocket and dropped it behind a barrel. And he searched in his breast pocket for the small square of gauze in which a little glass vial was concealed. He felt its hardness with his thumb, crushed it with his nail to release the vapor it contained. The postantidote, as it were. But this made sense, left a man free to choose the right time, the right place. He held the piece of gauze close against his nostrils, inhaled deeply. It took him off-guard, nearly knocked him over. Sort of intensified smelling salts, that was all it was. He had just taken too deep a breath of it. He sniffed the gauze more cautiously, as he had been taught to do. Either it was a stronger brand than the vapor he had inhaled after practicing the spray gun

43

on the dogs, or he had been more shook than he realized and breathed in too much too quickly too violently. His eyes and throat smarted, but his head was clear. He looked into the courtyard, judging his next step. And this was it, here in this crowded place with everyone mesmerized by the dancer on the stage. The woman up there was really turning them on. Her long black hair had escaped from its coil and fallen loosely down her back almost to her waist. Her heels rippled, smashed, beat, changed the rhythms as easily as the guitarists' fingers. Her body circled, the flower dropped to the floor. Laner slipped out of the doorway, keeping close to the wall, moved along it slowly.

Some people from the back tables had filtered along the sides of the courtyard, stood there trying to get a better view of the dancer's intricate steps. They made an adequate screen for Laner as he worked his way along the wall. He stopped once or twice, briefly, to watch the stage and look interested in the show. He even called *"Olé!"* with the rest of them. There were only two things necessary in this game, he decided: put on an act and keep it going; choose your moment and use it. No one saw me, no one is paying me any attention, he thought in rising exhilaration.

Gustaf Torrens and Ed Pitt were sitting silently in their back corner. Torrens was tense, worried. Pitt was bored; the black man wasn't letting this music reach him, perhaps on principle. And he was still smarting under Torrens' earlier rebuke about his language. Laner had been included in that rebuke, but Pitt was nursing it as his own. "Clean out your mouths!" the Swede had told them. "Cut out that talk when you're around me." Torrens was too damn square, thought Laner as he neared his table. Come to think of it, all those people back in Moscow were a bunch of squares. Too many regulations, too much preaching along with teaching. What did rules and orders have to do with ideals? I'll match mine against his, any day, thought Laner as he nodded for Torrens and slid into the chair beside him. But much of his exhilaration was dying away. He hadn't even dropped the piece of gauze at Torrens' elbow, as he had meant to do. A nice touch of high drama. But not now. He gave Ed a small hand-clenched sign.

"Cut that out!" said Torrens. "Where have you been?"

"Looking around." Laner's exhilaration was gone. Cut that out, cut this out; that was Torrens' way of handling things. I say nothing, Laner decided. Nothing at all. Not here, not now.

"What have you been doing?" Torrens asked, his voice low and intense. His blue eyes were fixed in a hard stare.

"Just proving a point."

Pitt was no longer bored. He knew as little as Torrens, but he knew Laner better and he sensed something interesting. "You made it, man?" he tried.

Torrens was baffled. His worry changed into anger. "Made what?"

Pitt's grin split wide across his face. "Tell the man," he mocked in his best Alabama-bound accent. "The man wants to know."

Torrens' lips tightened, but apart from that he paid no more attention to Pitt. "What are you holding in your hand?" he asked, reaching out so quickly that Laner was caught by surprise. Torrens unfolded the crumpled piece of gauze, looked at it in disbelief. Then he palmed it quickly, raised his hand to his nose, and sniffed the gauze to make sure. He dropped his hand into his trouser pocket. When it came back onto the table, it held only his pack of cigarettes. There was a long pause while he lit a cigarette. Pitt's black eyes were sparkling with delight. "We'll talk later," Torrens said.

"It's a job you should have done yourself." Laner was on the defensive and resented it. "What was the idea, anyway, of letting a pig live in this town, snooping around in comfort? I did you a favor." He gave Pitt a knowing glance. "One less."

"Right on." Pitt went into a sudden fit of silent laughter.

"You complacent fools," Torrens said. "You loose-brained—"

"Shut it! Cool it, man, cool it. We traveled a long way without your help. We'll start traveling a longer way tomorrow." Pitt's low voice was contemptuous, the words spat out in a slow drawl. "Just you get us on board that ship. That's your job, man. We'll do ours."

Torrens looked at them both. "I said we'd discuss this later." He smoked his cigarette slowly, stubbed it out thoughtfully. "We leave here as soon as this dance is over." He made an effort and smiled for both of them. He sat there, controlling his anger, waiting for the final bars of music. Then he rose with the rest of the audience, applauding as enthusiastically as any of them. He signaled to the boy who had waited on their table, paid, applauded some more, then gestured with a nod toward the exit through the wineshop. "Slowly," he told them, and his voice was pleasant and at ease. "No hurry."

Laner and Pitt recovered their cool, followed him leisurely. Pitt looked back at the stage where a new dance was starting. "They call that rhythm?" he asked superciliously. He shook his head pityingly.

Laner felt good. The Swede had admitted, in his own way, that Laner had been smart; why else all this pleasant talk as they went through the wineshop? Was Torrens only making a smooth exit?

Once they reached the street, would he start lecturing again? No, he was talking quietly, but in friendly fashion, about their plans. No questions, no inquisition. Yes, thought Laner, he has accepted what I did. He was impressed, all right. And why not? That was one for their textbooks.

Torrens halted at the nearest corner. "Well, seeing that we lost our transportation, we'd better look as if we were saying good-bye here. I wonder where that friend of yours went?"

"The beard? Back to the beach to play his guitar," Pitt said.

"Or driving nonstop to Madrid at ninety miles an hour," Laner said. "Don't worry about him. He's a five-year-old." But why are we saying good-bye right on this street corner?

"He had no idea of what you were?" Torrens asked casually. "It's dangerous to leave loose threads—"

"No loose threads. He's just a spoiled baba," Laner insisted. "He lost his temper and walked out. That's always his solution. It's kind of good to be free of him."

"We suffered him a long long way," Pitt said. "Picked him up at American Express in Madrid."

"Why did you pick him up?"

"Why not, man?" Pitt's voice had a touch of contempt, disguising his resentment at being questioned. He looked away, studied the distant lights.

Laner said quickly, "He had a car, he was coming south, he had a nice fat check from dear old mom right in his pocket. Good cover, you know. That's what he was for us."

"And you had no idea that he was Reid's son?" Torrens went on quietly, easily.

"Never heard of pig Reid until we were driving and singing our way to Málaga. Never saw him until tonight."

"And what did young Reid say about his father?"

"He just dropped a couple of sentences. He had a father who lived in Málaga, worked for the CIA. Big joke."

"And he was coming to see his father?"

"Nah," Laner said scornfully. "You don't get the picture. He just wanted to have a look at his father. Because mom forbids it, I guess. He's just a mixed-uptight kid." Laner paused, enjoyed his small joke. "Forget him, Torrens. He didn't talk with his father. And he can't—not now." Laner paused again, hoping for some praise. He wasn't being given any more reprimands, but Torrens might add a word of praise. Yes, Torrens was doing that in his own close-mouthed way. Torrens was holding out his hand. Laner took it, was given a warm shake, was astounded to feel a card left in his palm. Pitt was given the same treatment.

Torrens was saying heartily, "Good-bye." In a lower voice, he added, "The cards tell you where you'll each find a room for the night. Destroy them as soon as you are alone."

"But I thought—" began Laner.

"You'll have to wait one more day. Until your travel arrangements are complete."

"We were to leave in three hours—" Laner began again.

"You can't leave until your papers get here. There has been a delay. Don't look at me. That is not my department. You'll leave tomorrow. So I have been assured."

"Your American is slipping," Pitt told him. "So I have been assured," he repeated with high amusement.

Laner asked worriedly, "Tomorrow when?" The sooner he was out of Málaga, the better. He had been counting on leaving tonight.

"Around this time. A man will contact you at each of your hotels—he will use the recognition signals you exchanged with me. And stay in your rooms until he comes. Don't go wandering in the streets. You could be picked up for questioning."

"Why?" No one saw me, no one paid any attention, Laner thought.

"Anyone who was seen at El Fenicio tonight may be picked up for questioning. The Spanish police like to ask questions. We were all noticed back there. Don't kid yourselves about that." He stared hard at Laner, then glanced at Pitt. "Is my American doing better?"

"What about our clothes, money—"

"You'll get them with your papers. Tomorrow. And you may be traveling separately. You knew that, didn't you?"

"No. We weren't told—"

"Of course not," Torrens said genially. "They never tell me anything either until the last minute." He watched some men walking along the street toward them. He spoke quickly. "Both of you take this street down toward the water front. Pitt takes the first alley to his left; you, Laner, take the one on your right. You'll find the addresses on your cards without any trouble. I'll phone them to expect you." He raised his voice to a normal level. The passing strangers could hear whatever they wanted to. "Well— nice meeting you. Drop in when you are next my way. Good night, good night!" He was off, heading for a telephone in the direction of the main street, its lights still bright at two in the morning, calling back over his shoulder in Spanish, "Have a good time in Madrid! Good-bye!"

Pitt and Laner stared at each other, then at the narrow street they had been told to take. It was ill-lit, deserted, a place that worked hard through the day and shut up tight by night. "Dullsville," Pitt said in disgust.

Laner looked back at El Fenicio. It now seemed an oasis in a desert of new buildings. "There are other wineshops. There's always plenty around a harbor."

"What bread have you got?"

"Not much."

Pitt pulled out his wallet, showed it was almost empty, too. "So we do as the man says. We stay in our little rooms, don't wander around town." His voice was bitter. He resented Torrens' quick good-bye that had left them both with their mouths open. "He's a scared cat," he said contemptuously as they started walking down the narrow street. Torrens was already out of sight.

"And scared of what?" Laner was derisive. "A clown tripped over his two big feet and fell off a staircase. Who's to prove otherwise?"

"You sure of that?"

"Sure I'm sure. No one saw me. No one paid any attention," Laner protested. He was about to give some details, but the anger on Pitt's face silenced him. "Hey, man, we've come right across Europe together—"

"And been bossed every step of the way."

Not every step, thought Laner. And without help and instructions, money and safe rooms, where would they have been? But he wasn't arguing with Pitt in this mood. Perhaps it was time they were traveling separately.

They reached the alley that branched to their left. "So this is where I spend my last night in Europe," Pitt said. He didn't think much of it, but he started along it.

"See you in New Orleans," Laner called softly after him. There was no answer. Laner walked on toward the next streetlight. He looked at the card Torrens had pressed into his hand, slipped it into his pocket. He felt the spray gun. He would have more ammunition for it—if you could call an ampoule ammunition—when Torrens sent his duffel bag tomorrow. What was Torrens scared of—that he had ripped it off, smuggled it across Europe, or that he'd keep on using it? Laner was smiling broadly. One test, that's all I needed, just to get the real feel of the thing. One test, that's all I wanted. And better here than back home. Safer is better, isn't it? Besides, the risk was justified: no one saw me, no one noticed a thing. Everyone in that courtyard had had his eyes on the dancer.

Some of the spring came back into Laner's light walk. With

confidence and caution, he appraised the small back street where he'd spend the next twenty-four hours. It was empty, so he could cross without delay to the number he was looking for, slip quietly inside its door. He was expected. The fat, white-faced woman at the bar stopped talking with a half-drunken sailor to give Laner a searching look and then nodded when he sat down at the nearest table. She brought him a glass of wine, asked for no payment. "Room three" was all she said, looking at the stairs beside him, and she went back to the bar. Sleazy, dirty, filled with smoke and nitwitted talk in several languages. Not the Ritz, Laner decided, but safe. There wasn't a boozehound in here who'd remember a thing tomorrow. He kept his eyes on the table, nursed his drink, waiting for the right moment to get upstairs unnoticed. An argument was starting. This was it. Torrens should see him now; he'd be less scared. Torrens . . . One thing you could say for that son of a bitch; he knew how to make quick arrangements.

4

For the first fifteen minutes or so after Reid had left him, Ian Ferrier paid no attention to the empty chair beside him, but concentrated on Pablo's excellent footwork. And after that, there was Miguel's singing. This was the part of flamenco he least enjoyed, but judging from the constant murmur of admiring *olé*'s from the courtyard around him, his taste was either poor or uninformed. Probably both, he thought with some amusement. The guitars were good by any standard. He listened to them, looked up at the stars, did some dreaming.

Then Constanza began her dance, and his eyes were drawn back to the stage again. Halfway through, he had a small qualm about the empty chair beside him: there was a thin line of people now standing along the wall nearby. He glanced at them briefly without turning his head, wondering what the hell was keeping Jeff. And in that split second he glimpsed one of the Americans from the back-corner table—the thin guy with the blond unwashed hair hanging over his brow—standing almost at the door. It may be difficult holding Jeff's place, Ferrier thought worriedly. Esteban, who had been circulating quietly among his patrons, might have had the same idea. He came over to sit down for a few minutes with Ferrier and show that the half-occupied table had his approval, excusing himself with Spanish politeness and a touch of sardonic humor. "Do not worry," he said in Ferrier's ear. "Señor Reid will soon be back. He likes to talk with Magdalena, and she has always much to say."

Magdalena? Ferrier was no wiser, but he nodded. It seemed simpler for a foreigner not to start talking during a performance. Esteban, as manager of El Fenicio and old bullfighter friend, could do as he damned well pleased and get away with it.

"You enjoy our flamenco," Esteban stated, the deep furrows in his face pulling up into a real smile, and his melancholy dark eyes lightening with approval. For a minute or so, he watched the stage along with Ferrier. Then he sensed increasing pressure from the

51

people standing at the side. "Excuse me," he said, rose, bowed, and turned to gesture to them with his hands. They obeyed him, of course. They moved back against the wall. Perhaps Esteban fixed them with those dark eyes of his in the way he had dominated many a bull in the old days. But, thought Ferrier, I bet they don't stay fixed; they'll be back, once Esteban leaves. The thin American with the hunched shoulders was no longer standing near the door. In fact, he wasn't anywhere in sight. Now where did he go? Ferrier wondered; and then, looking at the stage again, forgot his question, didn't even think an answer was important. Constanza was finishing her dance with a succession of fireworks from heels and castanets.

There was a short lull, a sense of waiting, a sudden silence, and then gentle guitars. Tavita rose. She stretched her waist, raised her arms, advanced one thigh. Softly, at first, she began to dance the story of two different loves, a story that had been danced this way for more than four hundred years.

Where's Jeff? Ferrier wondered irritably. He was seeing the most wonderful dancing he had ever imagined, and it was being spoiled for him. (There's something wrong, he kept thinking. Jeff had said he would be back in time to watch Tavita, and he had meant it.) As the dance progressed, from Miguel's pleading into Pablo's demands, Ferrier found he was looking at that door near him, almost as if he were trying to will Jeff to appear. But there was no sign of him. Give up, Ferrier told himself angrily: Jeff manages his own life; if he wants to miss Tavita, that's his business. From then on, almost to the end of the dance, he watched the stage determinedly, ignored the seepage of people along the wall beside him. They had returned, of course, Esteban now being seated at a table of bullfighters on the other side of the courtyard. One of them steadied himself against the back of the empty chair, as if he had been pressed forward unexpectedly. Ferrier glanced sideways, automatically. And beyond the stranger, who gave him a bow of apology, he saw a shaggy nondescript blond head. Ferrier's eyes swerved back to the stage, but the last minutes of violent passion and remorse, now being danced so magnificently by Tavita, were completely ruined for him. The young American had come out of that damned doorway; what the hell was he doing, slinking out in that way? Come to think of it, he had been in there quite a while, hadn't he? If he hadn't come out so carefully, so unobtrusively, Ferrier would have paid less attention. He signed quietly to the stranger who stood by the empty chair that he and his friend could have the table. Then he rose, just as quietly, and made for the doorway.

He entered a room that was dark and silent. A staircase ran steeply up the wall on his right, barely lighted by two naked bulbs on the landing that ran the full width of this hall. There were two entrances up there separated by a clock on the wall. There seemed to be a doorway, too, underneath the landing, down on this level. He had the uncomfortable feeling of being an intruder, and he hesitated, now mistrusting the instinct that had brought him here in such a hurry. The dusty blond American with the hunched shoulders and narrow chest might only have been searching for a men's room, although there was one near the wineshop entrance, much closer to that back-corner table, much more obviously in use than this place; or he could have light fingers and a drug habit to support, but there was nothing down here that could be lifted without the help of two men.

And where was Jeff? The silence worried Ferrier. No sound of voices, no laughter. He decided to try on this floor, first, and quickly skirted the foot of the staircase to reach the door under the landing. He almost fell over Jeff Reid, lying sprawled, face down, one leg twisted under him.

For a moment of complete shock, Ferrier looked down at his friend. He knelt, touched the body. It remained inert. "Good God, Jeff—" he burst out. The head turned a little, the eyes opened, the jaw unclenched, and Reid let out his first groan. His face looked ghastly under the feeble light that filtered down here from the landing; his tan had turned gray, his forehead was beaded with cold sweat, his white lips were bloodied where he had bitten them.

He said softly, "I thought it was that—that—that little creep coming back to make sure." He had a violent attack of shivering.

I'll hear about that later, Ferrier thought grimly. "I'll get help," he said, rising.

Reid made an effort. "Don't alarm the courtyard. Get Magdalena—upstairs. Blanket. Smelling salts."

"An ambulance is more like it," Ferrier said, looking at Reid's leg. Smelling salts?

"But first—blanket. Smelling salts. Fresh air. Pull me near the draft. Pull me!" His voice was desperate.

"You shouldn't be moved," Ferrier warned him, but he took Reid's shoulders, helping him to turn on his back, and then pulled slowly for the six feet necessary to get him away from the lee of the staircase. It must have been the worst kind of torture, but Reid endured it without screaming. He groaned several times, once bit back a yell, and then lay in the cooler draft of pure air with his eyes closing. Ferrier stooped to loosen Reid's collar and tie, and then was running two steps at a time upstairs. Afterwards, he'd wonder how he—twenty pounds lighter and two inches shorter—had managed to pull Reid's dead weight so easily, or even how his feet had seemed to fly up these stairs, but now he thought of nothing except Magdalena.

She heard the pounding of his feet on the wooden landing, came out to meet him as he yelled her name. He looked at her in amazement: she was old and slow-moving, not young, as he had imagined, and probably useless. He pointed down to the room below, grasped her arm to yank her over to the edge of the landing, from where she could see Reid. "Blanket—smelling salts." God, what was the Spanish for smelling salts? "Ammonia." In desperation, he dragged her into the nearest room, picked up a large shawl from a chaise longue, kept saying *"Sels, sels."* (That was French, but what the hell.) He lifted a small bottlelike vase from a table, threw away its rose, and then sniffed at it in mime. She understood. She nodded vehemently, and pulled a small flask out from the pocket of her wide black skirt, where it had been all the time. He took it, tested it, nodded back, and turned to leave. He pointed to the telephone now, and some of his Spanish came back to him. "Call a doctor. Call the hospital. Señor Reid has broken his leg."

"Yes, yes." She pulled the shawl away from him, shaking her head at man's wastefulness, and replaced it with a less elegant (and warmer) blanket from a chest near the door. "Do not disturb the dance!" she warned him in a deep hoarse whisper. He waved a hand, ran on. Magdalena might be old, but she was neither stupid nor useless. Apart from her initial horror and fear, when she had recognized Reid lying on the floor below, she had reacted with a cool sense of the desperate need for haste.

He ran down the staircase, noted that its only weakness was the railing: the treads were solid and firm, built to last like the rest of this place. There's something more to this than a fall and a broken leg, he thought. Reid was semiconscious. He had vomited, and he was shivering. Half-opened eyes looked up at Ferrier, then at the bottle of smelling salts. He nodded gratefully. Something more, Ferrier thought again.

From the courtyard outside came the abrupt silence of a dance that had ended, then the shouts of applause.

Tavita had noticed Reid's empty chair when she had risen to dance, and then as the music caught hold of her she had forgotten about it. Now, standing at the center of the stage with her arms held out for the applause that poured toward her, Miguel and

Pablo spaced behind her, she saw that Ferrier had left, too: strangers sat at that table. Her glance swept on to the rest of the audience, a proud smile of delight on her lips, anger in her heart. I never danced so well, she thought, and they missed it, Jeff and his friend. She bowed her head, let her arms drop to her sides. Raised her head, bowed again. Now the anger was being replaced by worry. She remembered, just in time, to turn to Miguel and then to Pablo, drawing them into the ovation, before she walked back to her chair. She shook her head, as she heard the demands for an encore of the last part of the dance. "Later," she called out, "later," and fanned her face with her hand. She draped her shawl over her warm shoulders, tried to pin back her hair into a coil, wondered how long she would have to sit there. She pressed her fingers to her brow and cheeks, eased the neckline of her dress away from her skin, fingered her hair again, and prepared in general for an exit.

"You look hot," Constanza said, not without malice. You are getting old, the large dark eyes were saying.

"I am hot," she admitted. "This dress is too heavy. I must change." She smoothed her hair again, found it hopelessly disobedient, shook her head over her little defeat, and rose with unconcern. "A *fandango*," she told the guitarists as she left the stage. "Keep it going. Get them dancing in turn. I'll be back in ten minutes." That will hold them, she thought as she made her way, with smiles and bows for the various tables, toward the doorway. Behind her, she heard Constanza's harsh clear voice calling *"Anda, anda!"* The little minx was taking charge. Let her, Tavita thought. I have more to worry about tonight than discipline.

As she stepped over the threshold, she looked back in Esteban's direction. Yes, he had noticed her summons. He would follow her. She started upstairs, got no farther than the first step when she became aware of the visiting American, Jeff's friend, standing in the shadows of the room. "You did not like my dancing?" she began, and then came over slowly, unbelievingly, to where he waited. She stared down at Jeff Reid. She kept staring. "Dead?" She burst into a stream of Spanish, her hands at her face.

"He is alive. He fell from the staircase and broke his leg. We are waiting for the ambulance. It should be here—"

"Fell? Impossible!" She swirled round to speak to Esteban, who had just entered, and again there was a flow of Spanish. Esteban made to close the door.

"No," Ferrier said quietly, "he needs the fresh air. Just keep your voices low." But who would hear anything outside? Flamenco blotted out all other sounds. I never heard the crash of Jeff's fall. And was it a fall? He couldn't understand all of Tavita's denunciation, although he got the idea that she was blaming Tomás: Tomás did this, Tomás tried to kill him. She looked, at this moment, as if she could kill Tomás herself. And so did Esteban. I'm glad I'm not this Tomás, whoever he is, thought Ferrier and glanced at his watch. Every three minutes, Jeff had told him; smelling salts every three minutes. So he knelt beside him, and applied the bottle again. Jeff was looking slightly better; his color was still strange, but the nausea had stopped, and the violent shivers. There was silence in the room. Ferrier looked up to see Tavita watching him. Her anger had vanished. She knelt beside him, touched Jeff's brow, smoothed back his hair. Then she rose, crossing herself quickly, and turned toward the staircase. There were heavy tears on her face.

"I must change," she said, her voice quite calm, even businesslike. "I have to dance." She ran up the stairs, lifting her wide skirt before her. "Magdalena! Magdalena!" No anger now; no tears; just her eyes on the clock. Halfway up to the landing, she remembered to call to Esteban, "Go back into the courtyard. Watch Rodriguez. Do not let him enter. If he is curious, keep talking. Keep him out of here!" She was running again, her dark-red skirt filling the stairway, her black hair fallen loosely down her back.

Esteban had been watching Reid with a mixture of compassion and worry on his gaunt face. "He will be all right," he predicted, and moved toward the courtyard. "I shall send Jaime to be with you."

"Who is Rodriguez?" Ferrier asked, rising, dusting off his trouser legs. Jaime, for Christ's sake—that kid! He wished he had Esteban's confidence about Jeff Reid's recovery, too.

"Captain Rodriguez is State Security," Esteban said, his face quite expressionless.

"Oh, the policeman."

Esteban almost smiled, and went into the courtyard.

Ferrier sat down cross-legged on the floor beside Jeff. He lit a cigarette, smoked it slowly, started to wonder. What was Tavita trying to hide? Allowing for that old business-as-usual, the-show-must-go-on routine, there was yet something else. Secrecy. Reid's accident was to be kept quiet; no one was to know about it, especially Captain Rodriguez. And Jeff, too, hadn't wanted any attention drawn to him. When Ferrier had tucked the blanket around him, told him an ambulance was on its way, he had said, "Stay here, Ian. Until it comes." Then he had made a special effort and added, "No fuss. Don't sound any alarm." At the time, Ferrier had thought Reid was trying to let Tavita's dance end without any distractions, but now he was beginning to believe that there was something more involved. Which, in the cold light of day, would seem ridiculous. Only, this was not the cold light of day. This was a room of shadows off a moonlit courtyard, with an injured man lying on the floor beside him. He finished his cigarette, decided he would have to alter his own plans, remain some extra days in Spain until Jeff was out of danger and had become reconciled to a long stay in a hospital bed. He might even have to cancel that side jaunt to northern Italy, perhaps even his visit to England. The tracking stations in both those places weren't official, anyway: just two interesting, and successful, amateur efforts that had aroused his curiosity and appealed to his sense of humor. In an age of giant, expensive machines, it was encouraging to see what a little money and a lot of human ingenuity could do.

Jaime came into the room, looking both alarmed and excited. He stood over Reid, and Reid—eyes opening at the sound of his footsteps—let out a small, strangled cry.

"Okay, okay," Ferrier said quickly. "It's Jaime." He looked at his friend curiously, offered the smelling salts again.

"No need—I'm feeling better. It's the leg that really bothers me now."

"It's the one that got busted before?"

Reid nodded.

"That figures."

"I was lucky that you—"

"Don't try to talk. Just take it easy."

"But I must—" Reid's face twisted with pain. He recovered, but hesitated, looked at Jaime.

"Jaime, would you please check on the ambulance?" Ferrier tried, in a mixture of Spanish and English. Jaime caught the meaning. He hurried toward the back of the room, disappeared through its doorway. So that's the way we'll make our exit, Ferrier thought, by some back entrance on a small street. No procession through the courtyard, no disturbance, no gossip. These people really knew the meaning of discretion.

"Has he left?" Reid asked. And as Ferrier nodded, he said, "You must phone tonight. Business. Important."

"Take it easy, Jeff. Nothing's so important as getting you—"

"Tonight. Make the call tonight!"

"All right, all right. Where?"

"To Madrid."

"What's the number?"

"Better write it down. There must be no mistake. You won't

find it in the book." Reid was speaking as if he had misgivings, as if he were persuading himself, finding good reasons.

"Have you pencil and paper I can reach? My stuff is in my jacket." And his jacket was now bundled under Reid's head. "Oh, here's a matchbook," he said, fishing it out of his shirt pocket. "Now all I need is a—"

"Try my pocket. Right-hand pocket. Quick, quick!"

Ferrier pulled back the blanket, searched, and found a pencil. It was an automatic one, small and slender, ornate to the touch, possibly made of silver, but it worked all right. "Ready and waiting."

Reid's voice was low. Ferrier had to bend over closely to hear the number clearly. The light was so bad that he struck one of the matches to verify that he had jotted down the figures readably and accurately: 21-83-35. He repeated them aloud, but softly.

Reid nodded. "Ask for Martin—don't write it!"

"I didn't," Ferrier said reassuringly. "I've just written the number. Not Madrid. Not Martin."

"Good. Tell him—tell him I can't keep the Monday appointment. The Monday appointment."

"Sure. You can't keep the Monday appointment."

"Tell him I'm laid up. For weeks. Hell, what a mess!"

"Do I include that?" Ferrier asked with a grin.

"Might do no harm." There was a deep sigh. Reid's eyes stared up at the heavy timbers in the ceiling as if he could find the answers to his problems up there among the decorated beams.

"What if I can't reach them?"

"He will get the message." There was a hesitation. "It's important. We've a lot of competitors."

"I won't forget." Ferrier pocketed the matchbook. "Here's your pencil back." He made a move to replace it.

"No, no! You'll need it. Don't lose it."

So Ferrier pocketed the pencil too. He was puzzled, but he kept silent.

Reid said, "Another thing—you'll find a lighter in my pocket. Take it. Keep it for me. Keep it safe. Safe."

Ferrier found the lighter. It was perfectly normal in shape and size, and smooth to hold except for one small bump in its center —an embossed emblem, some kind of decoration. By this dim light, it was difficult to see what it was, but it could be one of the service Zippos that everyone used to carry around with them. "It's safe," he said, slipping it deep into his trouser pocket.

"Don't use it," Reid was saying anxiously. "Just—"

"Sure, sure. Stop worrying. Take it easy, will you?" Ferrier smoothed back the blanket.

Reid was exhausted, but he was intent on speaking. The whispered phrases became spasmodic. "Martin will send—someone to take—charge—" There was a pause.

"Of the office?"

"Yes. Make sure he—he identifies himself. Get him to—write—"

"Write what?"

"Anything. It's the—the pencil that matters. He uses one—similar to mine." Reid didn't elaborate. Either his mind was drifting or he had something more important to say. "If something—something goes wrong—with me—" Again a pause, as if he were still deciding.

"There's nothing wrong with you that a couple of good doctors can't fix. So shut up, will you?"

"If it does," Reid persisted, "the lighter belongs to Martin. It was his. He will expect it." There was an attempt at a smile. "Sentiment."

Sentiment? Ferrier was perplexed, troubled. There must be real meaning to all this: a man who had made such an effort to speak through his pain must be taken seriously. "Don't worry," he said gently. "I'll see to it."

"You'll remember everything?"

"I'll remember."

Reid relaxed for the first time. "Thank God you've—you've a good memory." He closed his eyes.

There was a movement on the landing. Ferrier looked up quickly. Tavita was just about to come downstairs, her new dress billowing out in a froth of white and yellow. Her hair was perfect, her face freshly made up. She carried a pink cushion in one hand, held the railing with her other as she started down. Behind her, keeping step by step, was Magdalena, holding up the wide hem of the long skirt to keep it from sweeping the staircase. Everything Tavita did, thought Ferrier as he rose to his feet, had a sense of drama.

She came forward, holding out the cushion, saying, "Put this under his head."

"Just leave him as he is," Ferrier said.

Her magnificent eyes took him in, from head to toe. Her voice was cold. "He will be much more comfortable."

"What he needs is an ambulance. Did you telephone the hospital to make sure someone is coming?"

She bit her lip in annoyance, controlled her temper. She did not enjoy a reprimand, however tacit. "Magdalena made very sure. She even telephoned his own doctor."

I hope so, thought Ferrier. The waiting had put him on edge.

"Tavitita," Reid said, opening his eyes. "Don't worry. It takes more than a fall—"

"It was only a fall?"

Magdalena broke in. "I told you," she scolded, "Tomás was back in his room. He was nowhere—" She saw Ferrier looking at her. She took the cushion roughly, said in a mumble, "I told you it was a fall."

Tavita shook her head with real sympathy, regret, impatience —a strange mixture that fascinated Ferrier. The anger and fear she had displayed to Esteban had gone; so had her annoyance with him. "Oh, Jeff, Jeff!" she said slowly. (But she had trouble in pronouncing the first syllable, and it sounded more like Hyeff. Well, thought Ferrier, I can stop worrying about my lousy Spanish accent. We all have our tongue-twisting troubles.) "Why did it *have* to happen at this time?" She looked at Ferrier. "Please."

"Of course." He moved away quickly, stood just within the shelter of the doorway, looked at the stage with its tableau of bright color and postures, listened to the guitars instead of Tavita's voice. They are friends, he decided, not lovers; at least, not permanently. And the idea startled him. He had assumed, somehow, that Reid's interest in El Fenicio was a matter of passionate romance. That would have been his own interest, he admitted to himself. She was the most beautiful, tantalizing, upsetting, and annoying woman he had ever met. If he had had ten years of experience less, if he were in his twenties instead of the less vulnerable thirties, he'd be in love with Tavita and probably thoroughly destroyed emotionally. It might be worth it at that, he thought. He sensed her behind him, turned to look at her. "You make the most beautiful pictures," he blurted out, watching the angle of her head, the slender neck, the soft skirt ruffling out from tightly molded waist and hips.

She didn't even hear the unwilling compliment. "You are his friend," she said, studying his face. She looked at the steady gray eyes, the pleasant but firm lips, the marked bone structure that gave strength to his features, and found them reassuring. "I think you are a good friend," she added softly, her eyes lingering on his. "You will help me?" She didn't even wait for an answer, but—listening to the music, timing the moment for reappearance— stepped into the courtyard, and with that exquisite grace made her way toward the stage.

Esteban was beside him. "Everything is all right."

"Captain Rodriguez is not interested?" Ferrier asked with a small smile. And interested in what? He wondered if Esteban would tell him who Tomás was. Or why the feeling of secrecy, of some small conspiracy, inside this room. Or was all this quite natural, and Ferrier only sensed strangeness because he was a foreigner here, plunged into a setting and a group of people that were nothing like anything he had ever encountered before? He looked over at Reid and Magdalena. Goddammit, she *had* moved Jeff, replaced his folded jacket with that pink pillow. She was shaking out the jacket now, lamenting its creases and dust stains from the floor.

"The captain has left," Esteban said with obvious satisfaction. But if he was relieved, he was also thoughtful. "He left as soon as Tavita had finished her dance."

"He didn't stay long," Ferrier said, making conversation. He was more interested in the view he had from this doorway; here, unnoticed by the people in the courtyard, he could see the middle and front tables as well as the stage. The only table that was fully blocked from sight by the scattering of standees down the side of the courtyard was the nearest one, the one he had occupied with Jeff. As he watched, the little group in front of him moved slightly, parted just enough to let him see the heads of the two men who had taken that table, and then the gaps closed again and the table was hidden. Now if I had been that long-haired guy who slipped out of here, Ferrier thought, I'd have felt quite safe; I couldn't have guessed when people might move unexpectedly and let someone sitting at that table catch a glimpse of me. But why should I have wanted to feel safe? What would I be trying to conceal? "I think," he told Esteban slowly, "that you should keep an eye on the Americans—the ones at the back of the courtyard."

"But they have left, too." Esteban looked at him sharply. "Why should I watch them?"

"When did they leave?"

Esteban shrugged his shoulders. "Jaime will know. He was their waiter. But why—?"

"I was just curious." He turned away from the door. He looked at the staircase. A fall? Yes, that could always be possible—if Jeff had landed in a heap at the bottom of the stairs. But he hadn't. He had fallen over the side, about halfway up. And this wasn't a free-standing staircase, either: it had a decorative iron railing, not too strong to look at but high enough to reach a man's waist, and you didn't topple easily over that even if you had been running downstairs, had slipped, lost your balance.

Esteban said, "Do not be so worried, Señor Ferrier. The hospital is excellent. I know it well. I was there eleven times."

"Eleven wounds?"

"Seventeen," Esteban said gravely. "Some of them very bad; others just simple gashes from the bulls' horns. Do not worry. Señor Reid will walk normally again, as I do. He will be in good hands. The best."

"I'm glad to hear that," Ferrier said, equally gravely. He wondered.

"You must come back another night," Esteban told him. "Then you can enjoy yourself. Tonight was unfortunate." He gave that small formal bow of his, returned to the courtyard.

That's right, thought Ferrier: everything must continue normally, even Esteban in his appointed rounds. Seventeen wounds . . .

Magdalena had cleaned most of the dust from his jacket. She had removed his wallet and passport for safety while she had shaken vigorously, and they lay neatly on a wine barrel along with his car keys and loose coins. She replaced them all carefully and correctly, handed the jacket to him. These people really slay me, he thought. "Thank you, Magdalena," he said. "Tell me, who is Tomás?" The effect was immediate. Her eyes widened in horror. Then quickly she crossed herself.

"Was that for me or for him?" Ferrier asked. But she did not wait to answer; she was already halfway toward the door that young Jaime had taken. I bet she is going to warn him not to talk about Tomás to me, Ferrier thought. "How's it going?" he asked Reid.

"Could be worse."

"Yes. You could have broken your neck. You were damned lucky."

Reid nodded. He tried to say something, couldn't manage it.

"Save it. You can tell me tomorrow. Or the next day. I'll hang around." Where was that ambulance? Ferrier concentrated on it, as if by thinking about it he could bring it more quickly through the streets to El Fenicio's back entrance. His sense of helplessness increased his worry; he was a foreigner in a completely strange city. Back home, in a situation like this, he could have taken charge, or at least felt useful. Here, he had to wait and hope that an old woman and a young boy, who only understood half of what he wanted to say, would somehow get everything squared away.

And they did, too. Not badly, at that. When the ambulance arrived—without sirens or horns blowing madly—the stretcher-bearers were quick and gentle, the intern was efficient. "I'll see you into the hospital. Make sure you get the prettiest nurse," Ferrier told Reid just before the morphine hit him.

Magdalena was saying, as she gathered together the cushion and the smelling salts, "Stay here, señor." She pointed to the courtyard. "You will enjoy the dancing."

"The best is to come," Jaime assured him. "I shall find you a good table."

"Thank you, no." Ferrier hurried after the stretcher, leaving two worried faces looking blankly at each other. Now what had they been cooking up? he wondered, and then dismissed his question as idiotic. Why would Magdalena and Jaime want to keep him here, except as a matter of politeness?

"Señor!" Magdalena called after him. "Tavita would like to see you." He pretended he hadn't heard, and kept on his way.

5

Hospitals were places that Ferrier usually liked to avoid—big, antiseptic, impersonal factories for the cure of the suffering where a visitor felt lost in a mile of faceless corridors; depressed, too, with the innumerable doors behind which were people in pain, pain forever behind those doors, with beds never empty, continuously filled and refilled. Tonight, the usual gloom fell over him like a cloak as soon as he stepped into the reception room even if the Hospital de Santa Maria de la Victoria was small, one of the smallest in the city, and peaceful and seemingly capable. Bewilderment attacked him, not because of the length of interminable corridors—here they were short, with red-tiled floors burnished to a rich gleam under the subdued lights on the thick white walls—but because he was a foreigner in a completely strange place facing the totally unexpected. Not that he objected to the unexpected if his own choice led him to it. But an hour ago he had been sitting in a courtyard looking at the stars above him, listening to flamenco, and now he was grappling with a long question-and-answer form to give all the necessary information about Reid and his accident, how it happened and where and when. (The why of it was a question that kept lingering at the back of his mind.) The change was almost too abrupt; like the ice-cold pool after a sauna. But it braced him. A man could immobilize himself by asking questions that had no answers. He stopped wondering about the meaning of that telephone call to Madrid, and prepared to make it. 21–83–35. That's how he remembered the number. He checked with the matchbook and found he was right.

After all, he thought as he enlisted the help of the man behind the reception desk, hospitals were accustomed to telephone calls, both in and out. The man was elderly, sympathetic, and pleased to break the dull routine of a quiet night with some low-pitched advice. The call went through quickly enough from one of the public telephones in the adjoining waiting room—empty except for two sad-faced women huddled together at the end of a bench.

And there was only a brief pause at the Madrid end of the line before a man's voice answered. Ferrier gave the message, word for exact word, just as he had been given it.

It was a businesslike voice, speaking in Spanish at first, and then breaking into English as the man heard Ferrier's slight hesitations with syntax. No, Señor Martin was not there, but he would receive the message on his return. Who was calling?

"My name's Ferrier. I'm staying with Mr. Reid for the weekend."

"How did the accident happen? And when?"

"He slipped on some stairs. About an hour ago."

"How serious?"

"He says it's one helluva mess. I won't know exactly until I hear from the doctors. They are with him now. He's in the Santa Maria de—"

"Señor Martin will be sorry to hear about it," the cool voice said quickly. And the call was ended.

And who was that? Ferrier wondered. A secretary of some kind? He had spoken with self-assurance, with decision in his voice. Whoever he was, he was certainly a man in a hurry. In fact, if he had only waited a minute longer he could have had the doctor's report. Ferrier was lighting a cigarette and watching the cover of the matchbook burn into a twisted black ash when he heard his name being gently called from the doorway. It was the sister in charge, the rolled brim of the large starched hat that covered her hair nodding to him to make haste. Dr. Medina was waiting. So he dropped the remains of the matchbook into a potted plant and followed her, a ship in full sail, with her long, wide skirt down to her ankles and her broad swathe of white apron wrapped around the heavy gray dress. It was astonishing that anyone so bundled with clothes could look so neat and cool and businesslike on a warm summer night.

Dr. Medina was grave as he should be, but not pessimistic. Tactfully, he spoke in English, slowly, carefully, but with confidence. He was a confident man. "A compound fracture of the right leg—some complications because of previous injuries, but no cause for alarm—no break in the right arm bone, only severe contusions, a wrenched shoulder."

"Is he showing any more symptoms of sickness? His color was bad, at first. He needed fresh air—made me pull him over to the door and asked for—"

"You *moved* him?" Dr. Medina was scandalized.

"He was insistent. He seemed to know what he needed."

"Ridiculous."

"He was shivering violently, too."

"Possibly shock. I can't diagnose from a description. But I can assure you he is a man of normally excellent health. I am his own personal physician—brought here tonight as a matter of courtesy." He bowed to the sister, spoke rapidly in Spanish. She replied in her soft gentle voice, held out a bunch of keys. "Oh, yes," Medina said to Ferrier. "Señor Reid was conscious for a few minutes. He left a message for you. Can you understand Spanish?"

Ferrier's eyes measured the quiet face of the nun. She will tell me more than any busy doctor, he decided. "Yes. But please speak slowly," he told her with a smile.

She gave him the keys. "Señor Reid said you would need these. He wants you to come tomorrow—"

"Nonsense. Let him sleep all tomorrow," Dr. Medina said.

"—and bring him some things. His razor, books to read, his small radio from his study. Also the dictaphone on his desk and his engagement calendar."

"Incredible!" Dr. Medina said. "Is he going to turn his hospital bed into an office? Bring no such things, Señor Ferrier. And if you come along on Sunday, that will be time enough for him to have visitors."

The sister said sadly, "He made such an effort to give me that message. Perhaps it would be better not to disappoint him? If he isn't well enough tomorrow, then we will just keep these things until he *is* well enough."

Ferrier said, "When should I come? Around six?"

She nodded.

"*If* he is awake," Dr. Medina warned, "I don't want him disturbed."

She nodded again, a wise woman who knew when to stop making suggestions.

Dr. Medina bade her good night, rather formally, most correctly, and added his thanks. "Come on," he said to Ferrier. "I'll give you a lift back to the house. No—no trouble; it's on my way, and my car's outside."

"Tomorrow at six," Ferrier told the sister. "And my thanks, too."

She murmured something in Latin and turned away.

"Now we've been sanctified," Medina said as they went into the street. "Feel better?" His stiffness had vanished along with his slightly pompous bedside manner. He was easy and relaxed. "That place always makes me a little nervous," he confided. "But don't worry, your friend is in good hands. I prefer the other hospital, of course. That's the big Civil Hospital, west of the city. We have more laboratories and fewer crucifixes on the walls. Didn't you notice them back there?"

"Yes." Ferrier made no other comment.

"What are you?" Medina asked amiably. "Catholic or diplomat?"

"A heretic. You might call me an independent Protestant."

"Church once a year?"

"Not even that."

Medina laughed, but he was friendly. "You accept religion?"

"If it does good."

"Spoken like an old-time liberal." Medina opened the door of his small white buglike car. "What about coming home with me for some supper and a bit of an argument?"

"Another time," Ferrier said firmly. There was a scattering of people on the street, but for him this night was over. "Haven't got accustomed to Spanish hours," he admitted. He looked back at the hospital, with its high-walled garden at one side. There was a small chapel in there, with an old tower and the rest of it new. In the moonlight, the rest of the buildings looked new, too, even if the style of architecture was in an older tradition. "Rebuilt?" he asked.

Medina was busy maneuvering the car into the road. "There was a fire some years ago," he said vaguely. "Are you going to the bullfight on Sunday? It's a big day here. Twelve thousand people crowding to see it. That hospital won't be such a quiet little place then. Have you ever seen a bullfight?"

"Yes."

"You don't like them?"

"Not particularly. I'm on the side of the horses."

Medina was amused. "Typical American. A man of lost causes."

And just what cause is yours? Ferrier wondered. He spent the next ten minutes answering questions about his journey to Málaga, his impressions of El Fenicio and flamenco. They were just reaching the topic of Ferrier's job as they came to the long line of plane trees that lined the Calle San Julian. "Hey, stop! My street," Ferrier said. They had overrun it. "Don't bother to back and turn. I can walk the rest. Jeff's place is only a few houses away. I won't get lost." He shook hands, added his thanks.

"At least you won't get mugged," Medina told him pointedly.

Sharp to the last little dig, thought Ferrier. "That's right," he said. "All I have to do is fight off mosquitoes. Thanks again."

"Don't worry about Señor Reid," Medina called after him.

"He's as strong as an ox. And sometimes as stupid. But we'll get him well, in spite of himself." He waved as he drove off.

A cantankerous cuss, thought Ferrier, and on the young side for the role of curmudgeon. Medina was possibly in his middle thirties. In the hospital he had acted as if he were fifty, rigidly correct in dress and manner. Outside, the pressure-cooker lid had come off, and he was tossing out remarks as if he were a precocious kid without much thought behind him. But which was the real Medina? Come to think of it, which was the real Ian Ferrier?

And that was quite a question, he decided as he approached Reid's house. The short walk had done him good. The air was warm, perfumed from the gardens; the street was quiet, with only a few men strolling along as he was. Medina's remark about muggers had annoyed him, but it was true enough. It was a pleasant thing to be able to walk along a city street at half past three in the morning and not wonder what footsteps following too closely might mean. He drew aside to let three young men pass him. They were deep in an argument about football.

He might have strolled on, down to the end of the Calle San Julian, except that he had been right about mosquitoes. They were beginning to come out in full force. By dawn, they would be invading all those open windows in the houses around him, clustering on the netting over the beds like a swarm of sailors on a ship's rigging. He paused just long enough under the nearest street lamp to look at the bunch of keys that Reid had sent him and select the most probable one for the front door. He made his choice from size: apart from two obvious car keys, there were three miniature Yale types, which possibly opened drawers or cabinets, and a larger one of old-fashioned design fit for a main entrance. He opened the gate to Number Nine and started up the driveway. It edged one side of the garden, following the straight line of one of the boundary walls that separated Reid's house from its neighbors. The darkness emphasized the feeling of enclosure. Some people might call it privacy; others would term it suffocation. It was certainly peaceful. If people lived next door, you would never know it. This villa in its small garden was a world of its own.

Ahead of him, the driveway broadened into a small parking space at the side of the house where the entrance to the kitchen quarters lay. All that wing seemed pretty much asleep now, although it had been filled with voices and laughter and scoldings and general give-and-take when he had left his car there after dinner. Reid had explained. "Concepción's family. Part of it, at least. I lose track of their comings and goings, but why worry as long as she housekeeps and cooks and is completely dependable?" But it developed, a little to Ferrier's disappointment, that Concepción belied her name; the family consisted of her nieces and her cousins and her aunts, not to mention nephews and uncles or whoever decided to pay her a visit. She was a childless widow, but she was rarely lonely. It all evened out, Reid had said philosophically. Food bills might run high, but the house was well scrubbed and polished: Concepción made them work for their supper. A brood of relatives was something accepted without protest or revolt in this part of the world.

Ferrier could see the outline of his car now, standing at one side of the little yard. But just beyond it, almost opposite the kitchen entrance, there was a second car. It was Reid's. He recovered from his astonishment and walked on, branching off the driveway toward the front of the house. Someone had brought it back from El Fenicio and saved him a journey down there tomorrow. That was how he looked at it. He concentrated on unlocking the front door, wondering now why all the outside lights had been turned off. Perhaps Concepción was extra conscientious about electric bills to make up for her relatives' appetites. After some fumbling, he got the key into the lock. It worked. He batted off the mosquitoes from his shoulders and neck, stepped into the small entry hall. Here at least was some light, subdued but sufficient to let him take a few steps into the main room.

It looked ghostly with its white walls looming vaguely out of the shadows. Arched openings led to pits of darkness: on his left, the dining room; on his right, the study. Facing him, the wall had a long diagonal of steps, edged with twists and curls of black iron railing, mounting to the bedrooms above. Near the foot of this staircase was another arch, leading to a corridor that must reach into the back of the house. The geography was fairly simple, and if only he knew where the light switches were, then all his problems would be solved. What he wanted to do now was to get to the study, find some paper, and jot down Reid's requests while the details were clear in his mind. Razor, dictaphone, engagement pad, books. Oh, yes—a radio, too, just to keep Reid worrying about the state of this mixed-up world.

Ferrier made his way cautiously over the tiled floor, avoiding collision with the furniture—the pieces were fortunately few, but they were massive stuff, hand-carved and solid, painful for an unsuspecting thigh or shin bone—and reached a high-backed chair. He had sat there, that evening, and he remembered the huge wrought-iron lamp that stood behind it. It was dark in this corner, darker than he imagined as he had paused at the hall's threshold. He groped his way around the chair, cursing silently. His hands, held out blindly before him, struck a large vellum shade and set it quivering. He steadied it, cursed himself for having burned his matchbook, and fumbled for some kind of switch. Was it twist or pull? At that moment, a door opened somewhere down that kitchen corridor. Footsteps, light and quick, were coming in this direction. So Concepción wasn't asleep, as he had imagined. He was about to call out and give warning that he was there, that he couldn't find the damned switch; would she turn on some lights? But a man's voice was speaking, briefly, in a hoarse whisper. Concepción was answering. And Ferrier was standing there with his Spanish phrases stuck on his tongue.

"To your left!" she was saying as they came into the room, and she flicked on a wall switch that illuminated the staircase and the landing above. "Quick, quick!" She was dressed for bed, with a cotton wrapper over a nightdress, her lank hair in braids down her back.

The man moved swiftly. He was already halfway up the stairs. Then he seemed to sense something. He stopped abruptly, looked down into the room, reached into his jacket. It was that movement that kept Ferrier quite still, his lips now tightly closed, his eyes narrowing as he watched the man. Thick, dark but graying hair; black eyebrows; deeply tanned face, heavily furrowed; medium height, medium weight; well dressed. And armed.

"It is only Jaime," Concepción reassured the man impatiently. The boy had entered the corridor, carrying a suitcase. The stranger's hand came out from his jacket, and he started climbing the rest of the stairs. Concepción was at his heels, and then came Jaime with the suitcase. The strange procession vanished. In the upper hall, footsteps faded, suddenly ended.

Ferrier gave up on the lamp—no matter what he turned or tugged, it refused to light. He started toward the archway where Concepción had managed to make something work. And at that point, Jaime came running downstairs. He slowed as he saw Ferrier, completed the last steps hesitantly. Several emotions passed over his young honest face: astonishment, worry, fear. Then they cleared away as he noticed Ferrier's smile. "But, señor," he began, "we heard no doorbell. How did—"

"Keys. Señor Reid gave them to me."

"When did you—"

"A few minutes ago. Before you carried the suitcase upstairs."
Jaime's eyes widened. Anxiety was back.

Ferrier had reached the arch. He examined the array of push
buttons set into its heavy wall. "I was looking for some light to
get me into the study." He pressed several of the buttons as he
spoke, and the whole room lit up: four standing lamps, one in
each corner; eight wall brackets; two table lamps. "I certainly
got it."

Jaime was worrying about the suitcase. "An emergency,
Señor Ferrier. Esteban's house was full. No room left. There is
a bullfight on Sunday; everyone is coming to see it. So I have to
sleep here, and so has my cousin Pépé, who is a *banderillero*.
And we also brought his—his manager."

Ferrier noticed the hesitation. The pleasant thing about honest
people was that it really hurt them to tell a lie. "That one?" he
asked, pointing up the staircase. "One of the sixty-percenters?
No wonder he can afford to dress in silver-gray."

"Señor Reid has met him. Señor Reid knows my cousin.
Esteban said Señor Reid would not object." Jaime, still anxious,
followed Ferrier over to the study. "Esteban said—"

"Okay, okay, okay. You seem to know your way around here.
Can you find me a drink? Scotch, if there is any."

"I know where it is. I come here to help my aunt when there
is a big party." The words were tumbling out now as Jaime
could talk about something that was both real to him and true.
"And you would like ice," he said quickly. "Soda?"

Ferrier had to laugh. "I'd like all of that. But tell me, Jaime—
where did Esteban find keys for Señor Reid's car?"

"The Señorita Octavia had an extra key. Señor Reid gave it
to her. For emergencies."

"The Señorita Who?"

"Tavita."

So Tavita was in this, and Esteban, and Concepción, and her
two nephews. The family angle? "Is Concepción also the aunt of
Esteban?"

That broke out a wide grin on the boy's thin, worried face.
"She is his sister."

"And Tavita is—what?"

"Her father was the uncle of Concepción's sister-in-law."

"You've lost me. Better get that drink. And then get to bed.
You look as if you needed some sleep." As we all do. I'm ex-

hausted, Ferrier thought; slow-moving, slow-thinking. "Seems as if Concepción has decided to spend the night upstairs."

Jaime was shocked. "Oh, no, señor." Then he saw the joke, but resisted it. "My aunt does not behave like that. She is making the bed with sheets and—"

"Not a romantic type," Ferrier agreed. What had Reid called her? "Completely dependable." But Jaime was already on his way to the pantry for the ice. Ferrier sat down at the desk, began making his list for tomorrow. He heard Concepción returning downstairs, exclaiming as she came about the blaze of lights. She had gathered a good head of indignation by the time she reached the big room, and made for the study at express speed with some angry comments on Jaime's sanity. She stopped short at the door, almost sliding on the tile floor, as she saw it was Ferrier at the desk. She regained her balance, but not her tongue. He looked at the sallow face, now flushed either with haste or with dismay, at the straggling plaits falling over her shoulders, at her worried eyes. He lifted Reid's bunch of keys into view. "I know," he said. "You didn't hear the bell."

"I thought Jaime—" she said haltingly.

"He is getting me a drink. And then we'll all go to bed."

She nodded. Her large dark eyes kept watching him, as if they could learn what he knew or didn't know. "Jaime brought the car back," she tried.

"Most thoughtful of him."

Her eyes left his face, traveled to the telephone. She moistened her pale lips, frowned. She scarcely noticed Jaime as he returned with a tall glass on a small silver tray.

Ferrier finished the list, pocketed it. "By the way," he said quietly, "Señor Reid is all right. A fractured leg. But he is well." He looked at them quickly, caught the open dismay and contrition on both their faces. He felt slightly better about that: they had forgotten to ask about Reid, not because they hadn't been worried about him, but because they had bigger troubles. "Thanks, Jaime," he said, and took the drink. Again he noticed Concepción's glance at the telephone. "Do you want to call someone?" he asked bluntly.

She flushed again. "Perhaps Esteban? At El Fenicio? To let him know that—that Señor Reid is all right? He would want to know."

I bet that's the least of his worries tonight, thought Ferrier. "Go ahead." Rising, he picked up his glass. Why feel aggrieved that I can't finish my drink down here in peace? Why feel anything at all? This isn't my house. This is none of my business.

"Thank you, señor. When do you want to be awakened tomorrow?"

"I usually waken myself."

"Perhaps your breakfast tray at noon? It is very late now. And it has been a difficult day."

Was it thoughtfulness, or some necessity for an exact timetable? He couldn't help wondering about that. "Noon," he agreed. Eight hours of sleep seemed a pleasant idea. "Good night."

"Good night, señor." She nodded to Jaime to go with him, and picked up the telephone. Everything was all right, she was assuring Esteban as Ferrier began climbing the stairs.

Yes, he thought, everything is all right: Jaime delivered the merchandise and I asked her no questions. He didn't know whether to laugh or lose his temper. "You don't have to see me safely into my room," he told Jaime sharply. "I can find my own way. Good night."

"There may be a difficulty with lights," the boy said, a hint of a smile at the back of his eyes. It spread over his solemn face as he saw Ferrier's annoyance vanish. No more was said, but the silence was friendly.

At the top of the stairs, Jaime put his finger to his lips, led the way along the upper hall with a catlike tread that increased Ferrier's amusement. But he followed obediently. His room lay at the end of this hall, but before they were halfway there, Jaime paused at a narrow door. Again the finger went up to his lips as he turned its handle slowly, cautiously. What the hell is he doing? Ferrier thought in alarm; that man is bound to be awake. Who would want to look in on that furrowed face and wish him good night? Jaime opened the door just enough to let Ferrier see a steep flight of stairs leading upward between two walls of yellowed plaster. Then, carefully and silently, he closed the door. Ferrier pointed to the ceiling overhead, and raised an eyebrow. Jaime nodded, and resumed his tiptoeing toward the end of the hall. Again, Ferrier followed obediently. A couple of conspirators within a conspiracy, he thought, not knowing whether to laugh or worry. He returned Jaime's whispered good night with a nod of thanks, and watched the boy walk soundlessly back along the corridor.

A conspiracy? Ferrier looked around the bedroom. The word seemed ridiculous in this comfortable and welcoming place. Concepción had been in here and straightened everything out for him. Fresh pillows on that big, beautiful bed; mosquito netting undraped to encircle it. The room was high-ceilinged and cool; restful, too, with tall shuttered windows overlooking a quiet and peaceful garden. He would sleep well here, and all the better for knowing that the stranger had been tucked away in the attic and wasn't in the next room.

He locked his door—something he didn't usually do in a private house—and tested it. Then he emptied his pockets quickly, heaping their contents on the dressing table. He picked out Jeff Reid's pencil and lighter, examined them closely. The pencil was of silver, as he had guessed, finely ornamented with a light tracery of arabesques. The lighter was a type he remembered well; it was made of steel, dark in color, with its small Air Force emblem embossed in brass. It was just the kind of thing that Jeff would carry around with him as a memento of old times, a good-luck piece. There was nothing remarkable about it except for the intensity in his voice when he had said, "Keep it safe. Safe." Ferrier found a clean handkerchief, wrapped the lighter and pencil in it securely, and placed it under his pillow. He felt like an idiot, but at this time in the morning, he had no better ideas. I guess I just don't trust that man upstairs, he told himself, not even when he has been pushed into an attic.

Why the attic? Why the secrecy? Of course, you could rationalize the whole sequence of events. Concepción didn't like the man, was giving him no favors, no encouragement to prolong his stay. Yet, even if he was an unwelcome guest, her whole treatment of him jibed with the Spaniards' engrained sense of hospitality. Rationalizations were a nice easy way to find comfortable solutions, but they weren't working tonight. The only answer he could find to his questions was one without any proof: Concepción had been instructed to hide the man as securely as possible.

Why, why, and again why? His questions depressed him, because they brought back the feeling of some kind of conspiracy, and that was something he would rather not face at this hour. He needed sleep. The only questions that were worth staying awake for were those that could have definite answers. And he hadn't any, probably never would. It was none of his damned business, he told himself once more, as he stripped off his clothes.

He adjusted the louvers of the shutters to let in as much air as possible and stood at the window for a few minutes feeling the fresh coolness from the garden pour over his skin. The stars were fading. Shapes of trees were emerging more clearly; shadows were losing their rigid lines. The street was silent, the houses asleep. It was still and peaceful, and innocent. Not the kind of place where a man needed to carry a pistol around in a pocket of his silver-gray suit.

"Oh, shut up!" he said angrily, heard the first flight of mosquitoes coming in for their dawn raid and made a dive for the bed, switching off the last small light, pulling the net curtains around him. Smooth sheets, soft pillows took over. His eyes closed, and the questions, as voracious as the female mosquitoes clinging onto the closed net, stopped biting at his mind.

6

The morning light, clear and intense, scored the floor with sharply drawn lines, spread over the bed to touch Ferrier's face. He came alive slowly. Someone didn't close the shutters properly, he thought; someone left those damned louvers too far open. There was the sound of water flowing gently. Fountains? Granada? He opened his eyes fully, stared at the crown of mosquito netting far above his head. Not Granada, but Málaga. Granada had been yesterday's awakening. He closed his eyes again, but he knew that sleep was gone. So he swung his legs off the bed, pushing aside the net draped around him—the mosquitoes had retired for the day, he noted with approval—and stepped from the small rug onto the cold marble of the floor. He headed for the bathroom, wondering if he had left a faucet turned on last night. The puzzle was solved as he halted at a window. One of the girls who had helped serve dinner and raise the chatter level in the kitchen afterward was now down in the garden, watering the plants with a hose. Jaime was there, too, hindering her with advice. They were keeping their voices low, by command obviously. Such restraint was scarcely natural to either of them.

Ferrier swung back the shutters to let the morning air come unchecked into the room. Jaime glanced up as he heard them scrape. He looked so astounded that Ferrier, retreating with a wave of his hand, stopped at the dressing table, where he had dropped his small belongings last night, and picked up his watch to check on the time. Twenty minutes past nine. Five hours of sleep. He was adopting Spanish habits with a vengeance; he'd probably start thinking a two-hour siesta was the only way to pass an afternoon. One thing, certainly: Concepción's timetable had been thrown out of kilter. Jaime was no doubt now in the kitchen, spreading his astonishment.

77

Jaime was actually in the dining room. There, his aunt was superintending the washing of the floor. He beckoned her away from Angela, who was down on her knees, into the privacy of the pantry. (Pépé was in the kitchen, finishing a long breakfast.)

"He's awake," Jaime said.

"Impossible."

"He's awake."

"But he said—"

"I saw him at the window."

"He will go back to bed. You must have been talking too loudly with—"

"He has opened the shutters wide."

"Then he is mad. Does he want to turn his room into an oven?" Concepción, reverting to her usual role of capable housekeeper, fumed over that piece of stupidity, and then forced herself back to the problem. "I shall telephone El Fenicio and warn Magdalena. She can waken Tavita." Yes, that was a good solution, Concepción declared. Let Magdalena handle this.

"Tavita will not like—"

"She will have to. That is her worry." Concepción began preparing the breakfast tray. "This is ours."

"What about Pépé?"

"Tell him to leave. And fetch Maria from the garden. I'll send her and Angela down to the market." She put a plate on the tray, took it off, frowned at it, put it back again.

"I'll set the tray," Jaime suggested. "You had better telephone." He had never seen his aunt so flustered. "What about the man in the attic?"

"I took him food an hour ago."

"Is he really in such danger?"

Concepción's voice became vehement. "I do not care if he is." She lowered it quickly, almost hissed out the words in her intensity. "But he is putting us all in danger—that is what I care about. The sooner we get rid of him—" She didn't finish the sentence. As she left for the telephone, she added two descriptive words that left Jaime with his eyes wide and his lips breaking into an incredulous grin.

Ferrier had shaved, showered, and stowed away the lighter and pencil in his trouser pocket by the time the breakfast tray was carried in by Concepción. She looked better this morning, although her eyes showed nervous strain; there was a pleasant expression on her lips, a more amiable note in her voice, and competence in her movements. Her smoothly brushed hair and neat blouse and skirt became her more than the rag-tag effect of last night. Her confidence had returned, and she took charge efficiently. The tray would go on this low table, just here, before the opened windows; they must be closed, and the shutters too, before eleven o'clock, or else it would be impossible to sleep in comfort this afternoon; Señor Ferrier's yellow jacket must be cleaned and pressed at once; was there anything else, was he comfortable, had he slept well last night?

Ferrier gave up the idea of suggesting that he'd like his breakfast downstairs—he preferred his elbows on a table to picking off a tray—and asked for something to read. But that idea was forestalled. Jaime had been waiting outside the door with a bundle of American magazines and papers under his arm. He came in as Concepción left. And stayed.

At first, Ferrier thought it was politeness: was the coffee strong enough, the orange juice all right? And then he thought that Jaime might be trying to practice his English. But after five minutes of aimless questions, Ferrier began to wonder. He finished a piece of heavily crusted bread, avoided the sweet rolls, ignored the two thick slices of golden cake, poured himself some more coffee, picked up the Paris *Herald Tribune* that was four days old and opened it determinedly. "Doesn't your aunt need you downstairs?"

Seemingly not.

"You tell her," Ferrier said, "that there's no need to keep watch over me. I shall be here for another ten or fifteen minutes. After that, I'm going out. Simple, isn't it?" Once more, he didn't know whether to be annoyed or entertained.

Jaime was neither. He said unhappily, "I only wanted to talk."

"Then talk. About the man in the attic. How long does he stay there?"

"Not long."

"Who is he?"

Jaime shook his head.

At least, thought Ferrier, no more pretense about my cousin Pépé's manager. "Where did he come from?"

"From El Fenicio."

"And before that?"

Again Jaime shook his head. "I wasn't told," he said.

"His name? Come on, Jaime. You must call him something."

"We know him as Tomás."

"That is pretty indefinite."

Jaime nodded his agreement.

"When did he arrive at El Fenicio?"

"I only saw him last night."

"Last night seems to have been a strange one for all of us," Ferrier said. His voice had lost its sharpness. The boy was telling the truth as far as he knew it. Which was, Ferrier reflected, just about the most that could be said for any of us.

Jaime sensed the change and welcomed it. He liked to talk and he wanted to talk, as long as the man in the attic was left out of it. He said eagerly, "It was strange from the beginning. From the minute the four Americans sat down at that table in the back corner of the courtyard, it was very strange. The bearded one pointed out Señor Reid. And then the others—"

"Hold it, hold it!" Jaime's rush of words had brought a change in accent, and Ferrier wondered if he had misheard. "He pointed out Señor Reid? Are you sure?"

"It was Señor Reid, not you."

Ferrier stared.

"They were talking about your table. The black man asked, 'Which? The one in the yellow jacket?' The long-haired man added some words to describe you. I didn't understand them all—sometimes English is difficult to follow. The black and the long-hair laughed. But they stopped when the beard said, 'No. The other one.' And then, at that moment, Señor Reid turned around to signal to me. They were all silent. The man with the beard looked away. The long-hair said, 'So that's the big see eye eh man!' And the man with the beard was angry. Truly angry. I came forward to serve you, so I did not hear the words he said. The others were laughing at him. And so—he left."

"What did the man with the long hair call Señor Reid?" Ferrier asked slowly.

"A man who sees with his eyes."

"No, tell me—just as you heard it. Stop thinking of the meaning." Ferrier rose, found his pen and address book. He tore out a page. "Write the words here."

"But I don't write English. I don't read it. I learn it by ear."

"Then use Spanish words that have the same sounds that you heard."

"It is difficult. Spanish sounds are different."

"I know."

Jaime took the pen and wrote *Si*. He paused to admire it. "Yes, that is almost the same sound." Then he wrote, after some thought, *Ay*. "That is not the same, but it is close." He finished with *E*.

"It's close," Ferrier said softly. So that's the big CIA man.

. . . "What did Esteban or Magdalena think about this? Or Concepción?"

"But I told no one. Only you." Jaime broke into Spanish. "I thought you could help me understand that *see eye* phrase. It was new to me. How could Esteban or the others help me? Besides, Esteban gets angry if I listen to the foreigners talking. But how else can I learn English?" He put down the pen carefully. "I do not think Señor Reid was seeing so well with his eyes when he fell down the stairs."

Ferrier laughed in spite of himself.

"Everyone is talking about that," Jaime went on, encouraged. "Captain Rodriguez is asking questions about the American with long hair. He thinks he was carrying drugs, trying to hide them in the storeroom for someone else to pick up. Perhaps Señor Reid saw him, tried to get downstairs too quickly, and slipped and—"

"Captain Rodriguez told you all that?" Ferrier asked in surprise. If so, the captain was the most communicative policeman he had ever heard of.

"No, no. But it is easy to know what a man thinks by the questions he asks," Jaime explained kindly. "He asked questions about the long-haired one. He asked about the storeroom and who had entered it. And he notified the narcotics police, because they came to search all through its barrels and crates. They even went upstairs. That was after the dancing ended, so the performance was not disturbed. But the police were everywhere. That's why we—" He broke off abruptly, his excitement ebbing just as quickly. He wondered nervously if *el norteamericano* had guessed what he had almost blurted out. "Why do you look so serious, señor? The police found nothing. No drugs. Everything is well. No trouble for anyone. Except for the American with long hair. He will be in trouble when they catch him, unless he can give a good reason why he stayed so long in the storeroom. It is a private place. Señor, please do not look so serious."

"But drugs are a serious matter, Jaime." So the police raid was the reason that Tomás was brought here last night; that's why he was smuggled out of El Fenicio in such a hurry. "Is Tomás a man who deals in narcotics?" Jaime looked at him wide-eyed. "If he is, I don't give a good goddamn whether he is Esteban's cousin or the brother of Tavita's aunt. Out he goes! You should never have brought him here. Get him out."

"But he has nothing to do with drugs. Nothing. Believe me,

señor, Esteban would not allow that. He would not help such a man." Jaime's voice was stilted. His eyes now looked reprovingly at Ferrier. He moved across the room to the opened windows, closed the shutters. "Soon the sun will be too warm, and this room—"

"I know about that. What I don't know is about Tomás. What does he deal in? If not drugs, what?" Ferrier heard a car driving carefully toward the house. He moved quickly over to one of the windows, adjusted the louvers so that he could see out clearly, looked down at a dark-blue Mercedes now drawing up near the path to the front door. Jaime really had a pair of exceedingly sharp ears, he was thinking; the boy had heard that car several seconds before he himself became aware of it. Or had Jaime been listening for it?

"He is only a man who needed a place to sleep," Jaime said. "Nothing to do with drugs. Nothing like that."

"But why all the secrecy?"

"It is a matter of honor." Jaime's flat statement was final. His hurt pride struggled with a new anxiety, and lost. "Señor Ferrier, you have not finished your breakfast. This cake is—"

"I've had enough," Ferrier said abruptly. Anything, anything to get me away from this window. What am I not supposed to see? Why should these people think Americans don't have a pride of their own? Why the hell have I to pretend I'm stupid, easily maneuvered, pushed around like a pawn on a chessboard? He stayed at the window. A man in gray uniform had hurried around from the driver's seat to open the car's rear door and let a woman step out. She was slender, smartly dressed in white, with high-heeled black sandals glistening on her small feet. No hat on her smooth dark head, but short white gloves on her hands holding a patent-leather satchel. "Tavita," Ferrier said in amazement. "Isn't this rather early for her?" It was barely half past ten by his watch. She was walking toward the house now. The chauffeur closed the car door behind her, spoke to someone still sitting inside, picked up a small case from the front seat, and left in the direction of the kitchen entrance. Extremely quiet out there, Ferrier suddenly noted. All the small sounds he had heard earlier—the hosing of the garden, women's voices, a snatch of song—had floated away during his talk with Jaime, and he hadn't been aware of it. "Where's everyone?" He turned, saw the door close silently behind Jaime.

Tavita was standing in the middle of the big room, her arms folded, her head bent, as she listened to Concepción's complaints.

"I know, I know," she said sympathetically. "But what else could we do? Señor Reid will not object. He has met Tomás."

"But Tomás did not want to come here. He was angry, last night, when he learned where he had been brought."

"Where else could we take him at that hour?"

"And this morning when I fetched him something to eat and told him about Señor Reid's accident, he cursed us all. He called us fools and idiots."

"How very grateful of him," Tavita said softly, but her eyes hardened. "And did he say why we were fools and idiots?"

"He said that if Señor Reid was attacked—"

"Attacked?"

"—then someone knows who Señor Reid is. And that, he said, means danger. This house may be watched."

"But why?" Tavita shrugged off her own question. "We have other things to worry about." Attacked . . . this house may be watched . . . Tomás had too many fears and suspicions. No one could connect Jeff with Tomás. No one. "Tell him we are waiting," she said shortly.

"And now he's going to grumble about us being an hour early."

"What else could we do?" Tavita asked again. She seemed so sure of herself, so completely in control, that Concepción made no further objections. If she only knew how I felt, Tavita thought, she'd throw her apron over her face and start wailing. Why did this happen to me, to any of us? Tomás walked in from the street, and from the moment that Esteban gave him shelter in good faith, Tomás put his claws deep into all of us. Esteban, this morning, a saddened and wiser man, had made a bitter suggestion: hand him over to Captain Rodriguez; let him take his own chances. But Esteban did not have a brother who once had worked with Tomás.

"If only Señor Reid were here," Concepción said.

"Now, now," Tavita told her briskly, covering her own worries, "we'll manage without him. We'll manage very well." But she gave a start, almost as violent as Concepción's, when Jaime appeared unexpectedly at the head of the staircase and ran down toward them.

"He won't stay in his room," Jaime told them as he reached the bottom tread. "He says he has had enough." And so have I, Jaime's voice told them. "He asks questions, and I have no more answers."

"Why?" Tavita asked sharply.

Jaime had a special mixture of awe and admiration for Tavita.

As he looked at her now, and saw her fear, his own sense of failure deepened. He kept silent.

"At least you should have stayed in the corridor upstairs," Concepción scolded. "Get back up there. We don't want him opening doors—"

"He is not that kind of a man," Jaime said angrily.

"You said he asks questions."

"Because he is not a fool, either."

"Jaime," Tavita said, "how much did you tell him?"

He hesitated, evaded his aunt's eyes. Somehow there was no evasion possible with Tavita. "I did not have to tell him much. He knows."

"He knows about Tomás?"

"He saw him. Last night. On the staircase."

"Oh!" exclaimed Concepción, and covered her mouth with her hands.

Tavita hushed her quickly. She said with a smile, "Well, then —he saw Pépé's manager. Or did you forget to tell him that?"

Jaime shook his head. He said with some reproach, "The señorita knows that I would not—"

"I know," Tavita said gently. "But he didn't believe you."

"Last night, I thought he did. This morning, I know he did not."

Tavita raised one hand, stopped a threatened outburst from Concepción. "No harm done. We just alter our plans a little. I suppose Señor Ferrier heard my car arrive?"

Jaime nodded. "And he saw you. He wondered why you had risen so early."

"And what did you say to that?"

"I left."

Tavita laughed in spite of herself. "No wonder you ran out of answers."

Jaime's wounded pride stopped smarting. He hadn't failed, really; it had just been impossible to succeed. "He is a difficult man to deceive," he warned her, his voice dropping to a whisper.

"Especially when you didn't want to deceive him, in the first place," Tavita reminded him, her voice now as sharp as her perception. All wrong, she told herself angrily, I planned this all wrong. I should have taken Ian Ferrier into my confidence, treated him as I would have treated Jeff. Deception was stupid. And what is stupid is wrong.

"Why isn't he down here by this time?" Concepción wanted to know.

"Go upstairs, collect his tray, and find out."

"Me? After he saw me on that staircase last night? After I pretended—" She didn't finish, but shook her head vigorously. "I'll never be able to face him again."

"Stop the dramatics. We are wasting valuable minutes. I must leave in half an hour." Tavita looked at the miniature diamond watch on her wrist. She could never see its figures clearly, but she wouldn't admit that. She made a practiced guess. "In twenty minutes, at the most." What a hideous journey it would be. And again she thought, why did this have to happen to me? To me? "All right. If neither of you will do it, I'll find out." She moved toward the staircase.

"But you can't! It wouldn't be correct!" Concepción protested.

"Correct?" Tavita stormed, her dark eyes flashing, her head tilted back.

Temper, temper, thought Ferrier as he stopped at the head of the staircase and wondered if he should descend, after all, into this little maelstrom. Three faces stared up at him. "Is it safe to come down?" he asked lightly.

Tavita recovered first. She said, "Oh, it was just a small argument. Now settled." To Concepción, she spoke softly, quickly, so that even Jaime could only half hear her. "I leave in twenty minutes. Don't fail me. Say nothing, nothing, nothing to Tomás. About last night or the staircase. Nothing. It will only make his anger worse. Keep him calm. Calm." Concepción nodded, retreated against the wall to let Señor Ferrier pass. He wasn't paying much attention to either her or Jaime. He had eyes only for Tavita. And she was, Jaime agreed, looking superbly beautiful this morning even if she had scarcely had four hours of sleep. He noted that Señor Ferrier had changed into a clean shirt, knotted a silk scarf into its open neck, put on a green linen jacket. Too bad that Señor Ferrier was going to be disappointed, he thought regretfully as he watched them meet, the fair-haired man and the dark-haired woman, and then start talking as they walked toward Señor Reid's study. Yes, it was a pity the way this Saturday morning was being ruined for everyone.

Concepción tugged at Jaime's sleeve, reminding him to fetch the clothes that the chauffeur had brought. He turned obediently toward the kitchen corridor, but paused to register a whispered protest. "I hate this man Tomás," he said vehemently. His aunt looked at him. "Because he hates all of us. Why should we—"

"Go, go!" Her hand waved him on.

When he came back with the clothes, the study door was closed, and they could start climbing the staircase without being seen.

7

So we are friends this morning, Ferrier thought, as he felt the gentle touch of Tavita's hand, saw the warm smile on her lips.

"I am glad," she said simply.

"So am I," he admitted, lost in the depths of those large dark beautiful eyes. "I'm sorry about last night."

"Oh?" She frowned, began walking toward the study. "Oh, yes," she said, pinning down his allusion. "I asked for your help."

"Magdalena asked me to stay and talk with you, but—frankly —I thought Jeff was in more need of help at the time."

"That was the way it seemed," she said.

Ferrier felt that she had somehow managed to agree and yet disagree with him. "What was the problem?"

"I managed," she said vaguely. "How is Jeff? I telephoned the hospital this morning, but they said he couldn't have any visitors."

"Not until this evening. Perhaps not even then, if Dr. Medina has his way. He likes to lay down the law."

She was puzzled. "Does he? You met him?"

"At the hospital last night. Or, rather, early this morning."

"He went to see Jeff at *that* hour?" The warm smile came back to her face. "Then that proves he is a good doctor. Magdalena is devoted to him. Jeff sent her to Dr. Medina some years ago when she was ill and he cured her completely."

And you, thought Ferrier, are highly nervous at this moment; why else all this concentration on Magdalena or Medina? Anything perhaps except her own problem. If it was Tomás, then she had only halfway managed with him: he might be safely out of El Fenicio, but he was now stuck upstairs in the attic here. Was that what was troubling her underneath all that calm, cool surface?

"Yes," she was saying as they entered the study, "old Medina is a wonderful doctor."

"Old?" Ferrier was slightly startled. "He's about my age." And possibly about your age, too, my proud beauty, although it would be too ungallant to mention that. It was part of her astonishing attractiveness, though; she didn't pretend, in either dress or manner, to be tremulous eighteen or confident twenty-four, and yet she was young, age unguessable.

"Oh," she said, "then it was Medina's nephew—he must have taken Magdalena's call." She shrugged off her mistake. "I agree with you. He is a little—officious? But it was thoughtful of him to go to the hospital so quickly. Would you close the door? A little more privacy." She glanced back at the staircase, where Concepción hovered. "He is helping his uncle in his practice. He came here about two years ago."

I'm sure we don't need privacy to talk about Medina, Ferrier thought. Could this woman, who looked so calm and relaxed, really be nervous? "Is he Jeff's doctor?"

"Did he say that?" She laughed softly. "He would, of course. It is a strange thing—" She paused, perhaps choosing her words carefully. "Jeff finds him amusing. He gives interesting parties where you can meet so many different kinds of people."

"Do you go to these parties?"

She shook her head. "I do not find them interesting. I am—I am not political." Her voice became bitter. "I hate all politics. That is why it is so difficult to—" Again she broke off, looked at the safely closed door, hesitated, sighed.

"I have a better idea for privacy. Why don't we drive along the coast or back into the hills? Visit Ronda? We could find some *parador* where we could have lunch and—"

"I can't. I am sorry." The words were abrupt. She added gently, "I am truly sorry. I would love to spend the day with you. But I must return to Granada."

"So soon?" He managed to hide his disappointment, but not his surprise. Yet he ought to have expected something like this: she hadn't even sat down. She had dropped her bag and gloves on a corner of Jeff's large desk, leaned against it with one hand, her body half turned toward him, her face slightly inclined as she studied him. Behind her smooth head, there were brightly covered books in dark wood bookshelves against white walls. There were no curtains on the windows, only the tall shutters half drawn that sent wavering lines of sunlight over the bare tiled floor. It was a man's room, austere and practical, a strange setting for this elegant woman, who looked—stranger still—as if she was completely at home in it. He was the intruder here, not Tavita.

"Yes. Too soon." She hesitated, then began to speak slowly,

choosing her words carefully. "There is much business to be done. Next week, we prepare to leave for London." Now the words began to spill out quickly. "I have danced there several times. And so I have many friends in England. This time, it is for a holiday. There is much to plan; I cannot leave without arranging everything at El Fenicio, and in Seville, where I also dance. So—you see?"

He could see that part of it. He couldn't quite see why she had chosen this time of the year for a holiday, though, when the tourists were beginning to pile into Spain. Or perhaps she never had to depend on foreign visitors for capacity audiences. "What about Jeff? Aren't you going over to the hospital?"

"Not today. It is impossible. Jeff will understand."

"I thought you were very good friends." It was a mild-enough rebuke, but she was hurt.

And angry. Her eyes flashed, her head came up straight as she stared at him. "We are. He is one of my dearest friends. He will understand." She turned away abruptly, walked over to the window, faced the garden. There was a long silence. "Has Jeff told you about us?"

The directness of the question startled him. "No. Jeff doesn't talk about his private emotions."

"Of course not," she said impatiently. "He is a man. Not a little boy who must make a public parade of his own affairs."

Good, thought Ferrier; so we agree on that at least. He moved over to the two red leather armchairs that were grouped at the side of the window for a view of the garden, a pleasant arrangement for quiet talk. She did not turn around, but kept her back toward him, her face averted, so that even her profile was hidden from him. "A pity I'm not Japanese," he tried, "or else I could stand here for hours admiring the nape of your neck. But I prefer a full-face view. Come on, turn round. Show me that the eyes have it." Either she didn't understand him or she preferred to ignore him. How the hell, he thought irritably, can we hope for international understanding when we can't even find an international sense of humor? All right, all right, it wasn't much of a joke, but it stopped her tears, didn't it? No joke is altogether bad if it does that. And we certainly didn't need privacy to talk about Medina or an unlikely trip to London. "What's the problem?" he asked briskly.

She understood that question at least. She even found it comic, seemingly. Her brief laughter choked on itself. She pivoted round, looked at him. Her eyes were brighter than ever, as if the controlled tears had turned to stars. "Which problem?"

she asked bitterly. She broke into Spanish. "The problem that Jeff is not here? The problem that he is needed? The problem of how I send a message to him and get his answer? Or the problem of a man who is in danger and who endangers us all?" The words were pouring out now, quickening with each question. "The problem that everything has gone wrong—not according to *his* plans—and he doubts everything I try to arrange? The problem that he trusts Jeff but not the rest of us—contemptuous, suspicious, angry with everyone?" She caught hold of herself, realizing suddenly that even if Ferrier could not understand all she talked about, she had yet said too much. She tried to cover up. "Then there is the problem of Constanza—the dancer who made the performance start so late last night. She was going to dance in bare feet. For true flamenco?" The indignation was real, and beautifully dramatic.

And now, thought Ferrier, she's onto a problem that is more in her line; she can handle this herself. She often must have gone through variations of the same battle, like the devoted Shakespearean who is directing an Ophelia who wants to do a strip tease. We didn't need privacy for a discussion of Constanza, either; let's get this talk back where it belongs. To Tomás. "Quite a quarrel," he said placatingly. He was sticking to English, just to make sure. "But what has it to do with this man who is in danger? He's the real headache, isn't he?"

She ignored that, kept concentrating on Constanza. "I lost my temper—"

"No. Surely not."

Tavita noted the amusement on his face. "I had every right to lose my temper," she said stiffly. "It was the fault, of course, of that photographer from the big American magazine. He had her dancing on the beach, bare feet, dressed in floating gauze. *His* idea. For the American public, he said. Flamenco? I told her she could take all these tricks over to North Africa where they belong, bare her belly if she wanted to, but never *never* call that dance flamenco. Yes, as you say, quite a quarrel. And another problem: Constanza will wake up this morning and begin resenting what I said. That is the way she is. And I can't be there to keep her silent. What will she decide to tell Captain Rodriguez when he comes questioning? Oh, he will come to visit El Fenicio again. This afternoon, perhaps, as soon as everyone is awake—and talkative. Constanza has quick eyes. When I dance, I forget everything except the dancing, the music, but Constanza watches the audience—that is why she will never be a great dancer. She thinks she saw someone up on the balcony of my

room. I told her it must have been Jeff. I told her that he had
been leaving an invitation with Magdalena—an invitation for
me—to join you and Jeff in a late supper. Oh, Jeff and I often
do that, you know. It could be the truth."

Just as the holiday in England could be the truth, Ferrier
thought, and probably isn't. "And was it Jeff on your balcony?
Or was it Tomás?"

Her face went white. "Constanza only *thought* she saw someone. It could have been a shadow or—"

"Then why worry?"

"Because Captain Rodriguez is too interested in last night."

"Drugs?" Ferrier asked quietly. That was a question that still
troubled him.

"Ridiculous!" There was no doubt she found it so. "That was
only an excuse he used."

And again we are retreating from the main problem, Ferrier
thought. He brought it back. "In order to search thoroughly?
For what, then? For Tomás?"

"But he can't know about Tomás." She sounded as if she were
persuading herself. "None of us knew about Tomás until he
arrived yesterday. Not even Jeff." She noticed the disbelief in
Ferrier's eyes. "Truly," she said. "Jeff did not know who he was.
I had to give Jeff the signal that there was someone—a refugee
—from Cuba—who was upstairs waiting for him."

"Why?"

"But the refugees always did. Jeff always talked with them,
made sure they were what they said they were."

And learned something about Cuba that wasn't displayed on
guided tours, no doubt. "So he had an interview with Tomás?"
Ferrier instinctively touched Jeff's lighter, which lay deep and
safe in his trouser pocket. His anger surfaced. "And what was he
thinking of, dragging you and Jaime and all the others into his
damned business?"

She was puzzled. "Dragged? It was I who asked for his help.
Six years ago. And he gave it to me."

"You mean you involved him? Not the other way around."

"Involved?" she repeated in English. She didn't like that word.
She shook her head.

"Look—we were doing fine: you talking in Spanish, I in English. Let's keep on that way. It is much quicker. What I meant
by involved is—"

"I know what it means. But it wasn't that way. I trusted Jeff.
And he trusted me. And so—as true friends—we worked together. It was all so simple at first. It began with my brother. And

then, a friend of his came next. And then a cousin of that friend. And then—" She shrugged her shoulders. "They are honest men. Not criminals. They do not come here to make trouble." That seemed to satisfy her that she had broken no laws, perhaps not even bent a few. Ferrier's doubts showed on his face. She said pleadingly, "But don't you see? Someone must help them to make a safe arrival."

It was a curious phrase, not only in the way she expressed it, but also in the idea that lay behind it. "Couldn't your police take care of their safe arrival? Or your immigration people?"

"And if *you* were a refugee, Señor Ferrier, how would you let them know you were coming? In advance?"

He shook his head. His question had been damned stupid, he realized. He had been thinking mostly of the risks Tavita and Jeff had taken.

"You could hardly write to our police and say, 'Gentlemen, I am leaving Havana, without permission, and will arrive in Málaga at pier Number Three on the eighth of June by the freighter *Santa Maria,* which will dock at six o'clock in the evening. Please have my papers in order so that I can land. Also, since I am a stranger in Málaga, please make arrangements to meet me so that I will not be kidnapped or knifed to death in a back alley in some drunken brawl.' You understand how it is, Señor Ferrier?"

"You made it quite clear."

"And did I make you angry," she asked sadly.

"With myself," he admitted frankly. I asked for it, he thought, and I certainly got it.

"Then you will help me?"

She had timed that question well. He said guardedly, "If I can." And here starts my involvement, he thought. No, not quite true. His involvement could be said to have started when he went to see flamenco danced in El Fenicio last night. Everything that had followed had, in its strange way, led him to this answer. He didn't like it. It wasn't of his own choosing.

"It is simple. When you see Jeff today, will you please ask him what I should do? Tell him that I have already done what he wanted: I have kept Tomás safe. And I will make sure he is safe —until I hear from Jeff. But he must send someone who is capable of dealing with Tomás. I am not."

"Why not?"

"Tomás is a refugee, like the others. But he is not like them, either. He does not intend to live in Spain, work here. He cannot.

And please—" her hand went up, and she smiled—"no more questions."

"No?" He was smiling, too. "I'm to help you with some guy and I can't even ask what his full name is?"

"Tomás is enough. He is already angry that so many people know he is here. He did not plan it that way, but how else could I manage?"

She was no professional, he decided. When she had to rid El Fenicio of Tomás, she had panicked, turned to friends and relatives. As for Tomás—was he really a refugee? Or was he a fugitive? He cannot live in Spain, Tavita had said. Yes, possibly a fugitive, and that much more dangerous. "A pity," he said gently, "to involve so many. And not from Tomás' point of view. I'm talking about Jaime and Concepción and old Magdalena. Oh, and wasn't there a *banderillero* called Pépé?" And now an idiot called Ian Ferrier, he thought wryly.

"I ask them to do no more for me than I would do for them," she said, eyes wide, head high. "And they know that." Then indignation and anger vanished, and her voice softened. "I like your concern, Señor Ferrier. I think I like you very much."

I wish, he decided, I could stop thinking and feeling what a beautiful woman this is, and keep my mind on the cold hard facts.

"But," she went on, "what else could I do, last night? Pépé can drive a car, but he did not know the way to this house. Jaime knows the way, but he is too young to drive—he has no license."

"Everything has to be kept legal," he agreed.

"You are laughing at me, again! If you had stayed at El Fenicio, you could have brought Tomás here quite safely—as Jeff would have done. And none of the others would have been involved." She looked at him severely. And then relented. "No, no, I do not blame you. I was a little angry because you do not take me seriously. I do not blame you any more than I blame Jeff's fall. If anyone is to blame for all this trouble, then it is—" She paused, frowning.

"Tomás?" he suggested.

"Or the man who attacked Jeff. Certainly, if Jeff were here he would deal with everything, and I would have no worries at all."

"Attacked?"

"That is what Tomás says. He may be wrong. He has so many suspicions. But why should Jeff be attacked? Perhaps the man— the American with the hair around his face like cobwebs, the one that puzzles Captain Rodriguez so much—perhaps he was trying to reach Tomás upstairs. And Jeff stopped him. That is what

Tomás must think, I know. You can see why he is so—so nervous. It was good that you did not speak or move when you saw him last night." There was laughter in her eyes, as if she were imagining the scene.

Not my most heroic moment, thought Ferrier. Every time he had remembered it, he had felt not exactly proud of his performance. Sure, he had been tired; sure, he had been thinking of a hundred things; sure, he had been startled. But usually his reflexes were quick. "An attack of paralysis," he admitted a little sourly as her laughter burst to the surface.

"You fooled the clever Tomás!" she said with open delight.

He felt better, somehow, that she was putting that interpretation on the hidden confrontation. "If you hate him so much, why help him? Why don't you walk right upstairs to the attic and tell him to clear out?"

The laughter faded. "You *do* ask difficult questions. But even if I could do that, Jeff would not want it. Yes," she insisted as she watched his face, "you will find that is true when you talk with Jeff."

He said nothing.

She became anxious. "You will talk with him? You will tell him what I said?"

"I'll see him for you."

She relaxed. She seemed to sense his doubts, though, for she said quickly, "I cannot risk getting in touch with Jeff directly. And I cannot risk using the telephone. So you must bring me his answer. To Granada. Will you do that?" She moved away from the window, passed him with a drift of rose fragrance trailing behind her, and went over to Jeff's desk. She knew in which drawer to find a piece of writing paper and pencil. "Here is my address. It is easy to reach—not far from the Alhambra Palace. You know that hotel?"

"I stayed there two nights ago."

"You walk south from it, and take the street, almost a country road, that runs along the edge of the high ground. The houses are few and so close to the cliff that their terraces look as if they were going to slip into the ravine. My house is the third, on your left. You will see its name on the iron gate: La Soledad."

"Solitude?" The name amused him, and so did her running description. She was writing while she talked. He joined her at the desk, looked over her shoulder. The letters were big and bold, but not altogether easy to read. He repeated the words to make sure. "Cuesta de San Cecilio. La Soledad. Vergara." He glanced at her. "Señorita Vergara?"

"Octavia Vergara. I was the eighth daughter in a family of fourteen—and the youngest. But Tavita is simpler. And here is my telephone number." She added that with a flourish.

"I thought you distrusted telephones."

"Your visit must appear to be—natural. So of course you would call me to let me know you have arrived in Granada. And perhaps ask me to luncheon?" There was a fleeting smile. "But be careful what you say. You are on your way to Madrid, you brought your rented car back to Granada, you would like to see me, possibly give me the latest doctor's report on Jeff?"

"I need no excuse for seeing you. And will you come to lunch this time?"

"I will say, I'm so sorry; but will you have dinner with me instead? The view from my terrace at night is magnificent."

"And when did you think this up?" He found it comic. Did she really think she had to spell everything out so clearly, that he couldn't invent his own telephone calls? "A perfectionist, I see." He took the piece of paper and folded it.

"You are laughing at me again! But why? What is wrong? It could all be true, couldn't it?"

Yes, he thought, it could all be true. She liked that phrase. A lie was not altogether a lie if it could be true? He laughed outright.

She went into a sudden small panic. "You *are* going to help me?"

That sobered him. "Yes. Why else would I have let you tell me all this?" He took out his wallet and slipped the folded sheet of paper inside it.

She gave a sigh of relief, and then a brilliant smile. She put out her hand, touched his arm lightly. "Thank you." Then she looked at her watch, couldn't quite read it, asked, "How long have I been with you?"

"About half an hour."

"What?" She picked up her bag and gloves, hurried to the door. But even these quick movements seemed graceful.

He just managed to get there first and open it for her. "Not quite half an hour," he reassured her. "What's the rush?"

They were out in the main room. Concepción was there, standing guard at the hall entrance. Jaime was at the front door. "You are late," Concepción was saying.

"I know, I know," Tavita told her impatiently. "Don't worry. We shall reach Granada before two o'clock if we drive quickly." She looked at Ferrier. "And miss the heat of the day," she added for his benefit. She waved a hand to Concepción, nodded reassuringly to Jaime as they passed him. "Good-bye, Señor Ferrier. Give my best wishes to Señor Reid."

"I'll see you to the car." He followed her outside.

"No need," she said firmly, and held out her hand. "My chauffeur is there to open the door." The gray-uniformed man, black-visored cap pulled well down on his brow, was indeed waiting. He was rearranging a pile of dress boxes on the front seat to make room for his suitcase.

"Let me walk you down this path," Ferrier said.

"No need. Please!" Then she noticed the small gray car that had drawn up outside the gateway and was now backing along the street to leave the driveway entrance free. A man got out. "So it begins," she said softly. She halted. She began talking vivaciously, as if their conversation was so engrossing that she found it difficult to leave. "Your name is strange: Ee-an. Is that how it should be pronounced?"

He nodded. "Ian. It's the Gaelic version of John. Not so strange. It's the same name as your Juan." The man, he noted, had entered the driveway and was walking briskly toward the house. "Rodriguez?" he asked as he looked away from the neat figure in its light-gray suit.

"He is alone. So there is no trouble. But Gaelic? What is that?"

"The language they speak in the highlands of Scotland. That's just north of England."

"I know, I know."

"Lots of Europeans don't."

"It is a place of mountains. That is why they have those peculiar dances."

"Why?" he asked, interested, almost forgetting Captain Rodriguez, who was now passing Tavita's car. The chauffeur was arranging packages and boxes. Magdalena's cracked old voice was shrilling out advice.

"But it is the same wherever you have mountains or rough country. The dancers leap. All their steps are high, light. But down on the plains or where the ground is more—more level, then people dance with a closer step to the earth. They do not need to lift their feet so much."

"The flatter the ground, the more they shuffle?" he suggested.

"But it is true. Have you not noticed the difference in the dances of your own American Indians? The Jicarilla Apaches leap. The Pueblo Indians beat the earth with each step."

"Now how do you know about—"

"One August, some years ago, I was in Mexico. And I went up

into New Mexico to visit the Gallup Festival. Why not? Many artists from Europe go there to see the Indians at their ceremonial — Oh, Captain Rodriguez! Good morning. Have you met Señor Reid's friend—Señor Ian Ferrier?"

Ferrier returned the captain's polite bow with a nod of his head. Whom has he come to see? Tavita or me?

The captain answered that question for him by saying, "Are you leaving, too, Señor Ferrier?"

"No."

"Just listen to Magdalena!" Tavita exclaimed. "She is cross at being kept waiting in the car. Good-bye, Captain Rodriguez. Good-bye, Señor Ferrier." She held out her hand to him. "I hope we meet again. I wanted to hear more about your astronauts." To Rodriguez, she said, "Señor Ferrier comes from Houston. He tracks things in the sky."

"The machines do that," Ferrier said. So she and Jeff had talked about him before he arrived. Ridiculously, he was pleased. He released her hand, still feeling the small secret pressure it had given his.

"I know, I know. And all you do is oil the machines."

That sounded like old Jeff, Ferrier thought. He laughed and said, "That's about it." She gave him a dazzling smile that was all his own. She turned away and walked toward the car, paused to call back, "And you will be sure to tell Señor Reid that I am deeply sorry about his accident? Do explain that I must be in Seville tonight, so I must leave this morning to let me break the journey in Granada. I shall go to see him next Friday, when I am back in Málaga." She waved, and walked on.

Ferrier had been looking at the Mercedes. The chauffeur was now closing the trunk, where he had been rearranging things—a busy fellow, that chauffeur, efficient—and was preparing to come into full view to open the door for Tavita. Are my eyes playing tricks, Ferrier wondered, or is that uniform less crumpled than the one I saw earlier this morning from my bedroom window? Where are those deep creases across the back? Ferrier took a quick step toward the front door. "It's cooler inside," he suggested.

Rodriguez was watching Tavita. "It is only a brief visit—"

"That suits me," said Ferrier. He was already inside the front door, and Rodriguez followed him. "I wanted to see something of the town before lunch at the *parador*." He led the way through the hall into the main room. "I'm delighted you speak English. My Spanish is—well, hesitant." From the driveway outside, they could hear the car being backed slowly toward the street. "But if you prefer to talk in it, I understand most of the flow. It's the speaking that I find a little baffling." He turned to face Rodriguez. "I suppose you came to ask about Jeff Reid. The latest reports were that he is resting comfortably—which means, of course, that he is sleeping off the painkillers they pumped into him." He pointed to a couple of hard chairs. "These look the coolest. Shall we sit over there?" And you are talking too much, he told himself. He relaxed a little when he heard the diminishing sound of Tavita's car as it traveled away at good speed.

Rodriguez shook his head. "It is only a brief visit," he said again. "A few questions." He hesitated, seemed to find some difficulty in explaining the need for them. "Friendly questions. Nothing official. You see, I am—well, I suppose you have already been told that I am attached to the police?"

Ferrier nodded.

"Please do not let that alarm you. I am here to ask your help."

"Oh?"

"A matter of—of background," Rodriguez said softly. His voice was pleasant, like the expression on his face. He was shorter than Ferrier, possibly in his mid-thirties. Black hair, thick and long on top but straightly cut at the nape of the neck, was held together by careful brushing and a dash of oil that added a gleam to the heavy curls. His brown eyes were calm, sympathetic; his round face placid, almost cherubic in its innocence. He was dressed carefully but not expensively. His light-gray suit and white shirt were immaculate, even if they were ordinary in cut and material. His shoes, black and highly polished, covered small narrow feet. His hands were neat and delicate. He was a man like a thousand others whom Ferrier had seen in the streets and cafés of Madrid and Granada. At this moment, as he looked around the big room with considerable interest, he seemed to be searching for a tactful start on those few questions. "Are you married, Señor Ferrier?"

It was an unexpected beginning. Ferrier recovered. "Not so far," he admitted with a cheerful grin.

"Then you live alone."

Ferrier's grin broadened. "More or less."

"On this scale?" Rodriguez' manner was amiable, almost humorous. One hand gestured vaguely toward the room.

"Hardly. But the style of living in America is simpler. We don't have many Concepcións around. Without her, this house would be one giant headache."

"Of course, Señor Reid entertains a great deal."

Now we are coming closer to business, thought Ferrier. "That's part of his job, I suppose."

"Certainly, he has many visitors. But never his wife or children. That must have been most disappointing for Señor Reid." There was a diplomatic pause. "He expected them, you know. Yes, for the first few months he kept hoping. But I understand that his wife refused to live in Spain. A strange woman. Do you know her?"

"I haven't seen her in years."

"What was she like?"

"Quite pretty," Ferrier said coldly.

"And seemingly quite determined. An unhappy combination for any man who married her."

Ferrier said nothing at all. Janet Reid had always been charming to him, but he had never been really comfortable about that. She had a way of dropping small acid comments about other friends of Jeff's when they weren't there to hear them. Ferrier had had no illusions that his back, once it was turned, wouldn't make an equally good target. So his pleasure in her company had been decidedly guarded. But she was Jeff's choice, made early in their lives when he was going off to Korea. No one had forced her to marry an Air Force pilot, yet she seemed to have an increasing resentment that Jeff wouldn't change his career to please her. Some women never knew when to let well enough alone; they didn't seem to realize that if they shifted a man away from what he believed in, from a job that he felt had to be done, they'd change him from a man into a eunuch.

Rodriguez said, "There was a separation based on incompatibility and then charges of desertion against Señor Reid and a divorce." He shook his head in disbelief. "I do not understand your American laws. He took the blame. But does that seem fair? It was she who had refused to come with him to Spain. She deserted him." Rodriguez paused. Quietly he added, "Why did he not defend himself?"

"Oh, he probably did not want any publicity—added bitterness —that kind of thing. Bad for the children." Ferrier drew a deep breath. I got out of that fairly well, he thought. Publicity was something that Jeff would try to avoid if he was connected with the CIA. Would that be Rodriguez' next question—why would Jeff want to avoid publicity?

"I think it was worse for the children that she never allowed them to come and see him in Spain. And when he went back to visit America, she kept them away from him even there. Is that legal? Why did he not insist that she obey the law? Or was she threatening him? With what disclosure?"

Ferrier looked blankly at Rodriguez. He was thinking now not so much of Jeff but of Janet. This was a new light on her entirely. If, that was, Rodriguez' information could be believed. "I know nothing about all that."

"Señor Reid never discussed his troubles with you?"

"No."

"But you are his friend, a good friend."

"He isn't the type to bellyache." Ferrier caught hold of a sudden rise in temper. "It isn't my business. And frankly, Captain Rodriguez, is it yours?"

"I do not think that you are qualified to judge what is, or what is not, my business."

And that was true enough. Ferrier had encountered too many critics of his own field of work whose arguments had been based on false assumptions. There were undercurrents that no one, standing at the edge of a seemingly normal stretch of water, could be aware of—unless he was a practiced diver and went deep below the surface.

"I would not be here," Rodriguez said stiffly, pointedly, "if the son of Señor Reid had not become mixed up in what is most definitely my business."

"Jeff Reid's son?"

"Adam Reid, eighteen years old, student, home address given as Twenty-ninth Street, North West, Washington, D.C."

The name was right. So—with quick mental calculation—was the age. And Jeff had inherited a small house in Georgetown from his father: the sum total of all that had been left him. Janet had taken that, too, had she? "Where is Adam? What has he done?" Ferrier asked worriedly.

"He has been in Málaga for the last three days. Or at least, near Málaga. He has been staying with some friends in Fuengirola, a few miles away."

Ferrier stared at the quiet Spanish face in disbelief. "He came to Málaga and didn't get in touch with his father?"

"Oh, he knew where his father's house was. He admitted he had searched for it. He had also found out Señor Reid's habit of visiting El Fenicio on Fridays. Didn't either of you recognize him there?"

"At El Fenicio?" Ferrier asked incredulously. "Was he one of those four Americans?"

"Three Americans," corrected Rodriguez. "The fourth is a

Swede who speaks English with an American accent, possibly because he has so many American friends who stay with him at Fuengirola when they are passing through Málaga. Adam Reid was the young man with the beard." He studied Ferrier quite openly now. "You didn't like to hear that, did you?" he asked not unsympathetically. "No, I suppose not. You cannot enjoy the idea that your friend's son actually pointed him out to his enemies."

Ferrier said defensively, "I'm pretty sure Adam had no idea of what he was doing." Damn, he thought a second too late, I've practically admitted I know that Jeff was identified.

"Possibly not. He is a young man who has little idea of how he can be used. His excellent American education never taught him about that." Rodriguez paused. "So you saw that incident when Adam Reid identified his father?"

"No." He doesn't miss a trick, does he?

"You must have heard about it, then?"

"Yes. Just a piece of gossip. I noticed nothing."

"Too bad. I had hoped you could testify that the light-haired American followed Señor Reid into the storeroom after the identification was made. Why did you go in to investigate? Any suspicions?"

"I was worried. Reid had said he wouldn't be long—"

"Why did he leave you? Did he say?"

"No."

"He did not mention arranging a party after the performance?"

"No. But he wouldn't tell me about that until it was all arranged."

"He is a man of surprises?"

"A man who doesn't raise false expectations."

"Where did you find him after his accident?"

"At the side of the stairs."

"Not at their foot?"

"No. At the side. Just below the halfway point."

Rodriguez relaxed, even smiled naturally. "How pleasant it is to deal with a man who tells me the truth. Yes, we found some evidence of where he had crashed down from the staircase. Someone—you?—dragged him away from there. Why?"

"He needed fresh air, a place where it circulated freely."

"Did you decide that? You were taking grave chances by moving—"

"I knew that. He insisted."

"Why?"

"He didn't explain."

"Did he say what had caused that fall?"

"No."

"Or who was there at the time?"

"Look—I didn't ask him questions. I was too worried about getting help for him."

"Did he seem—ill?"

"Yes."

"Have you any guesses? After all, neither you nor I believe this was a mere accident, a natural fall."

"Plenty of guesses, and no conclusions. The whole thing defeats me."

"Defeats you, Señor Ferrier? I doubt that. We called your Embassy in Madrid this morning about—another matter. I was talking with one of your friends there. You have a most impressive record. Analysis and interpretation. That is your special field, isn't it?"

So he checked on me, Ferrier thought. Of course he would. I ought to have guessed that right from the start. I was the unknown who entered a complicated picture, the vague outline that had to be filled in. "Before you found that out, what role had you chosen for me?" he asked sharply. "Someone who had gone into that storeroom to pick up a message or drugs left there by that young American? Did you think I was in some kind of dirty business with *him?*" he ended angrily.

"Now, please," Rodriguez said softly, unhappily. "You know well that I must check every small thing, however ridiculous it seems. Drugs? No. I never took that seriously, although our narcotics agents insisted on a thorough search of El Fenicio. A message? You mean some kind of espionage? Well, that might be more possible, except that some things we have learned since that unhappy incident last night make me now believe that you would have little in common with Lee Laner—that is the American you mentioned—or with his black friend, Ed Pitt. Or with their kind host at Fuengirola, the man with the Swedish name and passport of Gustaf Torrens. We will know more about him soon: we have been in touch with Stockholm. Yes, that unhappy incident—so unpleasant for Señor Reid—has turned out very fortunately for us. And very sadly for Lee Laner. Seemingly, he made a mistake last night. We do not know what it was. Yet. Perhaps Señor Reid will be able to help us with that problem. Are you quite sure he recognized none of those Americans in the courtyard last night, or Señor Gustaf Torrens? He made no comment about them?"

"He said he had seen a thousand like them in the last few years."

"Yes, that is what we are all to be made to think. One gets tired of the pattern; one stops looking at them; one accepts and asks no questions." Rodriguez took a small step toward the hall, a hint that he was now about to leave. "I apologize that I had to ask you so many questions of my own. But I hope that some of the things I have mentioned will explain the reason why I needed a few answers. So thank you, Señor Ferrier. I hope I haven't interfered too much with your visit to Málaga. Good—"

"One minute," Ferrier cut in quickly. He may be finished with me, he thought, but I'm not finished with him. "You owe me an answer. You didn't say what Adam Reid has done. And I've three other questions. Are you holding him? Where? Can I see him?" He was angry, and didn't care whether he showed it.

Rodriguez said stiffly, "You seem to think that we are unreasonable men. Your Adam Reid is now driving toward Madrid with nothing worse than a strong admonition to obey our traffic regulations. He is quite proud that he faced the Spanish police, but a little disappointed that he cannot charge us with having threatened, beaten, or tortured him." Rodriguez smiled bitterly. "Or will he?"

Ferrier said quietly, "Then he was arrested. Why? Because he was seen in the company of—"

"Not at all for that reason. The arresting officer did not even know Adam Reid had been at El Fenicio. It all began simply—like most trouble for young people. He was detained last night, or, rather, early this morning, for driving at high speed through the city and for blowing his horn repeatedly. As a foreigner who might not understand our traffic laws, he would have been allowed to proceed with a strict warning. But he did not have his passport. He could not remember where it was. He could not understand much Spanish. He could not speak it. So he was taken to the nearest Guardia Civil post, where an interpreter could be found. His manner was strange, but he was carrying no drugs. He was dressed poorly, but he had money and many traveler's checks. His only luggage was a small duffel bag with no change of clothes. He was—extremely unhelpful, until he heard that the American Embassy in Madrid would be notified, so that after proper verification they could issue him with temporary travel papers and he could proceed on his journey. It was then that he began to co-operate. He did not want his mother to be worried by any enquiries; she did not know he was in Spain—he was supposed to be traveling through France and Italy toward Yugoslavia. He even remembered where his passport might be—he must have left it in his suitcase along with the rest of his things at a house in Fuengirola. He was quite casual about the clothes. He thought it easier to buy new ones rather than go back to collect that suitcase. He had forgotten about the passport. He had been leaving Málaga in a very great hurry."

"Why?"

"He was evasive about that. Fortunately for him, I arrived at the police station just then, and I had seen the quarrel between him and his friends in the courtyard at El Fenicio. It was real. He was furious; and they were contemptuous."

"Had they traveled with him from America?"

Rodriguez shook his head. "They picked him up in Madrid at the American Express office. There is always a crowd of American students there. He had a car. They wanted transportation. They came south together. He was vague about them. He only knew they had been traveling in Europe for a year. That impressed him. That is what he really wants to do: travel, cash checks from his mother, travel, travel. Anything to postpone the days of growing up." Rodriguez shook his head in wonder. "Or don't Americans want to grow up? Is that why you have put youth on a pedestal?"

Ferrier ignored that. It would be difficult to answer, anyway. "So you let him go? Just like that?"

"He had been very helpful. In his own way. We learned the names of Laner and Pitt, and we had a short talk with Gustaf Torrens when we visited his house to find Adam Reid's suitcase." Rodriguez laughed, briefly, softly. "Strange how a young man who loses his temper and drives too wildly can draw attention, quite by chance, to a peculiar group of people. But that is what happens in my work. It has all the joys of the unexpected."

"You've had a busy morning," Ferrier said dryly. And now Adam Reid would be followed until he was safely out of Spain, just to make sure he was not making a habit of encountering "peculiar groups of people." Peculiar in what way? There had been no mention of morals; and drugs had been discounted. It could be something in the area of dangerous politics—not the simple voting kind that most Americans indulged in with open argument, but politics that throve on secrecy and bred conspiracy. Yes, there had been a hint of that in Rodriguez' acid comment about Torrens, "the man with the Swedish name and passport of Gustaf Torrens." An illegal agent? Whoever or whatever Torrens was, he must have spent some bad hours since Spanish Security had called on him for Adam Reid's suitcase.

"Extremely busy," Rodriguez agreed. "In fact, I did not get to bed last night. That was why I did not accept your offer of a chair. If I had sat down, I might have fallen asleep." He was moving definitely toward the door. "So if I have seemed a little slow, this morning, and taken up too much of your time—you will understand?"

Slow? Ferrier would hate to be interviewed by Rodriguez when the man had a night's sleep behind him. He followed the captain into the hall. There were several loose ends, left purposely so, and they bothered him. He would like to know more about Lee Laner; that could be one small step toward finding out about Jeff's accident. There was a connection somewhere, he felt.

"Yes?" asked Rodriguez quickly. "You have another question?"

It was almost, Ferrier thought, as if he had been waiting for a question. About Torrens, or Pitt, or Laner? "Yes. Would you let me know where young Reid is staying in Madrid? If, that is, you should just happen to learn where he is."

Rodriguez had noted the irony. He froze in disapproval. Then he decided to treat it as a small joke between them. "If," he said, "I should happen to learn where Adam Reid is, I shall certainly inform you. But I don't think you'll be able to persuade him to come back to Málaga to see his father. Was that your idea?"

Ferrier nodded. "I could try."

"I tried, too."

"Did you tell him his father was in the hospital with a smashed-up leg?"

"I did even more than that. I told him that his new friend, Lee Laner, might be to blame."

"How did he take that?"

"He refused to believe it. Naturally."

"Well, by the time he reaches Madrid, he may have thought it over. In any case, I'd like to talk with him."

Rodriguez shrugged his shoulders, pursed his lips. "It will be a waste of your breath. But I'll let you know. He's lucky, that young man."

Ferrier remembered the sullen, unhappy face that had glared blankly at the street outside this house. The truly lost generation, he had thought at the time. "Lucky?" He shook his head.

"Luckier than Lee Laner. We found him. Just one hour before I came here." Rodriguez was watching Ferrier carefully.

"Good. That may clear up—"

"We found him dead. Behind some crates in a warehouse near the harbor. A knife wound in the back. Pockets emptied, no identification." Ferrier was too startled to speak. His obvious amazement was the best answer he could have given. Rodriguez' sharp eyes lost some of their wariness. He even volunteered a morsel of information. "We are searching for his companion—the black man called Pitt. They separated last night. Strange, isn't it? They had traveled so long and so far together."

"There is something big at stake here," Ferrier said slowly. Far bigger than he had imagined.

Rodriguez nodded. "And it involves your country, I am inclined to think, rather than mine. Laner and Pitt were only traveling through Spain. Their destination? Adam Reid had the impression—vague, not definite, but still an impression—that it was the United States. At least, he had heard them talking about New Orleans. And a ship did sail for there, at dawn."

"That's where we may find Pitt. Unless he was killed, too."

"No. I don't think you shall find him either dead or alive. My own guess is that he was safely removed from Málaga by another route about the same time as Lee Laner was being eliminated."

Ferrier studied Rodriguez' bland face. You know more than you've told me, he thought. Naturally. But if one man had been "eliminated" and another "removed," then why did you come asking me questions? They are already out of your jurisdiction, both of them. Or is your real interest Jeff Reid? Good God, have I said anything to add to Jeff's troubles? Then he thought of Tavita, and her chauffeur in the fresh-looking uniform, the man with the peak of his cap pulled down over his brow, who had been so efficient with packages and boxes that somehow his face had always been turned aside. And he thought of Jeff's lighter, deep in his pocket.

"Yes?" asked Rodriguez politely. He was standing fixed in the doorway, watchful, expectant. "You were about to say?"

"I was just thinking this is one hell of a way to spend a weekend."

Captain Rodriguez nodded and turned away, walking with his quick light step toward the driveway, a neat figure in light-gray sharply silhouetted against the lush puce, pinks, and reds of geraniums and bougainvillaea. Ferrier retreated from the brilliance of color and light into the shadowed hall. He crossed the wide room, his pace quickening. He took the stairs at a run, three at a time. She didn't, he kept saying to himself, she didn't take Tomás out—right under the nose of Captain Rodriguez. Surely not . . .

But she had. The doorway to the attic staircase was innocently open, and the small room at the top was empty except for a narrow iron bed that looked disused and desolate, with its thin mattress and meager pillow stripped down to their faded stripes. The one small window was now closed. It looked and smelled like a place that hadn't been occupied in months. Only, on the cracked plaster wall that was marked with the blotches of long-dead and dried-up mosquitoes, there were five or six corpses showing signs of fresh blood.

He went down to his own room. From his window, he could see Rodriguez near his car talking with another neatly dressed man. Then Rodriguez stepped into the car, drove away. The man sauntered toward the deep shade of the nearest large tree. So the house was now being watched, Ferrier thought. Or guarded, as Rodriguez might say with a pained lift of his eyebrow. But that scarcely mattered now. Ferrier began to laugh. Yes, Tavita had managed it; she had taken Tomás out, right under Rodriguez' nose, and his, too.

8

All right, thought Ferrier, let's go through the motions: a look at the town, lunch somewhere—possibly at the *parador*, if it isn't too full of tourists all in search of a hilltop inn with an Arab fortress, Phoenician and Roman ruins for its neighbors. That's what I told Rodriguez, and I might as well let him see I follow my suggestions. That's one way of keeping life as simple as possible, and that's what I aim to do. Once I see Jeff this evening, and get his answer for Tavita, I'll hand back his damned lighter that's burning a hole in my pocket, and the pencil, get rid of the whole thing and head for Granada. One night there, and I'll desentangle myself—that may be difficult unless Tavita, instead of being woman, is playing conspirator; in which case I'll kiss her beautiful little hand and get the hell out and feel I'm lucky to escape. I've got my own work to think about, my own schedules to keep, and they are complicated enough without getting involved in a whole new scene. Let Rodriguez worry about his eliminated American, Tavita about her Tomás; and Jeff may be out of action for a while, but he has his Martin in Madrid to move the pieces around the chessboard. This is one game I don't belong in.

And having delivered this definite declaration of independence to a massive flowerfall of purple bougainvillaea that splashed down the wall against which he had edged his car last night, he switched on the ignition, decided there wasn't enough room to turn without sideswiping Jeff's Buick, and started backing down the driveway to the road. He braked quickly, stopped dead, swore. A yellow sports car, filled to the brim with a tight cluster of talking and laughing people, had swooped through the gateway and was already more than halfway to the house. It came to a halt just behind him. Thoughtful of them. There was nothing else to do but get out, with marked patience, stand by his open doorway and stare at them with a frozen mask for a face. They'd get the message.

If they did, they ignored it. The driver gave a friendly wave, eased himself out of a crowded front seat, reached over to the folded top and lifted a picture that had been balancing there with the help of a restraining hand from one of the men in the back. The other man there had his arms full with a dazzling redhead, who was sitting precariously on his lap. In front, there had been another lap-percher, a brunette, definitely uncomfortable and glad to slip out onto the driveway, leaving two blondes behind her. Four pretty girls, Ferrier noted, all with long hair swinging around their shoulders, all with bright shirts and beads and deeply looped earrings. The brunette was smoothing down her white trousers, ignoring the complaints from the blondes that they had been crushed to death. One hundred and twenty pounds, five feet four in flat-heeled sandals, thirty-six, twenty-four, thirty-six, all pleasantly disposed of in the right proportion. She had a merry smile, too, now directed at Ferrier. "Do you mind?" she called to him, and pointed to the garden. "It is so beautiful." And without waiting for his answer—he was admiring the pointing arm, smooth and firm and golden-tanned—she moved toward the nearest roses.

"Sorry," the driver said as he reached Ferrier. He waved the canvas he held in one hand back toward the car, where his five friends had now fallen silent and were studying Ferrier with various expressions: the two blondes were speculative, the redhead was interested, the two men were quietly measuring possible opposition. "We seem to have blocked you."

"It seems that way."

"I thought Jeff Reid might have been in your car. I promised to drop this off at his place." Again the canvas was casually displayed. It was roughly painted in bold green and purple slashes, possibly an impression of terraced vineyards, with white blocks for houses clustering along the crest of the steep hill and a sprinkle of leaning church towers, chrome yellow, heavy black outlines, under a flat stretch of indigo-blue sky. "He wanted something to doll up a wine catalogue for his American market. Is he at home?"

"No. He's in the hospital."

The stranger's thin, handsome face looked depressed, more for the fate of his painting than for Jeff Reid. He was tall, narrow-shouldered, fairly young—possibly around thirty, certainly younger than the two middle-aged men he had brought with him, although they were desperately trying to keep faces and waistlines taut and lean. They all had the same bleached-by-sea, tanned-by-sun look, hair that was most carefully cut into casual locks, Victorian sideburns, expensive sports shirts appropriately faded, and eyes that were unguessable behind large round dark glasses. "Do you hear that?" the tall one demanded of his carload. "In the hospital, for God's sake." There was a united protest. "I agree. We can't take this thing on a picnic." He waved the canvas in disgust, looked at Ferrier, removed his dark glasses to show intensely sincere blue eyes, and smiled with definite charm. "May I drop this advertisers' dream in the house? It can welcome Reid when he gets home—when will that be?—and he can put the check in the mail. I'm Gene Lucas, by the way." He had already started toward the house. "Won't be long!" he called back to his friends as Ferrier caught up with him. He looked quickly at the garden, made sure that the dark-haired girl was far enough away, said lightly, "Amanda is perfectly happy. She has a thing about flowers—four pots of roses on her scrubby little terrace—waters them, prunes them, prays over them, and gets nothing in return." The blue eyes were focused on Ferrier now. "Are you staying with Reid, or were you just calling to offer condolences?"

"I'm this weekend's guest."

"So you are Ferrier?"

Ferrier, leading the way into the hall, stopped short. "Yes," he said, with just enough of a rising inflection in the word to make it a question.

Lucas propped his picture against the wall, lost interest in it. He said quickly, no time to waste, "You telephoned Martin in Madrid. What's the trouble?"

Ferrier stared at Lucas blankly. So the painting had been just an excuse to get into the house for a quiet talk, and all that little act within earshot of Lucas' friends had been merely plausible justification for the visit.

"What's bothering Reid?" Lucas insisted.

"He didn't say." Ferrier did his best to look unconcerned. He slipped his hands into his trouser pockets, stood at ease. His right knuckles were touching the lighter. For a moment he was tempted to get rid of it, hand it over—this must be Martin's man—but his fingers now felt the small silver pencil, and he waited.

"You mean he got you to send that message without telling you what was on his mind?" Lucas was incredulous.

"The message told that, didn't it? He couldn't keep some business appointment on Monday. Simple."

"Come on, Ferrier," Lucas said impatiently, "don't give me this standoff. When Martin gets a message like that, it means an emergency. Send help. Rally around. So here I am. What did Reid tell you?"

"Nothing much."

"Look—if he trusted you enough to let you send that message, he must have told you what to say if anyone from Martin made contact with you."

Ferrier's hand closed around the lighter. Keep it safe: that was all Reid had said. And only if something more happened to Reid was the lighter to be given to Martin or to someone sent by Martin. But nothing more had happened to Jeff Reid. He was alive. The lighter would go back to him this evening; he could decide how to deal with it then. It would be comic, thought Ferrier, if Jeff handed it back to me and told me to pass it along to Lucas, and all this mild sweat for nothing. Except, I don't know who this fellow is. Sure, he comes from Martin—or so he says. But what about that silver-pencil routine? Jeff had been definite about that.

Lucas sensed his indecision, tried harder. "This could be urgent, and we are wasting time. Didn't Reid give you instructions before they carted him off to the hospital? No additional message for Martin? There has got to be something, you know."

"Why don't you ask him about that yourself? I'm seeing him around six this evening. Drop in at the hospital any time after that."

"Why not before?" Lucas asked quickly, a sudden show of suspicion in his eyes.

"Doctor's orders. Jeff's not on view until six."

Lucas' manner changed back to something more genial. "It wouldn't be a good idea for me to contact Reid directly. Why else do you think I came to see you?"

"That," Ferrier said, "is still puzzling me."

"I wonder. Ever heard of Laner?" The question had been offhand, but Lucas was quick to notice Ferrier's surprise. "So Reid did tell you about Laner?" Lucas pressed his advantage as Ferrier looked at him blankly. "Did he also mention the name of Tomás Fuentes?" he asked softly.

Tomás . . . Tomás Fuentes? "Wrong on both counts," Ferrier said bluntly. "Reid mentioned neither of them. I heard of Laner about half an hour ago—from a policeman who had as many damfool questions as you have. You know, Lucas, you not only puzzle me. You worry me. What the hell is going on? Who is Fuentes? What's he got to do with Reid?"

Lucas backed off noticeably. "He is just a rumor, a possibility. If he were here, Reid might know about it. That's all. I was only checking." He shrugged his shoulders, looked apologetic. "It's just part of the job."

"What job?"

"I'm in the same line of work as Reid. He told you he is with the CIA?"

"No." And, thought Ferrier, I've never known anyone in the CIA who went around proclaiming it as blatantly as this. What's Lucas trying to do? Impress me, get my full co-operation? Can this type really be authentic? If so, God help our country.

"That shook you," Lucas said delightedly. "At least I've had one success this morning. You're cool, Ferrier, you're really—" He jerked his head around to look at the doorway, all expression wiped off his face, the lean handsome profile now hawklike. It was the dark-haired girl. "Hello, Amanda. Getting impatient?"

Slowly, she entered the hall. "The others are. They are all over the garden. You'll have quite a time corralling them back into the car."

"You start work on that. I'll be with you right away."

"What makes you think Bianca would listen to me? She never does. Why did you have to bring her along? There is just one too many on this picnic." The voice was plaintive.

Ferrier had a feeling of disappointment. This complaining touch was the last thing he had expected from anyone as pretty as Amanda. He preferred her as he had first seen her, with a smile glancing over her lips. Now they were downdrawn and mutinous. But Lucas seemed pleased, as if he was taking her small show of jealousy as a compliment. "We'll soon be on our way," he told her as she wandered vaguely around the hall. She scarcely glanced at Ferrier. She stopped just beyond the two men, again rather vaguely, and began studying Lucas' vineyards.

Lucas turned back to Ferrier. "You can tell Reid I delivered on time. And I'm waiting for further instructions." He glanced at the girl, added, "I suggest a series—three more pictures. But if so, I'll have to start work right away. Let me know, will you, what Reid has in mind?"

Ferrier nodded. "What's your telephone number? Better write it down for me." I've given him his cue, he thought; now he will produce a little silver pencil and flourish it under my nose. Lucas is just the type to enjoy playing games like this.

"I'll call you," Lucas said. "Late this evening? If you have any news for me, we can make a date for tomorrow."

"Hold on, hold on," Ferrier warned him. "I don't know where the hell I'll be this evening. And I may have left Málaga by tomorrow."

Lucas studied Ferrier thoughtfully. "Difficult, aren't you? You know, I have the strange feeling that you could give me Reid's answer right now." He shook his head unhappily over such lack of trust. "Oh, well—I'll write down my phone number, and you can call me." He pulled a wallet from the pocket of his bleached linen shorts, found a scrap of paper. "Have you got a pencil?"

So he put the first move on me, Ferrier thought in annoyance. And am I supposed to produce Reid's pencil, hand it over nonchalantly?

Amanda had turned away from the painting. "It isn't really your best work, Gene. You've rushed it, and it shows."

"Thanks a lot," Lucas said coldly. "If you want to be helpful, where's that silly pencil of yours—the one you always carry around in that grab-all?"

"Would you like it?" She spoke with studied sweetness. She searched with maddening slowness in the white canvas bag that hung from her shoulder.

"Amanda! Come on!" Lucas was angry. "You're in a foul mood today."

A mood called Bianca, thought Ferrier. His hand came out of his pocket, empty. "I'll find something to write with," he said diplomatically, and started toward the study.

But Amanda caught his arm lightly as he passed her. "Here you are," she said, presenting him with a pencil. It was small and slender, made of silver, decorated with arabesque tracery. "Give this to the man. And tell him to hurry. Are we going sailing or aren't we?"

Ferrier took the pencil, resisted a second glance, passed it over, and hoped Lucas couldn't sense the jolt that had stiffened his spine.

Amanda covered his reactions beautifully. "I have the most wonderful idea," she told him. Her voice had lost its petulance, became warm and inviting. "Why don't you come along on our picnic?"

"He can't," Lucas said, scribbling down the telephone number.

"But why not? He looks like a man who has a long empty Saturday ahead of him." She spoke to Ferrier. "Do you know anyone at all in Málaga?" Her deep-blue eyes were sympathetic. "No? I guessed it. How awful. Gene—"

"No," Lucas said decidedly. He handed her back the pencil, gave Ferrier the slip of paper. "Now, get out to the car. Let's start moving," he told her.

"Seven of us in one car—that's really carrying the carefree bit too far," she said rebelliously. She turned to Ferrier. "We each and every one of us have a car—can you believe it? But we must all pack into Gene's, and laugh and wave—such jolly fun—and when he makes a sudden stop I'll be right over his windshield."

"You've never objected before to sitting on a lap—" Lucas began.

"Stationary," Amanda interrupted. "But not at the speed you drive." She looked angrily at the blonde girl who had come running up the steps to stand hesitating at the threshold as she saw the tight group of three. She had gathered some roses, fastened them loosely into her long hair, and held a large cluster of bougainvillaea against her breast. "Our flower child, Bianca," Amanda murmured.

"Why, there you are!" Bianca said with a delightful, two-rows-of-teeth smile. In spite of her name, she was definitely American.

"Yes, aren't we?" Amanda said blandly.

"Amanda—" warned Lucas. But Amanda was already out into the sunlight, walking quickly toward the car. Bianca wasn't quite as simple-minded as she seemed. She turned and ran, passing Amanda, dropping roses but reaching the car first.

Ferrier was grinning widely as he and Lucas followed. "Two pieces of advice: don't mix your drinks, and never mix your women."

"So I'm learning," Lucas agreed. "A little discipline is what is needed," he added, frowning in Amanda's direction.

"Happy picnic. I began to wish I were coming with you."

Lucas saw nothing funny in that. "We'll keep our contacts to a minimum. Phone me at that number I gave you—it's my answering service—but only leave your name. That will tip me off to get in touch with you."

"Do you really expect to hear from me?" Ferrier asked lightly, determined to keep everything as casual as possible. He hadn't yet made up his mind about Lucas. At first, he had almost accepted him—perhaps because he had been hoping for someone to arrive quickly and take charge. Then he had begun to think Lucas was a fraud—until he had asked the girl for her "silly pencil." If Lucas knew about that, he could be authentic. Lucas and Amanda, a very neat team, staging a quarrel as an efficient little smoke screen. These two working together? And yet, there had been something in the girl's manner, in the expression in her eyes when she had handed Ferrier the pencil, that puzzled him.

"Why not?"

"I'll have nothing to tell."

"You know what I think?" Lucas said softly. "I think you could tell me right now. Martin really won't like this delay one bit." His voice sharpened. "Not one bit."

Threats always angered Ferrier. He let go. "The hell with this Martin, whoever he is. The hell with you, too. I'm not in your line of work. You must be really out of your mind if you think Jeff Reid would pass on information to me. I'm a weekend guest. That's all. So shove it."

"You aren't the usual weekend guest," Lucas said stiffly, but he wasn't quite so sure of himself. He even became politely persuasive. "If Reid is lying trussed up in a hospital bed, can't phone, can't get messages out, who else would he use but his old and reliable—"

"Shove that, too." You try too hard, he thought as he stared angrily at Lucas. Then he changed gears. "You know," he said too innocently, "you're lucky. I might just have gone on drawing you out, and then turned in a nice piece on how the CIA spooks go chasing their shadows. *Life* might print it. Or what about *Ramparts*? It's just their idea of what the American public should know. Your Martin really wouldn't like that one bit, either. Now would he?" Ferrier's smile broke into a laugh. It sounded authentic, even to his own critical ears. Lucas moved quickly away, urging his friends to get into place. Bianca, of course, was already there, well settled into the seat next to Lucas.

It was an odd scene: a car overloaded with determined gaiety, heavy witticisms and light giggles, beads and flowers—there had been quite a rape of Reid's garden—and the faded, crumpled shirts denying their Dior and Cardin labels. Amanda wasn't joining in. She stood outside the car, her arms folded. Then she turned away, began picking up the roses that Bianca had scattered in her haste. Concepción had appeared—perhaps she had been watching all along from a distance—and took a firm stand at the corner of the house, brows down, eyes in an intense Spanish stare.

"Amanda!" Lucas called. He was angry.

"In a minute." She was carrying the roses to Concepción. "These have to go into water or they'll die."

Lucas swore, turned on the engine, went savagely into reverse, and backed the car down the driveway. Amanda stood looking after it. There was amazement on her face, a dejected droop to her slender shoulders. Lucas, giving her one last glance, must have been delighted.

So he has left her to work on me, thought Ferrier. But there are less crude ways of doing it. He's a son of a bitch. That little bickering act in front of me was one thing; this snub in front of a carload of gossips is quite another. Ferrier went over to the girl, touched her arm. She came back from her own thoughts, looked at him worriedly. She wasn't angry. Worried. She said quietly,

"The problem is how do I reach the dock in time to get on that boat?"

"I'll give you a lift down there, if that is what you want."

"It isn't. But it might be the best idea." She remembered the roses. "Let me give these to the housekeeper. She can put them in a vase." She turned to Concepción and spoke rapidly in Spanish. Ferrier watched her curiously; she really had meant what she had said about keeping flowers alive. A strange one, this. He reached his car, started the engine, and had the door open for her as she came running to join him. Concepción had melted, and even waved good-bye to them. "I apologized for my friends," Amanda said by way of explaining that small miracle.

"Your friends?"

"Thank you for that doubt in your voice. No. They come and they go, and Lucas groups them around himself while they are here. The affluent vagabonds." She sighed and shook her head. As they neared the street, she became practical again. "Back out to your left," she told him. "We go south."

"Do you really want to go sailing with that bunch?"

"No. But I'd better. For your sake."

"Mine?" That amused Ferrier. So did the plain-clothes policeman who stood patiently in the shade of a large plane tree. "There's a Security boy—the one who is trying to read a newspaper."

"Whose?" she asked quickly.

"Spanish."

Her eyes widened. "There is another back there, farther along the street. He seemed to be having trouble with his car. And he isn't Spanish. Lucas was much too pleased to see him when we arrived."

Ferrier adjusted his rear-view mirror. Yes, there was a man farther up the Calle San Julian. His car must be all right now. He was getting into the driver's seat. "A blue Fiat? It's taking off. After us, do you think?"

She nodded. "You're it. Now we'll *have* to drive to the dock."

"Why? I say the hell with Lucas and his giggle of lotos-eaters."

"I wish I could. But if I don't turn up for the picnic, he might start guessing that I had picked a quarrel just so as to arrange some time alone with you. Which I did, of course." She smiled as she saw she had forestalled his next remark. "But it won't be much—only a matter of twenty minutes or so. And it is perfectly logical that you would offer me a lift. It wouldn't be quite so explainable if we shook off that car on our tail—it is, isn't it?— and headed away together for some place unknown. Perhaps even a quiet rendezvous? That's the way Lucas thinks. He has the most intricate suspicions." She looked at Ferrier quickly. "You didn't fall for his act, did you? I mean, you didn't tell him anything? I must say I was scared. I stood outside the doorway, within comfortable listening distance, but there is just so long one can admire a bougainvillaea without attracting attention. When the others started to explore the garden, I thought I'd better come inside and start interrupting. For a very bad moment, I thought you were going to produce a silver pencil."

Here it comes, Ferrier thought: the question about Jeff and what else did he give you or what did he tell you, what did he discover.

But she was looking at the busy intersection they were approaching. "Keep on going. When you reach the big street, turn left. Again keep on going past the long stretch of park and flowers. Then past the bull ring—you can't miss it, it's as big as the Colosseum—and follow that avenue for about three miles. Then you make a right—I'll give you the sign when—and you'll be on the water front. There's a kind of fishing place there—boats and docks and restaurants and bars and beaches, all kinds of fun and games. The dock we are aiming for is bang in the middle of it all. Got it?"

He nodded, kept his eyes on the thickening traffic.

"Now," she said, "let's concentrate. I'm Amanda Ames. You are Ian Ferrier. You sent Reid's mayday message to Madrid early this morning; 21–83–35 was the number you called. And you asked that the message be delivered to Martin." She paused. "What's wrong?"

"Nothing." She had been quick to notice, he thought. He had identified himself solely as Ferrier over the phone. "Just wondering where you picked up the Ian. Are you a friend of Jeff Reid's?" But if so, why hadn't Reid told him to telephone her?

"No. We've never met. Any contact we have is made through Madrid. It was Martin who gave me your name. He would check on you, of course; probably through the Embassy. They know you there, don't they?"

Damned idiot, he told himself. He was so busy trying to find the complicated pieces of an intricate puzzle that the obvious things were escaping him. Of course Martin would be curious about him. "I only hope," he said, trying to reassert his intelligence, "that when Martin phoned you he didn't use that 21–83–35 line. It has been tapped, obviously. Unless, of course, Lucas is working with you."

"It has been tapped," she said curtly. Then she was lost in her own thoughts, and they worried her. "But that's another problem," she said at last. "And not yours."

"At least you've learned it exists," he said consolingly.

He hadn't been much comfort. She nodded her agreement, but she frowned down at the bag on her lap as if she were seeing it as a cluster of possibilities, and none of them pleasant. "Let's get back to us," she said, becoming businesslike again.

"Delighted." But not this way, Ferrier thought. Here I am with a pretty girl, a really pretty girl, face and figure perfect according to my taste, bright eyes, soft lips, and obvious intelligence. We are driving through a pleasant foreign town, heading for some beaches and the blue Mediterranean. It's Saturday, and there's a sunny weekend ahead, and all the traffic around us is showing it, everyone going somewhere with nothing but pleasure on his mind. And we are being businesslike.

"If you weren't driving," she said, "I'd ask you to write down the time you telephoned Martin. But I'll do it for you—if you'll lend me a pencil."

"What's wrong with yours?" he asked. But he fished for the silver pencil in his trouser pocket and handed it to her. "That makes me okay?"

"It's reassuring." She examined the pencil closely, handed it back. "Thanks."

"What else did it tell you?" he asked. He pocketed it carefully.

"It is Reid's. He must trust you a lot."

Here it comes, he thought once more. The question.

But it didn't. She said, "Martin got in touch with me this morning. He instructed me to get his reply to Reid. Will you take it? It's simple. Tell Reid to stop worrying. Martin has sent for reinforcements. They are on their way—arriving tonight. They will make contact with him. Definitely. So not to worry."

"Is that all?" No questions, he thought in surprise, no probing. . . .

"Isn't it enough? Help is coming. And in this game, that's all you want to hear when you are in a jam like Jeff Reid. Whoever arrives will get in touch with him and learn what all the sore trouble is about. It must be big. It must be fantastic." She lingered over that last word, dropping her voice, her eyes widening. "Ah," she said quickly, "there's the bull ring! Got your bearings?"

"Yes. And no."

"No?"

"What's your connection with Lucas?"

"I share the same courtyard with him. I have two rooms and a small balcony opposite his studio."

"How long have you been there?"

"Almost a year."

"And Lucas?"

"He was well settled in three years ago."

"How did he know about the pencil?"

"By accident. At least, I hope it was an accident. He was searching for some matches one night at a party, started looking through my bag, emptied it all out on a table with the usual masculine jokes about the things women carry around with them. The pencil was there among all the litter. He admired it. So you see why I nearly panicked today when I thought you might have believed him enough to offer him yours. It would have been an easy two and two for him to add together. He's no fool, even if his style is flamboyant American—the young, get-with-it, look-at-me crowd. It's good cover."

"Cover for what?"

She didn't seem to hear that quiet question. "Of course, today he was trying to act Establishment. But the truth is he has no real conception of how the American Establishment behaves."

"And how does it?" he asked jokingly. Establishment . . . a word imported from England along with the Beatles and miniskirts. Over there, it had validity: an army of permanent civil servants, nonpolitical, nonpartisan, outlasting all governments, a formidable block of quiet, unobtrusive, continuing power. But in the United States, where every change in administration brought new faces as assistants and advice-givers, where every cabinet member brought in his own men for guidance and counsel? Where most career civil servants were bypassed, sometimes for a four-year stretch, sometimes for even less, by the lawyers, journalists, professors, businessmen, and image makers? It was a very remarkable Establishment that rose to the top levels of power so swiftly and then dropped just as speedily out of sight. "How does it behave?"

She thought about that. "I don't know," she answered honestly. "But I do know that Lucas is quite sure he has the answer; and he hasn't, any more than those trendy movies—you know the type? Let's pull everything to pieces, leave no beliefs intact, ignore the good, emphasize the bad, down with the system, up with us." She shook her head sadly. "All these bright little boys and their intellectual pretensions . . ." She paused, tried to laugh. "I do know about that, at least. Once upon a time, I was one of the bright little girls."

He waited, but there was to be no further explanation, seemingly. He said, "So Lucas has been seeing too many trendy movies?"

"He doesn't need to. He was writing that kind of stuff when he was a sophomore. And now he really believes his own propaganda. He cooked up plenty of it in his underground newspaper. That was in Berkeley, 1964. I was there, too."

"You knew him even then?"

"Radicals together. He scarcely knew me. He was deep in the action. I was a very minor revolutionary. Then we went off—in different directions."

"And how did that happen?"

"Oh, with a small incident, which he played up big. He burned his draft card, although he wasn't in any danger of being drafted —he was a graduate student by that time. A public ceremony, with TV cameras notified in advance; after which he disappeared. Driven into hiding, fear of persecution, America in the hands of Nazis, the whole bit."

"And you?"

She looked at him with large and thoughtful eyes. "Are you just curious, or really interested?"

"Interested."

"I had a severe case of disillusionment. You see, at first I had really believed that Lucas' protest was honest. Then I found proof —I didn't want to believe it, but there it was, proof—that the whole thing had been staged. On orders. It was a performance. So all our protests on his behalf became performances; we didn't know it, but all our reactions were according to plan. That was the first shock. The second was when I learned that his disappearance was on order, too. The third was when a girl we all liked and trusted—a true liberal, an honest radical, a free and soaring spirit —was elected president of a really important student society and then announced to the newspapers that she always had been a communist. I suppose the idea was to make us think that if someone like her was a communist, then communists must be delightful people. But she had got most of the votes because she had always maintained she wasn't a communist. When I challenged her about lying, she told me she hadn't lied; she had only been following orders. And what benefited the cause was never a lie; couldn't be, by definition. Because truth was whatever was good for communism. Whatever hurt it was a lie." Amanda shook her head, sighed. "And so—I faced a big moment of real truth, my own, and nothing to do with Moscow's definition. It wasn't exactly a pleasant experience—who likes to admit he has been manipulated? I had been used: that was true truth. Three shocks like that, close together, made a bolt and a jolt. And then there was a fourth shock, much worse. One of my professors had spoken out frankly against the violence that was developing on the campus. So his office was invaded, his files were looted, and the manuscript of a book he was writing—ten years of work—was burned."

"And that was the end of the dream?"

"For me? Yes. It was no longer a dream, but a nightmare. And I woke up in stages. First, there were several weeks of honest reassessment. Painful. Especially when I heard two of Lucas' friends persuading many of us that the professor had got what he deserved; he was against progress, a reactionary professor who should be driven out of the university. But he wasn't reactionary; he was a liberal in the old-fashioned style. And the truth was that he had seen more clearly than most that the universities were being destroyed and reshaped as centers of political action. Bases for revolution, in other words."

"And after the weeks of reassessment?"

"Two months of misery while I got rid of my prejudices and collected some facts. Real facts. Not half-truths, not assumptions. A lonely, lonely time."

"There was no one you could talk with?"

"The old friends had dropped away. I was deep in the jungle of the New Left. I had to find my own way out."

"What about parents, family?"

She looked at him, asked sadly, "My sweet, progressive parents who never said 'No' to me and wouldn't face a value judgment in case it labeled them as illiberal? How could they tell me what was right and what was wrong? They never did, you know—perhaps because they had never really faced the truth themselves. They just won't believe there is any threat against our country except from the right wing. They don't see there is danger from the left, too. Although, in a way, that is making a value judgment—but they'd be hurt if I even suggested that to them. I don't want to hurt them. They fed me, nursed me when I was sick as a child, clothed me, supplied me with money, affection. And so I try to forget that every book and magazine and discussion in our house steered me in their direction—to the political left. And now that I've fought my way back to the center, they don't even listen when I try to explain what happened to me at Berkeley. They just look bewildered, and retreat. They tell their friends that Amanda has become apathetic. Apathetic!" Her voice was strained, close to tears. "Crazy, mixed-up parents," she said softly, unhappily. "I worry about them."

If only to distract her from this attack of gloom, he went back to Lucas. "And no one in Lucas' group tried to stop you? Or gave you an argument?"

"They were too busy planning revolts to notice mine. I just eased my way out."

"You told them you were tired of running the mimeograph machine and washing coffee cups?"

"Close enough," she admitted ruefully. "But at least I didn't graduate to a bomb factory. I saved myself from that."

"Who is Lucas working for? Peking or Moscow?"

"You really ask the hundred-dollar questions, don't you?"

"It's one way of learning the hundred-dollar answers. Or is he a free-lance?"

"No, no. Totally committed. Like me."

"That must be some courtyard you share."

"It has difficult moments." She dropped her voice. "When he disappeared in 1965, he went to the Soviet Union by way of Tokyo. He completed his training there. He is now working for the KGB."

He looked at her.

"You don't believe me?"

He hedged. "I think he's pretty inept for a trained agent."

"Really?" she asked coldly. "Yet you almost accepted him as an American agent, didn't you?"

He was annoyed. But it was true. "Perhaps I'm the one who has been seeing too many of these trendy movies." By God, he thought, that was doubly true.

"How was he inept?" she challenged him. "If I hadn't been around with my little pencil, you might have produced yours."

"Lay off," he said. "I'm stupid. Didn't you know?"

"Not stupid. Just unaccustomed. How was he inept?"

"He arrived almost too late. Another five minutes and he would never have met me."

"Wouldn't he? He had that painting he splatched up this morning after an early visit from his laundress. She is his message-delivery service, actually. He would have left it with your housekeeper, used it as an excuse to call on you this evening. Inept?"

She really loved that word, Ferrier thought. "I take that back."

But she was off and running. "Not Lucas. Do you know why he has a boat, and weekly picnics? When his guests are all prostrate with sun and food and that lazy Mediterranean feeling, he leaves them dozing on deck to the sound of his favorite records and slips down to his pint-sized but tight-shut cabin. He has a transmitter. It doesn't receive, but it sends. It isn't one of those big powerful jobs—that would draw too much attention—but he can easily reach the north coast of Africa. And he only needs to be a couple of miles off shore and he's safe from the Málaga police. There are hundreds of boats, all shapes and sizes, in these waters on Saturday afternoons. His messages are short, concentrated. Within ten minutes he can be back on deck, sprawling with the rest of us."

"And what do you do?" he teased her. "Signal your friends in one of those boats that it is time to start monitoring Lucas?" His guess must have been close enough, for she looked a little startled, and hesitated over her answer.

She never gave it. Instead, she exclaimed and pointed. "Here! Turn right!"

He had to make much too wide a turn, evade a trolley car and a psychedelic Volkswagen, with his mind still working over Lucas and his transmitter. We must have a listening post, he was thinking, but it would have an impossible task picking up all the garble of messages, some pure chat, some real traffic, that was being sent over and around these waters. The sure way of catching Lucas' reports would be to sail, discreetly, some distance away, and watch through powerful binoculars for Amanda's signal: a girl in a dazzling red swimsuit standing beside the mast, or a bright-yellow towel being draped over her shoulders as she rose to look over the side of the boat. "Is Lucas as important as all this?" he asked as he swung the car back into his own lane of traffic.

Again she didn't answer. "Neat," she said of his driving. "But we might have been arrested. Sorry. It was my fault. I was too busy talking." She was having an attack of worry now. "I talked too much. I should only have given you Martin's message, and dropped into chitchat about weather. But at least I've made sure you don't miscalculate on Lucas. Be careful, won't you? There really must be something fantastic at stake."

He liked her concern, even if it wasn't so much for him as it was for the job on hand. "Take care, yourself." He was driving slowly now, because of the increasing crowds, with many on foot. He could study her face for a moment. Incredible, he thought, that a girl like this could handle an assignment like Lucas. She was well qualified, that was true: her experience in Berkeley, with that small group of the radical left, made her a natural for this job. And yet . . . He frowned at a clutter of cars just ahead of him, slowed down more. There was something he had wanted to warn her about, something he could have told her right at the start of their talk but had postponed until he felt more sure of her. What the flaming hell had it been? he asked himself angrily.

"You know," she said slowly, "it could just be that the piece of information Lucas wanted was about those two men: Laner and Tomás—what was it?—Tomás Fuentes."

"There's nothing wrong with your hearing, even when you're lost in admiration of bougainvillaea. But cross off Laner. He was found with a knife in his back this morning. Spanish Security thinks he was eliminated. They are curious. But I don't think he was connected with Fuentes."

"Why not?"

"Captain Rodriguez didn't mention that name, didn't even hint at it sideways. That's his technique. Quite effective."

"Fuentes," she said thoughtfully. "Jeff Reid didn't speak of him when he handed you the identification pencil?"

"No." But he thought of Tavita, dark eyes under long dark lashes, cream silken skin with a soft blush over high cheekbones, shining black hair as tightly brushed and knotted as any ballerina's, and he wondered about her Tomás. He almost mentioned him, but he could see her dark eyes were smoldering ready to burst into fire, the blush on the cheeks had sharpened with anger, the smooth head was held high ready to denounce such a betrayal of her secret. That's what Tavita would call it. Less dramatically, he could admit it was perhaps an indiscretion, possibly a piece of foolishness on his part: Fuentes was only a guess in his mind. "This is as far as we go, I think," he said, looking for some place to park in the little plaza where the street ended and the water front began.

"Drop me here. The dock is only a minute away."

"In this crowd?" Besides, he thought as he edged the car into a free space, she may find Lucas and his merry crew have already set sail or chugged off. "What kind of boat does Lucas own?" In the rear-view mirror, he saw the blue Fiat coming cautiously into the plaza.

"It looks like a fishing boat, but he put in a souped-up engine. When he's in the mood, he can slip over to Tangier. That doesn't happen too often, nowadays, not since Tangier has become a little suspect. Hashish," she added. She nodded in the direction of four new-style Americans straggling past. "That's where they go, by the Algeciras ferry, to pick up what they need."

"You can tell them by sight?" True, they fell into a pattern, a new kind of mucker pose. Behind him, the blue Fiat was searching for a parking place. Let it, he thought.

"They are so obvious," she said. "Hashish must really do

something to the mind, or they wouldn't all be so stupefied. Six years and a day—that's where they are heading."

"Six years and a day? Is that what they get when they're arrested?"

"Standard minimum. No favorites played. And they can't believe it will happen to them."

"That's an old American weakness."

"I used to joke about it. Not any more." She was out of the car and walking fast, as if to work off some of her bitterness. He caught up with her. "Who pays for all this?" she asked angrily. "I don't mean *now*—that's just a matter of easy money from some deluded parent. I mean, who pays for it in the future?"

The future . . . He had his own nightmare about that, and there were so few he could share it with and ease some of its weight. Last night, he had almost unloaded part of it on Jeff Reid in the courtyard of El Fenicio. Strange how it had slipped out, as if it was a relief to talk with someone you could trust, someone who wouldn't retreat into disbelief or leap right into panic. "The future really worries you, doesn't it?" he said sympathetically. He looked at her and wondered. She wasn't so much older than these kids pushing past her right now, was even younger than some.

"Why else did I take this kind of job?" she asked. Then she shook her head sadly, almost pathetically. "I thought I could play one small part in helping my country against her enemies. But what happens when Americans become their own enemy?"

"Only some of us," he reminded her. "And only some of the young are dodging reality. Not all."

"I know, I know," she said with a touch of impatience. "Plenty of them are going to beaches to do no more than swim and sun and have a two-week vacation. It's a minority who have bugged out completely, or throw filth at cops, or scream dirt at college presidents, or set the libraries and the banks on fire, or make the bombs and collect their arsenals. But it's—oh, look—if you were a doctor and had a patient with cancer, would he really be consoled if you told him that it was only a minority of his tissue cells that had gone haywire? He would want to know what danger there was of the cancer spreading, wouldn't he?"

"We aren't just a collection of tissue cells. We're people. With minds of our own."

"After looking at some of the collection on these beaches, you won't believe that. We are such natural joiners and the drug people are such missionaries. Everyone must try it, come along with them. Spread the joy, man. And it spreads. That's why I'm so—so depressed." She was, in fact, pretty close to real tears.

He took her arm. "Come on, Amanda," he said gently, "I wasn't arguing with you; I was only trying to make cheerful noises. In all honesty, I'm depressed too. Only, we'd better not let these bastards grind us down. Is it Lucas? Has he been pressuring you with this kind of talk? Loaded words, propaganda phrases?" He lowered his voice, tried to make one small joke to lighten her load. "New hazards for our undercover agents."

She found that comic. Briefly. Then she looked at him. "Yes. As a matter of fact, yes. Like me to give you a small imitation? Lucas and his political pals gloat over these beaches. Oh, not publicly—they praise the kids at every party they attend, say they are the brightest and best, and blame everything on the system. But privately, they gloat. It's the only word to describe it," she told him anxiously, as if he were already disbelieving her.

"Okay, okay. They gloat."

"The beaches are symbolic, they say. The new American life style, squalid and sleazy and soft. Capitalist self-indulgence, imperialist decadence; it's all on the point of collapse—with calculated violence and the threat of terror to help, of course. A push here, a shove there, and it all falls apart. America is up for grabs. The tough-minded will win, and it is no longer fashionable for America to be tough. There's only one thing that worries Lucas and his friends. They have done the undermining, the preparing, the hard work for years. And their problem now is to keep the wild men—the Maoist revolutionaries and the militants, black and white—from trying to grab, too. Final control, as always, must be in Moscow's hands." She paused. Her voice became bitter. "And who says the Cold War is over? God in heaven, whenever I hear that, I begin to wonder if Lucas is right. He predicts America's future as one big cop-out."

Ferrier's face was tight and grim. "Is it?" he asked. He pushed their way impatiently through a density of beads and fringes, kinky hats and headbands, uncertain smiles and searching eyes.

"Newcomers," Amanda said, looking away from them. "Once they find a group to join, the eyes develop a sullen stare. Some will move on after a few weeks, go searching for a bigger and better beach. Others just let the weeks pass into months, even into years."

"And the Spaniards?" This was their beach, wasn't it?

"Fewer and fewer. They are the dispossessed."

"Lucas and his crowd must enjoy that a lot."

"You know your Lucas," she said.

"I've met his type." We've always had some of them around, he thought. The only difference now was that they were so confident and cocky, pushing their own particular brand of dope quite blatantly. He stopped, let go of her arm. They had come almost to the water's edge, blue sea sparkling far out into a misted horizon. The dock lay in front of them, an enclave of jetties with moored pleasure craft. On one side of this little harbor, the fishing boats —real, as yet unconverted to the tourist trade—had been pulled up onto a narrow shore, their nets set to dry in front of the street where the bars and small shops crowded together. On the other side of the harbor were several acres of tightly packed bodies. Day after day, week after week, months into years of sitting, standing, lying around . . .

Ferrier looked quickly away from two different worlds, each ignoring the other: the fishermen intent on finishing the work that had started before dawn, with a concentration that was in itself a disdain; the self-made exiles, linked together in their flight from reality, beginning a road without end. "Any sign of Lucas?" he asked abruptly.

Amanda had been studying the dock. At first, she didn't answer. Then, "Yes. They are just boarding." She averted her eyes from the two-masted, unrigged fishing boat, with its boldly painted prow. "See them? Let me know when Lucas notices us."

Ferrier nodded. "So we arrived right on their tail. We made good time, after all." And a pity, he thought. He had hoped they would be gone.

"That should please Lucas." She kept her back turned to the boat. "He will take it as a sign that I regretted my little tantrum. It was quite a performance, wasn't it? Too bad we had to meet that way."

"Too bad this is the way we say good-bye. Any chance of—?"

She shook her head definitely. "And I'm sorry. It was wonderful being able to talk, just to talk. That's the hardest part of my job—keeping silent when opinions that make me mad are flying around."

"It's hard," he agreed, and wondered how she could ignore danger so coolly. He stared with increasing hostility at the man who had taken a stand on the prow of the boat to get a better view. It also made a nice dramatic gesture. "He has just caught sight of us," Ferrier said quietly. He let his own eyes slide away to the jumble of people moving around the dock.

"How is his mood?" she asked tensely.

"He looked too goddamned pleased for my taste."

"That could be a good sign." She relaxed. "And now I start being sorry, properly subdued and contrite. Will this suit him?" Her face became hesitant, remote. "No, no—don't come with me.

Let's show him a quick parting, polite, no more. Good-bye, Ian. And my thanks." She turned away, gave him a casual wave, hitched her bag more securely over her shoulder. She pushed her loose dark hair from her brow, raised her hand to signal the boat. "Gene!" she called, and increased her pace. "Wait for me, Gene!"

For a moment, Ferrier watched the neat swing of her hips, and then started off for the plaza as if he had lost interest. He kept seeing Lucas' handsome face with its confident smile, and cursed the man silently all the way back to his car.

9

It was almost five o'clock when the message came from the hospital: Señor Reid was awake and ready, an hour ahead of time. Could Señor Ferrier come now? Señor Reid was most eager to see him.

"Fine," said Ferrier, both surprised and delighted. "Tell him I'll be there in—in about fifteen minutes." That, he thought hopefully, would allow five minutes for actual driving, five minutes for making sure of the right street, and roughly five for leaving and parking. He picked up his jacket from a chair in the study, along with a green cloth bag (a sentimental survivor of Jeff's undergraduate days) which he had already stuffed with dictaphone, radio, razor and soap and toothbrushes, engagement pad, and a small cassette player with half a dozen packaged tapes of classical music. The four books, which he had spent the last half hour selecting carefully from Jeff's shelves, were equally guaranteed to provide real pleasure; nothing aggravating or nauseating. A hospital bed was not the place to start your stomach churning with wild talk or furious sound. Within a couple of minutes, Ferrier was on his way.

People were now stirring on the Calle San Julian. The heat had been turned down slightly, the glare was cut by the plane trees, but Ferrier didn't envy the police guard on duty outside Reid's house. He saw no sign of the blue Fiat, which had followed him back from the beach up to the old Arab fortifications—where he had lunched leisurely and thoughtfully—and then had disappeared. Perhaps it had been replaced by that red Porsche or the gray Renault which just happened to be leaving San Julian along with him. It didn't matter much to Ferrier. Not now. Jeff Reid had recovered more quickly than expected. Eager to see me, thought Ferrier. Not half as eager as I am to hand over the lighter and pencil and all the rest of the paraphernalia, give the messages, and ask a few questions of my own. And after that, curiosity at least partly satisfied and my guesses proved either wild or well

131

aimed (that's important to no one except myself, but I'm the one who has wasted all this bright summer day trying to grope for meanings and rational explanations), I can bow out. And head for Granada. There's a little business to be completed there, of course; about a couple of sentences of business. And the rest is pure pleasure. Perhaps I might even leave for Granada late to-night. A drive over these mountains by cool moonlight, snowcaps pointed against a starlit sky . . .

He was in high spirits in spite of the sun-baked streets as he parked his car near the hospital. It was a less lonely place by day: the visitors, whole families of them, all ages, all sizes, were beginning to pile in. The hall was crowded, the waiting room already half full. He pulled on his jacket, gathered together a few Spanish phrases, and approached the busy desk. In this part of the world, a foreigner who made an effort to speak its language was given politeness in return. A pert young nurse took him in charge most willingly, parted a way for him through the turmoil of people and pointed him in the direction of Jeff's room. It was easy to find, the fourth door along the red-tiled corridor. His heel almost slipped from him on the high polish, and he entered with a joke ready on his lips about cleanliness preceding plaster casts, and then fell silent instead.

The place was filled with roses. Red roses, masses of them, brilliant against stark white walls. On a narrow high bed, leg suspended, swathed in plaster and bandages, was Jeff Reid, watching him with hollow eyes in a strangely drawn, startlingly bleached face. He shouldn't be seeing me at all, thought Ferrier; he should have taken some sleep producers and be dozing out of the reach of pain. I'll keep this short, and good-bye to any long talk with a hundred questions and all and all. "Hello, Jeff. Quite a setting you've got here. What do you think you are—a film star?"

"Tavita," Reid said, his voice strange, distant, all its usual resonance drained out of it. He gestured to the roses with his unbandaged arm. "It's her way of saying sorry that she can't come to see me. She hates hospitals."

"She'd have been here with me," Ferrier said quickly, "except that she had to leave for Granada."

"Oh?"

"I'll tell you about that, but first things first." Ferrier dumped the contents of the book bag onto a chair, took off his jacket, loosened his tie. The shutters were partly closed, the room's walls were old and thick, and there was a ceiling fan gently circulating; but even so, this place seemed to be getting warmer by the minute as its cool contrast with the hot streets outside began to lessen.

"There's a message from your company's office in Madrid. Martin is sending replacements to take charge for you. Soon. They'll get here tonight at the latest. Anyway, you can stop worrying. All's well." He heard Reid's small sigh of relief, pretended not to notice, began finding places for the radio and cassette player. "I brought some extras. Thought you'd like some Mozart, Bach, and Brahms. Okay?"

Reid nodded. "Play the Mozart."

"Now?"

Reid nodded.

Ferrier looked at him sharply. Was Mozart for pleasure or precaution? Had Jeff some suspicion that this room could have been bugged?

"I've been out cold for most of this day," Reid said as Ferrier inserted the cassette and started the Haffner Symphony. "Didn't know what was happening around me."

"Too loud?" Ferrier moved closer to the bed so that they could hear each other, even with a background of brilliant sound and their voices lowered to a minimum.

"Just right." Reid grinned. "Nice busy music."

Ferrier reached into his pocket, brought out the lighter and pencil. "Present and accounted for. Where do you want them?"

"That's the problem, isn't it?" Reid hesitated, looked around the room, shook his head. "This bed is hopeless. There is forever someone changing something, taking temperatures, feeling pulses."

"Want me to hold on to them?" Ferrier asked slowly. It was the obvious question, even if it was an unwilling suggestion.

"You have done all right so far. And thanks."

Ferrier pocketed the lighter, tried to look cheerful, said, "Perhaps you'll need the pencil? Identification?"

"I don't think I need much of that—who the hell would try to impersonate me as an Egyptian mummy?"

"Oh, *that*'s what you are. I thought you were giving an imitation of a Thanksgiving turkey trussed for the oven."

There was a small smile on Reid's pale lips. "That's just about as helpless as I feel right now. Okay, okay, leave the pencil. Put it with the rest of my things over on that small table. Make it look natural."

So Ferrier placed the pencil along the edge of the small engagement pad, angled the dictaphone beside it, laid the razor and toothbrushes on top. In the general clutter, the pencil was unnoticeable. He came back to the bed, lowered his voice even more. "Talking of impersonations," he said easily, "a fellow called Gene

Lucas came to see me around noon. He said Martin had sent him. But he didn't have any pencil on him. There was a girl with him who did—Amanda Ames. She gave me the message for you. She also told me that Lucas was working for the KGB. Know either of them?"

"Not the girl. Lucas—Lucas? There was a Lucas who turned up at one of Medina's parties. I didn't meet him, though. Only saw him across the room."

"About thirty? Six foot, dark-haired, blue-eyed, handsome profile. But what was he doing at one of Medina's parties? Medina's your doctor, isn't he? Or at least he goes around saying he is your doctor. Oh, I know, I know—he only assists his uncle, and it's old Medina who is your doctor, but Junior forces the pace, doesn't he? Why?"

"Don't worry about Medina. He collects a lot of strange birds at his parties. He likes to think of himself as an independent thinker—an original. You know the type."

"Yes," Ferrier said sourly, "just the type to be gulled by people like Lucas. That man's a smart operator. What was he doing at Medina's party?"

"Probably what I was doing—studying the strange birds."

"I wonder," Ferrier said with a touch of exasperation that was partly directed against himself. Why the hell was he talking about Medina when there were so many other things to tell Jeff?

"How did you handle Lucas?" Reid asked, going straight to his own particular worry.

"Gingerly. He made several feints, threw a couple of unexpected punches. He claimed he was a buddy of yours, said you both worked for the CIA."

Reid was quite silent.

"He not only knew about my telephone call to Martin, but he knew the meaning of that message. Highest emergency, greatest importance, rally around." Ferrier paused. "I don't like that, Jeff. It looks as if your Martin has more than a tapped phone to worry about. It looks as if—" He broke off, thinking of Amanda. That's what I wanted to warn her about, and couldn't remember it in time: not just a telephone call intercepted, but an informer—someone who had penetrated Martin's group—supplying the meaning of Jeff's cryptic message.

"As if we've been infiltrated?" Reid asked slowly. "Could be. Or Lucas might have been trying to panic you into telling him anything you knew. Emergency is a useful word. Properly applied, it gets quick reaction." He half smiled, as if he knew that old dodge well. "I'll pass on the warning to Martin. He will deal with it."

"You play it cool," Ferrier said worriedly. Or perhaps this was for his benefit: Jeff was trying to calm him down.

"Why not? All Lucas knows is that there is an emergency. That's all my message said. No specifics."

"He may not need them. He seems to have some information about a man called Tomás Fuentes."

Reid's eyes lost all expression. His face was carved out of wood, ridged and furrowed.

"Lucas has the idea that Fuentes may be in Málaga. He also thinks it is possible that Fuentes got in touch with you."

There was a short silence. Then Reid said hoarsely, "Let's hope to God that Martin gets someone here." He began cursing his helplessness.

"Take it easy Jeff. Easy. I don't believe Fuentes is any longer in Málaga. He's in Granada."

Reid looked at the red roses.

Ferrier nodded. "Someone called Tomás was smuggled up into your attic, early this morning. Today, around eleven, he was smuggled out again—dressed as a chauffeur."

Reid looked at him, astounded and horrified. "She's taken him to—"

"Yes. And she wants your instructions. I'll deliver them to her as soon as I can leave Málaga."

"The little idiot—"

"She didn't do too badly," Ferrier said. "There was a considerable crisis at El Fenicio last night. Captain Rodriguez had the place searched. He found nothing."

"Tavita, Tavita . . ." Reid's voice was almost a whisper. He shook his head, half-admiringly, half-sadly. "She doesn't know what she has got hold of," he said with sudden anger. "That man is capable of killing her, once her usefulness is over. He'd do anything, anything, to cover his trail. He has already murdered for it—in Mexico."

"You'd help a man like that?" Ferrier was incredulous.

"Personally? No. I'd like to see him dead and buried."

"What is he?"

"A part-way defector."

"You mean he is using us?"

Reid nodded. "That's his idea. He needs our help to get to safety."

"And then?"

"He expects to be vindicated, reinstalled. He didn't say so, of course. He's playing us along. He will need us if his private plans don't jell. That's my estimate. I think it's accurate."

"Reinstalled as what?"

Reid didn't answer. His face was set and grim, lined with pain.

"As what?" Ferrier challenged quietly. "I won't be much use to you unless I know the basic facts. I don't work well when I'm blindfolded."

Reid looked at him, then nodded his agreement. "He is KGB. High-placed, long-standing. He has been directing the Cuban branch of their Department Thirteen. Know it?"

Ferrier shook his head.

"It is one of their most important and most secret departments. Specializes in assassination and terror. It exists, Ian. Believe me, it exists."

Ferrier stared at the tense white face. He nodded, watched it relax.

"It has existed for a long time," Reid went on, his voice steadying. "It has had different names. In the last ten years or so, we've known it as Department Thirteen. At present it is concentrating heavily on the Disunited States. Why not? It's their big opportunity. And they'll make the most of it. It is training selected Americans, very willing Americans. The big push is toward 1976."

"Revolution?"

"You've heard the word recently, haven't you? Or are you one of those who don't listen to the radicals and militants?" Reid asked wearily. "The activists, Ian. That's the group I'm talking about. Not the disenchanted young, not the ordinary dropouts or politicals or protesters. The real hard-core activists."

"The ones with the ruthless ideals?"

Reid nodded, relaxed. "You've been reading the signals, all right. And haven't you noticed that, every now and again—when they are particularly cocky—their mask of innocent protest slips and out they come with their truth? Revolution. They've even named the date."

"They really mean it?"

"They mean it. As Hitler meant what he said. But who listened?"

"Even when they listened, they couldn't believe it." Ferrier remembered his father and his friends discussing this same point. He used to think his father's generation had been stupid or lazy, unwilling to make the effort to face unpleasant facts. "Then, as now," he said softly. "That's our handicap, too. We listen, and we can't quite believe. And there are so few of those militants, a small minority—that's the real stumbling block when we try to assess them. That and their wild rhetoric. Where does their put-on end and their truth begin?"

"With training. And money. And supplies. And a major propaganda effort to keep the rest of us confused. They've done well in that department, so far, and they'll do better once the Big Lie machine really gets behind them. Forged documents, false letters, the whole bit. Our smart Madison Avenue image polishers look like a kindergarten effort compared to the brains that are backing those guys. They are having fine fun with us. And we go on our bumbling way, thinking there must be some rational explanation for all our troubles, something we can cope with by fair debate. Fair? If they can't find an issue, they create one. And we swallow it, hook, line, and sinker. They now think we are the easiest catch. Why else have they become so sure of themselves, so arrogant? They—" Reid's voice had hoarsened to a painful whisper. Ferrier poured him a glass of water, steadied his head as he sipped it. Then Reid leaned back against the pillow, closed his eyes. "So few of them, you said. Yes. But how many honest men have believed their stories? How many have supported—"

"Take it easy, take it easy," Ferrier said. The leg is hurting him badly. "I'll call a nurse. You'd better—"

"Not yet, not yet. I'll have a long sleep once you leave." Reid opened his eyes, made a big effort at a small grin. "Pain," he admitted, "brings out all the worries. Sorry."

Ferrier went straight to the point. "What do I tell Tavita?"

Reid hesitated. "She must keep Fuentes in cold storage for twenty-hour hours. He will be taken off her hands. Definitely. And she mustn't panic him, give him any cause for alarm. He might decide to move on his own."

"Disappear?"

"We'd have little chance of finding him again."

"Who else is after him? The KGB, of course. And the Spanish government too?" Why else Tavita's nervousness about Captain Rodriguez?

"Yes; old history. Then, of course, Castro's agents want him silenced. And the Maoists would be interested in recruiting him— or in extracting information from him if he refused. And there isn't an intelligence service in the free world that doesn't want to know more about Department Thirteen's latest developments."

"I'd hate to be as popular as that," Ferrier said with unconcealed contempt. "And we are supposed to save his bloody neck."

"Meanwhile." Reid was equally sour.

"But what can we really expect from him—if he is planning to get back into power? You think he is actually hoping for that?"

"Yes. He might just manage it, too, if his ideas are vindicated and he is proved right and his friends get enough courage to see he is re-established."

"Then he won't tell us one thing of real value. It will be just another put-on."

"We'll get more out of him than he means to give. And even if he tells us little, it could be useful. You know from your own work—"

"I know." The smallest things, the scraps of information, could be valuable—whether they verified a supposition, or opened up a new possibility, or helped analysis, reinterpretation, better evaluation. "But can you trust what he tells you? Will there be any real truth you can dig out from a flow of words?"

Reid gave a strange small laugh, brief, ending in a grimace of pain. "His information is credible. I've found that out." He pointed to his grotesque leg. "Laner." He took a long breath, made an effort, said slowly, "That's the long-haired guy." He gave up, as if all the stretch of explanation he saw lying before him was just too much.

"I know," Ferrier cut in again, trying to spare Jeff unnecessary effort. Thank God he had got around to mentioning Laner; that was something Ferrier had wanted to hear from the beginning of this talk, but he had thought it wiser not to force the pace. And there had been other priorities. "He attacked you. How?"

"Spray gun." And then, as Ferrier frowned over that, Reid added, "Cyanide spray. Heart-failure effect."

"Was he after Tomás Fuentes?"

"At first, I thought he was. But—" Reid hesitated.

"He didn't go upstairs to search," Ferrier tried.

"Just came over—had a look at me—then left."

"He thought you were dead?"

Reid nodded. "And I just wasn't worth that risk. I wasn't so important. Why me?" He drew a slow breath, made an effort. "It only makes sense if Fuentes was telling the truth. About his recent trainees. Some of them are difficult to control: too confident, too eager for action, too intent on showing what smart boys they are. And that type always knows best. No matter how they've been disciplined or trained, they always think they know best. Dangerous element. Unpredictable."

"I admire your restraint. They are more than a bunch of super-inflated egos. They are fanatics, totally ruthless, blinded with hate, dedicated to violence." And even if Fuentes and his crowd called them young idealists, nobly committed, true revolutionaries, they still knew what they had recruited, what material they had to work on. "Don't tell me," Ferrier said sarcastically, "that Fuentes had a touch of remorse about what he was unloading on an unsuspecting world. Or could it be he was scared of having his operation blown by someone like Laner? Well—he can stop worrying about him. Someone else decided that Laner wasn't worth the cost of his training. He has been disciplined. Permanently."

Reid stared at Ferrier.

"His body was found near the harbor this morning. Knifed. Apparently—as Captain Rodriguez described it—in a water-front brawl."

"Rodriguez?" Reid was suddenly wary.

"One of my visitors today."

"What did he want?"

"He talked about Laner." And about Adam Reid, but that was definitely one topic not to bring up right now. "No mention of Fuentes. Which doesn't mean much, I agree. He may have heard the same rumor that Lucas was tracking down."

"Rodriguez . . ." Reid was worried. "I've always kept clear of him."

"You've never meddled in Spanish politics? Taken sides?"

"I've kept clear of that, too. Not my job."

"I had the feeling he knows about it."

There was a short silence. "So good-bye Málaga," Reid said slowly. He looked at the red roses.

Ferrier branched off quickly to another subject. "Is Ed Pitt—the black who was traveling with Laner—another graduate of Department Thirteen?"

Reid nodded.

"Rodriguez thinks he has been shipped out. Ultimate destination America?"

Again Reid nodded.

"We'll have to alert—" Ferrier cut himself off. Deeper and deeper in, he thought angrily; you take one step, then a couple more, and soon you are walking the full mile. Why the hell did I have to bring up the question of Ed Pitt? But he knew the answer to that. America needed no more assassins.

"There will be several such names. Once Fuentes starts talking. There's a man in Washington—Robert O'Connor. Knows about Cuba, about Vado. That's what Fuentes said. He will talk with him. He's been right so far."

"Fuentes? Or this O'Connor?" He is beginning to tire, Ferrier thought worriedly. He has a lot to say, too much perhaps, and so his mind keeps jumping.

"Fuentes named O'Connor. No infiltration there, no danger."

Ferrier hesitated, then risked it. "You don't trust Martin any more?"

"It's not that! It's just—" Reid's pain showed in the sharpness of his impatience. He closed his eyes, tried to control his voice. "O'Connor is the expert. He can take charge. He knows Vado."

"Vado?" Who the hell was Vado? Deeper and deeper in . . . "Just a minute," Ferrier said, moving over to the cassette player. The Haffner was ending. "I'll put on the Brahms Fourth." He began changing the neatly packaged tape.

"I was to go to Washington," Reid said as the music filled the room. "A quick trip. There and back. Ian, would you—if Martin is slow to reach me—it might be best—" He halted as a brisk knock sounded on the door. It opened.

The pert nurse came in, bouncing and cheerful. "And how is the patient?" she asked brightly.

"Fine," Reid said through his teeth. "Come back later and—"

"Fine, are you?" Dr. Medina asked as he entered the room. He nodded to Ferrier, looked in astonishment at the roses. "You receive your visitors in style," he said genially, and lifted the clipboard with Reid's medical record from the bottom rail of the bed. He studied it briefly.

"They are taking good care of me," Reid said.

Medina replaced the board and its careful notations. "Uh-huh . . . How's the pulse?"

"That has all been done," the nurse said in Spanish. "Señor Reid was fully examined an hour ago. All is going well."

"And why wasn't I notified as soon as he was awake? I left definite instructions."

The nurse said coldly, "There was no need. Dr. Medina, your uncle, Señor Reid's physician, was here when our doctors—"

"And how long have you been here?" Medina asked Ferrier.

The nurse looked at Ferrier pleadingly. So he said, offhand, easily, "Not too long. I was a little early, so I dropped in." He could feel the nurse relax. Antonio Medina might have little standing at this hospital, but she was scared of doctors. What one might call a well-trained nurse.

"I hope you didn't make him talk too much," Medina said severely.

"I did most of the talking. I brought him some music. Any objections?"

"Not at all, not at all. But a little less volume, please." Medina looked at Reid. "Are you strong enough to sign a contract? Ridiculous nonsense, of course. Business should be kept out of sickrooms. But there is a man outside who wants to see you for only a couple of minutes. He is from Madrid—some firm called Martin and Sons. He says the contract is urgent. Is it?"

Reid nodded, avoided glancing at Ferrier, who was standing frozen by the cassette player.

"All right. Just the signature. No discussion." Medina was being extremely competent. He told the nurse brusquely, "Send the man in." Then he turned to Ferrier. "Come along. We'll wait outside."

Ferrier looked at Reid, hesitated. Does he want that lighter, and how do I get it to him naturally? "By the way, Jeff, I also brought you some cigarettes. Would you like one now?" He produced his own pack, had his hand on the lighter all ready to deliver.

Jeff had caught his meaning. "Keep them. Meanwhile."

"I should think so," burst out Medina. "No cigarettes in here. And, nurse"—the young woman had returned with the man from Martin and Sons—"see that these roses are all removed before your patient goes to sleep again. They must not be left here overnight. You understand?"

Ferrier pretended to listen, but his full attention was now on the stranger. He was a medium kind of man, in height, weight, features, and dress. Nothing extravagant. A quiet manner, hesitant but friendly. The only touch of color to his dark suit and restrained tie was a small red carnation in his buttonhole. He carried a briefcase in one hand; the other, with a neat bandage on its thumb, held a brightly jacketed book, as if he had come prepared for some waiting around. Well, thank God he had at least come. Ferrier glanced over at the bed. Reid's face was less strained. The end of responsibility, thought Ferrier, and felt something of the same relief. "I'll stay outside. If you need me, press that button on the bedside table. What does it do?" he asked the nurse. "Rings bells or buzzes?"

"It turns on a light over the door."

"Every modern convenience," Medina said sarcastically. "Come along, both of you." His grasp on Ferrier's arm was gentle but definite. Ferrier disengaged himself, equally definitely, hesitated.

The stranger said apologetically, "This won't take much time." His voice was pleasant. American, proper Bostonian. "I'm sorry to break in on you like this, but I'm leaving Málaga this evening for Madrid." He turned to Reid, looked at the encased leg, shook his head with sympathy. "Too bad. Martin telephoned me about your accident, asked me to get this contract signed. It's urgent, seemingly." He was opening his briefcase, selecting a document. Ferrier followed the nurse and Medina into the corridor.

There was a mixture of people spilling over from the entrance hall and the crowded waiting room. "Six o'clock is the beginning of visiting hours," the nurse explained. "They'll soon be in the wards, and this corridor will be much quieter." She picked up a wandering child. "Are you lost?" she asked gently. "Shall I help you find your mother?"

Medina watched her leave, said, "Much quieter, but not cooler. Shall we move into the little garden?"

"I'll stay here," Ferrier said, glanced at his watch—eight minutes to six. He almost regretted his decision as more visitors came pressing into the corridor, packing everyone into a tighter mass. He backed against a wall with Medina, let the others be pushed past him. He could see the upper half of Reid's door, now on the opposite side of the corridor; and in spite of the broad shoulders and large bullet head of a tall fair-haired man jammed in front of him, he had a clear view of its signal light. But it remained unlit. All was peaceful. Even the jostling mass was still, now silent, almost somnolent in the rising temperature.

A gong boomed. Everyone jumped a little, was jolted into movement and excited talk. There was a brief confusion—the big man adding to it by turning too quickly, misjudging his own bulk and bumping into Ferrier. Profuse apologies, of course.

"De nada," Ferrier said impatiently, and shoved the man aside. The confusion was over as quickly as it had begun, changing into a steadily moving lane toward the main hall. And there was the man whom Martin had sent, caught up in the main stream of traffic, already halfway down the corridor. Reid's door must have opened when the big fellow had almost toppled against Ferrier. Damnation, thought Ferrier. "Hi there!" he called, and started after the neatly brushed head of medium-brown hair now bobbing along in the steadily flowing current. Then Ferrier stopped, feeling slightly foolish. Why should he speak with the man, anyway? There had been no signal from Jeff, no request for the delivery of the lighter. Either Jeff hadn't been too sure of his visitor or he was someone who wasn't important enough—another messenger, perhaps, like Amanda Ames. In a matter of seconds, the corridor was cleared. The voices had receded into the other wing of the hospital. The entrance hall, the waiting room beside it, were empty, too. Suddenly, it was all very lonely. "What was his name?" he asked Medina.

"How should I know?"

"Didn't he tell you?"

"I—I just met him. Is it important?"

Ferrier turned toward Reid's room. Quick, light heels came hurrying along the corridor from the hall. It was the young nurse, a little breathless. "Your friend has left," she told Medina.

"Not my friend," he answered sharply.

She looked at Medina. "But—"

"Never saw him before in my life." Medina followed Ferrier, stopped him as he was about to open Reid's door. "Don't you think Señor Reid has had enough excitement for one day? I'd advise a little rest now. You can come back later."

"I'd like to see him for a few minutes."

The nurse said, "He may already be sleeping. Dr. Medina's friend—sorry, doctor; I mean the man you brought here—told me that Señor Reid seemed rather tired. He wanted a little rest."

"Most sensible idea he has had—" began Medina. He stared as Ferrier pushed him aside, quickly opened the door.

"He is asleep," the nurse whispered, and moved across the room on tiptoe to adjust the shutters, darken the room.

"Best thing for him," Medina said in a hushed voice. "A little natural sleep—Ferrier, what are you doing? Don't waken him!"

Ferrier reached the bed. Reid was still, peaceful, his eyes closed; his head was twisted sideways on the pillow, his mouth half-open. His good arm was stretched toward the table, but even if he had had time to make it, his fingers could not have pressed the signal that controlled the light outside his door; the bed table had been pulled a few inches beyond his reach. "Open the shutters," Ferrier heard himself say. "Open the shutters, damn you!"

"Señor Ferrier!" Medina was scandalized. And then worried. "Is something wrong?" His voice was faint, almost strangled.

The shutters opened wide. The full light streamed in. "He is dead," said Ferrier.

"No, no, no!" shouted Medina.

The nurse came running to stand beside Ferrier, her eyes wide, her face in shock. She reached over to take Reid's wrist, feel it. "Dr. Medina," she called, "Dr. Medina—" She began pushing the emergency signals. He came forward slowly, unbelievingly, his eyes fixed with horror on Reid's inert body.

Ferrier didn't wait. He was out of the room, running down the corridor, pushing his way through a straggle of latecomers in the entrance hall, ignoring the startled looks and exclamations as he shoved open the front door and raced down the steps toward the street.

10

It was a narrow street, drawing back from the front of the hospital to form a little square. At one end was a park or gardens of some kind; at the other, the broad avenue that was a main thoroughfare. Ferrier hesitated, getting his bearings, deciding, his eyes searching. People everywhere, some in standing groups, others walking toward the hospital; cars everywhere, too, some parked, some moving slowly out into the narrow street. Boys on bicycles, children playing, women with baby carriages; old men sitting on a low stone wall, lost in late-evening thoughts. Which way? People everywhere, but where was the man with the smoothly brushed head and dark suit and a briefcase and a bright covered book?

Useless, Ferrier told himself, useless. Abruptly, he broke off that train of thought. If anything was useless, it was to start out saying it was useless. Sure, the man had had several minutes to lose himself in this crowd. But would he walk far in this heat? Or did he have a car parked near here? That was possible. Ferrier couldn't picture him making his way toward the avenue to wait for a trolley bus. He'd be too noticeable in his definitely American clothes; memorable, also, if he went searching for a taxi. A private car could hide him, get him out of the public eye. A car that was waiting as near the end of the street as possible, ready to slip into the avenue; that was the quick way back into the city, or out of it. Ferrier started toward the avenue, almost at a run. *"Dispenseme, dispenseme,"* he kept saying as he forged through the various groups. But that man, he was thinking, must have had just as much difficulty in making his way along this street, and he couldn't have risked drawing so much attention to himself, either. Unlike Ferrier, he wouldn't have forced the pace.

Most of the cars were parked; only a few were moving out, and these slowly. There was some kind of block toward the end of the street, now only a short distance away. A boy, circling on his bicycle, had skidded and fallen. No harm done, seemingly. A white Simca had braked just short of him. A policeman was pull-

ing him to the side, lifting the bicycle out of the way of the
blocked cars, yelling to the traffic to keep moving. A blue Fiat
was impatient, tried to edge past the nervous Simca, was given a
loud reprimand by the policeman, slowed back into place. The
driver leaned out to explain something quickly, apologize perhaps. The policeman had enough on his hands as it was—the
boy's family were swarming around—and, as the Simca speeded
forward into the avenue, signaled all the following cars to get out
get out get out. They did.

Ferrier, no more than thirty tantalizing feet away from the blue
Fiat, saw it make a light on the avenue, slip into a heavy stream
of traffic. He stopped, staring after it, helpless and angry. It was
the same car that had waited outside Reid's house this morning in
the Calle San Julian, the same car that had trailed him and
Amanda Ames down to the beach. And the same driver. The
passenger beside him, shoulders clearly visible as the car had
made its quick turn even if his face had been averted, wore a dark
suit, and the back of his head, brown-haired, was neat and
smoothly brushed.

Ferrier took a deep, long breath, started back toward the hospital. What could you have done, actually? he asked himself. Yelled
at the car, got the policeman to stop it, and then what? There
were no charges he could make except to sound wild, crazy.
There was no proof at all. Short of searching that man, of having
an expert standing by who could recognize a cyanide spray gun
when he saw it, there was no proof possible. He approached the
hospital steps, skirted the handcarts piled with bunches of flowers,
a brilliance of reds and yellows and pinks and purples, thought of
red roses and Tavita, and wondered how he was going to tell her.
And when. Don't panic Fuentes, Jeff Reid had said. Don't panic
Tavita, either, he told himself. Then suddenly he had his own
mild panic, thrust his hand deep into his trouser pocket. It was
still there, Jeff's lighter. My God, he thought in horror, I might
have lost it in that wild run along the street—it might have
dropped out, or it could have been lifted by pickpocketing fingers
when I got jammed in a crowd. But it was there. He reached the
steps, mounted them slowly.

"Señor Ferrier!"

He stopped and turned, saw Captain Rodriguez leave his car,
which had been parked across the little square in front of the
steps, and walk toward him. How long has he been there? Ferrier
wondered. The car looks well embedded in the row of automo-
biles over on that side of the square, and I saw it—yes, I'm pretty
sure I saw it when I came out of the hospital—but I didn't see

Rodriguez. What was he doing? Loitering behind one of those palm trees or ducking down behind his chauffeur?

"Yes," Rodriguez said lightly as he reached Ferrier and halted beside him on the top step, "my lieutenant was right. You are an angry man."

Ferrier glared over at the small gray car and its driver.

"He saw you come running out of the hospital and he—"

"Didn't you? Or were you tying your shoelace?"

Rodriguez' attempt at a friendly joke ended. He looked hurt, then angry. And then he decided to ignore the rudeness. "Something is wrong, I think," he said softly, studying Ferrier's face.

"Yes. Very far wrong." Ferrier made an effort, brought the harsh words out. "Reid is dead."

"What?" Rodriguez was bewildered. "I was waiting to see him —seemed better to let you finish your visit."

Much better, thought Ferrier bitterly. If Rodriguez had managed to place a bug in that room, all he needed was to let Jeff and me talk ourselves out. I wish I could see his face when he plays back our conversation. All he will hear is the Haffner and Brahms's Fourth and a mumble-mumble background.

Rodriguez recovered. His face was grave. "When did it happen?"

"Ten minutes ago. Perhaps less."

"And the cause?"

"They'll say it was a heart attack."

Rodriguez stared at the American, frowned. His lips tightened. He said stiffly, "Are you implying that our hospitals are careless?"

"No."

"Then perhaps I did not understand your English correctly?"

"Perhaps."

Rodriguez again studied Ferrier's face. I am a patient man, he reminded himself. "Let us go inside," he said politely, pulling the door open, stepping aside as he held it. "After you, Señor Ferrier." The golden glare of the street gave way to dim shadow; a warm breeze stirred around the hall from its ceiling fan. The sharp noises of traffic faded. There was an illusion of coolness and peace. An illusion . . . Ferrier looked around for Medina. He saw two white-coated doctors, a nurse, a few people grouped at the reception desk, two harried attendants, but apart from that the hall was almost empty now. Was Medina in Jeff's room?

"Tell me one thing," Rodriguez said. "Why did you go racing into the street? What were you searching for?"

So he did see me; may even have followed me, Ferrier thought.

"A man in a dark suit, carrying a briefcase. He had been visiting Reid. Just after he left, we found Reid dead."

Rodriguez' dark eyes sharpened. "What was his name?"

"No one seems to know."

"Nonsense. All visitors to private rooms have their names noted, along with their times of arrival." He moved over to the desk, spoke authoritatively, argued for at least two minutes while the reception clerk checked and rechecked his file, then came back to where Ferrier waited. Rodriguez was annoyed and puzzled. "There is no entry for that man. He passed through with a young visiting doctor called Medina, and it was assumed that they were colleagues, that the stranger had been called in for consultation." He controlled his temper, shrugged his shoulders, excused the hospital with one final word. "Naturally," he ended lamely.

"Naturally. But Medina doesn't know him. He was only showing the man the way to Reid's room."

"Did Reid know him?"

"No. But his credentials seemed believable. He came from some business firm that Reid deals with—an urgent signature was all he wanted."

"A strange thing," Rodriguez said softly. Ferrier's spine tightened, but he kept his face expressionless. "That man's dress, I mean," Rodriguez added. "He carried more than a briefcase when he arrived. There was also a book. And a noticeable bandage on his thumb. And a flower in his lapel. Did you notice those?"

Ferrier nodded.

"Did you see him when he left?"

"Only the back of his head. There was a crush in the corridor just then. The gong had sounded for visitors to move into the wards."

"Then you didn't see that he was still carrying the briefcase, but no book, flower, or bandage? But perhaps," Rodriguez added thoughtfully, watching Ferrier's eyes, "the need for that was over."

Ferrier looked at Rodriguez sharply.

Rodriguez was enjoying himself. "Yes, that interested me, too. It looks as if he might have used these little additions, for—well, for the purpose of identifying himself quite clearly to someone who was a stranger. It's quite a common method in some circles. It makes sure of meeting the right man."

Again he is prowling around Jeff, thought Ferrier; can't he leave him alone? Jeff is dead; Rodriguez' file on him is closed. And then he thought, But Jeff didn't need to see that kind of identification; all he needed was one small silver pencil.

Rodriguez said softly, "I seem to have shocked you."

I could cause Medina some real pain, Ferrier decided, if I were to open my mouth at this moment. So he kept it closed, tight. He nodded a good-bye, started toward the corridor, determined to find Medina and ask a few questions of his own. By God, he thought in rising anger, if my suspicions are right, if Medina actually did meet an assassin and bring him safely into Jeff's room . . . But at whose suggestion? Was he simply being used by someone like Gene Lucas, that plausible liar? Someone who knew Medina's vanities and weakness, and manipulated him skillfully? Medina could be just another Adam Reid, two of a kind, never realizing what they were doing, never knowing how much blame they carried. Nature's fools.

Ferrier turned the corner into the corridor, almost knocked over Medina. He had been talking to a grave-faced sister whose hands were clasped and her head slightly bowed as she listened, wordless, to Medina's small lecture. He regained his balance, looked around sharply at Ferrier, calmed down as he saw who it was. "I was just about to leave. There is no more that can be done. Heart failure." Then he went on lecturing the sister. She was, Ferrier noted as she raised her head to look at him sadly from under the sweeping brim of her white starched hat, the same one who had spoken with him last night and given him Reid's requests. Medina was telling her, "It was a grave mistake to let him have any visitors, any excitement. That was my advice last night, and it was correct. Most unfortunate that—"

"And what about the visitor you brought him?" Ferrier asked. "I?"

"Yes, you," Ferrier said calmly. He was conscious that someone else had just turned the corner to stand behind him. Perhaps a doctor, another nurse; or Rodriguez?

"That was nothing, a signature; it aroused no excitement. A matter of a few minutes. Nothing."

"So I am to blame?" Ferrier's tone was almost conversational.

"No, no—you did not mean to endanger Señor Reid. It was simply unfortunate—"

"And you are quite sure it was heart failure?"

"We all are." Medina was totally convinced, and perhaps glad that he could be so completely sure. No conscience at all, thought Ferrier, no misgivings, not one hint that he was puzzled or troubled or even sorry. He looked at Medina disbelievingly as the man went on talking. "They've taken the body into surgery now—an attempt to try to save him. The effort must be made, of course. But useless, I'm afraid. It was a quick, severe heart attack. We must face the cold fact that there is no miracle to be expected, not even here."

The sister's face tightened, but she kept her silence.

Ferrier said, "You told me that Jeff Reid was as strong as an ox. Your words. His last checkup—"

"Made by my uncle," Medina said quickly. And that disposed of that.

Ferrier resisted the old American solution: one to the gut, one to the jaw. Crude, Europeans said. But it would have been extremely satisfying, right now. And he couldn't even use a few jabs of well-aimed phrases—not the place, not the time. Phrases such as "Well, I'm glad you've recovered from your hysteria. What were you afraid of finding when you put on that performance in Reid's room? A death from unnatural causes? Thumbmarks on a throat, or signs of an injection in an arm? How fortunate it was so natural, a heart attack, nothing to be explained, something we all accept." But he resisted hard. He took a long, deep breath, let his eyes drift away from Medina's. He could feel the man relax. No proof, thought Ferrier; all I have is suspicions. If I had got hold of that stranger and his briefcase, forced him back to the hospital for questioning—but I didn't. He stared at the white starched wings floating in perfect balance over the sister's grave face. "Can I be of some help?" he asked her. Or do I just leave? he wondered. He felt useless in every way.

"Yes," she said, gave a small bow to Medina, and turned toward Reid's room. "If you would come with me, Señor Ferrier?"

He nodded, glanced over his shoulder to make sure that it was Rodriguez who was standing patiently a little distance behind him. It was. Ferrier didn't resist, this time. He said to Medina, "By the way, it may not be so difficult to find the name of the stranger you brought in here. Perhaps your friend Lucas can tell you who he is."

Medina looked at him sharply. You could almost hear him calculating how much he could deny, how much he should admit.

"Gene Lucas," Ferrier said quietly. The sister had stopped, looked around. Rodriguez, keeping tactfully apart, was studying the vaulted ceiling.

"An acquaintance—I scarcely know him." Medina was recovering.

"Even so, you could always ask him who the man was."

"But how would he know?" Medina was bewildered, a study in puzzled innocence.

"He knows the blue Fiat in which the man was driven away.

He also knows the driver." Ferrier nodded a definite good-bye, started along the corridor toward the waiting sister.

"Why should we worry about that man?" Medina called angrily after him. It was a good question, and a dangerous one. And a revealing one, too: everything I say will be reported to Lucas, thought Ferrier as he halted and weighed his answer carefully. But he was spared it. Rodriguez had moved forward, was answering for him.

Rodriguez said gently, "It is a matter of straightening out the records of the hospital. It is the least you could do, don't you think? You did escort the man—"

"He was a stranger to me."

"Dr. Medina, I saw you waiting outside the hospital."

Ferrier walked on slowly. So Rodriguez had seen it all.

Medina was saying, "I wasn't waiting. I was looking at the crowds. People interest me."

"My impression," Rodriguez insisted, "was that you stepped forward when you saw him and—"

"Then your impression was wrong." Medina's anger carried clearly along the corridor.

The sister looked at Ferrier worriedly. "Dr. Medina is a difficult man," she whispered. "He could cause us much trouble."

"Not so much, now," Ferrier reassured her. No one, but no one, told Captain Rodriguez that his impressions were wrong.

Rodriguez was saying, his tone satin-smooth, "In that case, I apologize. But first, let me identify myself, and then we can talk a little more." The voice faded. Ferrier looked back along the corridor. Medina and Rodriguez were leaving. The shock of Rodriguez' identification seemed to have silenced Medina temporarily. But he will soon get his second wind, thought Ferrier; he will stick to his story, and nothing can be proved otherwise. I was wrong about Medina. He isn't one of Nature's fools. He is a natural conspirator.

"Who is that man who speaks with Dr. Medina?" the sister asked.

He hesitated, wondering whether he should add to the load of her anxieties by mentioning police or State Security.

She took his silence as ignorance. "At least," she said, "he seemed to be a friend of the hospital. I hope he can persuade Dr. Medina that there was no carelessness, no—"

"I'm sure he will."

"A dreadful event. We are so sorry. So very sorry." She halted at the open doorway of Reid's room. "I thought you might take away the things you brought for Señor Reid. And there are some more of his possessions." She looked at the empty bed. "Was I to blame?" she asked in real anguish.

"No."

"But Dr. Medina seemed to believe—"

"No," he said again, firmly. "He was afraid of being blamed himself. That was all." And you were such an easy target, he thought, watching the honest anxious face with compassion.

She was shocked. With Ferrier. "But he is a doctor. Doctors don't—"

"I know," he said wearily. "They don't. Most of them don't." Most of them don't play politics, he added for himself. Nor do most priests, most ministers and teachers, and all the rest in dedicated professions. Most don't. "I'll gather together Jeff's things," he said, moving into the room. "What else can I do?" There must be a lot of formalities, he thought worriedly. And suddenly he felt drained of energy even at the idea of them.

"The hospital called your consul at once. He has notified Señor Reid's lawyer, who will take charge. Señor Reid had arranged everything in advance." She shook her head. "Did he foresee—did he have a weak heart?"

There had been no weakness about Jeff's heart in any way, thought Ferrier. "He was a practical man. A foreigner in a strange land. And please, sister, stop blaming yourself. Or I'll begin believing I'm to blame, too. But he wanted to see me. And I thought he was fine; a little weak, of course, but what else could you expect? Certainly nothing to worry about. I saw him eight years ago when he was in much worse shape. He was in the Air Force then, and he had crashed—" His voice dried up. He couldn't go on. He began picking up the books and razor, jamming them into the green cloth bag.

"I shall get his other things," the sister said, her voice and heels retreating into the corridor.

And pray for him, Ferrier thought; pray for all of us. That will give you some comfort.

Stop thinking about the past, Ferrier warned himself. The present has plenty of problems to be faced if you are ever going to see a future. He fitted the radio into the bag, dropped in the soap and toothbrushes, picked up the cassette player. It had long since finished the symphony and was now humming peacefully. He switched it off, added it to the collection. But the cassettes were missing. Had he already packed them? He searched in the bag. No; the cassettes were missing. And so, he realized, was the engagement pad with Reid's careful notations and marked dates.

The dictaphone was gone, too. Also the silver pencil. He was back in the present with a vengeance.

He left the empty room and its masses of red roses, found an assortment of sympathetic voices and a brown paper parcel waiting for him in the hall, came out into the low yellow rays of a setting sun. Most of the people had left, but the old men were still there, resting against their low wall. He hoisted the green bag over his shoulder, carried the parcel in his arm, and went searching for his car. A brown paper parcel, small and pathetic: some clothes, a watch and ring, a wallet, a key chain. He laid it carefully on the seat beside him, dumped the green bag on the floor. He sat for a full minute before he turned on the ignition, trying to control the hot rage that swept through him. Medina. And Lucas. Above all, Lucas. And there was some anger left over for a man called Martin who hadn't got here in time.

Why the hell does our side always have to drag its feet? he wondered bitterly. Why are we so casual about things that matter, always depending on luck to pull us through? Why do we spend so much time and energy and money and have so damned little to show for it? Why do the best men have to die while a lot of self-satisfied bastards argue the toss? What's smothering us in stupidity—carelessness, selfishness, or just that easy habit of taking everything for granted?

He started the car, let the engine turn over. The back of my hand to Martin. He and his outfit were the first to know about an emergency in Málaga. But it was the opposition who came, bright and brisk, sharp-eyed and foxy, with Plan One; failing that, Plan Two; and no doubt Three, Four, to open the crack in any door. And what is our side left with? Me. I'm holding a lighter and information about the possible whereabouts of one Tomás Fuentes. And I have not a notion to whom I turn these over, or where or how. My only hope is that Martin will give just one tenth of the attention to me that Captain Rodriguez or Gene Lucas has paid, but with Martin's average so far I don't have much faith in that. Sure—all sentiment aside—poor old Jeff was probably not one of Martin's most important agents; and I'm just one of Jeff's friends who happened to get in the way. But whether an agent's assignment is simple or complex, whether it's routine stuff or dealing with highly sensitive problems, you listen to him when he gives you warning. He's your man, out on point duty, your first line of defense. And that has an importance far beyond anything else. What use are the brains of government if they haven't ears and eyes they can trust in far-off places? Decisions are only as good as the intelligence they are based on. And a capable and loyal agent isn't so easily replaced. Señor Martin, you've just lost one. . . . The back of my hand and the toe of my boot to you.

He released the brake, moved from neutral into first. All right, he told himself as he edged carefully along the street to plunge into the avenue's thick traffic, you're committed. You solve the problem your way, with a lot of help from old Jeff. He had made a big effort, back in that hospital room, to pass on a few tips. Just in case someone silenced him? Yes, all that talk about being helpless—that meant more than you realized at the time. Washington, that's where you are going. There and back, all the way to Granada. These were the priorities: delivery of the lighter; Tomás Fuentes himself. Not a visit to Italy and then a pleasant week in England. Instead, four or five days of hectic travel and a search for a man called Richard O'Connor. No, not Richard: Robert. Robert O'Connor. And what's the quickest way to find him?

He began turning over in his mind all the people he knew in Washington who might help him cut through the tangles of red tape to approach Langley—if that was where O'Connor worked. People who could be trusted to be discreet. That was the problem. There were four he crossed off his list as soon as he had named them: decent-enough guys but blabbermouths, never could resist proving their importance by casual leaks to their favorite newsman. A fifth was crossed off, too: he carried political weight, had plenty of influence, but he was a foxy character who loved to polish his TV image. That left Ferrier with two, who could be guaranteed to keep their mouths shut and avoid publicity. Which of these two would be the quicker to act? Speed was needed as well as caution. The urgency worried Ferrier. That would be the biggest problem of all, and a complicated one, too. For a moment, he thought with regret of his own private plans, relatively simple compared with all this mess he had got into, now disappearing like a jet trail in the high blue sky, spreading fainter, thinner, into nothing. But again, it was a matter of priorities. If you couldn't face them by the time you had reached the age of thirty-seven, you were ready to be buried among the ruins. The sad discovery of the adult world was the permanent truth: you don't always do what you want to do; you do what you must.

The Calle San Julian was peaceful, no one loitering near the gateway to Number Nine. So interest had dropped, Ferrier thought hopefully; the KGB—like Spanish Security—had perhaps deactivated its file on Jeff Reid. Dusk was approaching, thickening perceptibly. Soon the twilight would end, short-lasting, bringing sudden night. Concepción obviously thought it was too early to switch on the lights, but the dark house was uninviting. Sullen and sad, it was already retreating into the spreading shadows of trees and bushes. It gaped blankly at Ferrier—no welcome there —as he drove up the short stretch to its side yard and parked opposite the kitchen door. He picked up the bag and parcel, stepped out into the warmth of a still evening. So quiet, he thought, everything was so quiet. The people in the next-door house must be away for the weekend; from over the high dividing wall, there was no sign of life, only the feeling of emptiness. And there were no voices from the kitchen, no radio, no laughter, as there had been last night. Had Concepción already heard the news? If she hadn't, he had better tell her right away, get it over with. He walked to the kitchen door, the light crunch of gravel under his feet breaking the silence.

The door was unlocked. He pushed it open. The smell was hideous. He switched on a light, dropped Reid's belongings on the nearest chair, made for the electric stove—a gleaming touch of modernity, like the giant refrigerator in a vaulted alcove—where a pot hissed venomously. Its liquid had boiled away, leaving a black mass of unrecognizable objects encrusted on its bottom. He pulled out his handkerchief, yanked the pot away from the burner, dropped it on the tiled floor. There was nothing to spill anyway. He turned off the burner, looked around the kitchen uncertainly.

It was mostly old-time style, with a few new additions, a mixture of everything from cooking to eating to sitting, and big enough to house a family of ten. Cluttered but clean. He opened the door again to get rid of the smell of fish glue, crossed over to the row of back windows to let more air in. Under their stretch lay the sink and a long tiled counter. Concepción had been at work there, preparing dinner. Bowls of diced vegetables, peelings and scrapings beside them, a knife on a chopping board, a half-sliced onion. He was worried now, as well as puzzled. He jammed his handkerchief back into his pocket, felt the lighter. He hesitated, thinking hard. And then he heard a small crunch of gravel from the yard outside. Someone was approaching the open kitchen door, and carefully. Concepción? She didn't need to walk with such caution. Quickly, before the visitor could see his hand go out, he dropped the lighter into the nearest bowl, made sure it was covered in its bed of chopped tomatoes. He backed swiftly away from the counter, moving as lightly as the man outside, reached the central table. He paused there, watching the doorway. No one entered. There was only silence.

He felt foolish, wondered if his imagination had overreacted.

No, he decided, someone was out there, someone whose foot had slipped on the loose gravel; someone who was now standing absolutely still, hoping he hadn't noticed. What is this? he wondered angrily. An ambush, a trap? And what has happened to Concepción?

He circled back to the stove, picked up the pot from the floor. Its handle had cooled slightly, was at least bearable to hold now. It was medium size, but solid, and nauseating to look at. The smell was clearing off, though. If he hadn't been so quick to put distance between himself and the bowl of tomatoes, he would have remembered to pick up the knife. Not that he was an expert with it; apart from the usual pistol practice, his training in combat had been of the unarmed type. Again he looked at the doorway into the yard. What was he supposed to do? Step right out from a lighted kitchen, a perfect target? He turned, made for a closed door behind him. This one should open toward the heart of the house, perhaps into the corridor that led into the main room. Once there, he knew the geography of the place—and the position of the light switches, he reminded himself wryly.

He opened the door, carefully, quietly, made sure there was no one waiting for him there, and then slipped out of the kitchen. He was in that corridor all right, and it was empty. Dark, too; no lamps had been switched on. Ahead was an archway framing gray shadows of chairs and couches, an interior still life, a study in twilight. He tightened his grip on his cumbersome weapon, walked softly, steadying his slow progress with his left hand against a plaster wall. At the threshold, he paused. Then, quickly, he stepped into the room. No one on the staircase to his left. But from his right there was a man coming at him with the butt of a revolver held high.

Ferrier swung the pot, hit the descending wrist, heard the pistol go clattering over the floor and the man curse. As the man made an attempt to lunge at him, he swung again, this time catching him on the side of his fat, round face. The man went down with a scream, and stayed down. From the direction of the kitchen came running footsteps.

Ferrier mounted two steps of the staircase, drew his back against the wall. His eyes were becoming accustomed to the grayed light of the room, but he couldn't see the fat man's pistol. It must have slid some distance over the tiled floor, was now hiding under a couch or chair. So I surprised them, he thought with some real pleasure, even if they were expecting me. All carefully planned, was it? He concentrated on that wide doorway. Come on, come on, he told the footsteps silently. They had stopped as abruptly as they had begun. The man was waiting just within the threshold. All right, thought Ferrier, I can wait, too. But he tightened his grip, lifted his arm, listened for the smallest sound of movement.

"Hold it!" The voice came from the center of the room. A small, thin man rose from behind the chair where he had been crouching. His pointed revolver, a silencer adding ominously to its length, was direct and menacing. He came a few steps nearer, no more than twelve feet away. "No," he warned Ferrier. "Don't throw that thing in your hand. Drop it! I will use this revolver if needed. You make a good target. At this distance, the poor light does not matter. Drop it!" The words were in English, heavily accented, but fluent. The manner was intense.

Ferrier checked his impulse. He could see the man clearly enough; therefore the man could see him. This was no bluff. A loaded pistol, aimed right at his chest, ended all bright ideas. He dropped the cooking pot. It thudded down a step, clanged against the iron railing, stuck there.

"Come here! Hands up! Up!"

Ferrier stepped down one tread. He glanced at the entrance to the corridor. There was a footstep there, as if the man was getting into position. There was, as yet, nothing to be seen.

"Face me! Come here!"

And leave my back unprotected to that third man on the threshold?

"All the way down! Move!"

Ferrier drew a deep breath, steadied himself. If it was to be a knife between the shoulder blades, he had had it. But if it was only to be a blow on the back of his head, he might—if he was quick enough—lessen its impact. He moved, and moved swiftly, leaving the protection of the staircase wall, stepping obliquely forward into the living room.

The man on the threshold, tall and powerful, came out of its shadows, arm raised and ready. The blow, aimed at the back of Ferrier's head, only tipped him, but even so he stumbled forward, pitched onto his knees. There was a stinging pain. He let himself slump into a heap on the floor, pretended to black out.

The man who had used the cosh stood uncertainly with it in his hand, looking down at Ferrier. The blow hadn't felt quite right to him, hadn't cracked the way he usually heard it. He raised his arm again.

"Enough!" yelled the man with the revolver. "Enough!" he repeated to the fat man, who had come over to join them, nursing his jaw. "Put away that knife! See what he left in the kitchen. He brought in two packages." To the big fellow, he said, "Quick! Search!"

They turned Ferrier over roughly, so that the back of his head fell sharply on the tiled floor. Suddenly, it was no longer pretense. The pain doubled, a tight band spreading around his forehead, pulling tighter. He blacked out.

11

Esteban rose from his knees, stood looking down at the American on the floor. "He is all right. He is coming back to himself." There were no wounds, no blood. "A knock on the head. That is all."

Concepción, sitting on the edge of a chair, her hair falling wildly around her shoulders, stared at Ferrier and said nothing. She wasn't even seeing him. Her mind was as numb as her wrists and ankles. She rubbed them in turn, slowly. And tears for the news that Esteban had brought coursed steadily down her cheeks.

Ferrier opened his eyes, gradually focused them to the blaze of lights around him. The Eiffel Tower was Esteban, dark face grave, furrows deep at the sides of thin angry lips. Ferrier sat up gingerly, the echo of pain reminding him to move cautiously. His brain cleared. He could remember. No concussion, he thought hopefully. He felt the back of his head carefully.

"Move slowly," Esteban warned him. He picked up Ferrier's wallet and passport, which had been thrown on the floor, and handed them over. "I came because I was worried. I had been telephoning Concepción for almost an hour. No answer, no answer, no answer. So I came. They heard me and they left. I did not see their faces. They went out through the front door as I came in from the kitchen. Three men—one was tall, fair-haired; two smaller. They scattered in the darkness. Then I heard a noise from the cloakroom in the hall. They had pushed Concepción in there, bound and gagged. The piece of cloth around her mouth was coming loose, and she was trying to shout." He looked worriedly at Ferrier, who had finished examining his wallet, and was now checking his pockets. "Did they take your money?"

"No." The money was there. So were the traveler's checks, and the driving license. But his pocket diary was gone, with its list of addresses, of appointments kept, of engagements to come. But more worrying than that, the slip of paper with Tavita's full name and address and number had been lifted.

159

"Then that is good," Esteban said. "But also strange. Why did they not take your money? They left the watch on your wrist, too."

Good God, thought Ferrier, looking at his watch, did all that happen within twenty minutes—from walking into the kitchen to waking up on this damned floor? He felt as if he had been out for hours, but even that had been only a matter of a few minutes. He climbed slowly to his feet, steadying himself on Esteban's arm. He pushed back into place the lining of his trouser pockets. The men had been rough as well as quick in their search; one pocket was badly ripped. Esteban was picking up his handkerchief, keys, Reid's keys, matches, all scattered over the floor. "They took my cigarettes and my pen," Ferrier said in wonder. What the hell did they expect to find in a pack of cigarettes and a ball-point pen?

"Where are you going?" Esteban asked sharply.

"To get some ice." His head was throbbing, but that was nothing compared to the nagging worry in his mind. He staggered off, down the corridor, toward the kitchen. Esteban followed him; and Concepción, with a little cry of fear as she found she was being left alone, followed Esteban. "I need some air," Ferrier said as he reached the kitchen, and made straight for the row of windows over the sink, leaving Esteban to deal with the refrigerator. The bowls of vegetables on the tiled counter seemed intact. He brushed aside the invading flies, reached into the bowl of tomatoes. It was there. The lighter was there. His worry ended. He gripped the lighter, pulled it out, had barely time to cover it with his handkerchief before Esteban was beside him, dumping an ice tray into the sink, telling Concepción to find a towel. Everyone is moving so damned quickly except me, Ferrier thought. There he was, handkerchief clutched in one hand, unable to get that hand into his pocket and feel natural about it. Esteban's quick eyes were studying him too curiously. So he walked slowly over to the large wooden table, sat down on a bench, and as Esteban gave more instructions to Concepción he managed to slip lighter and handkerchief into his pocket, and began to relax. He looked at his hand in amazement; it was trembling, just a little, just enough to make him angry.

Esteban noticed his frown. "I'll get you something to drink."

"No." The idea was enough to make him feel like vomiting. "A cigarette, if you have one."

"I know what to mix," Esteban insisted, and left for the dining room. Concepción was applying an ice-filled towel to the back of Ferrier's head. Her tears had dried, but she said nothing; and for that, Ferrier was grateful. In the jumble of his thoughts, of bits and pieces of memories, his mind kept coming back to one thing: Tavita's name and address had been taken, and he was worried by that. He didn't know why he should be, either, and that worried him even more. Later, he would try to puzzle out a possible answer. Now, it was only an instinctive warning. "Thank you," he said to Concepción, "I can hold it." He took the towel from her heavy hand, eased the pressure against his skull. Of all the damned silly ways to be knocked out, he thought angrily; they turn you over, and you are being so bloody smart pretending to be limp that you let your own head smash against a tiled floor. And yet, it could have been worse: if that blow from the cosh had really caught him, he would have been out for a couple of days at least.

Concepción was coming back to normal, too. She had gone over to the sink, started fussing with the bowls, exclaimed in anger over the flies, closed the louvers on the shutters. Then she noticed the lingering smell from the burned pot, and ran to the stove. "Where's my bouillon?" she called out sharply, and jolted Ferrier's head." Where?"

He had to laugh. Her whole world was falling apart and she was fretting over some liquid for a sauce. "It's on the staircase."

She looked at him with horror. "He's crazy," she told Esteban as he returned with two glasses. "The blow has—"

"It's on the staircase," Ferrier repeated. "Go and look." But she did not move. He took the glass Esteban offered him. The drink was sharp, aromatic, unpleasant enough to be good for him. Concepción was watching him warily. "How did the men get into the house? Did you see all three of them? Clearly?"

He isn't crazy, thought Esteban, and began sipping his brandy.

"One came to the front door," Concepción said slowly, and then as the memories came back her voice quickened with indignation and she broke into Spanish, rattling on and on. It was a short story made long; she'd keep remembering small details, retraced her sentences to get the facts in proper order. Esteban would break in and translate, just to make sure the American understood, and then add part of his own information. Between them, they did a fine piece of reporting, completely muddled and scarcely comprehensible.

Ferrier put down his empty glass—the concoction was working; his dizziness was over; the pain was now only a small reminder, and he could lay aside the towel. He said, cutting into a description of Esteban's repeated telephone calls to this house, "Fine, fine. So this is the way it was. A man came to the front door just after six o'clock. He was tall, light-haired, broad-shouldered, well dressed. He said he had come to collect the picture delivered this morning. And when Concepción argued that she had not authority to hand it over, he told her that Señor Reid had died, had no more need for it. And the two other men—"

Concepción broke in. "I was standing so shocked, so—"

"Yes, yes," Ferrier said quickly, gently. It had been a brutal way to break the news of Reid's death. "The two other men—one small and dark, with a revolver; the other black-haired, fat—had come through the kitchen. And they tied you up. They left you, bound and gagged, lying in the hall. They went to search the house."

"From the attic right down, and then—"

"Concentrated on Señor Reid's study." Searching the house for either Tomás Fuentes or at least some sign that he had been here? Searching the study for any possible source of information such as the lighter? They hadn't known exactly what to look for, that was at least heartening. But they had been thorough. They had had almost two hours in this house.

"They were angry," Concepción said, "and rough. I could hear them pulling out books and drawers. I was so—"

"Yes. And you heard the telephone start to ring around seven o'clock."

This was Esteban's cue. "Seven exactly. I had just heard from the hospital—"

"Where you have many friends," Ferrier said patiently. He had heard all about them, in considerable detail. "You called every fifteen minutes from El Fenicio, and then came to see what was wrong. I got here just about twenty minutes before you arrived. They heard my car and—"

Concepción said excitedly, remembering another point, "One called out, 'That must be Ferrier.' And the man with the gun, the man who had given the orders about searching, ran to the dining-room windows to see who go out of the car. Then he came back, and talked in almost a whisper, and they shoved me into the cloakroom and—"

"So they know my name, do they?" Ferrier asked. And they knew about Reid's death before most people: even Esteban, with all his friends, hadn't known until later. And they knew about the picture. The whole assignment smelled heavily of Lucas. Quickly arranged, a little stupidly, too. "Why on earth did they use the picture as an excuse to get into the house?" That was idiotic, a giveaway.

"But what other excuse did they have to keep Concepción arguing, while they made sure there were no others with her in the kitchen? Besides, they were well dressed. They could not pretend to be workmen."

Not so idiotic. Just too quickly arranged. Of necessity. And I was not supposed to be up and around, able to listen to Concepción's story. Come to think of it, Concepción might still be lying in that cloakroom. I didn't know there was a closet in the hall. I'd have stumbled back to the kitchen and then probably passed out. I might never have been able to get off that floor for hours, if that cosh had really struck full strength. Ferrier gave Esteban a warm "Thank you, my friend."

Esteban unbent. Stiff politeness gave way to cadaverous charm. He accepted the thanks with a nod, sat down opposite Ferrier. "Now, you must have a story to tell." To Concepción, he said, "Get me another brandy."

She turned on him. "You do nothing. You talk and talk. You came too late. I could have choked to death in that dark cloakroom. You don't look to see what has been stolen. You don't call the police. You—"

"No police," Ferrier said.

She looked at him wide-eyed. "I will call them now."

"No police," agreed Esteban. "This is not their concern."

"But—"

"Tavita wants no attention drawn to this house," Esteban said sharply. "If you tell the police about this night, Captain Rodriguez will hear of it. He is already asking too many questions."

Ferrier said, "So he did visit El Fenicio this afternoon. And saw that dancer—the one who had the quarrel with Tavita?"

Esteban was wary. "Constanza? Yes, he talked with her about her—her vision last night. But she is always having visions."

"She saw a strange man on the balcony, didn't she?" And perhaps, thought Ferrier, this will get him onto the subject of Tomás Fuentes; he could tell me a lot about that man's past.

But it didn't. Esteban shrugged his shoulders. "Ridiculous nonsense. It was Señor Reid, of course."

"Of course," Ferrier said smoothly.

Esteban turned back to Concepción, saw she was only half persuaded. Loyalty to Tavita was keeping her silent; anger against the men who had broken into this house, her house, deepened her frown. "Why call the police?" Esteban asked. "The men came searching, but they did not find what they were looking for. They took nothing. Except some cigarettes and a pen. Was it valuable, Señor Ferrier?"

"No." Ferrier thought of the other things gone from his pockets, decided that wasn't Esteban's business. He said nothing, either, about the empty chair near the kitchen door. The green bag and the parcel had both vanished.

"So," said Esteban, "no police."

"You were not the one to be left to choke to death in a dark cloakroom," she told him bitterly, and she went stumping into the corridor. "I shall see what has or what has not been stolen," she shouted back.

Ferrier said, "She wants these men found and punished." And so would I, he thought, so would I. . . .

"At a time like this," Esteban said slowly, "women can be very difficult. She is upset, deeply upset, by Señor Reid's death. So she turns her grief into anger." He frowned, remembering something even more painful. "Tavita, too, is upset. I have never known her to take bad news so—"

"Tavita knows?" Ferrier looked blankly at the gaunt dark face opposite him. "You telephoned her?"

"But of course. She had to be told."

And now panic would be setting in. If she were to blurt out this news to Fuentes— "Esteban, would you get Tavita on the phone for me? And please write down her address and number. She gave it to me but—but I seem to have lost it."

"Telephone her now?"

"Yes. At once."

"I do not think she will be able to talk with you."

"She will. Or her chauffeur will. What is his name?"

Esteban looked at him uncertainly, the furrows deepening around his mouth. Then he decided to make light of the question, treat it as normally as possible. "Matéo," he said, and rose. "I think I will go and pour another glass of brandy. What would you like, señor?"

So we are back to being formal again, thought Ferrier. "I'd like a call to Granada."

Esteban drew himself up to his full height. He stood, half-sideways, shoulders back, face aimed at Ferrier. All he needed was a sword and a cape and he would be coming in for the kill right over my left shoulder, thought Ferrier. He kept his eyes fixed on Esteban's. He did not speak. "Why?" Esteban asked harshly.

"Matéo," said Ferrier thoughtfully. "Yes, that is much safer than Tomás Fuentes."

There was a long silence. Esteban's eyes narrowed, his lips were compressed. "If I had my way, I would let our police deal with him."

I bet you would, Ferrier thought as he watched the thin, bitter face. "And what about Tavita?" he asked quietly.

"No trouble would come to her. I would make sure of that."

I bet you would, Ferrier thought again. "Give me five days, Esteban."

"For what? To save his miserable skin?"

"Five days. Perhaps four. And you'll never see or hear of him again."

"But you will not imprison him? Sentence him to death? No, no. You Americans lose yourselves in lawyers' talk. What I want is justice." He controlled his rising anger with a great effort. He looked at Ferrier intently. "Will you Americans never learn? When you help your enemies, you betray your friends."

"Did Jeff Reid ever betray his friends?"

Esteban took a deep breath. "Five days," he said, and turned on his heel.

Ferrier rose slowly to his feet and followed a silent Esteban into the corridor. He was moving carefully, testing his strength. Much steadier now. Almost normal. Even the pain had become only a small persistent ache. I'll manage, he thought; I'll have to. As he entered the big room, Esteban—drawn well ahead of him, walking with his decided stride, grace combined with anger—was reaching the study. So he *is* going to telephone, Ferrier thought. And that was one worry less.

It was old Magdalena who was speaking. The phone connection was clear, but her words were unintelligible. She was crying, and the effect of sobs on a flood of Spanish was disastrous. "Please," Ferrier kept saying, "would you get Tavita? I want to speak with Tavita." He looked around for help from Esteban, but he wasn't in sight. He had handed Ferrier the receiver without a word, placed a note beside him on the desk, and then moved away. "Magdalena! I want to speak with Tavita. With Tavita!" That was almost a shout. It got through. There was a choking intake of breath, then the sound of the receiver being laid on a table, then nothing. Ferrier nursed the back of his head, reminding himself not to shout for the next few hours, and waited. And waited. And then he began to wonder if Magdalena had walked away, forgotten the call, and the receiver would lie there and lie there. . . . One minute passed. (He had read Esteban's note: Tavita's address and number, as requested. And he had started going through the telephone directory to find the local Iberia office for information on flights to Madrid and connections to New York.) And then, well into the second minute, the receiver was picked up. A man's voice spoke. The señorita was indisposed, he announced in Spanish.

"One second!" Ferrier said sharply. He had visions of that receiver being dropped back onto its cradle. "Do you speak English? Good. I am Ferrier, Ian Ferrier."

There was a short silence. Perhaps of interest?

"I am Señor Reid's friend. I am staying at his house. Are you Señorita Vergara's chauffeur?"

Another pause. "Yes."

"Matéo? Then I can speak with you." I've hit the jack pot, thought Ferrier: Tomás Fuentes, himself.

But that was too direct, seemingly. "I shall find the señorita." And almost at once, she was speaking. As if, Ferrier thought, she had been standing near, waiting for Tomás Fuentes' command. Was Tomás taking full charge? If so, Ferrier didn't like it. He didn't like it one bit.

"Who is it?" she asked. Her voice was quiet and sad, almost listless.

"Ian. Ian Ferrier. I wanted to tell you that—"

Her voice came to life. "Oh, Ian—it *is* you. I am so glad you telephoned—I don't know what to do. Poor Jeff, poor Jeff . . ."

"Nothing has changed, Tavita. Don't be frightened. You aren't alone." Careful, he warned himself, careful how you say it. This phone could be tapped. "It's a bad time, I know, for you. But we'll get through it. Just trust me and—" He was speaking to nobody; the receiver had been taken out of her hand. And then came the man's voice. Son of a bitch, Ferrier thought, he was checking on me, making sure I was Ian Ferrier. Of all the suspicious bastards—

"You must excuse the señorita," Tomás Fuentes was saying. "The news about Señor Reid has been a great shock. May I take your message for her?"

"Tell her I saw Señor Reid this evening. He talked a great deal about her. I will come to see her in Granada. I think she would like to know what he said."

"That will be a consolation, I hope?"

"It should be." Ferrier's mind switched from the guarded phrase, from the importance of saying little yet meaning much, to the sudden starting of a car in the driveway. Esteban . . . Esteban was leaving.

"A great tragedy. For the señorita. For all his friends. For his business associates, too. He will be hard to replace. Death ends so many hopes and plans."

"He was a practical man. I am sure his affairs are well arranged."

"That is fortunate. When shall the señorita expect you here in Granada?"

"As soon as I get back from Washington." Ferrier could hear a small sharp intake of breath. "I'm taking the first flight I can get from here. Urgent business. You will explain that it is urgent to Señorita Vergara? That I shall return as soon as the business is accomplished, and come straight to see her?"

"And when do you expect that?"

"By Wednesday, I hope."

"Four days?"

"Five, at the most."

"But"—the voice was sharp—"you will miss the funeral."

That, thought Ferrier bitterly, was a reminder that people might question his absence from Málaga. "Señor Reid will go back home," he said, muffling his anger. "His lawyers will attend to that."

"Of course," Fuentes said quickly. He sounded well satisfied. "I will tell the señorita—"

"Make sure you do." Ferrier jammed the receiver back on the cradle, stood looking at it with tight lips and hard eyes. I agree with Esteban, he thought: this man is poison. Why the hell should I burst a gut getting to Washington to save his hide? He looked around the study, seeing it clearly for the first time. Complete disorder. Books pushed aside on shelves or toppled onto the floor, pictures pulled askew—a search for a wall safe possibly. Drawers were agape, contents rummaged; even the locked drawer in the desk had been successfully opened. All this, he thought, and Esteban walking out in cold anger. Was it worth it? And above all, a good man dead.

The attack of severe depression passed, leaving him with a renewed ache at the back of his head. He would call the airport later, when he had got over this spasm. He lowered himself into an armchair, leaned back carefully, covered his eyes with his hand. Worth it? Yes, he could hear Jeff Reid saying, yes. If we could root out even one trained assassin, with all his willing helpers—the people who will give him shelter, supply extra arms, cover up his movements with false statements, contribute money without questioning how it is spent, help his escape through the hidden exit routes, rally the gullible to his defense if he is caught —all that has happened in this one day in Málaga would be worth it. Even one assassin . . . And we can root out more. Worth it?

"Yes," Ferrier said wearily.

Concepción's voice was saying "Señor Ferrier?" hesitantly, worriedly.

He dropped his hand from his eyes, saw her standing at the study door. She had the ridiculous pot in her hand. She held it up, by way of apology. He signed to her to come in. "Esteban has gone. Will he be back?"

"No."

"I'm sorry. We did not part well."

"I know. He is angry."

"I'll be leaving tonight. You can't stay here alone, Concepción."

"Why not? There is a lot to do. And someone must take care of this house—until—until—" She shook her head, not knowing what arrangements would be made. "I have tidied your room, señor. The men searched there, too. They were everywhere. Why?"

He shook his head, grimaced with the pain that the small movement had stirred up. He rose to his feet, slowly, felt all right. If he could just remember to keep his head still for the next hour or so, he'd be fine.

"You should rest in your room, señor. And I shall bring you more ice."

"Do you know how to fix Esteban's cure?"

"Of course." She actually smiled. "It was I who taught him how to make it. An old cure."

"All right, bring me that. I'll go up and have a shower." A cold, cold shower. It felt good even now. He looked down at his clothes, crumpled and torn. He'd also feel better with a change— if he had anything left to change into.

Concepción gave one last look at the study, sighed, shook her head, hurried away to mix the drink for him. But halfway across the main room, she halted and turned in alarm. The doorbell had rung. It rang again. She looked back at Ferrier uncertainly. He glanced at his watch. A quarter of nine. Who came calling at a quarter of nine? There was a third ring, and then impatient knocking, urgent but light.

"I'll get it," said Ferrier. Then, as he entered the hall, he called back softly, "Did you lock the back door after Esteban left?"

"That is locked." She gripped the pot handle tightly, held it at the ready, followed him slowly but definitely into the hall. A comic but comforting sight, thought Ferrier. Not that she could be of much use, if more trouble was waiting outside; but he liked the way she had volunteered. All demonstrations of support were most welcome at times like these. "There is a light outside, over the door," she said quickly, switched it on. "And there's a chain."

Yes, he thought, it might be wise to hook the chain in place before he opened this heavy chunk of wood. Only then did he turn the lock, pull the door open for the few inches that the chain would allow. But whoever was outside was as cautious as Ferrier. He was keeping himself out of view—or perhaps out of range. "Who is it?" Ferrier asked quietly. He repeated the question in Spanish.

There was a small laugh. "Charlie Brown and the Peanuts Gang." The man was standing well back, drawn into the shadows; his voice was low, but clear enough to be almost recognizable. Not Lucas' voice, that was definite. "Hey, there! Turn off that goddamned light—the one in the hall, too."

Ferrier looked back at Concepción. "I think I know who this joker is," he told her as he switched off the lights. She said nothing, only stared at him fearfully as he unhooked the chain. I hope so, he added to himself, and swung the door open.

12

Tavita watched Tomás Fuentes end the call. "I will tell the señorita," he was saying. Would he? she thought bitterly. He had
taken control; he would tell her what Ian Ferrier had said if it
suited him. Taken control . . . We'll see about that, she told
herself, and turned away abruptly to conceal the sudden flow of
tears. It was the first time she had wept since the news of Jeff's
death. She had exclaimed, and lamented, and talked wildly; she
had put on a performance over which she had no control—hysteria, Tomás had called it. Quickly, she moved out onto the narrow
terrace, stood with her back to the room, her elbows resting on
the stone wall that dropped straight down to the second terrace,
with its wall falling down to a third. A ledge garden, Jeff had
described it, clinging to the side of a cliff. Far below was the
wooded gorge, and the little streets and crowding houses with
their cooking smoke now invisible in the darkness, and the rise of
other hills with their bright sparkling lights strung out like glistening beads. This was where Jeff had often stood with her, watching
night come to Granada.

She heard Magdalena's footsteps, heels clacking on the paving
stones with her firm solid tread. The old woman had brought her
a white shawl to throw around her shoulders, cover her throat and
bare arms against the cool touch of the rising breeze. Magdalena
stood beside her in silence—there was no need to talk; they had
known each other too long, too well—and then stirred uneasily,
spoke angrily under her breath, left abruptly. So Tomás had come
out here, too. The soothing, cleansing magic of this place had
gone.

But she refused to be driven away, as Magdalena had been.
And she refused to ask questions. Or take orders. From now on,
whether Tomás knew it or not, she was going to be in control. It
was the only way to deal with such a man. Show him one small
weakness, and he had you by the throat. I have dealt with black-
mailers before, she thought: some made demands by calling on

your pity; some made threats by rousing your fears. Tomás had done both. But no more, no more, she told herself. Don't let him see, don't let him even feel, how helpless and weak you are. But you aren't alone. Remember that. That's what Ian Ferrier had said: "You aren't alone." So remember it.

Tomás Fuentes looked at the lights of Granada. "Strange," he said, "this is my first visit to Granada."

And your last, she thought bitterly.

"What, no comment on that? You surprise me, Tavita. Don't you think it is comic? I know much of Spain, and yet Granada so close to Málaga—is the one city that I never entered."

"That explains why it remained so peaceful during the troubles."

"That explains why you chose it. A dream world. Buried in history of long ago. An anachronism—"

"Peace is never an anachronism."

"Would you like my professional advice?" He studied her cold silence. "I shall give it to you, in any case. This kind of city, Granada the peaceful, Granada the proud, will be the first to flare up when the troubles begin again. And they will, Tavita, they will." She had turned on him with flashing eyes. "And they always start where it is least expected. Why? Because of a sense of guilt. Take any place where people have been spared war, ruins, starvation, cruelties, and what do you have? Well, at first—when others are suffering—they are afraid that the suffering will come to them, too. And when it doesn't, they are grateful. And then they grow a little smug. They see virtue in their escape. They begin to believe they are so clever or so tolerant or so generous that there is no reason for anyone to start trouble, that they are secure forever. And as the one sop to their conscience, which is secretly bothered that they have suffered so little while others have suffered so much, they develop a sense of guilt. And it is this sense of guilt that betrays them into the hands of their enemies. When the challenge comes, they hesitate, they argue, they are divided among themselves. They refuse to see it, in its full threat. Therefore they do not act. And action is the only answer to challenge. But how can a man take action when he is wearing a hair shirt next his skin? The hair shirt of guilt. It weakens and distracts. And once his enemies know that it is there, they grip where it hurts most. They have him. A man who has a sense of guilt is easily manipulated. And he is always the loser." He smiled as he looked at her. "Are you listening? Do you follow what I have been saying? No, I suppose not. Enjoy your dream world, Tavita. It won't last long."

"Not if people like you are around," she said angrily.

He laughed. "Women, women. One cannot talk with them. They reduce everything to the personal. You and I, and I and you. Have you never wondered why there are no famous women historians? Too emotional, too personal."

"I do not wonder about such things. Just as I do not wonder why there are no communist historians who can be trusted."

"Tavita, Tavita," he chided her. "You should read more, and think more. You waste your life. With your name, your following, you could serve—"

"I keep myself out of all politics," she said coldly.

He looked around the terrace, then back at the long, low stretch of house. "Yes, you have done very well. But don't you ever think of those who are poor and hungry?"

"I think of them. I was one of them."

"And you never forget it, not even just a little?" he teased her. She was beautiful with her eyes flashing indignation. What an effect she could have on people—she was one of them, more believable than any red duchess.

"I was poorer and hungrier than ever you have been, Tomás. You left. You made a nightmare world, and you left us to live in it. And now you come back to sneer at dreams—"

"I was talking of a bigger stage than the one you dance on. I was talking of something nobler than your own personal ambition. I was talking of service to—"

"To the people?" she cut in, mockingly. "Which people? *All* of them or only part of them—the part that will follow you and your masters? You say I am uneducated. I have not read all the books you have read. But I have my own thoughts. Have you your own thoughts, or are they borrowed from your approved reading list? And I have my beliefs, Tomás. Stupid beliefs, you would call them. But is it stupid to give people joy and pleasure, to show them the meaning of grace and beauty, to make fire stir in their veins and proud memories come alive to lift their hearts?"

"You always put on a beautiful performance, Tavita."

She looked at him. He was not as amused as he pretended to be. I can disguise my anger, too, she thought, and restrained the words on her tongue. She masked the emotions in her eyes, let her lips relax. "Thank you," she said, cool and detached.

Unexpectedly, he slipped a hand under the shawl, gripped her arm, gently but firmly, pulled her slowly toward him. "What a waste of time to quarrel like this. You have me as your guest for five days. Let us make them agreeable. After all, you are the great believer in giving joy and pleasure. No, no, I am not laughing at you." He caught her waist, held her firm. "Strange as it may seem, I—"

"Five days?" She looked at him disbelievingly. "Four days," she insisted, and kept her voice matter-of-fact. This was not the first time she had slackened an arm around her waist with the careful use of words and tone. A slap on the face, an attempt to struggle only aroused most men to prove they were stronger than you; the schoolteacher's voice and manner usually acted like a bucket of cold water. "I heard you say four days." The arm was still holding her waist, but it had not tightened.

"And Ferrier said five."

"Why five?"

"He is going to Washington."

"At a time like this?" she asked sharply.

"Business. Urgent business. Tavita—"

"You men! You make promises. You don't keep them." But Ian Ferrier will keep his, she thought. I heard his voice. I know what he meant. *Nothing has changed. . . . You aren't alone. . . . Just trust me. . . .* And I do. "What business in Washington?"

He hesitated briefly. "Reid's funeral. Something like that."

"And then Ian Ferrier comes back and takes you to safety, is that it? Did *you* send him to Washington to get help?"

"Of course not!" He was angry. The arm slipped from her waist. "I have nothing to do with the Americans. Ferrier is coming here as *your* friend, to help *you*. He is taking the place of Reid. That is all. Americans are easily bewitched into doing whatever a beautiful face tells them to do." That, Tomás thought, makes it quite clear, and it is important that it should be clear. Later, if she talks of these days—and as a woman, she would talk—she will only remember that I have had no connections with the Americans, that I did not seek them out, that I did not deal with the enemy. His momentary fear passed, his anger faded. He withdrew his hand from her arm, pretending he needed—quite naturally—to rest it on the wall as he looked down at the terraces below him. "How many?" he asked, changing the subject. He had not risked exploring the narrow terraces, linked together by stone staircases, in broad daylight. There could be too many eyes. There were other houses along the top of this ravine, other terraced gardens; and across the gorge, there were paths and roads winding through the woods. He had spent the long afternoon in the main room while Tavita had locked herself into her adjoining bedroom for her siesta, and Magdalena had retreated to the only other room on this floor, the studio, to doze peacefully among the artist's easels and pictures of flamenco dancers performing in torchlighted taverns and courtyards, of guitarists absorbed in playing, of Tavita in fifty different costumes and as many movements. He had wondered vaguely what kind of man this painter, Tavita's great friend, had been. No doubt one of those dilettantes with money.

Tavita was listening to the far-off drift of children's voices, playing far below in the small plaza with its strings of colored light bulbs to mark its boundaries. "There are two more terraces," she said.

"And all planted like this one? With flowers and fruit trees?"

He was now doing his best to be friendly, she thought. "Much the same."

"What's this one?" He reached over, touched the top of a tree that grew on the terrace below.

"Apricot."

"An ingenious man, your artist. How did he get all that planted on a narrow terrace? Money, money, money. It works miracles."

"He was only following the plans of other ingenious men. The terraces were first made centuries ago by the Arabs. He restored their work, replanted. That was all. And he had money. He was a lawyer, a very good lawyer."

"And these paintings in the studio?"

She looked at him angrily. "I told you not to go in there."

"Oh, a sanctuary? With old Magdalena as its guardian angel?" And when she didn't answer, kept staring at the large clear circle of moon now rising above the sprinkle of stars in the dark velvet sky, he said, "A lawyer who had a secret passion for flamenco dancers . . . Well, well—how fortunate for the little Tavita. Was he old?"

"Yes," she said calmly. "He was your age."

That silenced him. For a little. Then he said irritably, looking down at the small church tower rising from one side of the *plazuela* and the string of colored lights, "There they go again. These bells . . . Do they never stop ringing?"

"Nine o'clock," she said softly. "Time to leave. Have you enjoyed your view of Granada?" He looked at her sharply. "Only a small part of Granada," she went on, "but even so, it is something to keep you company for the next four—no, five days." She turned on her heel, walked quickly into the house.

He followed her, moved rapidly around the big room so that he blocked her path. "I am *not* leaving Granada," he warned her.

"Of course not. But you are leaving this house. You didn't imagine that I would keep you here? My friends will start visiting me tomorrow. I never know who will come, or when. And the servants will be back at ten o'clock. This morning, I telephoned them from Málaga and gave them the day to visit their relatives."

"How gracious of you."

"I control my household efficiently," she said coldly. And you, too, Don Tomás Fuentes.

"Where am I going?" he asked abruptly.

"To another house—it was my home for many years. You'll find it quite comfortable. And safe."

"Can you drive the car? I am not having any other chauffeur called in to help us. I want no—"

"We don't drive. We walk."

He stared at her as if she had gone mad. He pointed to his suitcase, which lay outside her bedroom door, untouched since he had dropped it there.

"Do we walk through the streets, carrying *that?*"

"You carry it. And we do not go through the streets."

"Then—"

"Quietly," she advised him, "speak quietly. Magdalena is downstairs in the dining room. Don't attract her attention—unless, of course, you would like to do that." She gestured impatiently to him, and he stood aside to let her pass between the crowded groupings of chairs and cushions and tables. "Wait here!" Quickly she moved over to her bedroom door, a massive panel of carved wood framed by two delicate stone pillars upholding a lightly decorated arch, and vanished from his sight. He had scarcely time to decide whether to obey her nonchalantly, or to treat her small commands with contempt, before she returned. She was holding a long key in her hand. She pointed with it toward his suitcase, didn't even slow her pace while he went to pick it up, and was already in the small semicircular entrance hall, her high heels lightly tapping on the paved floor, as he began to leave the room. He dropped his dignity and increased his pace. She's going to take me out of the front door and put me in some room over the garage, he thought as he entered the hall. He stopped in amazement. He had been wrong.

Tavita was standing before one of the carved wooden panels that curved around the hall. Gently, she was pushing aside one strip of its arabesque decorations. It moved slightly, just enough to uncover a small keyhole that had lurked under a formalized flower. She inserted the key in this lock, and twisted it until there was a click. Then she pressed her shoulder against the panel. It swung inward. She reached into the darkness at keyhole height, found a switch, turned on a light. She signed to him to follow, and stepped into a short, narrow corridor.

Tavita locked the panel behind them—this side of it was bare of ornament and disguise, its only addition being a large grip of wrought iron that let her close it firmly and quietly—and led him to the other end of the corridor, where there was a second door. It made no pretense of being anything else, strong and serviceable, held closed by a large iron bolt. This she opened slowly, carefully, so that it only scraped but did not screech. And again she reached into the darkness beyond the door and switched on the light. Or, rather, a series of lights: far-spaced bulbs, unshaded, linked by exposed wiring that was neat enough even if it looked like an afterthought. Actually it was a replacement. Near each bulb there was an iron bracket fixed into the white limestone wall. Once, the long downward stretch of corridor, tunneled out of the rock, had been lit by torches.

Tavita watched Tomás' face with a touch of amusement. "It is safe to talk here," she said. "But we must walk as we talk. It is a long way down."

He regained his breath, took his bearings. The corridor was twice his height and broad enough for two to walk closely if not comfortably. It was entirely of limestone; ceiling, walls, floor, stairs, all were a ghostly white under the reflection of the lights. It descended steeply, but it was so carefully planned that the downgrade seemed almost gentle, leisurely. There were groupings of steps, three or four to form a short staircase; and then a sloping stretch of the stone floor, sometimes only the length of a few paces, at other times as many as ten or twelve full strides. It ran fairly straight, curving slightly in a few places where the grade was steeper. The air was sweet and cool. There must be slits in the rock, he thought, although he could see nothing; how else could torches have burned there to light the steps? "Expert engineering," he admitted, as he caught up with Tavita, "but not the brain child of your artist. A reconstruction job, like those terraces?"

She nodded. "They were all in ruins, falling to pieces, like the house itself. It was his grandfather who did the reconstruction."

"Another painter?" he asked sardonically. "Also a lawyer?"

"A lawyer. But a musician."

"Always the perfect Spanish gentleman," he said mockingly. "It's astonishing what you can do if you have enough money so that you can neglect your own business. Pay others to do all the work and bring in the profits, while you devote yourself to higher things."

She let that pass, although her lips tightened and there was a glitter in her magnificent dark eyes that outshone the light beside her head. "Four steps here, two of them slightly crumbling," she said, and stepped down carefully.

He saw them just in time. *I could have twisted an ankle there, even broken a leg,* Fuentes thought. He decided not to goad her with any more remarks about her lover, now moldering in some ornate tomb no doubt designed by his grandfather—or was it another discovery, another bequest from the Arabs fallen into ruins and beautifully restored? He would have liked to risk that remark, but he wasn't too sure of his facts: would Christians use Arab tombs, or did Arabs have tombs? She'd be quick to point out his ignorance, and she had already snubbed him too much this evening. *A beautiful woman with quick brains was a deception. Take care with this one,* he warned himself: *she isn't the witless doll you thought she was.* He decided to watch his step, literally as well as figuratively, and kept his eyes on the ground before his feet. His sense of direction told him that they were traveling away from the terraced garden and its outfacing over the gorge. "Your house," he said with extreme politeness, "stands on a ridge. Is that it? And so we are now going down the opposite slope from the one I saw. But where?"

"Into the old town."

"Into the town?" He was worried.

"Busy and crowded. But quite safe."

"But where does this corridor end?" he insisted.

"At a little house inside a patio. I lived there, at one time. It is not unpleasant."

"Who owns it? You?"

"In a way, yes. I pay for its upkeep. But it is no longer connected with my name. Esteban Seriano now holds the lease."

"Esteban? Does he use the place?"

"That is not in our private agreement. He will have it all, furniture, everything, when I have no more need of it."

"And none of his friends will come knocking at its front door? You are sure of that?"

"Quite sure," she said acidly. "You will find it completely secure. Only occasional visitors stay there—friends of mine." She paused. "Usually friends," she added bitingly, and looked at him.

"Did they know about this corridor?"

"Very few."

"And Esteban, and Magdalena?"

"No."

"But Reid knew of it?" he asked shrewdly.

"Yes."

"You must have trusted him a lot."

She stopped. She turned to face him. "I would have trusted him with my life." She looked quickly away, hid the sudden betrayal of tears.

"An American?"

She was silent for a few moments, walking on with increasing speed. "I never thought of him as anything—except as a good man. An honorable man. That, I think, is too hard for you to understand. We shall not discuss him."

All he was left to admire was the back of her head, held high and proud, with its thick dark hair smoothed into a heavy twist at the nape of her neck. Her shoulders were enveloped with the silk shawl, its long fringes swinging over her hips, her legs under the sway of her skirt were perfect in symmetry, the ankles slender yet strong. Spain produced some magnificent women, he thought, and then frowned at this outburst of chauvinism. "Not so fast," he called to her. "I am carrying the suitcase. Remember?" He changed it to his left hand. There was nothing valuable in the case, nothing that could give away his true identity: a small cosmetic kit, with peroxide, hair dye, changes of clothing, some extra ammunition for the pistol, a knife he prized, a few carefully forged documents he might need if his present passport (Argentine citizen, Juan Blanco Jiménez, of Buenos Aires, rug importer) needed to be destroyed.

She slowed her rapid stride, but did not look around.

"How much farther?" he tried.

"Three hundred meters, no more." She still did not turn her head.

All right, he thought, I shall talk to the nape of her neck, and resist making the obvious remarks such as "You must know this route extremely well. Did you always go up this way to visit your artist?" Instead he said amiably, "But we've already come that distance, haven't we?"

"Less."

Three steep steps, then ten long strides on a descending slope. "The Moors built this, did they? Must have taken them a few years."

"They had plenty of time."

"Yes, they were here for centuries. Almost seven? They must have begun to feel that they owned Andalusia. I have heard stories of Arab families, now in Morocco, who took away the keys of the house they built, and have them yet. Of course, they have only been out of Granada for five hundred years. That leaves them two more centuries to wait, and equal the record set by the Christians."

She didn't answer. Her head was held even higher.

"Are there many of these corridors?"

"Several."

"Well known?" he asked quickly.

"This one isn't."

"You are sure?"

"Quite sure. The records say that this was one tunnel that fell into complete disuse and became impassable."

He said musingly, "Why did the Moors build them? They lived on the heights, yes. But they could take a troop of cavalry whenever they wanted to visit the Spanish quarter."

"Some did not always want a troop of cavalry along with them. And by night, it was dangerous to ride down to the city. They were pulled off their horses and had their throats slit."

They walked the remaining distance in silence.

At the end of the corridor, there was a stout door similar to the one at its beginning. As Tavita slid aside the giant iron bolt, he looked back at the way they had come. Incredible, he thought, and was impelled to speak even if he had determined that he would say no further word until she began talking again. "What lay above our heads? Streets and houses?"

She nodded, pulled the door open. Again, just as at the entrance to this long white tunnel, there was a short space leading to another door. And again, this door opened with the long-stemmed key and a peculiar twist once it was plunged deep into the thickness of the lock. She noticed his curiosity. "Enough security?" she asked with a touch of contempt.

He didn't answer. Yes, there was enough security to please even him, but he would give her no satisfaction by looking impressed. She switched on a light, and he followed her into a small interior room, more like a large closet except for its decorative paneled walls—the excuse for the door that, now closed, made one of the panels, with its keyhole hidden under a movable design. Most ingenious, he thought, and now it is time for you to take charge. He moved ahead of her, entered a larger room. She had switched on two small shaded lamps which cast a benign glow around him. Probably safe enough, he decided; there were windows on either side of a large door—the front entrance to this apartment, obviously—but they were heavily shuttered on the inside, their louvers completely closed. These little pink lamps could attract no attention outside.

He explored quickly, thoroughly. There were two other doors

from this room. One led to a bedroom with a window and an interior bathroom. The other took him into a small tiled kitchen, shelves filled with canned foods from meat to fruit, a rack of wine bottles, a miniature stove and sink, a refrigerator jammed into the old fireplace under a high mantelpiece.

Tavita had followed him, watching his quick inventory. "Yes?" she asked, noting his frown.

"Who cleans this place?"

She looked at him impatiently. "Are these domestic details really necessary?"

"Yes."

"Esteban has a cousin who comes in every week, just to make sure everything is safe and undisturbed."

"When does she come?"

"On Fridays. Don't worry, you'll be gone before she comes again."

"She never asks questions about bed linen or towels or empty cans and bottles?"

"Why should she? She is well paid. She needs the work. She is a cousin. Of course she asks no questions."

"How does she enter?"

"By the front door."

"She has her own key?"

Tavita said with studied boredom, "She has Esteban's key."

"She might use it any time."

"She won't. She does not intend to lose this job."

"She will wonder about your visitors here."

"She thinks they are Esteban's friends," Tavita said curtly. "I told you I've no connection with this place any more. I haven't been near here for years. Now, come along—I want to show you the patio outside the front door."

"One second," he said, and pointed to the kitchen window. "Where does that face?" He crossed over to it quickly.

"Only onto a small interior courtyard—just like the bedroom's window. A breathing space, actually. Not even the sun can look in on you."

He opened the shutters, looked out, saw a blank wall only a couple of arm lengths away. "What lies above us?"

"A wing of the museum."

He stared at her.

"Come here," she told him, and led the way back into the main room. She switched off the lights. "This is the only place where you have to be careful when you turn on a lamp. Make sure, then, that the shutters are tightly closed." She had moved over to a window, adjusted the louvers, let broad slats of bright moonlight come slanting over the tiled floor. "There's the entrance to the museum," she said, and pointed out at the patio. So he had to follow her, after all, and look. She drew aside, keeping well out of touch, he noted as he studied the layout of the courtyard.

He could see it clearly through the iron screens that covered the window with a light and intricate pattern. (But strong enough, he thought, to bar intruders: this ground-floor apartment was well protected.) The patio was spacious and pleasant, its paved floor bathed in moonlight, with an edge of deep shadow along one side. There were slender pillars, forming a shallow colonnade, on either side of a large doorway that stood directly opposite him. It must lead into a street filled with traffic. He could hear a distant steady murmur, like some unseen sea breaking in constant muted rhythm, from the world outside. But here, in this courtyard, there was only silence and emptiness.

He picked out the museum entrance to the right of the gateway, pillared and arched and heavy with stone curlicues. "Museum of what?"

"Oh, things of old Spain—wood carved and painted, silver-work, iron screens, leather, lace, embroidery and furniture and—"

"When does it open?" Arts and crafts, he thought. Always popular. People everywhere. Could be dangerous.

She opened her eyes wide. "Oh, *Madre de Dios*," she said impatiently. "How should I know? It was always closing for lunch when I was having breakfast."

"Does it open again in the afternoon?"

"Three, perhaps four o'clock."

"And closes for the night?"

"Around eight. I think."

"Is it a busy place?"

"Busy, busy, busy—particularly on Sunday afternoon. Then the Spaniards come as well as the tourists. It will entertain you, help pass the time, but don't open the louvers too wide. Tourists are always prowling around, always curious."

That was what he had feared. Constant movement out there in the patio. He would have to make sure everything was closed tight, suffocate in darkness, keep still, listen to the heavy footsteps trudging above his head on the old wooden floor of the museum. "So I'm locked away, am I?" Four or five days of this . . .

She smiled. "Now you will know how women used to feel, watching the world through shutters and screens." Her amusement vanished. She added coldly, "You aren't a prisoner, and you know it. You can walk out through that gate any time you wish. And good luck to you."

He studied the entrance gate, kept his temper down. "It looks impregnable at this hour," he said.

"There is the key to this house." She pointed to an elaborate piece of black metal, almost a hand span in length, that hung on the wall beside her front door. "And the caretaker will let you out of the courtyard—he is a veteran, who has his apartment right beside the gate."

He took command again. "What is that shop on the left? Opposite the museum entrance," he added impatiently as she glanced out in the wrong direction.

"A tinsmith's. He spreads his wares in the morning outside those windows, takes them in again before nine in the evening. He is an excellent workman, employs only expert help."

"Popular with the tourists?"

"He has many customers. So has the leather shop, next door to him."

"And the other doors around the patio?"

"Once they were apartments like mine. But the museum now owns them, displays replicas of old Spanish rooms." She moved back to the nearest lamp. "Close the shutters before I turn on the light," she warned him.

He gave one last look at the peace of the courtyard, then blotted it out of sight.

She seemed to read his thoughts. As she switched on the table lamp, she said, "I should not risk taking a late stroll out there once the moonlight fades."

"Ah—the loyal veteran who guards the gate?"

"And two other disabled veterans, custodians of the museum, who live in its basement. If they knew who you were, they would take you to pieces, even if one has a wooden leg and the other a hook for a hand. Your legacy to them, Tomás Fuentes. It keeps their memory alive. Or do you think we have all forgotten?"

"Some have," he reminded her, and scored a point. A good point, for she had nothing to say. He went on to improve it by adding, "You would be surprised by the number of recent contacts we have made—"

"So?" she interrupted angrily. "Then why did you come to me and Esteban for help? What was wrong with all your good political allies?"

He switched back to the courtyard. "All right, I don't take any postmoonlight or predawn stroll. Not even when the veterans are sleeping off their brandy."

"If they were, there is always the tinsmith. He lives above his shop. They say he works for the police in his spare time."

Now that was an interesting piece of information, he thought. "Too bad," he said. "A place like this, with so much coming and going, would make a perfect drop."

"A drop?" She had turned on another lamp, was looking around the room as if she were giving it one last check.

"A place—" he began, but did not finish. She couldn't care less, obviously, about a place where couriers could leave or pick up secret instructions. She was too engrossed with being the perfect, if unwilling, hostess. Women were really fantastic. He said, "When Ferrier gets here, how do you let me know?"

She pointed to a telephone on a small writing desk in one corner of the room. "I shall call you before he comes down the long corridor."

"What?" he asked sardonically. "You use an ordinary telephone? No private line between this house and the love nest perched on the cliff?"

She faced him, eyes blazing with anger. Then she said, her voice low but intense, "It will be safe. When I call, the telephone will ring three times, and then break off. Within one minute exactly, it will ring again. This time, you can pick up the receiver. I shall do the talking. It will be brief."

"Don't mention anything important!" he warned her quickly. "Nothing—"

"Of course not!" she flashed back at him. "It is enough if you hear my voice. Then I shall interrupt myself, apologize for speaking to a wrong number. The call is over. Your voice is not heard. You are safe."

"And what if, in your excitement, you do call a wrong number?" he teased her.

"Then the person to whom I was speaking would certainly tell me so. If it was a woman, she would be annoyed. If a man, he might try a little conversation. But you do neither. By your silence, I will know I *have* the right number."

He burst out laughing. "Amateurs are really—"

"One last thing. I do not know what time of day you will leave here."

"Surely night is the obvious time—"

"Too obvious, perhaps. Besides, it is also too quiet. Get rid of that suit"—she gestured to the chauffeur's uniform—"and wear one of your own. Look like a tourist. You cannot carry your case, of course. You will leave it behind. I shall see it is destroyed."

"Listen," he said angrily, "I will think up my own way of escape. Why not come back up to your house? Leave in darkness."

"You leave from here."

"More dangerous."

"Less dangerous. There may be friends visiting me. I may even be watched. You caused trouble at El Fenicio. There are people who have questions about that, and they will search for an answer."

She was thinking no doubt of that little State Security man—Rodriguez. But there were others who were interested, too, and able to move more quickly. Reid's death—no accident—bore witness to their speed and efficiency. A good operation, even if it increased his fears for his own safety. He wondered if he should let drop the fact that Reid had been murdered, but then decided it wouldn't be worth the extra shock he'd give her. With woman's lack of logic, she would blame him for Reid's death, making him its entire cause. And that could be really dangerous: she might even forget what trouble he could raise for her brother, turn him over to Esteban right away. Yes, that would be highly dangerous. And unjust. For it was a vain, emotional, irresponsible creature like Lee Laner who had really been the cause of Reid's death: Laner had made Reid helpless, an easy target set up for the assassin. Yet come to think of it, even Laner was not to blame. It was the unknown informant, the one who had told Laner who Reid actually was. Without that little bit of help, the chain of Reid's bad luck could never have been forged.

"And so, you leave from here," she repeated. She waited for a sharp contradiction, but he was strangely silent. She moved into the small room with its paneled walls.

She isn't even going to say good-bye, he thought. Well, if she doesn't want the usual last word, I'll give her it. "All very cozy, but you've forgotten one thing." She turned to look at him. "Books," he said sarcastically, waving his hand around the over-furnished room. "Pink shades on the lights, cushions, paper flowers, embroidered mats, all a man could desire. But what the devil do I read? Five days and—"

"Ample time to think your great thoughts," she said, and she was smiling. "Or, over by the telephone, you will find paper and ink. You might even write your memoirs. She unlocked the door, stepped over the threshold, pulled the panel back into place behind her. By the time he reached it, she had already locked it once more. He listened, but he could not even hear the bolt sliding free on the second door. She would be entering the main corridor now, fastening that door securely. Then she would stride, lithe and sinuous, head high and triumphant, up the stairs and the sloping floors, until she reached her own security. And she would be laughing.

He struck the paneled door with his fist. Twice. The pain brought him back to cold sense. He turned sharply on his heel, returned to the main room. He switched off the stupid little lights on their spindle-legged tables, felt his way to a window, opened shutters and glass pane, let the air stream in. It was bland, tepid. Not the cool breeze that had drifted over the high terrace, bringing the perfume of ripening apricots and night-flowering vines. He gripped the iron screen, shook it. I am trapped, he thought in a hot surge of anger; if she wants to betray me, she has me trapped.

Would she betray me?

No. Not until I am safely away from her and her people. Not until then. "We shall see about that," he said softly to the silent courtyard. "We shall see."

13

Ian Ferrier had swung the door open, but only far enough to let him bang it shut if the face of the cautious visitor turned out to be unknown. He might have a pistol in his hand or he might just happen to have a voice that sounded like Ben Waterman's. Ferrier wasn't in much of a trustful mood tonight.

But it was Ben, all right. He stepped smartly into the hall, closing the door behind him on the dark, silent garden, saying quickly to Concepción in his execrable Spanish, "No, leave that hall light off. Please!" He moved past her into the big room, turned to face Ferrier, and stared. He shot a second glance at Concepción, who followed them slowly, uncertainly, and his stare intensified. "What's that for?" He pointed to the half-raised cooking pot. Then he looked at the chairs out of place, rugs wrinkled, one floor lamp fallen, and—through the wide doorway of the study—disorder complete. "I wondered why you were so damned slow to open that door," he said, "but I must say—" He looked around him again, shook his head.

"It's all right, Concepción," Ferrier said. She wasn't even aware that she was gripping the pot as a weapon. "This is one of my friends. Would you get him a Scotch and soda? I'll have another of Esteban's specials." That reassured her. It also got her out of the room. "What the hell are you doing in Málaga? Thought you were going to Toledo for the bullfight this weekend?"

"That's tomorrow. Might make it yet." Waterman had a soft, gentle voice with traces of Atlanta clinging to it; a most deceptive voice. In Korea, where Ferrier had first met him after the cease-fire—both twenty-two and already realists—he had been one of the toughest reporters who wouldn't take an evasion for an answer or an excuse as an explanation; in the Philippines, he had been one correspondent who had left the bars of Manila for Huk territory; in Vietnam, around 1958, he had penetrated to remote villages that had been converted to supporting the Vietcong and

187

found—as an incentive to unanimity of opinion—the leaders of the anti-communist opposition impaled on high posts for all to see; in Washington, where he and Ferrier had come together again in the early sixties, he had frankly disliked his editor in chief, longed for overseas assignments, and eventually exchanged the newspaper world for government service. As a press attaché, he had been moved around enough to please; and perhaps exhaust, his curiosity about other places, other people. Or perhaps the times were out of joint. At present, he was stationed in Madrid, a pleasant appointment as well as a difficult one, which of course made it interesting. But when Ferrier had seen him last week for a long dinner and a catch-up talk, Waterman was thinking of resigning before his next transfer, of getting back to reporting and the United States again. This time, he was going to explore his own country. And he was also going to explore the new mushroom growth of little magazines and get-with-it newspapers that gave peculiar left twists to facts and events. That was the need, right now: an enquiring reporter (and the more the better), belonging to neither extreme left nor extreme right, who really went to work on the lower levels of his own fourth estate, exposing their sources to some bright daylight, getting into the dark corners of paranoiac rumor and calculated misrepresentation. Yes, that was where the biggest news story lay right now. In the USA . . . Dangerous? Well—there might be a little trouble, he had admitted gently. His soft-blue eyes had looked as engaging as the rock face of Gibraltar.

He had that same expression in his eyes now, as he crossed over quickly to the study to get a full view. He was a compact man, of commanding height, with a face as deceptive as his voice. It was round, soft, with a highly pink tan and a fuzz of curly fair hair far-receding from a clear, untroubled brow. "Anyone else here?" he asked. "Just you and the avenging Fury? Good."

And no questions about what happened, thought Ferrier. That means Ben has something else on his mind. "What are you doing here, anyway?" Ferrier insisted. "Or is this part of your job?"

"Only temporary. I'm the innocent middleman. Co-opted and brought kicking and screaming away from the pleasures of Toledo. We got here around half past six, and I tried to telephone you. No answer. Later, we learned you were at the hospital. We also learned about Jeff Reid. So I'm no longer kicking or screaming, but the sooner we get this over with, the better."

"The middleman?"

Waterman looked at him. "You're slow on the uptake tonight."

He didn't usually have to explain and double explain to Ian Ferrier.

"Slightly thickheaded. Give it to me straight. Are you in Jeff's line of work?"

"No. I'm here for one reason, and that's you. I know you. I can say definitely, 'Yes, this is Ferrier, friend of Reid's.' And there are a couple of real superspooks outside in your garden right now, wanting to meet you. I also know them—mild acquaintances, but enough to assure you that they are the real thing. Not phonies. Not impostors. They and you can take each other at face value. And that, so help me, is why I am here."

"Two of them?"

"There's a third tagging along—Mike, a young fellow who watches everything and says little. He's some kind of subordinate to the big guy—one of the top—who came all the way from Washington. He's calling himself Smith at the moment." Waterman smiled. "But he is for real. Believe me."

"I didn't hear you drive up."

Waterman's smile faded. He looked worriedly at Ferrier. "You really do need reassurance, don't you?"

"By the carload."

"That kind of day?"

"That kind of day."

"Then it looks as if this introduction job of mine isn't the harebrained idea I thought it was."

"It isn't. How did the four of you get here?"

"We came to Málaga separately, got together as soon as the news of Reid's heart attack reached us, and then traveled in two cars to a nearby street. We parked them there, at some distance from each other, and then drifted into the garden about ten minutes ago. The chap from Madrid, Martin is his name—"

"Martin? So he actually got here," Ferrier said bitterly. "What the hell kept him?"

"Well—he's pretty strong on security. He arranged all the timing and maneuvering. You'd think he expected KGB cadres at every street corner. Mr. Smith from Washington was getting a little impatient; but of course this isn't really his field of operations—he may outrank Martin, but in Málaga he has to take Martin's advice. I suppose—I'm out of my depth, Ian," he added frankly.

"So am I. But keep swimming hard. All right. Let's have them in." Mr. Smith from Washington, and his sidekick, and Mr. Martin from Madrid. Suddenly, Ferrier's headache cleared: that was what a good flash of anger could do.

"Keep your dragon lady out of it." Waterman nodded toward the dining room, where Concepción had made a reappearance. She was bringing a tray, with the drinks, a folded towel, and a load of ice. Waterman raised an eyebrow at the huge bowl of ice cubes. "Do we look as thirsty as all that?"

"I had my head banged up a little."

"Who bashed you?"

"Later, later." Ferrier took the drink from Concepción, swallowed it quickly, began to feel almost normal. At least he was able to think ahead clearly now. Quickly, definitely, he gave instructions to Concepción. No, absolutely no dinner to be prepared; but he would be pleased if she would make some sandwiches—something simple like ham or cheese, the kind of sandwich that Señor Reid had sometimes asked for, hadn't he? Good. Some of those. To be wrapped and put into the refrigerator. That would let her get to bed; yes, she was to go to bed and try to get some sleep. Not to worry about anything. Some friends might drop in to visit him later on. Yes, make enough sandwiches; no, he didn't know how many were coming; just make a dozen sandwiches, that was all. And get to bed, and not to worry. Understood? He added his thanks for all she had done, patted her shoulder gently, and she left without one protest.

Waterman looked at Ferrier with a touch of admiration. Yes, he was thinking, Ian has a way with women, the young and the old, the plain and the pretty. "You really like them, don't you?" That's what got through to them, one and all.

"Let's have your friends in," Ferrier said brusquely.

"Do you feel well enough to face them?"

"I'll manage." That was something he couldn't have truthfully said half an hour ago. It was a cheering measure of his recovery.

Waterman started moving quickly again. He went into the hall, slightly opened the door, avoided the bright moonlight, kept to the pools of dark shadows. He found the three men waiting under the nearest palm trees. Martin was the most impatient. He didn't speak his grumbles at being kept waiting so long, but they were clearly expressed in his abrupt movements, in his way of forging ahead without even listening to Waterman's quiet explanation. The man who was calling himself Smith was definitely interested. So was Mike, who risked a whispered comment: "Looks as if our quick hop across the Atlantic was worth it after all."

"Sh!" said Martin angrily. He was the first to go inside. He waited in the dark hall until the others had slipped through the half-opened door, locked and chained it, moved over to a wall switch, turned the hall light back on. Then in a tight little phalanx the three men came into the big room. (Waterman kept tactfully apart, a mild demonstration of his own independence.)

Which is which? Ferrier wondered as he stared at them and they at him. The youngest was easy to place; Mike, the subordinate, in his late twenties, neat and crisp and squared away like a small frigate between two ships of the line.

"This is Smith, just over from Washington," Waterman said, and indicated the man Ferrier had been studying with a very cold look. So the other one is Martin, Ferrier thought, and transferred the cold look to its proper target. Martin was the older of the two—in fact, he was the oldest in the room by about ten years. He was fairly tall, carried himself with authority, was half bald (his dark hair hadn't lost its color, though), and had a white-skinned face as if he had never been touched by a Spanish sun. His features were good, his expression would be pleasant enough once that slight scowl of impatience faded, and his movements were quick, decided. At present, he was adjusting the shutters, barely looked around for a brief nod in Ferrier's direction as Waterman introduced him. Waterman said, with his own touch of impatience, "Look, Martin, there's nothing to be seen through these cracks in the shutters—you tested that from the garden. Just lights on, that's all we could see."

"Too many lights," Martin said. He had a rich and imposing voice, mellifluous. "You'd think a party was going on here." He moved over to the master switch at the foot of the staircase, fiddled around with it, dimmed some of the lamps. He then chose a seat beside one of those, smoothed down his neat dark-blue jacket, seemed quite content to sit there and outstare Ferrier from his chair in the shadows.

He knows his way around, Ferrier was thinking as he remembered his own battle with the lights last night; he has been here before. What's making him so aggressive? Is he suffering a touch of guilt for getting here so damned late?

Smith said quietly, "It seems to me as if there has indeed been some kind of party here," and he glanced sympathetically at Ferrier. "Did you arrive in the middle of it? Or were they waiting?"

"Waiting and ready."

"What did they get?"

"Not what they hoped to find."

Martin broke in. "And what was that?" He was polite now, friendly, as if his head of steam had slackened off.

Ferrier didn't seem to hear. The back of my hand to you, he told Martin silently, and walked over to the drink tray. He had a raging thirst. "Scotch and soda here," he told them, and poured himself a tall glass of Perrier, not his usual tipple but at present the wisest. Esteban's special wouldn't quarrel with spring water. He added several lumps of ice, kept one of them to hold against the back of his head, tried to look nonchalant, as if this were perfectly normal behavior, and came back to where Smith stood.

"We'll have a drink later," Smith said. He was a man in his early forties, tall and thin, with jutting craglike features and amused brown eyes. His hair, with a strong wave in it but closely brushed to his head, was prematurely white. His face and hands were deeply tanned. He wore a thin gray summer suit casual in cut, a white shirt, and a narrow dark tie. His voice was quiet, almost diffident; his smile was equally shy and deceptive, Ferrier decided. For all his understatement, Mr. Smith was a man of definite quality. He was cool, perhaps extremely capable, certainly sharply observant. He also knew when not to offer gratuitous remarks and paid no attention to the lump of ice being held to Ferrier's head. He took off his jacket, threw it over a chair, said, "Mike, see if you can open a few more windows in that dining room over there, let some air blow through." And he silenced a possible objection from Martin by adding, "Just keep the louvers at a safe angle. And then, you'd better get onto the telephone. Call the airport, reach our pilot. Tell him and Max to be ready in about two hours—no, make it nearer three. Around midnight."

Ferrier felt dismay, then annoyance. That's the way it goes, he thought bitterly. In and out. Just enough time in Málaga to learn of Reid's death, pick up any loose information, and then leave. Or are they trying to show me that if I want to play this cool, they can be cooler? Sure I was downright rude to Martin, sitting like a presiding Buddha over in that dark corner, but I owed him that. And I'm feeling better for it, better by the minute. He dropped the remains of the ice cube into an ashtray, said, "Are you returning to Washington?"

"By way of Madrid. Yes."

"Could I hitch a ride?"

Smith studied him for a moment. "Why not?"

"Good. You'll save me a lot of travel time."

"Urgent business?"

"Most urgent."

Smith let that pass without even an upraised eyebrow.

Ben Waterman was puzzled. They had all got off to a wrong

start, somehow, and he couldn't tell why. "Do you want me to stay, or do I melt away?" he asked, and looked at Martin and then at Smith. He wasn't sure who was in charge here; until they had entered this house, Martin had assumed command— for one thing, he did know this section of Spain, while Smith was only the visitor from Washington who had come here on special assignment. Whatever it was, it must be of abnormal importance. Interesting . . . But how did Ferrier figure in all this? And what was making him so damned wary and non-committal? If he had something to tell, why wasn't he coming out with it?

Martin had sensed this, too. "Stick around, Ben. We may need you to introduce us all over again." He was watching Ferrier with tolerant amusement. "I thought I was cautious, but—" He shook his head.

Waterman said half-angrily, "Look, Ian—believe me! These guys are authentic."

Smith said quickly to Waterman, "You might help Mike with his efforts to get through to the airfield."

"Sure," Waterman said, and poured himself another drink while he waited for Mike to deal with the last window. Mike was young enough—twenty-eight—and new enough at his job perhaps to drop a joke or two that would give an old journalist just one small lead, something to chew on, like a stone popped into your mouth to help you get across a desert.

Ferrier stopped studying the glass in his hand. "The nearest phone is in the study," he told Waterman.

"The place that is all messed up?"

"Badly?" Martin asked. He was on his feet, ready for an inspection.

"That's where they concentrated."

"What did they take?"

"I wouldn't know."

"Then how were you so sure," Martin said sharply, "that they did not get what they hoped to find?" He didn't wait for an answer but was already halfway to the study.

Ferrier looked at Smith. "I slipped up there, didn't I?" he said dryly. So Martin was no fool, he had brains and he could use them. That at least was some reassurance; Ferrier began to lose the feeling he was dealing with a first-rate bungler, all smooth outside with a big nothing interior. There were several of these around, nowadays; they were glib and personable, holding jobs that were too big for them, always just managing to run hard enough to catch up. Their pretensions were matched only by their self-promotion and their carefully polished image. In certain jobs—politics, education, communication, defense, security —their ineptness could be disastrous for the entire nation. (In business, it was the workers or shareholders who could get hurt; in the arts or entertainment, it was public taste that could be either offended or lowered. In both cases, it was limited damage, affecting only some groups in the country, and bad enough. But not as lethal as what the incompetent could do when they had slipped into jobs dealing with the national interest.) Even a small-scale, low-as-yet-on-the-totem-pole bungler could do as much damage as the simple match that set off an old-fashioned fuse.

Smith's reply was long in coming. Then it was only, "You've had a bad day. Let's sit over here." He chose a couple of chairs on either side of a small table, with a lamp between them. No shadows for him. Or perhaps this was what he'd call "inducing confidence," Ferrier thought. God knows, I need some of that. He sat down, keeping his silence as a protective wall around him. But it was vulnerable, he knew: he had as good as admitted that he actually knew what the break-in artists might have been searching for. "Cigarette?" Smith asked, offering his pack. "I know," he added quickly, "it's S.O.P.—put the poor guy at his ease. But I wish you would talk with us. If my use of 'Smith' annoyed you, it is simply because I am supposed to be weekending in Maryland, right at this minute: I'm nursing an attack of twenty-four-hour flu, instead of being outdoors enjoying myself with the rest of the family. And as for the reason that brought me flying over here—" He paused, smoothed back a lock of white hair that annoyed him. "Or is that unnecessary?"

You know damn well it's necessary, Ferrier thought; you've taken my measure, blast you. I've got information I consider so valuable that I am not turning it over to the first man who comes along, whether old friend Ben says he can vouch for him or not. I've just seen too many people today who've been indoctrinating me in caution. "I'd like to hear it."

"Briefly," Smith said, "my particular field of interest is Cuba. So, although I never met Reid, and he wouldn't even know who I was—he worked under Martin's direction—I've been including some of his reports in my general homework. He made excellent summaries of his talks with several Cuban exiles here is Málaga. What he thought was significant usually turned out to be important; what he termed untrustworthy or exaggerated was just that. A good man. We'll miss him." He sounded as if he meant it. Ferrier nodded. "In the last two days, we've had some rumors that a man who was thought to have died in a fire on a fishing vessel off Mexico—all very believable, all seemingly authentic—is actually alive and in Europe. Possibly in Spain, although that was hard for any of us to believe. Now, since this man had had a good deal of importance in Cuba, I was extremely interested. And because Reid had always been so reliable and perceptive, I gave instructions that any report from him, no matter what it was about, was to be sent to me at once." He turned his head to nod to Martin, who had returned from the study with a heavy frown on his handsome face. Smith went on, "And so, that was why I was pulled out of my bed at dawn this morning to hear that Reid had just sent an emergency call to Martin, using you as his stand-in. Frankly, that added even more urgency to his message. He must have been—" Smith hesitated.

"Desperate," Ferrier acknowledged with a small smile, and found he had relaxed completely. Added to what he knew, this all made sense. "Yes, he was in a tight spot, and there was no other help around." He looked at Martin. "Where the hell were you?"

The frown on Martin's face deepened, but he decided to ignore the question. He said to Smith, "Mike made his call to the airport. I told him to try to straighten up the study. Waterman is helping him. That will keep them well occupied for the next half hour. Okay?" Then he concentrated on Ferrier. "As you were saying, what was it that the intruders overlooked? What did they hope to get, and didn't? A message, a piece of information, from Reid to me? Do you know where it is? Have you got it?"

"It was to be sent to Washington."

"I'll make sure of that," Martin said icily. "That's the usual procedure, Ferrier." Then he seemed to remember Smith. "Of course, we have a very special courier here with us. Reid's information couldn't travel in better hands. But—perhaps the quickest way for that message to get across the Atlantic will be to code it and send it from Madrid." He was talking to Smith now. "I'd better know what's in it. Then I'll know what action I have to face here." He turned back to Ferrier, held out his hand. "All right, I'll take charge of it."

Ferrier didn't move.

Smith said, "I think Mr. Ferrier is taking that information to Washington himself."

"But that's nonsense!" Martin looked angrily at Ferrier. "We could damn well get it—we outnumber you. So don't play coy—"

"Take it easy, take it easy, Martin." Smith shook his head wearily. "We are all on edge. Reid's information is obviously urgent, but I think Mr. Ferrier has good reason to know that better than you or I. He was here today. We were not. That gives a certain perspective." He looked at Ferrier. "What has been happening in Málaga? I'd like to hear it."

"We know the situation—" Martin began testily. This was all a waste of time to him. Reid's information was what mattered.

"Do you?" Ferrier asked. "Do you know, for instance, that you've been infiltrated?"

"What?"

"A man called Gene Lucas came to see me around noon. He said he was CIA. He wanted to know if Reid had passed any information to me, so that he could take it and hand it over to Martin."

"*What?*" Martin said again. "Lucas? He's KGB," he explained quickly to Smith. "A minor agent, but effective."

"Didn't Amanda Ames report to you that Lucas came here today?" Ferrier asked, puzzled.

"No," Martin said grimly.

Then Ferrier remembered the picnic. "She is possibly still out on Lucas' boat. They went sailing. That's why she couldn't report."

"Possibly." Martin's voice was cold.

"And I don't think Lucas is so minor. He was certainly on his toes. That's the kind of day it has been: the opposition has been all over the place, and we've been nowhere."

"On the contrary. I made contact with Washington. I made arrangements down here. I sent Ames to reassure you and Reid. She delivered that message to you?"

"Yes. But the opposition knew about that, too. Lucas and his friends have been right in on this, from the minute I sent Reid's message to Madrid, well before dawn this morning. I telephoned from the hospital, wasted no time—"

"They knew about my instructions to Ames?"

"They knew that you were sending, or bringing, someone to make contact with Reid this evening and get his information. Lucas made sure that would not happen. He had Reid silenced before you could arrive."

"It was a heart attack," Martin said slowly. But he was alarmed. Smith was sitting quite still, his eyes on Ferrier.

"An induced heart attack," Ferrier said. "One of those hydro-cyanic-acid jobs, I think, sprayed from a pen.

"Proof?" Martin asked quickly.

"There never is. That's the whole idea behind such a weapon, isn't it?"

"How do you know about it?" Smith asked.

"Jeff told me. That type of spray pen or spray gun, or what-ever Department Thirteen calls it, was used on him last night on a staircase in El Fenicio. But he jumped in time. That's how he smashed his leg."

"At El Fenicio?" Martin thought that over. "Any connection between these two attacks on Reid?"

"No. At least, I don't think so. But it was Jeff's description of the first attack that made me suspect the second."

"Suspicion but no proof?" Martin asked. "Isn't that what you are really saying?"

"You might call it a demonstration of proof when the murderer took several items from Jeff's hospital room; anything that might have contained a recorded interview, made either on tape such as you find in a cassette or on some kind of micro-wire that could be disguised in—well, in any small object Jeff might carry around with him. Also, the murderer made a neat exit, with one of Lucas' men acting as his chauffeur. Also, the three thugs who came searching here were directed by Lucas."

"Proof?" asked Martin.

Ferrier's lips tightened. "I'm too goddamned tired to go into details. You take my word for it. Or not. As you like."

Smith looked at the room and said diplomatically, "I'd take this upheaval as a slight demonstration of proof, too." He gave Ferrier an encouraging nod.

Martin said, "How did you learn about Department Thirteen? From Reid? And in what connection? The cyanide pen, or some-thing else?"

He's trying to find out about Tomás Fuentes, Ferrier thought. He hesitated. "I've just been trying to show you that your group has been infiltrated," he said slowly. "That's what you should be worrying about right now."

"I am. And if Reid was an example of the blabbermouths I've had foisted on me—"

"That's enough, Martin!" Smith's voice was cold and sharp.

Martin got control of himself. He looked at Smith, shrugged his shoulders, and said, "Sorry. I've been overworked and over-worried." He looked at Ferrier, and saw it was too late for any kind of excuse or apology. The damage had been done. Ferrier was watching him with undisguised contempt. But Martin made one last effort. "Reid did tell Ferrier too much," he protested mildly enough.

"Who else was there to tell?" Ferrier asked. "Actually, he told me little. We didn't have much time together. He told me just enough to get this into the right hands—in Washington." He pulled out the lighter from his trouser pocket. He held it up clearly. He took a little pleasure in the way Martin stared at it, took a step forward toward it. "No," he said, pocketing it again, "it goes to Washington. Those were Jeff's instructions—practically his last words. I'll carry them out."

"So that's what he was using," Martin said. "There's equipment in the study that can play it back to us," he told Smith. Then he beckoned to Ferrier. "Come on, let's not waste any more time. This is urgent."

"I know." But Ferrier didn't move.

"What else do you know? What kind of report is inside that lighter?"

Ferrier shook his head. "The subject of that report will talk only with a certain man in Washington. The subject insisted on that. And that's all I know."

"The subject, the subject," mimicked Martin. He obviously found Ferrier's caution slightly comic. "Let's get down to a name. Could it be Tomás Fuentes, alias Vado, alias Adán, alias Cristóbal, alias—" He stopped abruptly, noticing Smith's face.

Smith said, "I had no idea you were such an expert on Fuentes."

"Sorry. I didn't intend trespassing. Put it down to academic interest. Frankly, I thought I'd better do a little research, with all these wild rumors floating around."

"Have there been so many of them?"

"Oh, a slight exaggeration on my part. Just the one rumor, the same enquiry, over and over again in the last twenty-four hours. Actually, I don't quite believe it. Fuentes had too much of a reputation here to risk putting a foot back on Spanish territory. My own theory is that there could be an impostor, using the Fuentes name in order to get our attention—perhaps our help." He was watching Smith's face. Ferrier caught Smith's eye, gave one small shake of his head. Let Martin blunder along in his own inimitable way, Ferrier was thinking; Fuentes isn't his special interest, anyway—that much, I've just found out. He's the type who overthinks and underacts. But he can feel, too, damn him: for Martin had glanced around quickly, as if he had almost sensed some imperceptible communication between Ferrier and Smith. Martin transferred his full attention to Ferrier. "I think I succeeded in surprising Ferrier. You have heard some of those names, haven't you, Ferrier?"

"You surprised me all right." And now, Ferrier was thinking, I can stop worrying about Reid's last incoherent, wandering sentences. They made sense, after all. Fuentes and Vado were one and the same man, and Mr. Robert O'Connor in Washington was the expert on both of these names. So, in their way, were Smith and Martin. . . . "In fact, you astonished me. Who is the blabbermouth now?"

Martin was about to speak, decided not to, bottled up his anger inside tightly closed lips.

Smith said philosophically, "Well—it looks as if Ferrier is going to carry that lighter all the way to Washington."

"Stubborn idiot," Martin said under his breath.

"Stubborn? Yes. If he weren't he might not have that lighter safe in his pocket. I rather like men who are stubborn about the right things." Smith turned to Ferrier. "Who is this man in Washington? I may know him, get you quickly to him. That's what you want, isn't it?"

That's what I want, thought Ferrier. He hesitated briefly, measured Smith carefully. "O'Connor," he said. "Robert O'Connor."

There was a short but intense silence. Then Martin burst into a fit of laughter.

Smith said, "Oh, shut up, Martin! It's no joke." He shook his head worriedly.

"He'll never believe you. Not this character," Martin said, and went into another round of laughter.

Smith rose to his feet, called out to the study. "Mike! Ben! Can I see you for a minute? Yes, both of you." And when they came into the room, he said, "Mike, write down my name—yes, my name." He waited while Mike scribbled quickly on a page of a small notebook. "Tear that out. Fold it. Give it to Ferrier." Then to Waterman he said, "Tell Ferrier who I am. Go ahead —tell him!"

He's Robert O'Connor, thought Ferrier, and unfolded the slip of paper that Mike had handed to him. *Robert O'Connor*, it read. "This is Bob O'Connor," Waterman was saying. Ferrier handed the paper back to Mike. "You want to burn this, I suppose?" he asked with a good attempt at a smile. Then he pulled out the lighter, handed it to O'Connor.

O'Connor pocketed it carefully. And definitely. Martin watched it disappear, hesitated, as if he was about to speak and wasn't quite sure how to phrase his suggestion. O'Connor got in ahead of him. "You'll be late," he told Martin, consulting his watch. "It's after ten o'clock."

"A few minutes won't hurt. Developments here—"

"I can handle them, I think. And you shouldn't keep Reid's lawyer waiting. He will need some careful instructions."

"He's capable. Why don't you join us for a quick dinner? He may have more information on Reid's death. And then I'll see you safely on board your plane."

"I'll manage. Don't worry about me. Besides, all the topics you'll be discussing are a little outside my field. Strictly your business, aren't they?"

Martin got the message. It was a gentle reminder of their separate responsibilities: Reid was his to worry about—burial arrangements, disposition of effects, checks made at the office as well as here, notification of nearest and dearest as well as of associates, plans for his replacement; Tomás Fuentes was all O'Connor's. True, there had been a slight overlap: Reid had made that secret report, and perhaps it did deal with Fuentes. If it hadn't been for Ferrier's definite statement that the lighter was intended only for O'Connor—yes, thought Martin, I could have made out a case, a good one, to let me listen to the playback. He said, "I am of course curious about what Reid had to say."

"Of course," O'Connor agreed warmly. "If there's anything that needs your attention, we'll let you know immediately. And thanks for all your help. Look me up when you next come to Washington."

"You're leaving at midnight? I'd better assign two men to make sure you get onto that plane without any trouble."

O'Connor joked that suggestion aside. "You think we'll be hijacked?" Then he turned serious. "You've more trouble on your hands than we have. Infiltration—if Ferrier is right about it—is a major problem. I think I know where to start."

"I can handle it. I think I know where to start."

"Then you're lucky. Usually it's a nasty, heartbreaking, mind-tormenting business that can take months. I know." O'Connor was definitely sympathetic. "I went through it, a couple of years ago. It practically paralyzed my work. And I kept wondering if I was suspecting the wrong man."

"In this case, it's a girl. A fairly recent addition. Sent me by Washington."

"Foisted on you?" O'Connor asked pointedly. He began steering Martin toward the hall.

But their progress was slow, for Martin kept talking. "More or less. About a year ago. She came with a lot of heavy support —an uncle in a position to convince important people. She's clever, there's no doubt; puts on a good performance. And attractive. Washington said she had the right background for one of my assignments. She is a lapsed communist. But who can trust that? They revert—"

"Not always. I have known some who meant what they said. And they do know, more than most people, what we are up against," O'Connor reminded him sharply.

"Sure, sure. But this one could be a good double agent. That idea has been worrying me for some time, actually."

They had reached the hall. "Then you'd better take some action on that," O'Connor said, and put out his hand. Martin took it. The good-bye was made, but Martin did not leave. He dropped O'Connor's hand, turned to look back at Ferrier. "Something wrong?" O'Connor asked. His impatience was thinly veiled.

"Ferrier," Martin called over, "you're so quick to smell infiltration—what did you think of Amanda Ames?"

Ferrier's face was tight. He had heard the conversation— who couldn't have? But he wasn't prepared for Martin's question. "No!" he blurted out angrily. "Not Amanda. She's all right." And she had never been a communist—that was the whole point of her story. He almost said that, then realized that Martin could have a powerful answer: she never had any true story to tell—that was the whole point of being communist. So he kept silent, his eyes fixed on Martin unwaveringly.

"Indeed," Martin said dryly. "And how long were you with her?"

Ferrier suddenly saw where he was being led. But he didn't dodge this question, either. "About an hour." I must sound like a fool, he thought.

"And you find she is quite above suspicion? In one small hour?" Martin was overly polite.

Ferrier said nothing. He could feel Mike's sympathetic but speculative eyes studying his face. Thank God Ben Waterman had gone foraging in the kitchen.

"She is, you see, an extremely attractive young woman," Martin said to O'Connor. "Puts on a good performance, as I told you. But there is one thing she can't charm away, and that's the fact that there were only five of us connected with the Málaga listening post: Reid, two men with whom I've worked for fifteen years, Ames, myself."

The words were spoken clearly enough. Ferrier saw Mike's look of consternation, heard him swear softly under his breath at such indiscretion. "Don't worry," Ferrier told him. "It was all carefully calculated." Fool of the year, that's me. That's how I'm made to look. Anything I say, from now in, will be weighed twice. Askance—good old word that could hardly ever be used —is the way they'll look at me. Then he laughed openly. Askance was the exact expression on Mike's face. "I laugh so that I may not weep," he said, and got a twenty-eight-year-old stare in return. "Or curse," he added bitterly. Amanda Ames? I listened to her today. I got more of a message than Martin ever sent. . . . Or was I wrong? Hell, that was the worst of the Martins in this world: one good sneer from them and your confidence started crumbling. That was what had been intended of course, he reminded himself; but his confidence stayed shaken.

He heard the front door close. Mike said, "Stupid old bastard, I thought he'd never leave. What got into him?"

O'Connor came quickly back into the room. "He's just trying to show he is completely in control. Today has been a bad day for him. That's all." Then he asked sharply, "Where's Ben?"

Mike said, "He got hungry when you started talking about dinner. Muttered something about sandwiches."

O'Connor glanced at his watch, took the lighter from his pocket. "Let's get with it. I'd like to hear what this has to tell us." He held up the lighter. "Martin says Reid has the equipment—"

"Yes. It's there. Well disguised. Not touched. Looks like part of his stereo setup."

O'Connor tossed over the lighter. "Let me know when it's all ready to go." Then he turned to the very silent Ferrier. "You gave me a small signal when Martin was discussing Vado. Or is it now Fuentes?"

"Fuentes."

"You don't think he is a fake?"

"He's the real thing."

"How do you know that?"

"Because he made contact with two people who knew him in the old days. He used them to meet Jeff Reid."

"Friends of his?" O'Connor asked quickly.

"Far from it. But they are going along."

"Blackmail perhaps? That sounds like Vado—Fuentes. Who are they?"

"Esteban and Tavita, the—"

"Ah, yes—El Fenicio? Tavita was Reid's friend. She came into some of his reports—a crazy pair, but effective. . . ." O'Connor was briefly entertained by some memory. "So Fuentes is in Málaga," he added softly.

"He was in Málaga. I saw him last night. Just over there." Ferrier pointed behind him to the staircase.

O'Connor recovered from his shock. "You are certain?"

"Well—I am now. I didn't know who he was at the time. He didn't see me. I thought it better not to step forward. He had a gun ready for use."

"When did you learn who he was?"

"This morning, when Tavita smuggled him out disguised as her chauffeur."

"Tavita told you who he was?" O'Connor was tense.

"No. But I—"

"You guessed it?" O'Connor was trying to hide his disappointment. From the study, Mike's cheerful voice called that he was ready and waiting. "Coming," O'Connor answered irritably, but he didn't move.

Yes, thought Ferrier, as he watched O'Connor's expression change from disappointment to doubt, there's that old askance look making its bow again. Thank you, Martin, thank you very much. I'm just the susceptible guy who takes women at their pretty-face value and twists the facts to suit his dramatic sense. "I had bits and pieces of information," he said angrily, "I made some deductions, I saw some definite evidence. Add all that together—and if you call it guessing, then it's okay with me."

"Oh, come on now," O'Connor said, breaking into a smile. "Did you talk this over with Reid?"

"Yes."

"And he believed you? But, of course, he must have. Or he wouldn't have told you about me, would he?"

That at least was a gesture. Either that or O'Connor was a smooth operator. Ferrier said flatly, "It was Fuentes I saw."

"And where is he now in Málaga?"

"He isn't. He's in Granada. He was there this evening. I telephoned Tavita, and he took the receiver away from her. So I spoke with him—"

"He actually spoke with you? What about?"

"I disguised it a bit. I passed on the word I'd be visiting Tavita."

O'Connor's highly intelligent face was bewildered. "You'd better start at the beginning." He looked up quickly as Ben came carrying a tray loaded with food into the room. "Go and make some more sandwiches," he said impatiently.

"But I just have," Ben told him. "The itsy-bitsy dainty little things on the lace doilies are Concepción's idea of a man's bite. The jumbo slabs are mine. Take your choice. And here's a tubful of beer."

O'Connor exchanged glances with Ferrier, shook his head, sighed, then shrugged in resignation.

Ferrier nodded toward the study, where Mike stood waiting. "I think you'll find the beginning starts in there. I only came in on the second act." Then he added with a gleam of humor, "But that, of course, is just another of my guesses."

O'Connor looked at him sharply. An answering smile appeared on his thin worried face. He lifted a couple of sandwiches, a can of beer, and headed for the study. "Okay, Mike. Get something to eat. I'll call you when I need you." He closed the door quietly on them all.

14

Esteban walked among the tables, making sure that everything was ready for tonight's performance. It was early yet—half past ten: the first people wouldn't arrive at El Fenicio until after eleven, and these were usually tourists. Saturday night was filled with them. "Make sure," he warned the waiters, "that the front tables are kept for our regulars. And no one—no one—is to sit here. This table stays empty all night." He tilted the two chairs against it as if it were already occupied. And in a way it was. Esteban could almost see Señor Reid sitting there in his favorite place. He turned abruptly away, walked to the back of the courtyard, stood there and looked at his domain. He wondered what kind of performance would be given tonight. The dancers were quiet in the dressing room—except Constanza. Death saddened her, she had kept saying, as if to explain her excessive tears. No doubt. She was sentimental. But death also excited her, for she kept talking talking talking. About nothing important, thank God. At least she was remembering Esteban's serious warning. She was no longer mentioning the man she had glimpsed, or thought she had glimpsed—Esteban hoped he had shaken her out of that notion—up on the balcony of Tavita's sitting room. She hadn't even mentioned it to Captain Rodriguez, this afternoon. And she'd have the lead part in the dancing tonight. But Esteban wished she could control her tongue, have some proper dignity. Death gave meaning to life, and should be treated with respect. The final act faced all of us; a friend's death was but a preview of our own.

Jaime was saying at his elbow, "Dr. Medina is here."

It was the younger one, the nephew. He didn't look happy. His usual smile was missing, although his voice was friendly enough. So Señor Reid's end was troubling him, too, thought Esteban, and he bowed slightly as he murmured a conventional welcome, feeling more sympathetic than usual to the man. (His uncle was another matter: *there* was a real man, someone who deserved both trust and admiration.) Young Medina said little at first. Then he saw a tall man entering the courtyard behind him, and spoke with a rush of words. "Here is someone who is devoted to flamenco," he said, indicating the newcomer. "He wanted to arrange a small party tonight for a group of American friends. I promised I'd introduce him to you and see that he got two good tables with a clear view of the stage, and persuade you to arrange a little supper for them as well as providing your best wine. Is that possible, Esteban?"

"The tables at the front are already engaged," Esteban told the stranger. "And we serve food only if you order it well in advance. I am sorry. But otherwise we would be delighted to have your party here." He waited for the introduction, but Medina was walking on, down the courtyard, toward the door near Reid's table. "Dr. Medina!"

"I am just going to see Magdalena, deliver her some pills for her arthritis," Medina called back.

Esteban started after him, a heavy frown on his dark face. The stranger stopped him by asking, "And when should we arrive to catch the show?"

"It starts at midnight."

"So early?"

"Tonight, yes." Esteban looked at him warily. The man spoke good Spanish, but with a strong American inflection.

"And when will Tavita herself be dancing? We can't miss that."

"I am afraid you must."

"You mean Tavita is not appearing tonight? But this is Saturday—"

"I regret, señor."

"When will she be dancing here again?"

"When she next visits Málaga." What did I say wrong? wondered Esteban, noting the flicker of interest in the stranger's blue eyes. "She dances here on Fridays and Saturdays. She is in Seville for the rest of the week."

"In Seville? That's disappointing for us. Too far to reach for tonight's show," the stranger added with heavy humor. "I hoped she might have been dancing somewhere near Málaga, just a few miles away."

Esteban inclined his head, said nothing.

"Will she be dancing in Seville tomorrow?"

"I don't know her plans," Esteban said coldly. Again he noted the flicker in the stranger's eyes. "I can give you two tables down here, señor. Would these be agreeable?"

The man looked in the direction of Esteban's pointing arm. "Well," he said slowly. "I think I'd better discuss this first with my friends. They particularly wanted to see Tavita. You understand?"

"Of course," Esteban said, bowed slightly, watched the stranger leave. For one second there, he had felt the old warning instinct. You stood at the side of the ring with the cape folded over your arm, you studied the bull's wild entry, noted the way it carried its head. Did the horns hook to the left? Or the right? How many thrusts of a *pic*, how many planted *banderillas* would it take to weaken the neck muscle just enough, lower the dangerous horn, bring these two lethal points even, give you a one-in-ten chance to escape a savage wound? Then you moved out to test the bull, swirling the cape, side-stepping, running, watching; always watching the horns and the way they were held. And sometimes your instinct about a bull could be as valuable to your life as the way you studied it. Instinct, a small warning bell sounding a moment of fear, arousing minutes of extra caution. And now, as Esteban's eyes followed the stranger out of the courtyard, there was that momentary fear in them. It passed. It always did. But he was suddenly twice as alert.

Quickly, with light steps, he walked toward the door Medina had entered. They met inside its threshold. Medina was in a hurry. "I didn't find Magdalena so I left her medicine with one of the girls. Good night, Esteban."

"No need to rush. Your friend has already gone."

Medina halted abruptly. "But I didn't expect him to wait. And he isn't my friend. He's a patient, a new one. Came into my office this evening with a strained ankle. Nothing serious. We started talking about flamenco. He's American, of course. They always know so much about flamenco and bullfighting, don't they?"

Esteban wasn't amused.

"Did you arrange two good tables for his party, later tonight?"

"He changed his mind."

"Ah, yes. Another American habit. But he will return some other night and bring many people. He will end by believing he discovered El Fenicio all by himself." Medina tried to edge past Esteban.

"What is his name? So that I will know it when he telephones about a reservation—some other evening," Esteban added smoothly. But he didn't step from the doorway.

"Name? Oh, one of those strange American names, hard to

remember. Leavis, Livis, Loamis—something like that. I'll check with my records, if you like, and get the right spelling. Pronunciation, now, is another matter," he said jovially. "I must go. I'm in a hurry. I have another house call to make before I can start enjoying my own Saturday night." He made his way into the courtyard.

Which girl? Esteban wondered as he moved quickly toward the dressing room. Constanza? Faquita? Maruja? Surely it would have to be Constanza the talkative, he thought gloomily, the girl who never could resist an audience. He stopped at the door, looked at the three dancers in various stages of readiness, each of them giving orders to the old woman who pressed and stitched for them. Silks and satins hung from hooks in the wall, billowing out dangerously near the little tables with their pots of creams and powders and rouge and hairpins. "What did he have to say?" Esteban demanded of Constanza. "And you know the rules: no men in this dressing room."

"But he's a doctor!"

"What was he doing here?"

"Nothing, nothing. He came looking for old Magdalena. Some pills or something." Constanza was more interested in choosing her dress for tonight. She favored the flame-colored one. "What about this?" she asked him.

"He just gave you the bottle of pills and left without one word?"

"He congratulated me. That was all."

"On what?"

"Well—I just happened to mention I was dancing the *seguidilla* tonight. And a Saturday night at that!" Her large brown eyes glowed with triumph, then veiled themselves in Maruja's direction.

"And you told him Tavita had gone to Granada."

"I didn't!" Constanza was frowning at her three pairs of shoes, trying to find the best contrast to her dress. "Maruja told him."

Maruja, brushing her long smooth hair with slow steady sweeps, said sarcastically, "When Tavita is called away so suddenly, who else but our little Constanza could take her place?" She dodged a thrown shoe, aimed her hairbrush in return, exchanged criticisms that became more specific as they mounted in volume.

Esteban shouted above the uproar, "Suddenly? What did you mean by telling him 'suddenly'?"

"Because it *was* suddenly," Maruja yelled back. "She left

while we were still asleep, didn't she?" Then she turned on Constanza again. "And another thing, duchess—" she began. Esteban didn't stay to listen. He left them facing each other, hands on hips, insults now flying over Faquita's head. They were good friends. The storm would soon end. By the time he reached the courtyard, the screaming had slackened into an occasional afterthought. Then there was silence, broken by full-throated laughter.

He took out his folded handkerchief, carefully mopped his brow. It had been hot in that dressing room, in every way. The warm air seemed cool by comparison but more insipid, even with all the fragrance of flowers around him. The girls must splash on that carnation perfume as if it were water. No wonder the bills ran so high, no wonder money never could be saved. There had been enough powder spilled on the dressing tables to keep a face covered for a year. But he had other worries now. Or had he?

Constanza had kept her promise: no more excited gossip about a strange man on the balcony last night. So what had Medina learned? Nothing much: perhaps no more than he might have guessed. And why should you worry about Medina? he asked himself. No reason at all. The man had an unfortunate tongue, quick to wound others. Inquisitive? Rumormongering? No, these were not Medina's faults. But why did he not speak of Señor Reid's death? Then he put it down to Medina's manners; they had been picked up abroad when he had been sent by his uncle to Paris and New York to learn medicine. Some men, like certain wines, did not travel well.

By the time Esteban had reached the back of the courtyard and passed through its arched entrance into the wineshop, he had talked himself into believing that his worry has been excessive. On the counter, a large tray of tumblers, all polished and downturned, was ready for the night's trade, but there was no sign of Jaime. Quickly, Esteban crossed to the doorway to the street, empty now but soon to be filled with taxis bringing in the Saturday tourists, and found Jaime standing just outside, as expected. "What's so interesting out there?" Esteban asked sharply. "You have plenty to do inside."

Jaime stepped back into the wineshop. "It's a very fine car but only good for driving at night," he decided aloud. "By day, the sun would roast and the dust would choke you. You might as well ride on top of a donkey for all the comfort you'd get. Now if I had money like that American, I'd buy a yellow car

—just like that one—but its top would be closed. And there would be air conditioning inside, and I'd have—"

"What American? What yellow car?"

"The one that was waiting for Dr. Medina. Just a little distance along the street. And could it start! They went zooming off, just like that." Jaime swept the linen towel in his hand sideways, cracking it like a whip.

"The tall dark man was waiting for Medina? The American who was in here asking for two tables?"

Jaime looked at Esteban curiously. "Yes. He came out first, and I followed him—politely, of course—to see the car drive off. But it didn't leave then. So I came back in here and polished some more glasses until Dr. Medina came rushing through the wineshop. Now the car will start, I thought. And I was right. It was off and away before I even got to the door."

My instinct warned me, Esteban thought. There is danger.

"Something wrong?" asked Jaime anxiously.

"Those three glasses!" Esteban pointed to the tray. "There is lint on them." He turned abruptly on his heel, stalked into the courtyard, then stood there irresolutely, staring at the empty stage.

What to do now? Call Tavita and upset her still more? Warn her about something he could not name?

Or he could call Ferrier. But what good would that do? Ferrier would ask five days, he thought bitterly. Besides, what could I report? A man arrived here, used Medina to get a few minutes alone with me and ask questions about Tavita and where she is. Not direct questions. Not exactly. But his interest was definite. And I was too clever. I tried to draw his attention to Seville. Now the man would wonder why; now he would know that I was trying to keep something hidden. Who was he? A police spy, an agent for Captain Rodriguez pretending to be an American? Who?

Yes, my instincts warned me all along. There is only one way to remove the danger from Tavita, from El Fenicio, from everything we have built together. And that is to remove Fuentes. Permanently.

Esteban walked back toward the telephone in the wineshop. But the first batch of taxis had arrived. Excited women with pink faces and short flowered dresses, fat men with glasses and light jackets, they all came jumbled in from the street, halting abruptly, looking doubtfully at the small dimly lit room, calling out they had come to the wrong place, what was that address, where's our guide—stop him paying off the taxis—hold them, hold everything. "Ladies, gentlemen," said Esteban, "follow me, if you please." He beckoned to them, silencing the small confusion, and led the way into the courtyard. His telephone call would have to wait. Perhaps wait until tomorrow. Time to decide. Time to make sure that his story was perfect in all details, bringing no disaster to Tavita. Yes, he needed time— not Ferrier's four or five days—but just enough to be quite sure in his own mind that he was acting wisely.

He bowed for the ladies, who were pleased with the tables he had given them, and sent Jaime running to get the guitarist on stage. Yes, he assured the gentlemen, this courtyard would soon be full; yes, it was old, quite historic; no, the dancing would not start until almost midnight, but it was good to come early and secure the best tables. Tonight, he answered all these usual questions with good grace. After all, he had to thank this group of tourists. A telephone call to Captain Rodriguez was not something to be made on impulse.

15

When O'Connor came out of the study, twenty minutes later, he was no longer smiling. His face was grim. He said nothing at first, just walked up and down the full length of the living room for several turns, head slightly bent, eyes fixed on the floor in front of him as if he were finding a solution there. Then he stopped in front of Ferrier. "When are you expected in Granada?"

"In about four or five days. I didn't know how long it would take in Washington to—"

"Four days . . . That gives us a little leeway. But I think we had better act as if it weren't there." He gave a brief nod to Ferrier, eyes easing from their worry. Well, thought Ferrier with a surge of relief, he doesn't think I've messed things up completely. "Ben," O'Connor went on, "we still need you. Sorry. But you know this part of the country well, don't you?"

"Andalusia? Yes. Alice and I spend Easter in Seville each year, and branch off to Córdoba, Granada, Ronda. It's—"

"Where is Alice now? Waiting for you in Toledo?"

"No. She's with the kids and a visiting sister from—"

"Good. Just a couple of days more, Ben. Perhaps less. Nothing indiscreet, nothing to involve you. We'll keep your status simon-pure."

"Which means," Waterman told Ferrier, "he needs someone to drive his car."

"You know the roads," O'Connor said persuasively, "and possibly—if I remember you—all the short cuts, too. By the way, would you drive Mike out to the airport? He is leaving pretty soon."

Mike was startled, but he said nothing. So we've got something, he thought as he rose and followed O'Connor toward the hall. Quickly, his mind reviewed the various plans O'Connor had laid out for him on their journey to Málaga. If it had all been a false alarm, they both would have returned to Washington, trying to console themselves with the fact that at least they had made the effort, at least they had checked. If there had been only a report from Reid, then they both would have returned to Washington, and no consolations needed. If there was not only a valuable report but also serious complications, O'Connor would stay behind while Mike high-tailed it to Washington, sending out en route a call for reinforcements or whatever additional help O'Connor might need. If there was no report worth sending on to Washington, but a completely fouled-up situation, then they'd both sit out the next few days in Málaga until the dust settled and they could see what had to be done. It's Plan Three, Mike was thinking as he reached the hall: me for Washington. He could feel the adrenaline beginning to pump into his veins.

"Good luck," O'Connor told him, shaking hands, passing over the lighter discreetly. "No delay. You know whom to reach. Also, have the FBI called in on this—get Bill, if possible."

So it's their headache, too, thought Mike. We are on to something really widespread. "I'll do that. Will you phone the airport, let Max know I'm on my way? I'll avoid the main entrance, use the side gate." He slipped his hand into his pocket, left the lighter safely there, brought out a scrap of paper. "Here's the airport number—I jotted it down, thought we might have to use it again." He glanced over at Ferrier and Waterman to check if they had noticed the lighter disappearing into his pocket, but his little subterfuge had worked. Waterman was washing down last mouthfuls of a sandwich with his Scotch, and Ferrier was paying no attention at all.

"Granada is the place," O'Connor was saying. "And I'll need all the help I can get. Double the reinforcements, if that's possible. Get Max to handle it. Tell him—" O'Connor paused, looked across the room at Waterman. "Ben, what's the biggest hotel in Granada?"

"The Palace. It's also the best."

"Ian—do you know it?"

"That's where I planned to stay." Ferrier was amused, both by his promotion to first name and by O'Connor's gentle diplomacy —old Ben wasn't to feel left out, although the answer to O'Connor's unspoken question couldn't come from Ben. Ferrier gave it. "It's handy for everything. Plenty of short-term tourists, but restrained. Its situation couldn't be better." Within walking distance of Tavita's house. Ferrier wondered if O'Connor had got his meaning.

O'Connor had. "Sounds good. What's the Granada airport like?"

"There isn't any."

"*What?*"

"That's right," Waterman said. "It used to handle light planes, but no longer. It was closed down a couple of years ago."

O'Connor's shock changed to frustration. "Are you sure?"

Ferrier said, "Why else do you think I had to rent a car to get here from Granada?"

O'Connor shook his head as he took a map of Spain from his pocket and unfolded it. Goddammit, he thought, this really will slow everything up: no easy escape. Twice as difficult, twice as dangerous. For we'll be on our own—no help from the authorities here—in a city of over one hundred and fifty thousand people, and no airport. And the nearest airports seemed to be either at Málaga or at Seville. And of course there was Cádiz, still farther away from Granada but only a few miles east of Rota, where there was an American naval base. Too far perhaps, but an interesting speculation, at least. "Ben," he asked, "how long does it take to drive from here to Granada? Three hours, with all these mountains?"

"Less if the traffic is light. Depends on the time of day."

"And from Granada to Seville?" From the map, the road was longer but possibly easier. "It's well over two hundred miles."

"Around four hours if you put your mind to it."

"Thanks, Ben." O'Connor folded the map, shoved it back into his pocket. "Now what about getting Mike to the airport here? We're in a bit of a rush."

"Oh?" Ben put down his glass, rose to his feet. "Sounds an important young man," he said as he looked over at Mike.

"Don't put ideas into his head. And I want you to hurry because I expect you back here. To collect me and drive me to our hotel and let me stretch out on a nice flat bed. Dammit, Ben, don't you ever need to sack out? I've been traveling since—"

"Sure, sure," Waterman said. "Time zones. That's what kills everyone."

Ferrier said, "Use my car and save yourself walking a couple of blocks for yours. Come on, Ben, I'll see you out and lock the back door after you."

Mike called to Waterman, "I'll meet you down near the front gate." He waited until both Ferrier and Waterman had left the room. "So you'll be in Granada. Palace Hotel. Reinforcements make contact with you there."

O'Connor nodded. Strange how talk of a nice flat bed made

him realize how tired he actually was. He got hold of himself. "Max will be in charge of them. They'll be his hand-picked men."

"Special action?" There was a touch of envy in Mike's voice.

"You never can tell. I want them in Granada by noon tomorrow."

"That's pressing hard."

"Max can manage it. He has connections in Seville; some good friends there. And in Granada. Tell him to head back there once he sees you safely transferred at Torrejon." That was the American air base just south of Madrid.

Top security and high speed combined, thought Mike. "No problem," he predicted. "The problem would be if you tried to keep Max out of Granada. He has had a pretty disappointing evening." Max had stayed on board their plane at the Málaga airport, kept out of sight from any inquisitive eyes. Which would make him, of course, doubly valuable in Granada: a fresh face, nonidentified and unexpected, was always a definite asset.

"We didn't need him here, as things turned out. But we do, in Granada. Tell him that. We'll need him. And three cars, with Spanish registration. And one light aircraft, capacity for six or seven, waiting at Seville."

"That's how you are getting out of Granada?"

"It's the surest way." The road to Seville might take longer to drive than the one back to Málaga, but it was straighter and simpler, with no high mountains to face, and less chance of an unexpected ambush. Hell, thought O'Connor—listen to me putting in the orders and I don't even know if we are going to deliver. But certain basic arrangements had to be made; they couldn't be left to wild inspiration at the last minute. "Okay, Mike. That's all. On your way."

"What about your flight across the Atlantic? I'd better warn them, when I transfer at Torrejon, to expect you and some friends—when?"

"Just tell them to expect us." He had almost forgotten that hop back across the Atlantic, perhaps because it seemed such a small problem compared with reaching Seville and getting safely away from there. Somehow, Seville worried him: it might be too obvious, and the opposition could be as well organized there as they were in Málaga. Our one hope is speed, he decided. If we could be in and out of Granada before the opposition even learned we were there, then Seville would be no trouble at all.

"Can't have you taking a commercial flight," Mike said with a grin.

"Not you, either," O'Connor said quickly. "We don't want either of us being hijacked to Cairo or Cuba." The idea appalled him: that would really muck up every goddamned thing. But he smiled, opened the door. "Take care."

Mike patted the lighter, deep inside his pocket. "It's part of my skin." Not even Max would be told about it. "See you in Washington."

O'Connor watched the young man ease his way out onto the steps, vanish into the shadows of the garden. He stood there for a brief minute, listening to the silence of the night. And he thought of all the recent arguments and uncertainty about America's youth. Well, that was one worry he didn't share. He had met too many young men and women—not connected with his work, either—in the last ten years, who knew some history, recognized some facts about the world, and didn't cop out from responsibility. Good luck, Mike. He closed the door.

Perhaps the trickiest part of Mike's journey might be boarding the plane at Málaga without being spotted. (He had restrained himself from giving Mike instructions about that; they would only have been a demonstration of a lack of confidence. Mike was good, or he wouldn't have been brought along on this trip.) Certainly, if Ian Ferrier was to be believed—and he was inclined to believe him at present—the opposition was very much alive in Málaga. "All over the place," Ferrier had said. "And we've been nowhere." Well, decided O'Connor, I'll hear Ferrier's story, all of it; whether his head aches or not, he has to spill it out tonight. No more delays. We're leaving the nowhere behind and getting somewhere.

Quickly, he went into the study, picked up the receiver, consulted Mike's slip of paper. It was a special number at the airport, connecting with the plane itself. As he waited to get through, he wondered if Ferrier had read much of Lord Acton. He would know the usual quotation that was bandied around frequently, these days: *Power tends to corrupt; absolute power corrupts absolutely.* But there were other passages in Acton well worth remembering, and one particularly applicable to the events in Málaga that had so depressed and angered Ferrier. *Do not overlook the strength of the bad cause, or the weakness of the good.* Yes, thought O'Connor sadly, that just about covers everything. *Do not overlook. . . .*

Ferrier heard O'Connor's quiet voice in the study as he returned from locking up behind Waterman. More telephoning, he thought, and dropped into the nearest chair. He wished it were his bed upstairs: a long cold shower and then cool white sheets, deep deep sleep and complete forgetting. At least, things seemed to be in some control now; that was an improvement. He glanced at his watch. Just after half past ten, and all was—if not well— certainly better than expected. Even his head had stopped feeling like a lump of clay balanced uneasily on top of his neck. It was tender to touch, sharp to remind him to treat it gently. But that was little enough. Considering. Two seconds slower, just one hesitation lasting an intake of breath, and that blow would have caught him full on the back of his head. Which proved one thing: when you move, move. And no wasted argument.

"Now," said O'Connor, coming into the room and drawing up a chair across from Ferrier, "I'd like your complete story. We have just about three quarters of an hour before we can expect Ben back here. Time enough?"

"If I stick to the essentials." Ferrier had been over them so often in his own mind, today, that there was no problem about marshaling them into order. "They begin at El Fenicio. I was sitting at Reid's table, waiting for his return." Clearly, quietly, without emotion, Ferrier began as concise an account as possible. Apart from the subject, it might have been one of his reports back home on recent developments in the Soviet fractional-orbital bomb system.

O'Connor listened well. No interruptions, no raised eyebrows or politely repressed amusement, no quizzical comments or half-veiled criticisms. He really listened. And the result was that Ferrier, his confidence in O'Connor growing steadily, finished his report well within the time limit.

"And that," said O'Connor after Ferrier ended, and he had caught his breath, "is a considerable that. Isn't it?" He looked at Ferrier for a long minute, then rose and poured a couple of Scotches. "Reid did a fine job. That recorded conversation with Fuentes is absolutely vital. Our thanks to you, Ian, for making sure it reached safe hands."

"There's one footnote I should add. It's Jeff's own impression of Fuentes. He said you should be wary of the man's over-all strategy. His tactics, meanwhile, are to give you just enough information to tease you along, get your help; and once he reaches wherever he wants to go, he is cutting himself off from you, lying low, clamming up, waiting. Waiting until his enemies in Cuba are discredited. Then he hopes to be reinstated. He is only a temporary defector, who will give nothing away that could really damage his return to Department Thirteen. That is his real aim."

O'Connor was thoughtful as he handed Ferrier his drink.

Then he repeated grimly, "Give nothing away that could really damage his return . . . Well, let's see what we can do, shall we?" He raised his glass, and they both drank to his promise. O'Connor's voice came back to normal. "Frankly, there were some parts of your story I didn't like at all."

Ferrier's sense of accomplishment left him. He looked at O'Connor, his eyes narrowing.

"They got Tavita's Granada address. Right out of your wallet. Not good, not good."

Ferrier relaxed. "I know," he agreed. "It links her too closely with me. Could be dangerous for her."

"Or vice versa. It was in her handwriting, too. That's going to interest them—they're probably checking on any autographed photographs of her, right now." O'Connor rubbed his brow worriedly. "And I didn't like that whole silver pencil bit. Reid's was lifted from his hospital room—they are probably taking it to pieces looking for microfilm—and Lucas knows the girl Ames carries an identical pencil. That's danger right there for her." He looked at Ferrier, said carefully, "Unless, of course, Martin's suspicion about her is right." He still kept his eyes on Ferrier. "No comment?"

"I don't believe she has sold out."

"Why not? Because she cut loose from the Wild Left at Berkeley when she found her group was being manipulated by communists?"

Ferrier shook his head. "That's a good story—always has been —but there was more than that to her. It was the way she reacted when she saw the kids at the beach. The lost ones, the lotos-eaters, searching for the never-never land. It hurt her to watch them. It hurt me. Blown minds, unhappy eyes, sullen mouths. All of them crowding together for the only courage they know. If Amanda had been just another version of Lucas, either she would have walked past them without a qualm—accepted the scene as one proof that America was on the skids, that her theories about the West were right—or she might even have risked a little gloating just to see me squirm. But no. The scene hurt her. Hurt badly. She's worried about the future of the country. Really worried." Ferrier took a deep breath. "So the hell with Martin. He has been infiltrated and he chose the easiest excuse. That's all."

"Martin must have had good reason for whatever he said." O'Connor was playing stranger to all this: the dispassionate observer who did not want to trespass on a colleague's responsibility.

A reason, certainly; but I might not call it good, thought Ferrier. "Is Martin important?" he asked frankly. "Is his section, department, group, whatever you call it—is it important?"

"Everything is important in this kind of work, big or small."

Ferrier had to smile. "Well, is his particular setup important in a big or a small way?"

"I'd imagine," O'Connor said cautiously, "that its significance is growing, now that the Soviet fleet is all over the Mediterranean."

"In that case, infiltration is really something to worry about."

O'Connor broke his neutrality with a definite nod.

"Then," asked Ferrier angrily, "why doesn't he go after the man who delayed sending you my telephone message? I phoned Madrid from the hospital before three in the morning, Málaga time. You didn't hear about it until dawn, Washington time. There's a six-hour summertime lag between Spain and our eastern seaboard. Whatever happened in all those extra hours to a simple little message that didn't even need decoding? You could have received it last night."

O'Connor said nothing at first. I was in the office until ten o'clock last night, he was thinking; I could easily have received that message from Málaga before then. "I take it you don't think much of Martin's efficiency?" he asked with a smile. But his own feelings were bitter. He masked his worry. "Well, Martin is out of our present operation now. We don't need his assistance. I have other sources." Max, for instance. Max won't drag his feet, or let others loiter, either. "As for the Ames girl—Martin could be right about her, you know. To be frank, he has a reputation for being cautious. Not imaginative, not daring. But quietly capable. He has been in this kind of work for twenty years. One of the old hands." Too old? wondered O'Connor. That delay in the delivery of the message from Málaga could have been absolutely disastrous. As it was, there had been irreparable loss: an agent dead. And there was now a feeling of emergency that was too tight for comfort. So let Martin clean up the mess in his own back yard—no doubt he was already investigating who was asleep on the job and why—and we'll concentrate on our own problems, O'Conner decided. He glanced at his watch. "I'll need your help in Granada, Ian. Will you give it?"

And what would he say if I refused? "I'll vouch for you," Ferrier said with a grin. "That's what you want, isn't it?"

"It's the quickest way of approaching Fuentes. You will get in touch with Tavita, meet Tomás Fuentes, and then assure him I'm the real O'Connor and no substitute."

"That should be simple enough."

"Check into the Palace Hotel tomorrow morning. Around nine. I'll be there ahead of you. But pay no attention to me at all. Have breakfast, read the papers, study the view, and then—soon after ten o'clock—call Tavita."

"Call her? From the hotel?"

"Why not? What else would a man be expected to do if he carried Tavita's address in his pocket? Make it a friendly call, really friendly—alone in Granada, hoping to see her as much as possible, can you spend the day with her beginning now? Right away, the sooner the better." O'Connor stopped abruptly as he noticed the amusement on Ferrier's face. "Sorry. I won't need to brief you on how to talk to a woman. Okay, okay. Handle it your way. And after the call, you set out for Tavita's address. You've got it?"

Ferrier passed over the sheet of paper on which Esteban had written the full directions. "I've memorized it this time," he said pointedly. "You can keep it."

O'Connor studied it. "How far from the hotel?"

Ferrier repeated the directions that Tavita had given him. "A few minutes' walk," he ended.

"Good. You'll reach it easily by half past ten, and I'll be right behind you. Ben and I will leave the hotel by car, drive around for a little, then past Tavita's house. He'll drop me there quickly, and I'll be at the front door in a matter of seconds. Have the old girl—Magdalena?—ready to let me in. No waiting. Ben will drive on; get back eventually to the hotel. That way, there will be no cars parked anywhere near Tavita's house—neither yours nor mine. Got all that?"

Ferrier nodded. "And afterward?"

"You can relax and enjoy Granada." Unless, of course, there were complications.

"Yes?" asked Ferrier, watching O'Connor's eyes.

"That's what I'm hoping for you, at least," O'Conner said blandly. "Plans have always got to be elastic—strong enough to carry the load, flexible enough to stretch a little."

"Like the fat lady's girdle."

"Just about," O'Connor said, and broke into a broad smile. He gave one last look at Tavita's address, took out his matches and struck one into a flame. He watched the piece of paper catch fire, curl up into a thin sheet of black ash; then he dropped it onto an empty plate, mashed it into fragments among the bread crumbs from the sandwiches. "Most determined handwriting," he observed. "Whose?"

"Esteban's."

"Ah, yes—the ex-bullfighter. You know, that was another thing I didn't like in your story."

"Esteban? A very decent man," Ferrier said quickly.

"Which also means a simple, honest man who sees things in strict black and white. He hates Fuentes, doesn't he?"

"But he's devoted to Tavita."

"Then he has had a real battle raging in his mind for the last two days." O'Connor shook his head in sympathy.

"Should I call him? Tell him I'm on my way to Granada. No delay, now."

"The only wrong thing with that idea is that I don't want anyone to know we are moving in so fast. Surprise is our best weapon." Our only one, O'Connor thought worriedly. But where the hell was Ben? Had Mike taken off safely? Was Max now being briefed, starting to make his plans, sending some special messages of his own? "Fuentes is a tricky customer," he said, trying to stop thinking about Mike's journey. "He will have his own ideas about where he is going. Reid was right: Fuentes is using us, for a small *quid pro quo*, to reach his hiding place. He must have had this planned for months."

"Switzerland and a numbered bank account," Ferrier suggested.

"How much did Reid actually tell you about Fuentes?" O'Connor asked quickly.

"Just what I've already told you. Enough to warn you—in case the lighter got lost."

Strange, realized O'Connor, that this man knows more about Fuentes than anyone else except myself. And in one thing, he added to that, he actually knows more than I do. He knows how Fuentes looks. "Sorry about the early start tomorrow. But I don't want you—" He broke off as the telephone rang. He glanced at his watch again. Something wrong at the airport?

"Do I take it?" Ferrier asked.

O'Connor nodded, rose with Ferrier, followed him into the study, stood impatiently by.

"It's Martin," said Ferrier, covering the mouthpiece. "For you."

O'Connor swore softly, took the receiver. He listened patiently. "Nothing to worry about," he said at last. "Mike is needed back in Washington, that's all. I'll travel on with Ben to Madrid, stop off at a couple of places and meet some people there. Might as well, while I am in Spain . . . Yes, yes. I know there isn't any flight out of here on Sunday morning. We'll be driving. . . . All right. If you have uncovered anything urgent, you can reach me in Granada. At the Palace. We should be there around lunchtime. . . . Ferrier? No, he won't be here tomorrow. . . . I'll tell him, but I think he'll see to his car himself. . . . Sure, sure, he'll let the housekeeper know to expect Reid's lawyer. Good-bye. Thanks for all your co-operation. . . . No. Nothing to worry about, I assure you." He replaced the receiver quickly, making sure of an end to the call. He stood looking at it for a few moments, then went back to the living room.

O'Connor was frowning. Surely, he was thinking, Martin didn't expect me to give any serious information over that phone? Besides, it is none of his business, anyway. Possibly he's just trying to give the impression of being tremendously efficient. "Well," he asked Ferrier, who was being tactfully silent, "did you piece that conversation together?"

"Some of it," Ferrier said frankly. "You weren't bothering about any conspiratorial whisper, were you?"

Something else was amusing O'Connor. "At least we know Mike is safely out of Málaga." He laughed outright at the way the information had come to him. Sideways, as it were, in the form of a mild complaint. "Martin got worried when he heard I wasn't on that plane."

"He had someone watching the airport?"

"Just in case of a crisis." O'Connor looked at Ferrier with a mischievous gleam in his eyes. "Changing your mind about him being ineffective?"

Ferrier let that go. "What was that bit about my car?"

"He offered to have someone take it back to Granada for you if you were traveling off in another direction."

"Obliging of him." So Martin had noted the car's registration plates.

"It was meant kindly. Oh, yes—and another bit of fussing: nothing is to be removed from here. Two of his men are coming to make an inventory. Close examination of everything. So tell the housekeeper to leave things as they are."

"If," Ferrier said wryly, "she'll let two strange men enter, after what she has been through tonight. She'll probably call the police."

"We'll let Martin handle that," O'Connor said generously. "Now where was I when his call interrupted us?"

"Early start. And you didn't want me to do something."

"That's right. I don't want you taking any risks on that road to Granada. Keep the speed down, will you?"

Ferrier caught the full meaning. "Don't worry. I'll make sure of getting there."

"That's all I want. If you are followed, don't try to—" He cut off, listening intently.

"That's the old Mercedes." It was moving carefully up the drive toward the yard.

O'Connor was on his feet, grabbing his jacket, pulling it on as he hurried Ferrier toward the back of the house. "If you are followed," he repeated, "don't try to outdistance them. Play it safe; keep everything natural, unworried."

"Okay, okay," Ferrier said reassuringly. He unlocked the kitchen door. Ben Waterman was waiting outside, handing over Ferrier's car keys with a happy flourish. He was in good spirits and all ready to tell them of some small triumph—that was the look in his eyes—but Ferrier never heard it, for O'Connor caught Waterman's arm, said, "Later, later," in a low voice. Together they headed down toward the front gate. Ferrier locked the kitchen door, went quickly through the long passage to try to have a parting glimpse of them from the dining-room windows. But he could see nothing. They must have left the moon-silvered stretch of driveway for the mixed shadows of the garden.

He wasted no more time, himself, but made for the staircase. He did not switch off the lights, deciding that a plunge into blackness would mark O'Connor's exit too definitely. He was equally careful about the lights in his own room, relying on the one at his bedside already turned on by Concepción when she had tidied the place. She had done more than that: the clothes he had given her for cleaning and pressing that morning were all hanging neatly in the wardrobe. Which solved a small problem. A man who liked to travel with only one bag couldn't afford to mess up his two jackets within twenty-four hours. Twenty-four? Even less than that, since he had sat down at a table in the courtyard of El Fenicio.

He was slowing up. He fumbled with his alarm clock, but made sure—careful, now, careful—it was set for five. That would give him time to pack, leave a note for Concepción (inventory, plus thanks, plus a more practical token for his gratitude), and set him well on the road before six. He placed the clock on the table close to his pillow, stood looking at it, stood thinking of tomorrow if only to stop remembering the pain of this day.

Then he got hold of himself, moved quickly. He stripped, showered, fell into bed, drifted away. Into sleep.

16

It was the easiest time of the week for a drive over the mountain highway. There were no trucks, no farmers' carts, today; and, as yet, only some early-rising tourists (the busloads would come later) and a few Spaniards in compact Simcas setting out for Sunday visits to their families. The olive groves sloping down to the wide valleys were empty of workers, and from the bleached walls of distant hill towns came the occasional ringing of bells, far off and dreamlike. The road was narrow—a two-lane job—but well surfaced and beautifully engineered. Ferrier kept to a safe forty on its higher reaches, made up to a steady seventy on its flatter stretches once he reached the high plateau that led toward Granada. Now and again (very much now and again), there was a small roadside village with one short dusty street closely lined by simple houses, a large church, a sleeping café, an unobtrusive police station on its outskirts. Here, he dropped his speed to a polite fifteen miles an hour, avoided all yelping dogs and straying chickens, didn't alarm the black-clothed women making their way to early Mass, didn't attract any evident interest from the couple of grave-faced men of the Guardia Civil who were already on duty. But the car—make, color, vintage—would be noted; its number remembered. The way of the transgressor was not made easy in this part of the world, thought Ferrier. Here, church and state never slept.

His spirits rose like Granada's three hills as he saw them come into view with their background of snow-tipped mountains in the distance and their clustering Moorish palaces, Christian towers and spires, woods and walls and ramparts and cliffs. Overhead was blue sky, a mounting sun, but the air was still fresh and cool. In every way, the day had begun well. He was almost half an hour early, he had not been followed. He would have plenty of time for a real breakfast (he had broken his fast with a handful of grapes and a hunk of bread, picked up in his hurry through Concepción's kitchen) and an intensive study of his map of Gra-

225

nada. He never liked feeling baffled by a place; get to know its layout and it became friendly. Even now, from his last visit here, he could find his way through the half-old, half-modernized town, trolley-car lines threaded through narrow streets, colored electric lights strung in garlands overhead, medieval squares and plane trees and flowers and Moorish-style courtyards, to start climbing up toward the high ground where the Palace Hotel stood. There, in front of its entrance was a large slope of triangular space where he could park his car among a hundred others. He noted the mixture of registration plates, as well as the markings on some giant Europa buses of the opulent-tour type arranged neatly side by side like a row of howdahed elephants. Dutch, German, English, Swedish, French. Two of them were being packed with overnight baggage, preparing to leave. So he would find a room, all right, and that worry was over. He put on his jacket, buttoned his collar, tightened his tie, gave his bag to a uniformed boy, and entered the large, discreetly busy lobby. First stage completed, he thought. I've arrived.

He telephoned Tavita. She was half awake at first, and sharply annoyed. Then there was a moment of absolute astonishment, disbelief. And after that, excited and tremulous, a touching welcome. When could she see him? Soon—soon? How wonderful, how marvelous. Come and have breakfast and look at the view she had promised him. In half an hour? She'd be waiting. "But of course I ought to have known," she ended. "It's the fourteenth, isn't it? Fourteen always makes me happy." If anyone had been listening to their talk, he would have thought it only meant two people were planning a most enticing Sunday. A pity, thought Ferrier as he left the hotel and took the quiet road south from the giant triangle, that it wasn't true. The trouble about this kind of job was that—quite contrary to popular opinion and movie scripts—it played hell with your sex life. In between crises, no doubt an intelligence agent relaxed and enjoyed himself; but among the harsh realities of physical danger and intellectual tension, the passionate lover became a romantic myth. When too much was at stake, a man sobered up. He had to. Strangely enough, he was perhaps more of a man for doing just that. Which, decided Ferrier, was an uncomfortable truth for someone who had always been set on his own pleasures. You're miscast, he told himself; you are too damned selfish for this type of work. All right, all right, let's get it done. Second stage completed. You are on your way.

La Soledad, like the rest of the scattered houses along this road, was almost hidden by its high wall. Only its tiled roof was visible. If the name had not been delicately scrolled on an elaborate iron gate, he would have passed it by. There was a driveway, straight and steep, swerving sharply as soon as he passed through the gate, descending right below the wall to reach a small turn-around for cars in front of the main door. Magdalena was there, waiting for him, pulling him into a hall before he had even taken his bearings. All he had time to note was that the house was of one story, with no windows on this side, and smaller than he had expected. The entrance hall was small, too, semicircular in shape, paneled with elaborate wood carvings, and fairly dim. But the room into which it curved was large and flooded with light from a wall of floor-to-ceiling windows. Outside was a narrow terrace, the tops of trees from a lower terrace, and, beyond all that, a view—down over a fall in the land to the cluster of small roofs far below, to foreshortened church towers and bald patches of little plazas; across that and up to another rise, covered with trees. And then, to his right, all the sharp slopes eased out into a plain that stretched to the horizon, meeting blue with dusty gold.

"So you approve," Tavita said behind him. She held out both hands to him as her greeting.

He took them, stood looking at her. "And of you, too." She had dressed simply, in a long white caftan, soft and loose. No jewelry. Little make-up. Smooth hair brushed to a gleam of dark silk, heavily knotted at the nape of her neck.

"I kept you waiting," she said.

"I was five minutes early."

"Come inside. We can talk better there. Sounds carry." She led him back into the room, one hand still in his. She faced him again. Suddenly, her magnificent eyes were filled with tears. "Oh, Ian—what went wrong? He was such a strong man, so—"

"I know. I know. But we must talk later about Jeff. Now there is urgent business."

"What?" She was shocked. She drew her hand away.

"Tomás Fuentes."

That was all he had needed to say. She drew a deep breath, steadied her emotions. Intensely, low-voiced, she said, "I hate that man. He is a spoiler. Of grief and of love and of all that is true and honest." Angrily, she kicked aside a floor cushion, sat down on a couch. "All right, then. Business. What business?" She began pouring coffee from a pot on the brass tray on the low table at her side. "Magdalena!" she called sharply to the hall. "You've forgotten the honey. And what are you doing by the door?"

"I asked her to watch it," Ferrier said quickly. "There is a man who is coming to see you. He wants to enter quietly without any waiting. As I did."

"To see me?"

"You. And Tomás."

She stopped pouring the coffee, set the copper pot down on the tray with a crash, almost upsetting the cups.

"Careful," he said, taking the pot from her hand. "This table doesn't look as if it could stand many shocks like that one." Mother-of-pearl inlay balanced on four wood-lace legs. He finished the pouring, set the cup in front of her. "Drink this." To Magdalena, who looked as if she were deserting her post, he called over, "Stay there! Tavita can do without honey this morning." He looked at Tavita with a grin. "Can't you?"

She nodded, half smiling. "So you just walk into my house and take charge, do you?" But she drank the coffee obediently, ate half a slice of cake, took the cigarette he had lighted for her, relaxed. "Who is this man?" she asked quietly.

"He comes from Washington."

"But so soon?"

"He had come over here to see Jeff. He saw me instead."

"So that is why you did not have to go to Washington? But where did you meet him? And how?"

"I'll tell you about that later," he said, trying to keep his voice easy, curb his impatience. There was no time for any explanations, only time enough to make her trust O'Connor. "He is going to help you. He will solve all our problems." I hope, I hope. . . .

"Did Jeff trust him?"

"He would have trusted him."

"And you?"

"Yes."

She thought about that, watching his face. Then she shrugged her shoulders. "Then I suppose I must."

Thank God, he thought; no questions that have to be parried, no tactful evasions to be made.

But then she said, "Surely he is not here alone?"

"I think we'll just trust him to arrange all that, too."

"Is he an important man in Washington?"

"His enemies think he is." Why else would Tomás Fuentes have picked out O'Connor for help? "Where is Tomás' room, by the way? Can he hear us talking?" This was a strange house, not small and one-storied, as he had at first imagined. There were other floors beneath this one; that much he had guessed from the layers of terraces outside.

She shook her head solemnly.

"He is downstairs?"

She shook her head again, crumbled the remaining half-slice of cake, ate a small mouthful. "It's so dry without honey," she told him.

"Tavita! Where is Tomás?"

"Safe. Completely safe. But not here. See"—she added delightedly—"I can produce surprises, too."

"Not here?" He was horrified.

She relented. "We can reach him easily. Within ten minutes, fifteen at most."

"How?"

"By walking." She watched him with amusement. "Ian, Ian—you must trust me as much as I trust you. Did you really think I would keep that monster in the same house as myself? I would never have slept at all last night if I knew he was here. In any case, it was a bad-enough night. I was only beginning to sleep when I was awakened at nine. The telephone. A call from—from the International Associated Press, yes, that's who it was. They are writing some articles about Granada, and are interviewing several people. Photographs, too. How we live. That kind of thing. They want to photograph me here—in the studio—dancing, of course, and in my best costumes."

"And what did you say?"

"I told them it was impossible for the next four or five days. After that, I would be delighted." She looked at him anxiously. "Why not? The articles will be published in London and New York, perhaps even in Paris. Important for me, Ian. Truly."

At least, he thought, she had put them off for four or five days—keeping them away from this house as long as she had expected to wait for him.

"Of course," she went on with a touch of regret, "if I had known you were coming here today, I could have arranged for them to photograph me tomorrow. Even tonight. Tomás will be out of Granada by then, won't he?"

He didn't answer that question. For one thing, he did not know O'Connor's plans; for another, the less Tavita knew, the safer she would be. "They telephoned you at nine? From where?"

"I don't know. Long-distance, I think."

"Early for Sunday morning, wasn't it?"

"But they are arriving in Granada today. They wanted a—a preliminary talk—preliminary?—yes, that's what they wanted this evening. You understand," she added placatingly, "they must look at the studio, see if it has suitable lighting, all that kind of thing." She saw she was worrying him somehow, so she changed the subject. "Now you see why I was so cross with you when you called—until I realized it was you, actually you. I was trying to fall asleep again. Such a hideous night. And yours? You must have had an early start. More coffee?"

He glanced at his watch. "No, thanks." And now he was worrying why O'Connor was late. Six minutes. Not much. But later than expected.

"We'll go out to the terrace, and I shall point out the view. And you can tell me all about your own work. Or is it very secret? Is that why you don't talk about it?" She had risen, coming onto her feet in one lithe movement from the soft cushions of the couch, not even needing the hand he had put out to help her.

His own work . . . He hadn't given it more than five minutes' thought in the last thirty-six hours. If a vacation was measured by absolute change, then his trip to Spain scored high. "Not so secret. Not usually, at least."

"Then tell me about it." She walked slowly, gracefully, each step almost in the motion of a dance, toward the terrace door.

Command performance, he thought, and smiled as he shook his head. "No. It isn't the kind of job that interests most people, not unless they are doing it." Or could understand the basics. But it always seemed a bit pretentious to emphasize its intricacies; specialization was usually boring to the uninitiated.

"So dull as that?"

His smile broadened. Hers was the usual reaction. "Well," he said lightly, "it keeps me from confusing shoptalk with conversation."

"Shoptalk?" That was a new word to her. She swirled round to face him, her wide caftan billowing out.

"Talking about one's work."

"Oh," she said. That was a new idea to her too. She thought about it, didn't like it. "But what is wrong with that? Why shouldn't I talk about dancing and audiences and performances I have given?" she demanded.

"No reason why you shouldn't. And no reason why you should. You don't need to talk about yourself. Every movement you make tells me who you are." Even the way she was stepping onto the terrace, right now, was pure Tavita.

She swirled round again, her eyes laughing. And then, as they glanced past him, they became cold and appraising. He turned round, too. Robert O'Connor was standing at the threshold of the room. In the hall behind him, old Magdalena was locking the front door. Hell, thought Ferrier, I never even heard him come in.

O'Connor took a few steps into the room, glanced around it quickly, selected a corner far away from the windows. "Sorry about the delay. And we'd better keep away from that terrace. There's a fine view of it from the trees on the opposite side. That's one of the reasons I'm late. I was over there just about twenty minutes ago. Saw you standing outside, Ian."

"So you were studying the lie of the land, were you?" I might have guessed.

"And the general layout of this house. It helps."

"Not this time. He isn't here."

O'Connor looked at him. Then he looked at Tavita. His face, in spite of his control, tightened visibly.

"He's in Granada, all right," Ferrier said quickly, and went back to the terrace door where Tavita still stood—she was obviously waiting for O'Connor to come forward and be presented—and closed it as he pulled her gently inside. "Come on, Tavita," he urged her, "you heard the man. We'll keep well out of sight of those windows."

"Is he afraid?" she asked cuttingly. She did not resist Ferrier's arm, but she came unwillingly.

O'Connor said, "Yes, I'm afraid for you, señorita. There was an attempt to follow us here. That is the second reason why I am late." He broke into fluent Spanish. "My apologies for this intrusion, and my regrets that I did not think it wise to come over to the window and greet you properly. Now would you have the kindness to ask your maid to leave us?"

She gestured to Magdalena, who plodded down the stairway at the side of the room. "All the way, Magdalena!" she called after her, and they could hear the thump of heels take a second flight of stairs, diminishing gradually until there was only silence. Tavita studied O'Connor carefully. "Who tried to follow you? The police?"

"I don't think so. There are others who are as much interested in Tomás Fuentes as the police."

"Who?"

O'Connor exchanged a quick, despairing look with Ferrier. "It would be safer for you, Señorita Vergara, if you did not know—"

"Who?"

"His old comrades," O'Connor said briefly.

"So this is why you help Tomás Fuentes?" Tavita looked at them reprovingly. "Now that sounds something that could be true. That is something I can believe. Not that you came all the way from Washington to save Tavita, but that you came to steal Fuentes away from his communist friends." She was delighted as she noticed the consternation on both their faces. "I don't like them, either, señor. Please sit down." She chose a chair backed well into the corner he had selected. "Is this safe enough?" she asked him mischievously.

Ferrier could almost feel the edge of the words tipping O'Connor's tongue: We are not here for fun and games, señorita. He caught O'Connor's eye again, shook his head almost imperceptibly. Play it her way, Bob, he told him silently; it will be quicker in the end.

O'Connor masked his impatience. "It's too bad we can't risk going out on the terrace. It must have a superb view. An interesting house, altogether. Quite old, isn't it? You have restored it with great taste. The pillars around that doorway, for instance—"

"Ah, you noticed?" She was pleased. "I must take you on a little tour."

Oh no, thought Ferrier, and repressed a groan. He gave full marks to O'Connor for his restraint.

"After all," Tavita said, "you do want to meet Fuentes."

"If that is agreeable to you." O'Connor was almost too polite.

"Nothing is agreeable to me at this moment," she said angrily. "I can think of more pleasant ways to spend a Sunday morning than having to think about a man such as Tomás Fuentes. He ruined yesterday. He ruined last night. He—" She looked at Ferrier, who was watching her worriedly. She relaxed, sighed. "But we must think about him, I suppose."

"And quickly," Ferrier said. "Even if he is out of this house, Tavita, he is not out of your life. So let's get him moved away from Granada."

"And this gentleman, who has no name, will take charge of that?" She looked at O'Connor, as if she had not yet made up her mind about him.

"I am traveling under the name of Smith," O'Connor said.

She waited, but he said nothing more. "And how long did you know Jeff?"

"I first heard of him," said O'Connor carefully, "about six years ago, at the time you and he arranged for your brother's safe arrival in Málaga."

"Jeff told you about me?" And my brother, she thought worriedly.

"Only in the greatest confidence."

"What did he say about me?" What did he say about my brother?

"He admired you. He trusted you."

She looked searchingly at O'Connor, trying to gauge the truth in his words. She said, "Nothing but compliments? How pleasant! And not even one small weakness?"

"Perhaps one," O'Connor said with a smile. "Fourteen is your lucky number, isn't it?"

That silenced her. "It isn't stupid superstition," she said at last.

"Jeff didn't say it was."

Again she studied O'Connor. "Why should he have told you all that?"

"To get our help. Your brother would not be alive today if he had not been given a great deal of help as he left Cuba."

Her eyes widened, as if she were seeing O'Connor in a new perspective. Yes, thought Ferrier, she underestimated him: his unassertive manner made her think he knew less than I said he did.

"How is he, by the way?" O'Connor asked evenly.

"He is well." She kept looking at O'Connor as if she were trying to find any other meaning behind the quiet, friendly voice.

"And the others who followed him out of Cuba? Safely established in their new lives?"

She nodded.

"Good. We want to keep them that way. So let's get Fuentes out of Spain."

"Can you really silence him? The only way," she added slowly, "may be to kill him."

Ferrier stared at her.

Even O'Connor was startled. Momentarily. "There is another way." At least, he thought, I'm going to try for it. He pulled a map out of his pocket, unfolded it, brought it over to where Tavita sat, stretched it on a little table beside her knees. "Here we are," he said, pointing to the road outside her house. "And Tomás Fuentes? Where is he?"

Tavita had dropped all her little plays and pretenses along with her doubts. Her smooth head bent over the map as O'Connor knelt beside her. "Calle de los Mártires. He is in a house on a courtyard near the end of that street. It's small, lies down in an old part of town." The map was baffling her, but she wouldn't admit it.

"Which old part of town? Over here? Just below your terrace?" I went through that district today pretty thoroughly, O'Connor thought hopefully.

"No, no. The other way."

It would have to be, thought O'Connor. "Down the hill? Or does it—"

"It's just off that big main street," Tavita said, delighted that she had found something she could recognize.

"I think I've got it," Ferrier said, remembering his study of his own map. "There's a Church of the Martyrs down there somewhere. Yes, just there, on the corner of that main street and a couple of others." And behind the church, there were several small unnamed streets winding around aimlessly. "It's one hell of a cluttered district." He pointed it out to O'Connor.

"Find the little street with the museum on it," Tavita said. "That's the Calle de los Mártires."

O'Connor found the museum.

"And that is where the courtyard is," Tavita added.

"At that museum?" O'Connor could see a whole new set of problems, each raising its ugly little head to leer at him. I'll have to get down there at once, he thought worriedly, even postpone meeting Tomás until I have an idea of where he is situated. How could you propose a plan for a man's escape if you didn't know what you were up against? And this meeting with Tomás Fuentes would be no social call; it would be hard business all the way.

"You don't need a map," Tavita said, watching O'Connor's close study of it. "I shall take you there."

"No," O'Connor said most definitely. "You stay here."

She pushed the map aside, rose to her feet. "I shall take you—"

"No," said O'Connor.

Ferrier said quickly, "It's safer for you to stay here, Tavita. And quicker for us, too."

"But there's no hurry, Ian; Tomás is safe. Unless, of course, you wanted to take him away this morning." That sudden idea delighted her. "What time is it?"

"Almost eleven."

"On Sundays, the museum doesn't close until one o'clock. Until then, there will be several people walking around the courtyard. But," she added honestly, "it will be much busier in the afternoon, when the museum opens again around four o'clock.

It will have a big Sunday crowd—until eight. That is when the museum closes for the night, and the courtyard begins to empty." She looked at O'Connor, who was frowning over the map, memorizing the network of little streets, calculating the precautionary detours that would be necessary. "You must take him away before then. I insist on that."

O'Connor looked up at her, raised an eyebrow. "Indeed?"

"Yes. By nine o'clock the courtyard is quite silent. The big gates are closed. A dangerous time to leave. You would be most noticeable."

O'Connor rose, folding the map, slipped it back into his pocket. "It's always the way," he said to Ferrier, shaking his head. "I spent more than a good hour studying the approaches to this house and now I find Tomás is in another part of town altogether. We'd better get down there at once. Separate, but within sight of each other."

"Did you listen to *anything* I was saying?" Tavita demanded.

"Every word," he assured her. "But we won't move Tomás out before one o'clock. I have to talk with him, make arrangements—"

"And how do you expect to talk with him? Go up to the front door, and knock, and wait for him to answer? Stand outside and *wait?* Oh, no. Impossible."

"The front door opens directly into the courtyard?"

She nodded. "And faces the main gate."

"Is there a back or side entrance?" O'Connor's face was grim. Yes, he thought again, it would have to be a house that stood in full view of every bloody tourist. "Or did everyone have a good look at him when you took him there?"

She shook her head. "No one could possibly have noticed him." She moved quickly over to the telephone, picked up the receiver, began dialing. "I'll let him know you are coming to see him."

"For God's sake—" O'Connor began.

"Tavita—" That was Ferrier.

Both were too late. The telephone was already ringing at the other end of the line. Ferrier reached her. "Please," he said softly, "put that thing down." She shook her head, her eyes amused. And then he saw that her lips were counting silently.

"Three rings," she said as she replaced the receiver but kept her hand over it. "Now we wait for one minute. Tell me when it is over." She kept her eyes fixed on Ferrier. To O'Connor, who had come to stand beside the phone, she said, "You must stop worrying. I am not a stupid woman."

Indeed you are not, he thought, but he remained worried. His impulse would be quite disastrous, he knew. He wanted to wrench the phone away from her, pull its wire right out of the wall if need be. And that would be the end of this tenuous truce. Intently, he watched her pick up the receiver again as Ferrier signaled the end of the minute. She dialed quickly, but he noted the number. "Ana?" she was saying. "Have you finished the alterations on my black dress? I need it right away. Immediately. Bring it— Ah, *perdone Usted,* wrong number." She jammed the receiver back in place as if, Ferrier thought, she wished the cradle were Tomás Fuentes' face. "See?" she asked them, and added a triumphant smile. "I, too, have my arrangements," she told O'Connor. Then she walked with a long easy stride across the room to a door on its opposite wall. "Only a few seconds," she called back to them. She opened the door and disappeared into her bedroom.

"If she thinks she is going to walk us down into town—" began O'Connor, and then fell abruptly silent. He was glad he had done just that when Tavita returned almost immediately, her clothes unchanged. She carried a shawl over her arm, a key in her hand.

"Now," she said, "I take you on that little tour." They exchanged glances, followed her into the hall. She paused at the top of the staircase to the lower floors, listened carefully, found nothing to alarm her. Then she approached one of the hall's carved wooden panels. Gently, she pressed one of its decorative arabesque carvings aside and revealed a small lock. She beckoned to them to come close, watch the way she inserted the key and twisted it and then pushed the panel open. She switched on an interior light, stood aside to let them enter a short narrow corridor. She closed the panel behind them, secured it with a small bolt. "Now we can talk," she said. "And please watch everything I do. And remember it. You will come back this way by yourselves." She led them to the heavy door that blocked off the end of this cramped corridor, unbolted it, let Ferrier swing its weight open for her. "That was more than Tomás Fuentes thought of doing," she said as she stepped into the darkness beyond and flicked on another light switch.

Ferrier closed and bolted the door after them, turned to see what kept O'Connor standing so still and speechless. Then he, too, stared at a long slope of white tunnel, carefully carved out of the limestone, adequately lit by well-spaced bulbs, which began its descent almost at his feet and went on down and down.

Tavita threw the shawl over her shoulders. "It's always cool here. We can move quickly. No danger. I shall warn you when there is a step that is beginning to crumble. And you can ask me all the questions you want."

Not all the questions, thought Ferrier, as he watched her take her lead so confidently. She knew these steps and stairs by heart. How often had she used them, and when? He followed O'Connor, letting him be closer to Tavita, listening to his questions about small streets and the parking of cars and the bus routes and the trolley cars and the available taxis and the kinds of shops and the types of neighboring cafés and the museum's attendants and the caretaker at the gate of the courtyard, while he looked at the white walls between which they passed, and wondered.

17

They had come to the end of the long descent. They passed through a door, stood in a short stretch of corridor with another door facing them. "As far as I go," Tavita said, and handed the key to O'Connor. "I never want to see that man again. I'll wait only to make sure you can open the lock."

Ferrier noticed the expression on her face as she watched O'Connor. She is really afraid of this man Tomás, he thought. He said, "Don't worry. We'll make sure that everything is locked or bolted when we return. And thank you. You have been magnificent." That brought her back to normal again. She gave him a warm smile, touched his arm. Then, business-like, alert once more, she listened to the key being gently turned. She moved back quickly, re-entered the beginning of the long climb toward her own house, signed to Ferrier to close and bolt its door after her. He watched her briefly before he shut her out of sight, rejoined O'Connor, who was waiting for him with unexpected patience. Or perhaps O'Connor was as nervous of the next few minutes as Ferrier was. "Who goes first?" Ferrier asked wryly. It would be his place, of course; he could identify Tomás Fuentes, and Fuentes knew him.

O'Connor took out a small automatic, checked it carefully, slid it back into his right-hand pocket. "Insurance," he said briefly, and pulled open the last door. He locked it securely behind them as they stepped into a small room. It was paneled, dimly lit, and empty. Ahead of them lay another room, presumably larger, slightly more illuminated by a soft pink glow. And silence.

There's no one here, thought Ferrier at first. He exchanged glances with O'Connor; then together they walked into the circle of light from a table lamp, carefully placed to throw its small beam over the threshold. "Stop!" a voice said from the shadowed side of the room. Another lamp, its shade tilted to face them, was switched on and held up so that its light could strike them fully. He's holding a gun on us, thought Ferrier and stood quite still, keeping his hands well in view. O'Connor did the same. The tense moment of scrutiny was over. "All right," the voice said; the lamp was put back on its table, the shade straightened, and the hand with the revolver slipped into an inside pocket of the silver-gray jacket and came out quickly, adeptly, but now empty. "I did not expect two men," the voice said. "But welcome, Mr. Ferrier—or do you still call yourself colonel?"

"No."

"And your friend?"

"Robert O'Connor."

"So soon? From Washington?" The hand was ready to slip back into the open jacket.

O'Connor said, "I came to Málaga when I got Reid's message."

"Then he did get in touch with you. But how?"

"Through me," Ferrier said.

"And when did you two meet each other?"

A cagey bastard, thought Ferrier. "Last night—after I tried to telephone Tavita."

"Tried?"

"You took over, didn't you?"

O'Connor said brusquely, "Come on, Vado. No time for games. Do you want our help or don't you?"

"So Reid managed to make a report on me. Quite a feat, considering he was flat on his—"

"I transmitted the report," Ferrier said. He frowned, looking at the man who stood well back in the shadows. "Switch another lamp on, will you?"

"What's wrong?" O'Connor asked quickly, and turned on another light. "Isn't this Fuentes?"

"The voice is the same one I heard on the telephone. The height and weight are about right. So is the suit. But I wouldn't say he was definitely Fuentes if it hadn't been for that movement of his hand, reaching inside his jacket for his revolver." Ferrier enjoyed the look on Fuentes' face: astonishment, then a touch of embarrassment soon smothered in annoyance as that overready hand dropped down to his side again. "I saw that same movement when he was on the staircase of Reid's house. Early yesterday morning," he added for Fuentes' benefit, and got rid of some of the disbelief in those large brown eyes. "The housekeeper and the boy were taking him up to the attic."

Fuentes recovered. "Your credentials get better and better," he said acidly. "I wish I were as sure of your friend."

"You know, it would have been much simpler if you guys weren't so damned cautious about being photographed for each other's files."

O'Connor's manner hardened. The quiet voice changed to cold intensity. "What do you need, Vado? A few details about Department Thirteen? Some names—such as Sanchez and Rosa and Guzman and Vermeeren? Or shall we talk about Feodor, Brown, Vladimir, and—"

"Enough, enough," cut in Fuentes, and stopped the flow of information. He glanced at Ferrier, who was watching him with open amusement. "And what interests *you* so much?"

"Just what the hell have you done to your hair?" The heavy dark thatch with its streaks of gray was gone. In its place was a half-shaven head with a thick bob of rusty white circling its back. The texture of the hair had changed with its color; it was now coarse, slightly fuzzed, instead of being smooth and gleaming. The artificial baldness had heightened his brow, seemed to alter the shape of his head. His eyebrows had changed, too—no longer emphatic and black, but sparse and blond. Even the hue of his skin appeared lighter, the lips almost anemic and formless. Only the furrows on either side of his mouth remained the same, and it would take more than pancake make-up to disguise them.

"Experimenting," Fuentes said curtly. "I did not expect any visitors today."

"Or any other day?" O'Connor asked, his eyes on a map of Spain roughly folded on a small writing table. "Were you really planning to take off on your own?" We got here just in time, he thought as he continued his slow tour of the room.

"Five days would have been too much in this place."

"It's cozy." O'Connor was now standing at the kitchen door.

"Not so cozy with that air shaft," Fuentes said. "Someone could get down from the roof with a rope ladder."

"The windows are heavily barred." And no way out on this side of the house, O'Connor decided. It has to be the front door.

"That wouldn't stop a fire bomb being thrown in through my bedroom window, or the kitchen's. And hear those footsteps overhead?"

"Visitors to the museum?" suggested O'Connor. And there was one thing he particularly didn't like: the old fireplace in the kitchen now partly blocked by a refrigerator. Fireplaces meant chimneys, and chimneys meant other fireplaces. He glanced up at the ceiling, wondering what the room above contained. The sooner we get Fuentes out, the better; but let's keep him calm about this place—just in case our arrangements get fouled up and he has to stay for one more night. Perish that thought, but it could happen. "You are safe enough here," O'Connor said as he came back into the room. "It's the street outside that you have to worry about."

Fuentes looked at him sharply.

"You've stirred up more trouble than you think."

"More?" Fuentes obviously didn't believe that.

"Your ex-comrades have been asking about a man called Tomás Fuentes. Yes, they've dug up your old name."

"Where were they asking?"

"In Málaga. They've connected you with Jeff Reid, and no doubt with Tavita. If so, they will move into Granada."

Fuentes swore steadily for a stream of seconds, ended in a frowning silence. "They'll trace me here," he said at last. "I knew it, I knew it—this place is a trap."

"Not this place. Tavita's own house could have been one. But there is no known connection between Tavita and this little love nest. At least, not for the last six years—so she told me on our way down here."

"They'll find the connection, if they search hard."

"They will. But this is Sunday, and all offices are closed; no available records about Tavita's holdings, past and present, until tomorrow."

"They'll talk with Esteban."

"He isn't likely to give out to inquisitive strangers. But the sooner you leave Granada, the better. We have the men, right here, and the cars. I'll get you to Madrid—or just south of Madrid. Put you on a private plane, capable of a long flight. You wanted to go to Switzerland. Isn't that right?"

Fuentes stared. "Reid turned in a very full report," he said acidly. A slight pause. A sudden worry, intense enough to escape through the mask. "Who read it besides you? Martin?"

It was Ferrier's turn to stare. How the hell does Fuentes know about Martin? Or perhaps these boys know far more about us than we know about them. It was a disturbing thought. Humorous, too: since when did I start saying "we" and "us" so easily?

O'Connor looked at Fuentes thoughtfully. "So far, no one has heard that report except me."

"Heard? Reid dictated it?" There was alarm in Fuentes' eyes.

Better than that, thought Ferrier as he watched Fuentes; old Jeff got you to dictate it, yourself. How does that send you, Tomás? There's real danger for you—your own words, your own voice. Ferrier glanced over at O'Connor. How was he going to play this? Tell Fuentes the bad news, or string him along?

"Briefly," O'Connor said. "He hadn't much time. Don't worry. The report is safe."

A neat evasion, thought Ferrier. Most of that taped conversation must have come from Fuentes. But O'Connor wasn't going to press that point now, seemingly. He was more interested in studying the shutters that covered the windows flanking the front door.

"Do you have it?" Fuentes asked.

"On me? Of course not. Too dangerous." There was a small gleam of humor in O'Connor's eyes as he studied the Spaniard. "Turn off the lights, would you? I'd like a look at that courtyard." As the room went black, he opened the louvers of one shutter carefully. The patio was just as Tavita had described it to him. But it was more crowded than he had expected; its voices had been muted by the thick walls and door of this house. Yes, there was plenty of movement out there, people of all kinds, all ages, tourists predominant, a constant stirring and thickening and thinning. Enough? "Ian, come and see this layout. Interesting?" As Ferrier took his place at the window, O'Connor studied the younger man's expression. Yes, he was interested, all right; he'd remember it. O'Connor glanced at the illuminated hands of his watch. Eleven-forty. The museum shut down for lunch and siesta at one. His thoughts raced, kept coming back into the same pattern, as if some sixth sense was pushing them that way. Try it, he told himself. If it doesn't come off, you'll lose nothing; you'll just move him out this evening as you originally planned. "Okay," he said, "switch on the lights." He closed the louvers tightly, fixed them back in place. "Are you going to trust yourself to me, Vado, or are you going it alone?"

"Do I have a choice?"

"Yes. It's between risk and stupidity."

"You're the risk, I suppose? I hope you are a good one."

"Then we leave together?"

"When?"

"Now. Or almost. As soon as Ferrier can reach the Palace and contact my man. We ought to be out of here five minutes before one."

Fuentes looked at him with a slight attack of admiration.

But he overcame it easily enough, reverted to his sardonic smile. "I have a mustache to add to this fantasy." He gestured to his face.

"All you need is a change of clothes—something you didn't wear in Málaga. Forget the mustache. You'd have to glue it on hair by hair, or else it looks fake. Have you any colored contact lenses in your box of tricks?"

"Yes. Would you like to choose which color, too?"

O'Connor ignored the hint of derision. "It's *your* face. Suit it. Now, let's move. Start cleaning up—leave no evidence of what you've been doing to your hair." He caught Ferrier's arm, started with him toward the anteroom, stopped and looked back.

Fuentes had not moved. "You surprise me in one thing. No conditions for helping me to escape?" He glanced at Ferrier. "And not to Switzerland. I have other plans."

That's for my benefit, Ferrier thought. I'd almost believe him, if I didn't doubt that honest smile.

"You know the conditions," O'Connor said. "You talk. I want the names, and fields of operation, of all Americans who have been trained, or are being trained, under the direction of Department Thirteen."

"When do we talk? And where?"

"You can start once Ferrier leaves. And we'll finish it near Madrid, when I catch up with you again."

"You aren't traveling with me?" Suspicions were rising visibly.

"As long as I stay in Granada, your comrades will stay— waiting for me to contact you. So I'll remain here and keep them guessing. You'll travel with a very good man. He has had his instructions. The only change in them is the timing. With luck, we'll be eight hours ahead of schedule. Come on, Ian."

But again they were stopped. Fuentes said, "Let us get one thing straight. I will not travel in a car that is obviously American, or with men who seem to be American. There must be no apparent contact between me and you."

"We can manage that."

"Also, I have certain stipulations about the way I convey my information to you. I do not talk or use a dictaphone. You will provide me with a typewriter and paper, leave me alone in a secure room. You will have that list of names and work zones, neat and clear. Talking can be so diffuse. You agree?"

Cool, thought Ferrier, as cool as they come. He is not going to have his voice identified in any way with the information he is passing on. Just several sheets of typed paper, safely impersonal, which he can deny he ever typed once he is reinstated.

I can hear him now, rhetoric flying, about American imperialists and their conniving machinations.

"Agreed," O'Connor said. "Any more demands?"

"Demands? Stipulations. If they are not acceptable, you can leave with Ferrier."

"Don't tempt me."

Fuentes relaxed. He had won that round. O'Connor was angry. "I have other necessary requests—passport, papers, money, which you will supply. Nothing extortionate. I am not a capitalist. But we'll leave the discussion of those details until you get rid of him." He nodded at Ferrier.

"Come on, Ian," O'Connor said, and shook his head warningly. Ferrier followed, his own anger simmering. He took the key from O'Connor, forced his mind back to the business on hand. O'Connor was saying, "You'll find Ben Waterman in the Palace bar. He'll direct you to a man called Max. Pass the word: I need Max now, a couple of his men, two cars. Then you leave the hotel and drive your own car down here. They will follow, park where you park—as near the museum as possible. Max will tail you when you start walking to the museum, but he must stay out in the street. And the instant I see you coming through that gate into the courtyard, I start easing Fuentes and myself out of here. As soon as Max sees me, he is to head back to his car. I'll follow, steer Fuentes into his arms. After that, Plan B goes into operation. Got everything?"

Ferrier nodded. "Plan B," he repeated. Whatever the hell that was. He began trying the lock, felt the key grip and then turn.

"If I don't see you in the courtyard five minutes before one o'clock, then we'll postpone everything until this evening. Need my map?"

"I have one. Don't worry. I won't get lost." He pulled the door open. Back to the old jogging, he thought. But what would it be like uphill?

Of course, remembered O'Connor, he knows his way around a map—any map. The little unnamed twists and turns that showed streets too small or insignificant to be identified would be no puzzle to Ferrier; he was accustomed to a bird's-eye view. "Okay. See you at the hotel—but before six. Sneak into 307."

I'm promoted, thought Ferrier, and repressed a joke about inner circles in smoke-filled rooms. "See you before six," he said. "But now, if I were you, I'd keep my right hand on that automatic." He closed the door behind him, locked it securely. He could still see O'Connor's serious face, slightly startled, slightly amused, as he reached the second door, bolted it firmly behind him. He started up the first slope, mounted the first steps at a slow even run. Interesting, he thought, to see how long he could keep up this pace in a steady ascent. He had just about an hour, all told, before he came walking through the front gate of the museum courtyard. Possible? He'd make a damned good try.

O'Connor heard the lock turn, securing the door which now looked only like part of a paneled wall, and came back into the room. He was thinking of Ferrier as he glanced at his watch. Would he manage it? Ferrier was capable of it—strong enough physically, lean, well muscled, no apparent flab; and he was quick enough mentally to improvise his way around some unexpected snag. Otherwise, I wouldn't have sent him out on this job. But yet—O'Connor stopped short, stared at the revolver that pointed at his chest, stared at Fuentes who held it so steadily.

"Take your hand away from your pocket," Fuentes told him. "Don't be foolish. We don't want any loud noises frightening the tourists. You will notice that I have a silencer already in place. You don't. So I could risk shooting you if necessary. But you couldn't risk shooting me. So place your pistol on that table beside you. Now come forward. To this desk."

"What—" began O'Connor angrily. But he was already guessing what Fuentes wanted. If Fuentes had intended to kill him, take off on his own, O'Connor would already have been dead.

"To this desk!" repeated Fuentes. "Now empty your pockets. Take off your watch. Cuff links, too. Put them all on the desk." He kept his eyes fixed on O'Connor's hands as they obeyed his command. "Now, do I have to search through all these things to find the miniature recorder you are carrying around with you? It would be simpler if you tell me how it is disguised. That would save me breaking open this handsome watch, for instance."

"I need that watch, damn you."

"Then open it for me."

"You are wasting—"

"Only a couple of minutes. Two minutes wasted, but years saved. Mine, O'Connor. I do not intend to have any recording of our talk fall into the wrong hands. And it could. Such things happen, don't they?"

"Why should I carry such a device?" The puzzle is, thought O'Connor, that he suspects me but never suspected Reid. I hope to God he'll answer that question, not leave it floating around.

"At least you don't deny it outright. And you are clever enough to know the only answer. Of course I must be suspicious of you: you were coming to meet me; you would not come unprepared. So open that watch. It seems the most likely candidate—a little thicker than normal, you'd agree? Oh, just a little thicker—not enough to be noticed when worn, only when handled and examined." He had picked up the watch, glanced at it, looked back at O'Connor. "I'll smash it on the floor, grind it with my heel," he warned. "A pity to destroy such an expensive piece of equipment. Made to your special order?" He held it out.

O'Connor took the watch, opened the back, extracted a flat coil of thin wire, handed it over.

"So delicate, so miniature, so dangerous." Fuentes examined it briefly. "Yes, quite similar to a watch I have. A little more elegant, perhaps." He pushed aside the cuff links contemptuously. "Useless," he said of them. He moved over to the table near the door, pocketed O'Connor's automatic with a flourish. "I'll return it when we are ready to leave. But this—" he held up the little coil of wire—"this I shall now destroy. A little fuel from my lighter, and a match, will make is quite unuseable." He was in excellent humor now; even expansive. "I notice you don't carry a lighter. Reid did. But—" he shrugged— "that's all it was. A simple ordinary straightforward lighter. Of course, he hadn't expected to be meeting me. And he was young. It takes an old dog to know all the tricks and apply them."

And sometimes a young dog can outsmart the old, O'Connor thought. "Did you examine his watch, too?" he asked sarcastically.

"I did. One of those wafer-thin fashions, quite uninteresting."

"You're a nimble-fingered son of a—"

"No compliments, thank you. We'll get on very well without them. No reason why we shouldn't have an amicable arrangement between us for the rest of our tour. It is much pleasanter, that way. Improves the quality of information. You agree?"

O'Connor nodded, put the contents of his pockets back in place, fastened his cuff links, strapped on his watch. "Let's get this place straightened up."

"That won't take long. First, let us have a clear understanding about my journey."

"Oh, yes—those final requests, as you called them. They *are* the final ones? No afterthoughts when you are in Madrid?"

"I know exactly what I need. No direct transportation to Switzerland. Munich will be far enough. And the plane will be a private one, and not American-owned. You will furnish me with a passport, papers, adequate travel money, a car, two suitcases with clothes—all West German. You will do that?"

"It can be managed." And then to draw any possible attention away from that careful phrase, O'Connor added, "I just hope your German is good enough."

"It's fluent. I worked in West Berlin for two years."

So, thought O'Connor, he will probably head for a German-speaking area of Switzerland. That could be his ultimate hideout. "Between 1957 and '59?" he asked.

Fuentes looked at him. "What made you think I was in West Berlin then?"

"Oh, just a couple of clever assassinations. Unexplained heart attacks, weren't they? Rebet. And Bandera. Two important anti-communists wiped out neatly."

"Not so neatly as we had hoped. You learned about it."

Yes, thought O'Connor, through a defector. . . . But he decided that would be a tactless reminder. "Don't be long in there," he told Fuentes, now carrying the miniature coil of wire in modest triumph toward the bedroom. "Want any help?"

"I can manage. I don't need much time. We can start having our first real talk in ten minutes. A general survey. We'll leave the particulars until I get that typewriter. Oh, by the way— the typewritten report will be quite lengthy, depending on the way you treat me, of course. I'll hand it over to you once we arrive at the Munich airport and I step off the plane."

O'Connor began to laugh. "You really know how to milk a bargain down to the last drop. And what's to stop us taking that report when we damn well want it?"

"You know the answer to that, and it is no joke. How many defectors would apply to the Americans for help if they heard I had been badly treated? Such news gets around. And without defectors and high-placed informants, where would you be? Groping in the dark. Fumbling your way through a maze of guesses and suppositions. Why, you wouldn't even have known the cause of Rebet's and Bandera's deaths if their executioner hadn't developed a misplaced conscience and come running to you!"

The bedroom door closed firmly. O'Connor glared at it, then turned away. Oh well, he thought grimly, let's keep Fuentes happy; let's allow him the last word. This time.

18

Interesting, Ferrier had thought. Disconcerting, too. He only managed two thirds of the distance before he was forced to drop into a walk. He tried to keep his pace brisk, his breathing controlled. Even so, the last pull up the final slope—it seemed steeper than any other part of this strange progress through the long white tunnel—was a sudden assault on every part of his body. Breathing became irregular, taking a gasp of air where he could find it; hot saliva scalded his throat and chest; there were tremors in tightened thigh muscles, and enough thumpings through his head to start up last night's pain all over again. He reached the first of the two doors at the top of the ascent, pulled it open, bolted it behind him with some difficulty; but whether that was from an overtense hand forcing too hard or his rising excitement, he wasn't sure. He leaned against it for almost a minute while he steadied himself. Then he walked at a normal rate, feeling more in command of his body, to the last door. I managed it, he was thinking, I managed it, and in better time than I expected when I was two thirds up that tunnel.

He eased the door only slightly open, stood there for interminable moments, listening for any sound of footsteps or voices in the hall. Nothing, except the beat of his heart pumping steadily. Quickly, he pulled the panel wide, stepped through, locked it securely. As he adjusted the scroll of carved wood to hide the small keyhole, he heard a voice in the big room just around the curve of the semicircular hall. He froze instinctively. Tavita's voice, speaking a torrent of Spanish. Then silence. Again speaking. Silence. Speaking. She's on the telephone, he thought, and walked into the room.

Tavita's eyebrows went up as she turned to see who it was. "So soon?" Then she covered the receiver with one hand. "And where is your friend? Has he already left?"

"He will see you later." Ferrier handed over the key with a

kiss for her outstretched hand. "With our thanks. And admiration." Tavita's annoyance disappeared. He added, "Will you have dinner with me tonight? I'll collect you around ten o'clock."

"It will all be over by then?"

"Hope so." He had already started back toward the hall.

"Ian—wait!" She spoke quickly into the telephone. "Call me back later. I think I can arrange an interview at ten o'clock this evening." She dropped the receiver, came running after him. "These people," she said in mock disgust—actually, she was pleased by their attention—"they are so eager to talk with me. They say they have a date-line."

"Deadline." He had reached the front door, opened it cautiously.

"Oh!" The expression on her face told him she didn't care for that word so much. "We'll have dinner here tonight. Come at eleven and chase those interviewers away." She stamped her foot to draw his attention to what she was saying. He was now looking up the driveway, studying the front gate.

"I'll come at ten and keep an eye on them." The road outside seemed empty. He tried to guess what to expect there. Surveillance of some kind?

"You hurry too much," she told him laughingly. "You look like a Red Indian—a blond Red Indian." Then quickly serious again, she caught his arm as he stepped into the driveway, gestured toward the garage. "Take my car—the big or the small, whichever you need. They are yours."

A small one? He had already thought of the car he had seen her use in Málaga, and discarded the idea: too noticeable, too imposing, too much Tavita. It would have drawn everyone's attention in the parking space outside the Palace. "The keys?"

"In the cars, of course. Where else?"

He was already at the garage door before she had finished the question. He swung it open, saw a compact Simca colored the usual light cream. It was ready to go, too, with the keys just as she had said. He waved his thanks, accelerated and got neatly up the hill of the driveway, nosed cautiously out of the gate.

Yes, two men were walking along the road, measuring their distance perhaps, for they turned to retrace their steps. Keeping watch over the house? He put on speed and passed them just as they were realizing a car had come shooting out of the gateway. He had averted his head, but he managed a glimpse of their faces in his rear-view mirror as they swung round to stare at the car's number. He hadn't seen them before. Could be anyone, he thought as his suspicions subsided: just two nondescript types in quiet gray suits, taking a stroll through the neighborhood while the wives and kids were at church.

The road was otherwise deserted. He risked breaking local regulations about speed limits, bounced along merrily for about four hundred yards, then slowed down as he reached the parked cars massed in front of the hotel. He eased the Simca into a modest position beside an overwhelming Rolls. As he switched off the ignition, pocketed the keys, he was remembering Tavita's "Ian—wait!" and his own stifled groan. So you waited, wasted three minutes, and gained at least ten. And regained your breath and recovered your normal color.

Ferrier walked smartly into the hotel, past the little shop at its entrance where lace fans and worked leather and Toledo letter openers and fringed shawls and postcards and wood carvings were drawing the usual crowd of visitors, and headed straight for the bar. It was a pleasant room with plenty of daylight—windows opening onto a long narrow terrace. He glanced around the tables. Only two of them occupied. At one, there was a broad-shouldered man with a tanned face, strong features, a handsome head of dark hair, an elegant suit in the sharpest French style that contrasted with his equally French, slightly tired, slightly bored expression. He looked as if he had spent an interesting Saturday in bed and was wondering what to do with Sunday noon. And at the other table, her back turned to the Frenchman—possibly as a mild rebuff to any possible ideas now forming inside his mind—there was a girl. A most attractive girl. Amanda Ames. She knew exactly what to do on a late Sunday morning. She was putting in time sipping coffee, writing postcards, and paying no attention to anybody. Ferrier averted his eyes quickly, walked straight ahead to the wide doors onto the terrace. This was not the moment for any delay, however attractive. And Ben Waterman had better be there, he thought worriedly.

He was. Ferrier's tension relaxed. Ben was sitting at one of the long row of tables on the narrow terrace—all terraces in this part of Granada seemed to be narrow, with nothing below them except a steep plunge of cliff—and he was enjoying the sun. He was almost alone; the other tables were empty except for a couple of young Spaniards in neat dark suits. His face was tilted up, his eyes closed, his light fuzz of hair ruffled with the breeze, his spread of newspapers anchored by heavy ash-trays and quite forgotten. There was a bottle of light Spanish

beer in front of him, half emptied, and a glass that was full.
I could use some of that, thought Ferrier. He touched Waterman lightly on the shoulder. "Wake up, Ben. Help needed." He
sat down, lifted the glass, had a long drink. "D'you mind?" he
asked as Waterman's eyes opened and focused.

Waterman said peevishly, with the usual annoyance at having
been wakened from a beautiful cat nap in the sun, "Hey—order
your own."

"No time. I need Max. Would you get him?"

"What's this—some kind of emergency?" Waterman came
fully awake. "Action at last, eh?"

Ferrier became aware that the two young Spaniards had
fallen quite silent. So he shook his head and said, "Nothing like
that. Just another conference, I guess. Where do I find him?"

"He's in the bar."

"The Frenchman?" Ferrier finished the glass, poured some
more beer carefully. So that was Max, on whom so much
depended.

Waterman was smiling broadly. "From Montpelier, Vermont.
Do you want me to tell him you're here? But why—"

"Yes. Tell him. And keep your voice down." Ferrier glanced
at the two Spaniards seven tables away.

"No need to worry about them. They're Max's watchdogs."

"Did they scare away everyone else?" The loneliness of the
terrace was a surprise.

Waterman lumbered to his feet, gathered his papers. "Sunday
begins at one o'clock for the in crowd." Then as a waiter came
out, he said breezily, "Well, I'll just tidy up and meet you later."
He moved away, took charge of the waiter, too, steering him
back inside the bar with a nothing-needed-here explanation. At
the doorway, he almost collided with Max, who had seemingly
decided to stroll out and have a look at the view from the
terrace. Apologies, of course. And a small aside slipped in by
Waterman: "That's Ferrier. Wants to talk with you."

Max nodded briefly, and stepped onto the terrace.

Waterman hesitated. But he hadn't been invited, and he could
think of no reasonable excuse to join them outside. Between
them, they've driven me away from the pleasantest front porch
in Granada, he thought with annoyance. What has Ian got to
say to Max, anyway?

Ian Ferrier was saying exactly what O'Connor wanted said.
He only added one thing. "Look out for tricks." He didn't have
to add Tomás Fuentes' name.

"That's my business," Max said. He had a quiet, incisive voice. An incisive man, Ferrier thought. He watched him rise, light a cigarette as he rested his elbows on the terrace wall, look intently at the steep plunge below him. The bedroom eyes, the bored manner were gone. "Give us five minutes. Take off then. I know where your car is parked. I'll be ready to follow." He glanced along the terrace, caught the attention of the two young men, nodded slightly, and left. They decided to leave, too.

Ferrier finished his beer, let the young men pass his table. They walked like Spaniards, dressed like Spaniards, were arguing politely about García Lorca and his poetry, but Ferrier wondered what part of the States they were from. Southern California, New Mexico, or just good old plain Nebraska? He'd never learn, of course; but it made interesting speculation. Who'd place him as Montana? Then he rose, too—he was ahead of time, but he wanted to get in place and not risk any delay—left a tip, and braced himself for his walk through the bar. Amanda Ames . . . It was too much to hope that she'd be still so engrossed in her postcards that she wouldn't look up. And she's the most attractive piece I've seen in years, he admitted now. Except Tavita. But Tavita is something quite apart from any other woman I've ever known. Possibly too much for one man to handle. Is that why she has never married? And who the hell are you to speculate about the reasons why people don't choose to marry? You've always found plenty of good ones for yourself.

He stepped into the bar. There were now about eight people at various tables. But no Amanda. So that problem was solved.

The lobby was more crowded, yet cathedral-like in its restraint. Outside the expensive souvenir shop, he saw Ben Waterman. To his amazement, Waterman stopped him.

"Hello, hello," he said, as if he hadn't left Ferrier only a few minutes ago. "Just choosing a fan for Alice. The black or the white, what do you think?" He had his hand on Ferrier's arm, pulled him over to look at the window display, stood close.

"For God's sake—" Ferrier began in a low, intense voice. His annoyance changed to shock as he glanced inside the little shop. He'd recognize anywhere that smooth dark-brown hair plastered over a neat round head: Jeff's visitor, Jeff's killer. He was buying a guidebook, spreading out its folded map for approval.

"I know, I know," Waterman said just as quietly. "I'm helping a lady in distress. She slipped this to me so that I could slip it to you." Waterman did just that, inserting a postcard neatly into Ferrier's pocket. Then he released the arm, eased away from Ferrier's side to a more normal stance. "She's the pretty girl in the bar. The extra-pretty girl. Don't tell me you've stopped noticing," he added with a laugh, then raised his voice to normal. "All right. It's the black lace. And if Alice doesn't like it, I can blame it on you." He moved into the shop.

Ferrier turned quickly away from its window—the man inside, too busy examining the map, hadn't noticed him. Or had he, and the guidebook was only a disguise? Ferrier searched for a cigarette, felt Amanda's card in his pocket. What the hell was she up to? But thoughts about her were quickly driven out of his head by a second shock. Two men had just entered the hotel, passing him without a second glance. They stopped to ask directions from the white-gloved pages who were on duty near the potted palms, then headed for the bar. They noticed me, Ferrier thought, but they have an appointment to keep. For half past twelve? His glance at his watch told him he had ninety seconds to reach his car.

Ferrier moved quickly out of the hotel, pausing only to light his cigarette and look around him. He was brooding about those two men: one black-haired and overweight, a round fat face set in a nervous smile, the pessimist who carried both a gun and a knife; the other dark-haired, too, but small and thin, with a stream of commands backed up by a long-nosed revolver—equally aimed last night at Ferrier. And where was the third of that trio? The tall blond man, powerful shoulders, arm upraised as he stepped out from the shadowed doorway into Jeff's living room? As long as I carry this bump on the back of my head, thought Ferrier, I'm not likely to forget him. Only, I didn't see his face. I'll need him grouped beside his two comrades to make sure it's the same guy. And *there's* one that could be a likely candidate—good God, it's the same big bruiser who blocked my view of Jeff's door in the crowded hospital corridor. The man had been standing near a dark-blue Fiat, talking with a friend. As soon as he had glimpsed Ferrier, he turned his back. Too obvious, Ferrier decided. What was the friend like?

Ferrier was curious enough to make a small detour to reach his rented car, which was parked not far from the hotel door—one advantage of getting here bright and early. He had a quick side look at the friend. His depression increased. It was the man who had trailed Amanda and him to the beach, the man who had driven Jeff's murderer safely away from the hospital. So they were gathering here, a bunch of vultures.

Meeting whom? For they weren't following him, that was sure. The big fellow and his friend had started to saunter to the hotel's entrance. So they were all here, all of them, Ferrier kept thinking. We were supposed to be so damned smart that we slipped out of Málaga unnoticed, came into Granada quietly and carefully—and they are all here. And to add to the irony of the situation, as the two men reached the hotel, Max came strolling out.

Ferrier stepped into his car, the ignition keys ready. Twenty seconds to spare, but he might as well start up the engine and begin to move. It wouldn't start. He tried again. Again. Again. Just an asthmatic wheeze that kept protesting, louder and louder, across the wide plaza. So that's why they weren't following me—didn't have to—what did they do to this damned thing? They had heard it, for the big man and his friend had turned at the hotel doorway to watch. Max had heard it, too. He had been about to get into a car that had already drawn out of its parking space. He stopped, seemingly giving his driver some directions; his back was to the hotel, his face looking in Ferrier's direction.

Ferrier was out of his car, walking rapidly to the little white Simca. Keep your eye on me, Max, keep your eye on me, he said silently as he stepped in and didn't risk any more glances at either Max or the hotel entrance. The Simca's engine turned over nicely. He backed it out from its sheltering place beside the huge Rolls, started slowly at first, his eyes on the rear-view mirror. Max must have climbed into his Mercedes, a nice powerful 280 but restrained in appearance, nothing flashy, not even too large in size; it began moving, too. And behind it came a Renault in subdued gray, not as old as it had been made to look, and much stronger in horsepower than might be expected. Ferrier put on some speed as he headed out of the plaza, noted with relief that the little caravan was not too obvious: the Renault even tried to pass the Mercedes and was waved back by the chauffeur.

Then suddenly, ahead of him, traveling straight toward him in the direction of the hotel, Ferrier saw the big yellow sports car. It was in a hurry. He had time to turn aside his head, pretend to reach for something in the tiny back seat, and avoid being noticed. But Gene Lucas, who was driving, only had his eyes on the Renault, which was again edging out as if to pass the Mercedes. There was no Bianca with him today, no clutter of liberal chic to lighten his journey. He was alone, a large suitcase his only company. He looked hot and tired, dust-covered and tense. A man, thought Ferrier, who is almost late for a most important meeting. Then he put aside all speculation and turned the blunt hood of the little Simca down into town.

Ferrier had decided not to play coy, become too involved in small twisting streets in the hope of greater safety. The most direct route was the best. Security lay not in detours but in the unexpected speed of O'Connor's decision. Their abrupt departure from the hotel was a help, too. So were the main streets, now crowded as Sunday came to life. Even Max and the Renault that followed were hard pressed at times to keep Ferrier in sight. For once, he thought, we've caught the opposition off balance. He began to enjoy himself.

He found a parking place in the lee of the Church of the Martyrs, set out quickly for the museum, with only seven minutes to spare. He glanced back as he approached the big gate to its courtyard. Max had arrived. His car had drawn up about fifty yards away, well to one side of the narrow street, the driver at the wheel, the engine idling. The Renault was behind, looking for a free space.

All right, thought Ferrier as he saw Max leave the car, here we go. He walked into the courtyard, paused inside the gates (do you see me, O'Connor, is this clear enough?), and looked around as any stranger would. Then he turned toward the museum steps. At their top, he was stopped by a middle-aged man in gray with an iron hook for a right hand. "The museum is closing," he was told. "In ten minutes, we close."

"I could have a look at the main hall."

"No. A waste of your money. Come back this afternoon." The man was tired, but the brown eyes were friendly even if the lips looked severe under a heavy dark mustache. "There is a lot to see. It takes more than a glance."

A gentle reprimand, thought Ferrier. "Of course. It was just my disappointment at arriving so late." And now, he thought, I'll have to put in time, waiting for O'Connor to leave. Or else I'll find myself walking out with him and Fuentes. And there they were—yes, there they actually were, already out of the house and with no one seeming to notice or pay any attention to the two men who were skirting the courtyard at the slow pace of interested tourists. Either you could say O'Connor was lucky or you could credit him with being quick to choose his moment. Whatever it was, luck or skill, it was bringing him safely into the colonnade that stretched along the other side of the broad patio. He was leading the way, about six paces in front of Tomás Fuentes. They didn't seem to have anything to do with each other.

The attendant broke off his advice to the foreigner about what he could expect to see inside the museum, said shrewdly, "You like architecture? Yes, that colonnade over there is old, fifteenth century. It was built before Columbus sailed for America." His iron hook waved in the air as he pointed. (Ferrier controlled his flinch, not so much at the hook, but at its direction. If Fuentes had seen that, he was likely to start running.) "It's just as it was—except for the tinsmith's shop in the corner near the gate. Commercial." He shrugged his shoulder, pursed his lips. Then he turned to warn some youngsters to take the steps more carefully, limped back to his post at the museum door to watch the visitors who were starting to trickle out. Ferrier joined a small group of them, followed their slow progress down the broad stone stairs. Now he could watch the colonnade in safety.

And it was worth watching. O'Connor, walking leisurely, was past the tinsmith's shop and strolling toward the gate. Fuentes had just reached the tinsmith's, seemed interested by its window display, then halted at its door. He was kneeling, tying a shoe-lace. And Ferrier almost halted, too, in his surprise. For as Fuentes rose, he slipped something under the door. Or touched it? Or what? (Had he actually slipped something—an envelope, a letter—something that had disappeared as quickly as it had appeared in Fuentes' hand? Ridiculous, Ferrier told himself: you are just too damned suspicious of that character.) Now he was following O'Connor again, walking a little more smartly to make up for lost seconds.

Ferrier came down the last two steps into the courtyard, let the thickening clot of people jostle around him. His impulse was to cross over to the colonnade, have a look at the tinsmith's door. But it wouldn't be particularly wise to draw the attendant's quick eyes back in that direction; he had already noticed Ferrier's interest. Once was understandable; twice would be emphasis. So Ferrier walked thoughtfully toward the gate. Possibly, he decided at last, he had imagined too much: Fuentes might only have been steadying himself as he rose. But with a man like Fuentes, you came to expect tricks. He enjoyed them, that was the truth of it. The detailed attention to his disguise must have given him a lot of pleasure. He was determined to be a winner, even in the smallest things. His dark suit, for instance, must have had a much larger chest size than his light dapper gray. Yet it had been well filled, as if he had added several inches to his girth and a full twenty pounds to his weight. Padded, or bulging with his special possessions? His movements had also changed: stride shortened, head and shoulders pitched slightly forward, hands scarcely swinging. From across the courtyard, he had seemed older, a little stiff in his joints. Thorough, that was Fuentes.

The narrow street was busier now. Ferrier could risk walking smartly toward the church, cutting through the flux of people trailing out from the museum courtyard. Ahead of him, he saw a door being closed on Max's Mercedes, and at once the car started moving, careful not to brush any of the pedestrians. Then, reaching a freer space, it increased its speed to the legal limit. Ferrier barely glanced at it as it swept past him. He noted, with interest, a man sitting beside the driver. Max was in the back seat with Fuentes, who was now wearing a tilted beret to add a new touch to his bald head. Behind them came the Renault, not too near, not too far. There were three men in this car—two unknowns, one recognizable. He was one of the two young men who had quoted poetry on the hotel terrace. I bet García Lorca is far from his mind now, thought Ferrier. And Max has increased his quota. He has taken along not a couple of men, but three, excluding the drivers. That makes five of them to back him up, if need be. Max, I like your style.

Ferrier reached the Simca. (He hadn't even caught a glimpse of Robert O'Connor, which was as it should be.) All over, he kept thinking, all over. Good-bye to Tomás Fuentes. All over, and thank God for that. Then he remembered Amanda's postcard.

He pulled it out of his pocket, switched off the ignition. The writing was hurried, and depressed—its line descended in a trailing slope. Like Jeanne Moreau's mouth, he thought. An unhappy sign. The message began bravely, ended strangely. *Can I take you up on that lunch? I'll have a table for two o'clock. Inside. If you're late, don't worry. I'll wait.*

He turned the card over. It was a colorful view of a garden restaurant, a sort of green terrace, with a venerable building as close background. This, the descriptive small print told him, was the Parador Nacional de San Francisco, where Washington Irving, the celebrated American writer, had spent many happy years being inspired by the great beauties of the Alhambra. Which beauties? Ferrier wondered irreverently. Then he became serious again as he looked at Amanda's writing. *I'll wait.* It wasn't the kind of phrase that a girl as pretty as Amanda Ames ever needed to use. Translated, it probably meant *Vital that I see you.* And it had better be: the last thing he needed today was luncheon with a charming question mark; what he wanted right now was an hour stretched flat on his back, with his eyes blissfully closed. It was the warm sun pouring into the little front seat of the car that had made him feel the full extent of the effort and strain of these last twenty-four hours. All over, he thought again.

He slipped the card back into his pocket, turned on the engine, forced himself to stay awake as far as the hotel. He'd cat nap in his room. Leave instructions to be called at a quarter of two. The Alhambra grounds weren't far away from the hotel—a few minutes by car. And the *parador* was at the edge of their walls; no problem in finding it. Cat naps were no problem, either. There had been many times when he had lived on them for several days.

I'll wait. . . . Pathetic and sad. Or was that just a part of the act?

19

Ferrier was twelve minutes late even before he reached the *parador* and annoyed with himself. (He had not allowed for the possibility that he might be followed from the hotel. Perhaps it had been a false alarm—he was inclined to think not —but he had taken the precaution of a roundabout route instead of the direct road.) He managed to find a small space for the Simca near the gatehouse, with a tip for the gray-coated attendant—the quadrangle was full of cars—and that added some more minutes. Then he had to make his way through a garden with fountain and cloisters, all very charming except that he was in no mood to appreciate the attractions of a sixteenth-century convent; and after that through a series of small rooms—elegant in the Spanish style, with wood beams, white walls, tiled floors, native rugs, hand-woven linen massively draped, dark rich colors, heavy candlesticks, wrought iron, large bowls packed with bright flowers. Beyond all this was the dining terrace and garden, filled with tables and crammed with guests. People everywhere, indoors, too. Amanda had certainly chosen a lonely spot for her rendezvous. And he had come too far, must have passed the room where she waited. He was closer to being twenty minutes late when he found her, tucked away at a corner table with her back to the room. He had been looking for a girl in a blue dress, and she had changed to brown. In spite of his annoyance, rapidly mounting, he had to smile.

She noticed his smile with relief, brushed aside his apologies. "You *did* come," she said thankfully. "After I sent that card—"

"How did you know it would reach me?" He had taken the seat on her right, the chair opposite her being already filled with a white silk coat and her white duffel-bag type of purse.

"Simple. From where I sat in the bar, I could see the back of your friend's head. When you went out to the terrace, he turned his head and began to speak in your direction. I couldn't

261

see you, but who else was there? Unless he was talking to himself, of course."

They shared a laugh, small, tentative. Then seriously, he looked at her. Her face was a little drawn and tired, but she really was a stunning girl. That brown dress, for instance—not a color he'd choose as his favorite, but it looked good on her, lightened by a white coral necklace that curved down to her breasts, lay between them. It was the quality of her skin, of a tan that wasn't too deep; honey and roses, he thought. Brown high lights were emphasized in her dark hair, lashes and eyebrows black, and those deep-blue eyes looking back at him so frankly.

"Yes?" she asked him.

"Oh, just admiring your earrings."

She was amused again. The earrings were simple little studs to match her necklace. She shook her head, as if he baffled her in a light way.

"So you saw me walk through the bar. Why didn't you say hello?" he asked.

Her voice dropped to a low level. "Too many strange people around. Gene Lucas' friends were all over the place—oh, not staying at that hotel. Lucas is, though. They are meeting there, right now. In my room."

"What?" He was taken aback, and showed it. He looked around quickly, just to make sure they wouldn't be overheard even speaking as quietly as they were. The well-spaced tables reassured him. Indoors wasn't as tightly packed as the open terrace. And the tables were self-absorbed, buzzing with tourist talk in several languages. Although none of the other guests were bothering to lower their voices, the only distinguishable words were an emphatic no or a clear yes that shot out from the mixed brew.

Amanda had been saying, "Lucas came panting along—he had arrived a little late—and asked me if he could use my room to meet a few friends. His own room wasn't ready to receive him. He said. It could be true, it could be a lie. You never can tell with Lucas."

"But you didn't have to let him—"

"But I do. Or are you forgetting my job? It is to penetrate the Lucas setup. I'll never do that by refusing—" She stopped as his hand touched her arm, warning her that a waitress was approaching. "Sherry," she told him. "Amontillado." She kept silent after that until the girl left, watched him curiously. "You look so dubious, Ian. The waitress will bring you real Scotch, just as you ordered. They are geared for foreigners at these inns. They're tourist industry."

"Dubious?" he asked jokingly. Had he really let his feelings about Amanda's job show so clearly? And there was a twist there: Amanda's job, according to Martin last night, might be just the opposite of what she had stated so calmly. Her mission might be—if Martin's doubts were on the right wave length—the penetration of Martin's Málaga network.

"Too much word," she agreed. "Something half-strength would have been closer. You looked just a little—on guard, leery, expectant of the worst, slightly skeptical. That was all. Or were you nervous about me? I shouldn't have told you about my exact job in so many direct words. I know—I shouldn't have. Only, I'm scared stiff, and you are the only person I know in Granada whom I can trust."

She was deadly serious, intense. Too intense. She'd be likely to break down any minute. So he tried to lighten the mood. "Come on, Amanda, you know better than to take anyone at face value. I could be—"

"You couldn't." She paused, then said slowly, "I heard about Jeff Reid."

He was silent.

Her voice dropped even more. "It was murder. Did you know that?"

The blue eyes were fearful, sad, and so completely honest. Damn Martin, he thought, for the suspicions he planted. Martin would say right now that this could be a small probe to find out if he had any proof of assassination, and if so—as the only person so far who had any evidence to offer—Ferrier was putting himself in some real danger by admitting it. He looked away from those blue eyes. "How did you find that out? Or am I making you break security again?"

"How I found out doesn't matter. What I've found out is the important thing. Ian—remember that man Lucas asked you about yesterday?"

Tomás Fuentes. "I remember," he said carefully.

"He is in Granada," she said, almost in a whisper. "That is why Gene Lucas is here."

And much good it will do him, Ferrier thought with a touch of satisfaction. He hoped his face was totally blank of expression.

"And that is why Martin sent me here."

"Martin?"

She nodded. "At least, I now think that is why. Martin didn't explain, just told me to leave early this morning for Granada. He had reserved a room for me at the Palace. He said Lucas was going to be there."

"And when did you see Martin?" Last I heard, Ferrier thought, Martin was going to start investigating. A strange way of making an enquiry, to send a suspect right into the middle of a highly sensitive, top-secret operation. Or was this some kind of test?

"I've never seen him. Just instructions and messages."

"And when did you get this one?"

"Late last night—almost half past eleven—I got a phone call to go to—" she hesitated—"to a place where I pick up any important message. When I got there five minutes later, I was given a number to phone. There was a woman at the other end. She told me to hang up and wait. I did. When the call came through, it was from Martin." She tried to smile. "He's a most untraceable person. I suppose it is necessary. Only—yes, I do get irritated. The others who have dealt with me—more important than Martin, I think, although that's possibly sacrilege—well, they just don't behave like that. Careful, yes; but they keep everything simple and direct. I don't think Martin trusts anyone."

"Except himself?" Ferrier asked. Martin's supercaution was beginning to look comic, now that the Tomás Fuentes incident was definitely closed as far as Málaga was concerned. Trust Martin to fuss and blow smoke screens after he arrived too late. I suppose, Ferrier was thinking, Martin wanted a part of the action and some of the credit. This wasn't his business—O'Connor had made that clear—but Martin had the excuse that Málaga was his special thing and what happened there was his responsibility. At least, he was making it so. But in what an inept way: sending a girl on a man's errand—this job was far too tricky, too dangerous for Amanda to handle alone. And a girl of whom he wasn't sure, at that. "He's a fool," Ferrier said in sudden anger.

"Not that," she said loyally. "It's just his peculiar way. You know—"

"Here are the drinks," he warned her, as the waitress with the friendly eyes and fresh complexion came slowly into the room with a carefully carried tray. "And we'd better order, don't you think?" Service was dependable but slow; white starched aprons and intense concentration.

Amanda picked up a menu, looked at it without much interest. Her thoughts were far away from food. "You choose."

"Well, for the first course: some light talk. For the main dish: conversation. And we'll postpone all business until we are drinking our coffee. How's that?"

"Business may take some time," she said worriedly.

"I've all afternoon," he assured her. Sure, O'Connor had said something about slipping into Room 307 for a small chat; but if anything important had developed, O'Connor would certainly have sent for him, wakened him out of his brief sleep if necessary. And Ben had no doubt squinted at the postcard. They'd know where to find him.

"I have to leave by a quarter of four—at the latest."

"Then we'd better get the food on the fire. Have a good swig of that sherry. You look as if you needed it." And while she sipped the sherry, he decided quickly on gazpacho, broiled mountain trout, wild strawberries. For wine, there was a white *vino de la casa* which seemed to be going down well at other tables and would possibly arrive more promptly than some special Rioja, which would take more time in service. And lastly, at the risk of appearing a barbarian, he told the apple-cheeked waitress they must leave, unfortunately, what a pity, unavoidable, in just over an hour. Would she attend to that, please, thank you, that's very kind of you, it is possible?

Amanda watched the girl hurry away. "She likes your smile." Then she looked at him. "So do I. But it has been in short supply, today. Yesterday, of course, was pretty rough on you." Her voice trailed away, her eyes looked down at her glass. "Jeff Reid . . . Am I next on the list?"

For a moment, he said nothing. Was this why she was so upset? "Now stop that! You and I are going to relax for the next hour. D'you hear? Look, Amanda, I haven't had a decent meal since yesterday's lunch—and you haven't had one, either."

"I didn't even have lunch, yesterday. The picnic was a complete flop. It was really comic. We didn't get one nautical mile out of that little harbor. Something went wrong with the boat's engine, and Lucas twisted his ankle—beautifully staged, both items—and so we came back into port. Bianca and her friends were furious: they had all stripped down for a lazy afternoon and, instead of that, they had to put their clothes back on and take taxis to another beach. The one at the dock was much too crowded, they said. Lucas gave them the picnic baskets along with his regrets—sort of a consolation prize. Then he went off to find a doctor and get his ankle taped."

"And you?"

"I took a taxi and tried to follow Lucas," she said, much too offhand, and ended that topic abruptly. She lowered her eyes, became absorbed in the sherry glass. You can't tell Ian Ferrier the details, she reminded herself. She began twisting the glass in her hands, moving it gently around and around, like her own troubled thought. Lucas . . . Lucas and his two long phone calls from two different areas on his way home from the aborted picnic, setting the ball rolling madly. Visitors coming and going all that late afternoon. The brief summons Lucas had received by telephone, which sent him rushing out to that little art-supply shop where he would receive a fuller message. Then back in the studio again, another trip out around ten o'clock, another return home by midnight. And a late visitor, staying briefly, listening to Lucas on the subject of Fuentes, Tavita, Reid, Ferrier. And after the visitor had gone, Lucas had waited, paced around, waited. Finally, it came, the telephone call, the big one, making the appointment in Granada.

Lucas had done most of the talking but his voice was tight—it always went that way when he was nervous, excited—and his manner strangely formal. "Yes, sir," he had answered. "Certainly. I'll arrive in the morning. But I have a lunch engagement with some friends—unavoidable—and that may delay me a little. We'd better postpone that stroll until later. At four-thirty, if that suits you? And one other small change, I'm afraid. It would be easier to meet some place closer. The Generalife perhaps? We'd enjoy a walk through its rose gardens—they are particularly fine at this time of year. Well worth a visit. Pleasantly cool, nicely irrigated. You know it? Good. Yes, I agree, sir. Ingenious fellows those Moors."

That had been all—just two friends arranging a meeting for a visit to Granada. Two friends who shared a harmless interest in horticulture. Lucas' words had come clearly, subdued as they were, across the courtyard. Miraculously. That new listening device—an electric bulb that caught up every syllable and transmitted it to her room—was absolutely incredible in its performance. (Far different from the results she used to have from that other type of bug, which one of Martin's men had installed previously. Sometimes she had even wondered if Lucas knew it was there and had smothered it; but that had been finding an easy excuse for her own possible stupidity. If she had been stupid at all, it was to have persevered with the uneven quality of the old listening device—sometimes clear enough, sometimes totally inaudible.) Miraculously, she thought again. And such a simple innocent conversation. Even the use of "sir" had been geared for any Spanish ears listening at the telephone exchange. She had never heard Lucas use that word; never. Or was it a throw-back to his childhood, when he was brought up in a comfortable middle-class world? Someone who had authority spoke to him, someone of whom he was in awe, and out slipped the "sir." Was that it?

Ian Ferrier's hand had reached over to her glass, steadied it. He was saying, "Amanda! Amanda—the sherry is for drinking, not spilling. Or is this a libation?"

She gave up playing with the glass. "It's so hard to stop think-ing about—" She couldn't even tell him. She drank some sherry.

He waited for the end of the sentence, but it never came. "And you know what I'm thinking? I'm lunching with two girls. One is Amanda; the other is Ames."

"Oh, no!" she said quickly. She was indignant, but at least he had all her attention now. "I'm just the same girl you met yester-day. You liked me, I thought. And I liked you. We really got together, didn't we? There's no change in me. It's just that the whole problem has shifted, deepened. So I keep thinking about it. I don't know what is at stake—if I did, I wouldn't try to keep puzzling it out. But there is something big at stake, some-thing vital, something absolutely imperative. I can sense it. Don't you?"

Careful, he warned himself. How easy it would be to let slip that the worst was over. All that was left was the tail of the hurricane. It could have a nasty whip of its own, of course, but at this stage all you had to do was to hang on a little longer. At least, the end was in sight. "Could it be a false alarm? I mean—"

"This is for real."

"But if it's only your instincts—"

"More than that, Ian. Much more. It's Lucas and the way he's reacting."

"To you?"

"No, no. He takes me for granted, as usual. Do you know, he called me up late last night—early this morning, actually—was all excited about a trip to Granada with a couple of friends. The only trouble, he said, was that his car needed an overhaul, so would I lend him mine for the journey? And why didn't I come along, too? I'd like his friends—journalists touring Andalusia. Cool, don't you think?"

"So that's one time you refused him."

"No. I agreed. Martin had told me to go to Granada, and this seemed a perfect chance."

"But Lucas didn't arrive in your car."

She suddenly began laughing. "No. And it's really comic how that happened. We were packing our luggage into my Buick this morning, a little after eight. And the police arrived, wanted to see Lucas. It was something about a blue Fiat that had driven away from a hospital yesterday evening. Lucas told me and his two friends—rather dull types they turned out to be; they sat in the back of the car, let me drive because I knew the way, hardly spoke all the journey—anyway, he told us to get moving, he'd follow us as soon as he had dealt with Captain Rodriguez."

"Well, well, well," Ferrier said, a smile spreading broadly. "Amanda, you've made my day." He laughed, too, and then sobered up. "Too bad that Rodriguez didn't have a longer chat with him. A couple of years' chat, for instance."

"But it's odd, isn't it? Weeks and weeks go by, even months, with nothing special happening—just dull routine. And then, all at once, everything starts moving. The opposition is too alert, too intense, too active. Something important, something really big is developing. Complete crisis. And you keep worrying, wondering if you'll fail in your own small job just when you are needed, if everything will blow up and you'll have done no good at all."

The last phrase caught his attention, not only the words but also the way she said them. I could swear, he thought, that this girl is honest, totally committed in her own understated way. No flashing eyes, no wild rhetoric, just a very quiet and strong belief. And yet, he admitted, he had met some Marxist types who talked with restraint and sincerity; idealists, they called themselves. Yes, he thought, those self-proclaimed idealists. . . . Gene Lucas would fill that bill. But Amanda? "You really do worry too much," he said, trying to find some safe, noncommittal words. "That's no way to solve any problem."

"I know. Except there is one that just keeps glaring at me. That's hard to ignore, you must admit." She hesitated, then said, "I have learned something. Something that Martin ought to know about. And I don't know how to contact him. Have you seen him? Where can I reach him?"

Ferrier looked at her. "And what makes you think I could recognize him?"

"He told me he had met you. Last night, when he was giving me instructions over the phone, he said he had met you."

"I didn't know he was here."

"I don't know if he is. But there should be *somebody*. That's my whole trouble—complete breakdown in communications. I've waited around the hotel since I arrived. Not one sign, not one message from Martin."

Ferrier could guess the reason why. "Have you tried reaching him through Madrid?"

"He told me not to use that number. It's suspect. But you know that!"

Ferrier nodded. "I was thinking about something else—just forgot." He glanced at his watch. "Where the hell is that soup? You'll be late if we are not careful."

"But, Ian—this is really odd. Scary. I've been sent up here, and then I've just been left flat. This doesn't happen, Ian. Believe me."

He was looking around for the waitress. "I see her," he said with relief, and it wasn't because he was anxious about getting lunch on time, either.

"We can skip dessert if necessary," Amanda said. "There's a job Martin ought to do, or see that it's done. If I can't tell him about it, then I'll have to do it myself. That's all."

The soup arrived in stately triumph. "Now relax, Amanda," Ferrier told her as he watched her spoon playing around the edges of her plate. "Eat it up, all those beautiful vegetables and vitamins and things. Makes you big and strong and able to beat Gene Lucas."

She smiled, a small pathetic flickering smile. "Ian," she asked slowly, "after lunch—will you come with me?"

"Sure—I'd be delighted." That was one part of him. "As long as I can get back to the hotel before six." That was the other part of him. He was as divided emotionally as she was, he thought wryly. And then still a third part of him began to worry if he had been too definite with that mention of six. Reported back to Lucas, that little slippage might cause O'Connor some annoyance. Oh, cut it out, he told himself roughly: either you trust this girl because you feel you can trust her, or you believe Martin and think that everything she does or says has a double meaning.

She was saying, "Oh, you'll be back by then—easily."

"Where are we going?"

She glanced at the nearest table, and although her voice had been kept at the lowest murmur possible without becoming inaudible to Ian at her elbow, she decided not to risk even a whisper. "Later," she promised. "Besides, did I hear something about no business while we eat?" Her eyes were laughing.

So it's business we are going on, he thought. Too bad.

Suddenly, she was completely serious. She put out a hand, touched his arm. "And thank you."

She really meant that, he thought. I know she meant it. His

own appetite came back—for the last ten minutes, he had thought it had gone completely. "Ever been to the Grand Canary?" he asked. "I traveled that way en route to Madrid, a couple of weeks ago." But no business to be mentioned here, either. He would keep off the subject of tracking stations, and concentrate on the island itself. It was a likely starting point for some light conversation.

"The remnants of Atlantis?" she asked, interested. "Or is that just another myth?"

So they were off and going. . . .

It had been a pleasant meal, all two courses of it. (Yes, they had to skip dessert and drink the black coffee quickly.) "We can talk better in your car," Amanda said. She drew on the white silk coat, thin, reversible, with a brown lining to match her dress.

"You're in plenty of time. Almost ten minutes to spare."

"We may need it. I'd like to get there early."

He paid, and they left the little dining room engrossed in itself, came out through small gardens into the quadrangle. "My car's outside. Where is yours?" She was hurrying, he noted.

"I came by taxi." And then, more frankly, "Lucas borrowed my car. He says his own is still giving him trouble. Actually, he's afraid it is too easily noticeable. That's the real truth behind all his excuses."

It's April weather, thought Ferrier. Blue sky invaded by rain clouds. "The hell with Lucas," he said angrily.

"I agree. But not until we find out whom he is meeting." She stopped as he opened the door of a Simca for her, looked at him with her eyebrows raised. "Don't you trust your own car, either?"

"They fixed it good and well this morning. Wouldn't budge."

"We'll travel east, around the Alhambra. Keep it on your left." She stepped in, waited until he started the car and they were away from any curious eyes before she slipped off the coat and reversed it. She kept it over her knees. "It isn't too far."

"I thought you'd be too hot in that thing. It's smart, though."

"It's useful. I reached the restaurant in white. So I thought I'd better leave the same way."

"And where are we going?" he asked, patience ending, curiosity no longer hidden.

"The Generalife."

She had given it the full Spanish pronunciation, Hehnehralee-feh, spoken so quickly that he looked at her questioningly. "Oh,

yes," he said as he caught it, "the Generalife. Of course—roses."
He shook his head, thinking that if anyone had to have a weakness, then roses were a good one. So this was where Lucas was meeting someone or other, was it? Again April weather, bright sky marred by heavy cloud.

"Do you know it?"

"No. Didn't have time to visit it. I know its situation, though. Roughly, that is."

"How roughly?"

"It lies along a hill of its own, across a gorge from the Alhambra. Three-star view. Gardens and terraces, and gardens and terraces. Also three stars. Pavilions, summer residence for the Moorish kings. They kept the harem there during the hot weather. Four stars definitely."

"You do read your guidebook."

"All the interesting parts." They came through the big gates. "I turn left here, keep under the hill?"

"Yes. That other road is for people on foot. We'll get as close as we can by car. Saves time."

"For what exactly?" She still had not given him the details.

"Lucas is meeting someone there at half past four. Someone extremely important—perhaps his control, or at least his chief contact. I could tell that by the way Lucas talked over the phone with him early this morning. I have never heard Lucas be so polite, so old-fashioned: no hep phrases, no snappy retorts, no acid remarks. This man is important."

"So you have a bug in Lucas' room?" Unless she had been there personally, Martin would remind him.

She nodded. "I imagine the subject of their talk will be Tomás Fuentes. That was another conversation I overheard: Tomás Fuentes, certainly in Granada, perhaps connected with a dancer called Tavita. You know her, don't you?"

"This is her car we're in."

"Oh, God," Amanda said, and her face tightened. "Now they'll really start tying you up with her."

"What of it?" he asked sharply. "She was Jeff Reid's particular friend. Naturally I met her."

"And you know nothing about Tomás Fuentes?"

"I haven't one idea where he is, and I couldn't care less." He got his voice back to normal. "Where do you expect to find Lucas? Acres and acres of gardens." He glanced up the hillside to his right. It was terraced and green. A beautiful labyrinth.

"And lots and lots of pools and fountains. But there is only one garden where there are little irrigation channels running through long beds of roses, with sprays of water rising and falling in a light arch over the flowers. Definitely ingenious. And that is what we are looking for." She began drawing on the silk coat, brown side out this time. From its pocket, she pulled a chiffon scarf of a soft mauve-pink, tied it around her head, knotted at the back, let the ends hang loose.

"You have your own way of being ingenious," he told her. And discreet—no sharp colors to attract anyone's eye. "But with a tan like yours, you shouldn't cover up your arms. A pity." He was slackening speed, drawing into the parking area, obeying the atttendant's signals where to leave the car.

Her answering smile was absent-minded. She was looking at the other cars. "No sign of my Buick," she said with relief. "You never can tell with these people. They may come ahead of time, make sure it's all safe before they actually meet."

"You really believe they will meet?"

She looked at him in astonishment.

Yes, she really believed it. He switched off the engine. "How do we approach? Up that hill?" The path climbed between gardened terraces.

"I'll show you the way." She was opening the door. "Keep a little distance behind me. We'll meet in the patio." She hesitated, nervousness no longer disguised. "But keep me in sight. Don't lose me, Ian. Please!"

"I won't."

Then she said in a very small voice, "Geronimo!" and she stepped into the brilliant sunshine.

20

Amanda walked steadily up the path to the main entrance of the Generalife. There were several people taking this road: a few family groups dawdling, keeping a close eye on straggling children; some foreigners pausing every now and again to look back at the view of the Alhambra on the hill behind them, studying maps, frowning over guidebooks. A mixed crowd. It would grow as the afternoon lengthened—most visitors-to-come were enjoying Sunday dinner or their siesta. She could see no one she recognized.

She reached the underpass, a short tunnel that would bring her up into the main courtyard. In its shadow, she risked turning to glance behind her. Ian Ferrier was a little distance away, trying not to appear as if he was hurrying. She felt a sudden warmth, an excitement, a strange suspension in time. Then she walked on, before he would see that she had been standing there, looking at him. There was a smile in her eyes, a softness on her lips as she stepped out of the underpass and entered the courtyard. More people here. Quickly, she came back to reality.

There was no sign of Gene Lucas as yet. How cleverly he had chosen this place for his meeting: several ways in and out, many paths, a confusion of terraces, an abundance of shelter from thick cypresses heavy with age, distractions everywhere—bright colors of flowers, constant movement of people. She glanced at the little groups debating what route they'd take first, and chose two Swedish girls who had decided on the patio, handsome blondes with a gay line of chatter and a roving eye—but not for her. They didn't even notice as she followed close at their heels, then slipped away from their escort once she was through the entrance. Usually, when she came here, she'd stand just at this spot, looking at the long rectangle that formed a patio, open to the sun, whose floor was entirely covered with roses and flowers. Today, she didn't pause. The entrance was a vulnerable place. Quickly, her eyes searched, made sure. Lucas hadn't arrived.

273

She had chosen a path between two of the long straight beds of roses that ran the full length of the patio. Delicate sprays of water met in a perfect arch above the bright flowers, a curtain of crystal beads gleaming in the sun, shimmering at the touch of stirring air. It was a fragile wall, translucent, but somehow she felt it protected her. She relaxed. She stopped to admire some roses, waited for Ferrier. In a few seconds, he was beside her. "All clear, I think," she said softly.

And half an hour to wait. "Where do we go?" Ferrier had been studying the patio. About fifty yards long, perhaps more; and a quarter of that distance wide. Two walls with vines and shrubs on either side, disguising a drop to a lower terrace on his left, a rise to a higher terrace on his right. Behind him was the entrance he had just used—better keep away from there, he warned himself. Facing him, edging this incredible floor of roses, was a two-storied pavilion, white, simple yet fragile in the Moorish style, that stretched across the full breadth of the patio and ended it completely. The second story interested him. It had a wide, deeply recessed balcony that seemed to occupy most of the floor space up there.

She noticed the direction of his eyes. "That's where we go. We take the steps on the left."

They were narrow and steep, tucked away at the corner of the building as if the architect had wanted to keep them as unobtrusive as possible and not destroy the line of his pavilion. "Any other way out from that place?" He kept looking at the balcony. One thing in its favor was its depth: he couldn't see its back from where he stood.

"Yes. It's really a gallery. You'll see when you once get up there. Several rooms, and a side way out onto the terrace that lies above us. If necessary, we can always make a quick exit that way." She noticed his hesitation. "The gallery is so broad that they can't see us up there unless we come almost to its edge and look down on the patio."

"But can we see them?"

"You'd be surprised." She was already moving toward the steps.

She seemed to know what she was doing. But he resisted it, just a little. "I'll follow," he told her. He waited for a couple of minutes, walking around the stretches of roses, seeing nothing to alarm him. It was an innocent Sunday afternoon, a general assortment of the domestic. Families with children, old people alone, honeymoon couples speechless, younger people in chattering groups, two handsome Spaniards stalking two blonde Swedes, a gray-coated attendant with slow pace and supervisory eye. Reassured, Ferrier glanced at his watch—four minutes past four o'clock—and then briefly at the huge central balcony of the pavilion. A redheaded man and a fair-haired girl were standing at its front, elbows leaning on the balustrade. Otherwise, it was empty. Immediately, he was worried about Amanda. He headed with no more delay for the flight of stairs.

It was a steep, straight pull, discouraging for most leg muscles. His own reminded him they had already had their exercise for the day. At the top of the steps, there was a quick plunge into limited space, tortuous, shadowed: a twisting corridor of stone, a few rooms small and bare of furnishings; intricate carvings and designs around the occasional narrow window that was empty of glass, letting in the hill breeze and keeping out the stark sun; superb views for those who had time for them—neither Ferrier nor the young couple kissing blissfully in one dark corner qualified for that; and then, unexpectedly, emergence into bright daylight and the long deep balcony. It was roofed, enclosed on three sides, and obviously led to other rooms. A true gallery, in fact, spacious and simple and inviting. The red-haired man and his girl were leaving. Amanda was alone, drawn close against one side wall, almost at its center point. Her eyes were watching the main entrance to the patio.

He went over to her, stood beside her. "A good view of the gates," he conceded, "but you were vulnerable. I could have been anyone coming up behind you."

"I knew your footsteps." She was smiling. "Actually, I sneaked a quick look."

"How long have you been standing here?"

"Before you looked at your watch and saw the time was five past four." She lifted her wrist, comparing his watch with hers, glanced briefly to check. "You're a minute slow. Or am I fast?"

"From now on, I'd better take your word for it. And that's a lopsided apology. You were right and I was wrong about this place. It's safer than it looked." He half turned at the sound of footsteps—the old floors creaked well—but it was another couple, wandering hand in hand. Behind them, slowly, tactfully, came one of the uniformed attendants, making sure that historical monuments were given the proper respect. Ferrier rested a shoulder against the wall. "No wild parties allowed, I see."

"You'd have to go back five centuries for that. This was where the harem was kept. So my Spanish friends tell me. They may be romanticizing of course. It makes a good story, especially by full moon."

"You came here by moonlight?"

"Once." Her eyes kept watching the entry to the garden.

But not on business, he thought, and felt a twinge of jealousy that startled him. He tried to joke it away by looking around the empty gallery, saying, "Standing room only nowadays. A pity. No improvement at all on cushions piled on silk rugs, stars above, roses below, and the distant music of falling water." And Amanda with her hair falling loosely over her shoulders, her eyes on his, her lips coming to meet him. "Amanda—"

Her eyes did turn to meet his.

Neither of them spoke.

Quickly, she looked down at the entrance.

"Let's get this damn duty over and done with," he said, "and then—" And then what? He looked away, too, stared down at that bloody entrance.

Five minutes passed. "I hate waiting, this standing around," Amanda said.

"Will he come?"

"Lucas? Yes. That message was definite."

"Not a fake to draw you up here?"

"Not a fake. He doesn't know about my new little listening gadget. I had one, you know, that wasn't too reliable somehow or other. Then, just a month ago, an old friend from my training days was passing through Málaga, came to see me. He's an expert in electronics; it's his specialty. So he listened to my complaint, said he'd fix it for me. And he did. A new device entirely. He got it working, one Saturday afternoon—the picnic day, remember?—and I must say it is miraculous. He told me to keep quiet about it, though. And I have, until now. So that you can take the worried frown off your face," she added with a small laugh. "As for keeping quiet—I think he cadged the device from a friend. Unauthorized procurement of intelligence supplies."

"In other words, he took a short cut. Clipped the red tape. Sounds a sensible kind of fellow."

"And of course," she said, amused, "all I heard for four weeks was just political chitchat. One of those doldrum periods I mentioned at lunch. Then wow! These last two days—they've been something else."

"What about the old listening device, the one that spluttered instead of talking? Did your friend remove it, or leave it in place?"

"In place. Untouched. Not even examined."

"He's smart as well as sensible. Did he offer any explanation of what had gone wrong with the first gadget?"

"He thought it had been discovered, and put out of action when anything important was being discussed."

"And who would Lucas blame for it? You?"

"I don't think so. I hope not. . . . At least, he never gave one sign that he thought me anything except another of his little stupids. Good for making the sandwiches, lending him vodka when the Martinis ran out at his parties, emptying ashtrays, washing up, amusing his nonpolitical guests with light chitchat. Women's work." She shrugged that off, turned serious again. "We aren't the only opposition he has to worry about. There are the pro-Chinese communists. They're around, you know. In fact, they came into one of his private discussions yesterday. The KGB are nervous that the Maoists may try to kidnap Tomás Fuentes. Or that the CIA may get hold of him." She gave Ferrier a quick, searching look. "Just who is Tomás Fuentes?"

"Someone important to them, obviously," he said, trying to keep his voice offhand, his face blank of expression. "Interesting discussion you heard yesterday."

Her eyes went back to watching the gate. There was a long silence. "They are going to search Tavita's house," she said at last.

"How?"

"By pretending to interview her."

"My God—" And here I'm stuck, he thought grimly. He controlled himself. "Did you mention to anyone that you were meeting me for lunch?"

She saw where that question was leading. She didn't like it. "And bringing you up here to get you safely out of the way?" she asked angrily. "Trust me more, Ian. You don't, do you?"

"I've never met a girl who attracted me more."

"I know you like me. Just as you know I like you. But something has been coming between us all afternoon. What? Oh, forget it," she said bitterly. "But I haven't been using any bug in your rooms. If I do that with Lucas it's because he is the enemy. He is out to destroy us. Any way he can. Don't you understand that?"

"I know the facts of life. I'm not quibbling about electronic surveillance of an enemy agent. Or of anyone who is planning assassination or organizing sabotage or conspiring to seize power by force. We'd all have given a lot for some listening device or telephone bug that could have been planted on Lee Oswald long before he shot Kennedy." From behind them, entering the gallery, came a burst of giggles and cross talk in Swedish and Spanish. Ferrier glanced around: the two young men had caught up with the blondes, and what couldn't be understood was being mimed. It was a merry little party, and would get merrier. The girls came forward to have a quick look down at the rose garden, decided the gallery was too crowded with Amanda and Ferrier there, and retreated to explore the rooms. Ferrier grinned and said, "Now that's where I wouldn't condone any listening device. Nor would you."

She nodded. "Just so you know where the line is drawn," she said, relaxing visibly. "I'm not someone who snoops around into people's lives. I—"

"I know that," he said, and slipped his arm around her waist. "You don't have to be so defensive about it, though. Not to me, at least."

"Then," she asked very quietly, "why are you so divided about me? Why does everything go so well between us—and then, without warning, your guard goes up?"

"Perhaps," he said, and there was more truth in it than he liked to admit, "because I've been a fairly happy bachelor, everything arranged comfortably, simply, no extra cares, no ties on my freedom; and then I meet a girl who has beauty, intelligence, a sense of humor, a sense of duty, and her life is full of problems. And automatically my reflexes say, 'Danger, Ian, here's danger.' And instinctively—" His eyes hardened, his arm tightened on her waist. And Amanda's body stiffened, drew nearer to him. Gene Lucas had just entered through the gates.

He was walking slowly, partly sheltered by a family group that trailed around him. He was early by ten minutes. Once inside the patio, he separated from Papá and Mamá and little José and Maria and all the rest of the brood, and began his own separate stroll down one long flower bed. His face came into sharper focus. Today, he was a well-dressed man in the Spanish style (and it suited him—the Swedes would have adopted him on sight), with a seemingly quick eye for pretty girls that neatly disguised a more general interest. Not much missed him.

"Is he coming here?" Ferrier asked worriedly, noticing Lucas' direction.

"Why should he? You and I are supposed to be safely up in the Albaicín."

"The gypsy quarter? And how did we get there?" He watched Lucas stop at a display of roses and turn to look back at the entrance gate.

"Well—you were right—I did tell him I would probably lunch with you. I had to. He asked me what I was doing for lunch, when he came borrowing my room for his meeting with some people who were arranging an exhibition of paintings here in Granada. He thought they were interested in two of his; very exciting, big deal. He was sorry about the way he was neglecting me, but it was just one of those things. He couldn't even be with me this afternoon, as he had promised; we'd just have to postpone that daylight visit to the Albaicín and he'd take me there later this evening after dinner. And that's where I dug in my heels and said, 'But I've never seen it by daylight—that's the whole point—I want to see the gypsies as they live there, not putting on a performance for tourists. So I'm going this afternoon.' But not alone, he warned me; that would worry him. So I said that if he wouldn't come, then I'd ask you. He tried to look doubtful. But he was pleased. After all, he had tried to steer me into that suggestion, hadn't he?"

"The perpetual chess game. Pawn to Queen's fourth."

"But whose pawn?" she asked quickly. "I hope it was mine. That's the winning move, isn't it?"

"It's the aggressive one."

"Well, I'm tired of always reacting instead of acting. Let's see what this move brings us."

Lucas must have recognized someone who had entered the gate —there was a crowd there now—for he had stopped watching it and begun to walk slowly around. Bloody hell, thought Ferrier, I didn't see any likely candidate coming through the entrance. I was too busy being fascinated by Lucas, too absorbed by what Amanda was telling me. So he did want to get me out of the way this afternoon, he did want—Ferrier's thoughts stopped cold. He tightened his grip on Amanda. Behind a screen of fine water, Lucas was meeting his friend. The arch of spray hid them as they came together, but not enough from this high observation point. The man was Martin.

Amanda said almost in a whisper, "Before they leave, I must slip down there and get that man's photograph. I'll take the path through that high terrace on our left, circle back down to the entrance gates of the patio. I'll catch him there. Don't worry, it's safe enough: they won't be leaving together. He doesn't know who I am."

"I think he does. And there's no need to photograph him. I can identify him. It's Martin."

She turned to stare at him.

"It's Martin," he repeated. And that explains so much, he thought, and his own anger grew. "I'm sorry," he said bitterly as she looked back at the middle-aged man, tall, pale of face, quietly dressed, who stood beside Lucas. "Truly sorry." For doubts and suspicions and all the rest of the poison that Martin had given him to drink. Thank God he hadn't swallowed it whole, thank God for his own instincts. He had thought they were prejudices; he didn't like the guy, he blamed him for fussing too much and delivering too little—a day late and a dollar short, that had seemed to be Martin.

For a long moment, Amanda could say nothing. She looked down at that quiet figure unbelievingly. "So Lucas has known all along. About me. He's known. They've played me—" She took a deep breath. "Oh, no!" she exclaimed, white-faced with shock. "Are you *sure?*"

"Positive. I met him last night."

"Oh, no," she said again, but this time it was in protest, not disbelief. "And all my reports—he would pass on to Washington only what he wanted them to see. Careful selection. Nothing damaging about Lucas—nothing valuable. No wonder my reports got such little response. No wonder I seemed so—so ineffectual. Oh, God—what do I do now?" Her hand tightened on Ferrier's, holding it close to her waist. And then something caught her interest in the patio. "That's odd. They have scarcely talked, and now Martin is moving away. All the trouble they've taken, the risk— oh no, not for two minutes of talk. They could have telephoned for only that."

"He isn't moving too far away. He seems to—" Ferrier broke off. He was perplexed, uncertain, as he saw a third man approaching. It was Ben Waterman.

Amanda had caught sight of Waterman, too. "There's your friend—the one who delivered my postcard to you."

Ferrier had found the explanation. With a smile, he said, "He knows Martin. He has either followed him up here—that's the kind of wild thing Ben might do, just for the hell of it—or he came to admire the roses and caught sight of Martin." In either case, this should give Martin a jolt. "Let's see how Martin handles this," Ferrier said, his smile spreading. "Yes, very skillful. He has put ten feet between himself and Lucas. They don't even know each other any longer."

Then Ferrier's amusement ended abruptly. Ben Waterman had passed Martin without one glance. Ben Waterman had joined Lucas. Together, they began walking slowly along the stretch of rose bed, stopping now and again, walking, stopping, walking, and always talking, talking easily and quietly and intently. Martin followed at a discreet distance, keeping a watchful eye on everyone around them.

"What's your friend's name?" Amanda asked, almost in a whisper, drawing back instinctively as Martin's eyes were suddenly raised to the gallery.

Ferrier didn't speak. She looked at him. His face was tense, his lips tight. He has had a worse blow than even I had, she thought; this has hit him hard. She asked no more questions, just kept her hand on his. The pressure of his arm around her waist was almost unbearable.

Ferrier took a deep breath. "Ben Waterman."

"He's the important one. He arrived exactly on time. Half past four. Martin made sure that he'd meet the right man, quickly, without any doubts. Yes, that was it—Martin vouched for Lucas."

"I've known him for years," Ferrier said dully, still watching Ben Waterman, now half hidden by a screen of water. "And I never knew him at all."

"He could be working for us," she tried. "He could have been sent here to do the job I've done so—so badly," she added bitterly. But she didn't really believe it: this man Waterman was giving the orders. Of that, she was sure.

Ferrier got a grip on his thoughts. "Let's move out of here. I've got to get back to the hotel. There's a man I must see. At once." O'Connor . . . How much had O'Connor told Waterman about the Fuentes escape? About the journey to Seville with Max? Perhaps Fuentes had never reached there. "Come on," he urged.

"I can't. Not yet."

"I'm *not* leaving you here alone, and no argument about that. Look, Amanda—there is nothing more you can do. It's over. Done. Finished." And my job, now, is to get you safely down through these gardens to the main road. "Come on," he repeated, his voice sharp with worry.

"I must see if anyone else joins them—get a photograph—"

"And report to whom? Martin?" he asked brutally. But she came out of her shock, recovered some of her senses.

She looked at him helplessly. "I—I—" She shrugged her shoulders as if she had just fully realized how lost she was. But she did not move.

"Face it, Amanda. The job's over. And you are in danger. If you are found near this patio, it won't be only this assignment that's ended for you. For God's sake, don't you know the danger you're in?"

And so are you, she thought. I've put you in this danger. But the job's not over. Not yet. And you won't leave without me. What do I do, what do I do?

"There is one man you can report to, and he is at the hotel," Ferrier said in desperation. "He is leaving for Washington. This evening." And that got results.

"The man you must see?" She didn't wait for his reply. She began walking quickly, past the honeymoon couple who were wandering around hand in hand, past a group of school girls twittering excitedly under the careful gaze of a nun, past the young men who circled around them, past the attendant pacing his beat, and led Ferrier through the little maze of bare dark rooms and passages that brought them out on the upper slope of the Generalife's hill.

He let her choose the way down. She knew these paths better than he did. The pace was fast. By himself, he might have taken a longer route through the complication of terraces and Moorish architecture. The chief problem, now, was time. But they lost none. (He had stopped worrying about being discovered by one of Lucas' men patrolling these gardens. It was more likely, he decided, that the smaller fry had been kept well away from the patio: Martin would not want any of them to be able to identify him. Nor would Ben Waterman.)

"Congratulations," he said as he saw that their quick detour was bringing them back into the mix of people outside the patio's entrance gates. "When we leave the underpass, I'll draw ahead. Keep well behind me. I'll signal you if I see anyone. That stretch of road down to the parking area is too open for my taste." It was just the kind of place that Lucas might have posted one of his agents.

She glanced at the patio gates as he steered her wide of them. The crowd around them was bigger than ever. "Conditions are perfect," she murmured. "Too bad about that photograph."

"We'll do without it," he said sharply.

"Waterman talking with Lucas, Martin just ten feet away—wouldn't that be something?" she asked lightly.

"Let's not even joke about it," he told her. "Don't press our luck, Amanda." At least, he thought, her confidence is returning. Up on that gallery, six minutes ago—less—she had been a shaken girl. "I'll get to the car first, bring it to meet you at the foot of that road. Then you hop in. No strain. Right?" They entered the underpass. "Right?" he repeated when she didn't answer. "We'll keep separate. I'll scout ahead. If everything is okay, I'll be at the foot of the road with the car. Got that?" And if everything isn't okay, I'll get back to her, grab her by the wrist, and we'll lose ourselves among those terraces.

She nodded. "But I don't think we should risk being seen getting into the same car. I'll take a taxi. Much safer."

He halted, looked at her. "Safer for whom?" Was she worrying about *him*? He nearly laughed outright.

"For both of us. Lucas knows we are spending the afternoon together. We'll be less noticeable if we are separate."

True enough. But he didn't like it. "There may be no cabs."

"Then you'll just have to pick me up as you said. But we really shouldn't arrive at the hotel together."

"We have a perfectly good cover story for that."

"Not any more. We never could have visited the Albaicín, gypsies and all, in this short time. No—you had to leave after lunch—business appointment, friends to meet, something like that. And I took a taxi and went sight-seeing."

He glanced at his watch. A quarter of five. Better than he had hoped, much better. But not good enough for the Albaicín alibi. She was right about that.

"I'll see you at the hotel," she told him. "My room number is 403. I'll stay there until I hear from you."

"We'll be watching for you. And if I don't call you before six— if I get delayed somehow—go straight to Room 307. His name is Smith."

"Take care, Ian," she said quickly. "You are my one hope." She laughed, a little unsteadily. Then suddenly she reached up and kissed his cheek. "And thank you."

He caught her into his arms, held her as if he would never let go, looking into those blue eyes. He kissed her lips. Then he was out into the bright sunlight, following the visitors who were leaving, making his way against the current of new arrivals.

The smile lingered on her face as she watched him go. He merged with the stream of foot traffic, and she stepped out of the underpass, keeping her head down, her hands deep in her coat pockets. She felt the mini-camera. Too bad, she thought again. I was so close to some really corroborative evidence. Martin could not have talked his way out of that.

The smile had gone from her face. Yes, conditions were perfect. In this crowd, she was only one of hundreds. And even if she couldn't get the three men into one photograph, she might get them separately as they left the patio. Same background, same clouds, same light showing the same time of day, same shadows, same film . . . Yes, that would be one piece of evidence that no one, not even the expert liars, could contradict. She quickened her pace. If she didn't get down to that group of taxis, Ian would come up here after her. Cursing and swearing, but coming up definitely. He was probably watching her, now, as she came to the foot of the road.

She saw the white Simca pull out as she got into a taxi. "Just a minute," she told the driver. She watched the Simca cruise past, Ian looking at her, making sure she was safe. It put on speed. Near her, a touring bus stopped and poured out a batch of crumpled people. This is my chance, she thought, this is it. Quickly, she handed the man a large tip, said, "Sorry, I have changed my mind." She was out and away before he could shrug his shoulders.

She slipped into the crowd of tourists and was lost from sight.

21

Ferrier did not stop to phone O'Connor from the hotel porter's desk. He made directly for Room 307, not even bothering to take the elevator to the second floor and walk the third flight. There was no need for that now. Ben Waterman knew exactly where O'Connor was to be found.

Ferrier knocked quietly. "Coming," a voice called from the room. He waited impatiently, studied the giant brass ashtray lying flat on the floor near him with its smooth fresh sand impressed by a large coat of arms. Along the vast stretch of hotel corridor there were many bright ashtrays and a uniformed boy at work on his knees, emptying the few cigarette butts, changing the sand, polishing the brass until it gleamed, adding fresh sand, smoothing it arena-flat, and at last carefully pressing it with the imposing seal.

The door opened. One of the young men he had seen sitting on the terrace that morning looked at him enquiringly, and relaxed. "Good," he said. "Glad to see you." Then he glanced out, following the direction of Ferrier's eyes, nodded. "Yes, he's been busy all afternoon."

"Regular staff or special substitute?" Ferrier asked as he stepped inside.

"Well—he's older than most of the emptiers and polishers. And he has been keeping a careful eye on this room. Much good it has done him. We've been taking it easy."

Have you? wondered Ferrier. He nodded over to O'Connor and two younger men—strangers to him—who were all on their feet, heads turned to face the door. Their jackets had been thrown aside, their shirt sleeves rolled up, ties slackened, collars loosened. The two strangers had just finished closing a fair-sized attaché case, stood beside it protectively. A sender-receiver? Ferrier glanced away from it, looked at the room. It seemed perfectly normal, with the usual nineteenth-century furnishings, faded pinks and creams, brass bedsteads, and all. But the writing table had been drawn up close to the French windows that gave out on their

285

own balcony, and the connecting door to another bedroom was unblocked and half open.

O'Connor moved over to the dressing table, began pouring drinks for everyone. He was looking remarkably happy. "And where have *you* been?" he asked genially. It hadn't worried him too much, obviously. Then he looked curiously at Ferrier as he offered a glass of Scotch. "Have this. You look pretty hot and thirsty. In fact, you look damned worried. What's the trouble?"

Ferrier took the glass, added more ice, juggled it around as he looked at the two strangers over by the attaché case. "Are these Martin's men?" he asked quietly.

"No. They work with Max."

"Absolutely guaranteed?" Ferrier looked at the other young man. Yes, his companion on the balcony that morning had left with Max. He was possibly okay.

Three pairs of eyes fixed on him angrily. O'Connor's were perplexed. "Absolutely. That's Sam who let you in. You've seen him before, haven't you?"

"No connection with Martin at all?"

"None." O'Connor was emphatic, and cold.

"Do they know who he is?"

"We have discussed him a little." O'Connor sounded vague. "We are working as a close team. In the circumstances, there's a need to know—"

"Good. I can talk then. There's something you all very much need to know." Ferrier took a swallow of cool liquid, didn't even taste it. "Martin is in Granada."

"Is he now?" O'Connor said. He was surprised, but not alarmed. "Well, as long as he stays out of our hair—"

"He's working for the opposition."

O'Connor froze. "Do you know what you are saying?" he asked much too quietly.

"I know that I saw Martin meet Gene Lucas—by appointment —in the Patio de la Alberca—up at the Generalife."

"How do you know it was a definite appointment? Martin could have been trying a smart move with an enemy agent."

"Amanda Ames heard the appointment being made early this morning in Málaga. She intercepted a phone call to Lucas."

"Amanda Ames?" This was Sam, half-amused, half-pitying. "Didn't you know she came up to Granada with two of Lucas' men? If you are looking for someone who may be playing around with the opposition, you couldn't do better than start with her."

"That," Ferrier snapped at him, "is what you are meant to think. She came up here on Martin's orders. If there's any suspicion about a security break in his network, he can shift the blame onto her. He has laid all the groundwork for that, hasn't he? And if any information about Fuentes gets to the opposition, then Martin will say that she lunched with me today and made me talk too much."

"Did you?" O'Connor asked.

"I lunched with her. But I didn't talk about Fuentes."

"Was she curious about him?"

"She had heard his name in these intercepts early this morning in Málaga."

"And she never reported this to Martin today—after all, he did send her up here, didn't he?"

"He hasn't been in touch with her. He left her sitting in the cold. She didn't even know he was *in* Granada." Ferrier drew a long, deep breath. "I tell you, I saw him. I saw him identify Lucas clearly to a third man who had also come to that meeting at the Generalife. And that man was Ben Waterman." Ferrier could feel a wall of ice forming around him, right here in this warm room. "Ben Waterman," he repeated defiantly.

The four faces stared at him.

Sam glanced at O'Connor. Then he said to Ferrier, "I don't get the picture, frankly. That patio where they met is the one with the pools? Just below—"

"You know damned well it isn't," Ferrier said. "Roses and a special irrigation system. Amanda and I stood slightly back on that gallery, looked down on them without being seen ourselves. The fountain sprays didn't hide them from where we were standing."

"How did this meeting take place?" O'Connor asked slowly, watching Sam's face. Ferrier had been accurate, no doubt about that.

"First, Lucas came into the patio. Walked around for some minutes. Next, Martin appeared and talked with Lucas—briefly. Then he saw Waterman approaching, and he retreated a short distance, stood there, waited. Waterman passed him as close as this—" Ferrier took a step right up to O'Connor—"but they didn't even look at each other. And then Waterman stopped beside Lucas. They began walking, talking. They were still talking when we left. Martin walked, too, kept his distance behind them."

The details had made some kind of impression. The four men looked at each other, then back at Ferrier.

Ferrier said, "Waterman arrived exactly at half past four. That was the specific time Amanda had heard in Málaga. She told me about that before we saw them meeting." He shot a hard glance at Sam. "I didn't quite believe her just then, didn't know what to think. But she was right about all the details. Half past four and Waterman was there. She thinks he is the important one."

There was a long deep silence. "Ben would be flattered," O'Connor said. "I expect him here at six. He has been sleeping off too big a lunch. Sam—would you just check his room?"

That's something at least, Ferrier thought. He tried another drink, but found his hand was trembling. He placed the glass carefully on a table, sat down on the nearest chair.

"And," added O'Connor, addressing one of the others, "he hasn't seen you, has he, Burt? Why don't you get down to the front door and watch who returns to the hotel in the next half hour?" He looked at the remaining young man. "Al—I can't think what the hell to give you to do, but wander out, will you? Perhaps you should keep an eye on the Ames girl." He turned to Ferrier, who had slumped in the chair and put a hand wearily up over his eyes as if he were trying to blot out the whole Generalife scene. "Ian," O'Connor said, "what's her room number?"

Ferrier's hand dropped slowly. He roused himself. "Room 403. But she won't be back yet. We returned separately to the hotel. She took a taxi. She said it was safer." Then he burst out, "I wish we hadn't. I wish she were here talking with you people. She could give you—"

O'Connor said, "It was certainly safer. For you. She was right about that."

"For me?" Ferrier looked at him indignantly.

O'Connor said to Al and Burt, "Okay. Phone if there is anything urgent. Otherwise I'll see you around six." They nodded, gave one last searching look in Ferrier's direction, went out through the communicating door into the next bedroom, taking the attaché case with them. O'Connor waited until the outside door to the next room was also safely closed. He picked up Ferrier's drink. "Let me freshen this for you."

"Safer for me?" Ferrier was back at that question, and angry.

"Look—if that girl has told you the truth, she is in a decidedly tricky position. Right up on the high wire. Anyone who tries to share her act is also sharing the danger. Fortunately for you—come on, take this drink; you need it—fortunately, this is a crisis moment. And it passes. By tomorrow, if only we play our cards right, Tomás Fuentes will have been only a rumor. A big exciting rumor that petered out. Nothing to it, man. We'll leave tonight, looking disgruntled and depressed: another of those false leads. And the opposition—oh, they'll search for a few more days, put out more alerts, but they'll leave, too, equally disgruntled. Rumors happen all the time, and they are mostly false alarms."

"They'll leave with a broad smile all over their faces."

"But we have got Fuentes. And we have hidden that fact. And we'll keep on hiding it as long as we want it hidden." O'Connor's voice had been cold and hard. Then he looked at Ferrier, who was skeptical and depressed, said more easily, "Let me give you the good word. We've been in touch with Max, loud and clear. The first stage is accomplished. Just half an hour ago, Fuentes was leaving for Washington."

Ferrier forgot everything else. "But not from Madrid. There wasn't time enough for that." He rose, went over to the French windows, looked out on the balcony. This room was high up, and made higher by the drop beneath the hotel to a lower stretch of ground. It faced roughly south, southwest, judging by the sun. He came back to his chair. O'Connor was watching him, had already guessed what was behind this interest in the view outside. "Loud and clear?" Madrid was due north. Reception would have been more difficult. "The message came from somewhere to the south?"

"That's right," O'Connor said. "A little to the west, actually. From the Cádiz area." He was suddenly in excellent humor.

From Rota? "You had him taken straight to our naval base there? And what does Fuentes say to that?"

"He is peacefully asleep."

"He isn't going to Switzerland?"

"If he wants to go—yes." O'Connor's thoughts traveled briefly to Jeff Reid's lighter. It might be a powerful mind-changer. "After he has talked with us, of course," he added discreetly.

"How much co-operation will you get when he wakes up in Washington screaming double cross?"

O'Connor looked pained. "Don't tell me you are feeling sympathy for that son of a bitch? Do you know what he pulled on me? A gun. Complete with silencer. I didn't even have time to take your parting advice."

"He actually drew on you? Backing up more demands?"

O'Connor nodded. "You know, there was a very awkward moment when I realized he would have killed me, taken my papers, walked right out of that door into the courtyard—if only he had been closer to my height and weight and had more of my face structure. Yes, there he was, pointing that pistol at me, calculating what kind of chance he would have."

"But not all power comes out of the barrel of a gun," Ferrier reminded him. He looked at O'Connor speculatively. "Sometimes it comes from a hidden ace. Such as Fuentes' own words, in his own voice, recorded by Jeff Reid's lighter?"

O'Connor only looked bland. "By the way, the lighter is safe. Thought you ought to know that. A relief, isn't it? Yes, Mike arrived in Washington without any trouble."

But Ferrier hadn't finished with Fuentes. "Why beat your brains out trying to make the rumor theory work? Why not let Waterman and his friends realize you've got Fuentes, and out of their reach?"

"Three reasons," O'Connor said crisply. "One: Fuentes is not safely out of their reach at this stage, if they know where to look for him. Two: we'd have no chance of any co-operation from Fuentes if he knew we hadn't covered his tracks as we promised. You know what he'd scream then? That we kidnapped him, took him by force, against his will. He'd blame us to clear himself. And three: Tavita's own safety."

"Three valid reasons," Ferrier said slowly. "Kidnapping charges? That's pretty steep. But it's pure Fuentes. He'd never have any chance of a comeback among his own people if they didn't think he had been victimized. They'd make good propaganda mileage out of that, too." Then Ferrier smiled. "When do you play your ace?"

"Only if we must. And I hope it won't be necessary."

"That's one time he won't be able to come up with any excuse, any explanation. No charges, no more demands. A reformed character." Ferrier added bitterly, "I say he isn't worth saving."

"Our country is worth saving," O'Connor said quietly.

"In spite of its Ben Watermans and Martins. God, what a hell of a mess some people create for themselves. Why? Why?"

"I'll start asking that when I'm quite sure in my own mind what they are." O'Connor paused. "I think we should remember that Ben Waterman was responsible for getting Mike safely to the Málaga airport last night. Ben didn't run any interference, try any tricks. Sure, I know Ben hadn't any idea that Mike was going on to Washington, or that he was carrying that lighter on him. No one knew that. Not even you. I know, too, that he might have been just building up our trust in him. As you'd probably say in your present mood, it was all a part of the old confidence game. But we ought—"

"Dammit, I've got every right to my present mood."

"I understand fully," O'Connor said. "But isn't it possible that your interpretation of the scene in the patio was a little colored by the Ames girl? She may be—"

"I saw him."

"Were you close enough to be sure it was Ben and not some quick-change artist imitating him? Remember Fuentes and his skill? That's possible, you know, it's quite—"

"Possible," Ferrier interrupted sharply, "but not true." His voice was harsh. "Look, do you think I *enjoy* saying it was Ben?"

"No, no. Please—" O'Connor looked at him unhappily.

Ferrier insisted, "I saw him. He was wearing a dark-blue suit, tightly cut, Spanish-style."

"If so, it's the first time he has worn it." O'Connor sighed, frowned. "Ian, mistakes can be made. But if you didn't make one—" there was a long pause, a deeper frown—"you can be sure that neither Martin nor Waterman is going to get away with it. Be sure of that," he added grimly.

"How would you handle the problem?"

"Not here. We couldn't deal with it here. It takes time, for one thing, to verify all the facts, make sure the suspicions are justified, trace all the leads we discover."

"So we play along with them, now, as if nothing had happened?" Ferrier didn't stomach the idea, and he showed it clearly.

"We wouldn't give them any valuable information, of course. But one thing is vitally important: we must not arouse their fears. We don't want them secretly skipping out for asylum in Moscow. So take it easy, Ian. Don't probe, don't test them. Don't—don't anything. Got that?"

"Martin will be the easier for me to handle. I don't like him, and he doesn't like me. But Waterman . . ." Yes, that was another matter altogether. I'll have to stop remembering him as a friend; I'll have to keep thinking of him as a Soviet agent. What is his role? Martin is a double agent, obviously. But Waterman? Just a highly trained man who had been skillfully directed into sensitive spots? No, he must be more than that. What's his specialty? Propaganda, disinformation, or simple espionage? Or is he a future contact for the Marxist underground in America? He speaks of making a close study of their newspapers—that could be his future cover. Or is he connected in some way with Department Thirteen? Why else is he so involved in tracking down Fuentes?

O'Connor came out of his own long silence, said angrily, "We are way ahead of ourselves. Nothing is proved. Nothing is certain. Nothing." There was a definite pause while he got his control back. "By the way," he said, forging into a pleasanter subject, "you must have made good time up that tunnel. You did a first-rate job. We are all grateful. I was a little worried that Tavita might delay you. She's a powerful delayer, that woman. All the feminine tricks and hesitations."

Ferrier was worried, unhappy, restless. He rose, searched for a cigarette. "No delay," he said abruptly. "She was on the telephone when I arrived. Some journalist wanted to interview her this evening. Big deal. Except—Gene Lucas is setting up a fake interview with Tavita. It's his excuse for entering the house."

"How did you learn that?" And O'Connor did not like it.

"From Amanda. And unless you start believing her, the opposition is not going to leave Granada disgruntled. They are going to leave with some hard information. Sure, they won't find Fuentes at Tavita's. But they'll question her."

"They most certainly will."

"She may deny everything. She doesn't scare easily."

"That," said O'Connor, "will depend on how they ask their questions. And don't think that these boys will hold back just because she is famous, popular, a woman who would make page one on any Spanish newspaper. When is that interview?"

"I didn't have time to ask Amanda." And that was a bad slip on my part, thought Ferrier. "But—" he thought back to Tavita's final remarks on the telephone—"Tavita said she probably could arrange an interview for ten tonight."

O'Connor threw up his hands. "Which gives them a pretty good tip that she expects Fuentes to be gone by then. She might as well have said the all clear sounded at ten." He rose, paced slowly to the window, smoothed his hair with one hand, and let his mind grope for a possibility. "They'll step in earlier, try to get Fuentes before we can move him from Tavita's house. Yes, that's how they may well be planning it. They'll arrive any time between now and eight o'clock. Certainly before nine. They'll figure that we'll be on the scene as soon as it is dark enough." As indeed we would have if Fuentes had really been hidden at Tavita's place. That was exactly what I was planning this morning when Ben Waterman drove me around on that scouting expedition. Ben Waterman . . . Oh, for God's sake, surely not. O'Connor swung round and glared at Ferrier. If any other outsider had brought me that story, O'Connor thought, I'd have laughed him out of the room. But Ferrier is no fool—that's the damnable part. "Look, you'd better get around right away, see Tavita. Tell her that the safest thing for everyone, herself included, is to keep saying that Fuentes was only a rumor. Just that. Nothing more."

"What if I got her away—took her out for a drink, kept her out all evening? They'd search the house, and then leave."

"And come back tomorrow to question her. They won't leave without hearing her story. I think you'd better tell her there is some real danger—" O'Connor stopped, listened, went quickly over to the door, let Sam inside.

"Sorry I'm late." Sam seemed a little more subdued than usual. He avoided O'Connor's eyes. "I've been searching the bar, the terrace, the public rooms, the shops. Waterman wasn't in his own room."

O'Connor stared at him, his lips tightening. He glanced irritably at the telephone, which had chosen this moment to start ringing.

"The bed wasn't even slept on. The maid had turned it down for his siesta. But not one dent, not one wrinkle. Virgin-pure. His gray suit was hanging under his bathrobe in the closet." Sam looked over at Ferrier, gave him a nod. "Boy," he said softly, "did you call it!"

O'Connor was too busy answering the telephone to make any comment of his own. ". . . He did, did he? What color of suit? . . . All right. Stay on the job, Burt. Tell Al to keep a sharp watch for the Ames girl. Let me know as soon as she arrives." He put down the receiver slowly. He said, "Waterman has just returned to the hotel in a taxi. He's wearing a navy-blue suit." Then he sat down, kept his eyes fixed on the wrinkled rug at his feet. "Well," he said at last, " we listen to Ferrier. We've been warned. And if we can't act on that, we shouldn't be in this business." He paused. "We'll deal with Waterman. And Martin. I'll make sure of that," he added softly. He raised his head, looked at Sam. "For the next few hours, we just follow the plan. No change. And play it easy—no jokes, no bright remarks."

"From me?" Sam was all innocence. Then he turned serious. "I'll be careful. Don't worry." And then one last crack, "Won't even mention Kim Philby."

"If you do, I'll send you back to Max with your guts hanging out."

"Pure Hieronymus Bosch," said Sam cheerfully. He noticed Ferrier's quick glance. "Another *aficionado*?" he asked with interest. "Have you seen—"

"Keep that for later," O'Connor said. "We have plenty of other problems to solve."

"Don't we always? And thank God a double agent is seldom one of them. Martin is the first I've met. I've heard of them— there isn't an intelligence agency that doesn't get infiltrated. But Martin's a first for me." He sobered, watching the deep depression settling on O'Connor's face. "Look at it this way, Bob. You've completed a successful mission—"

"Not yet."

I know that, thought Sam. He went on determinedly, "And as an extra bonus, you've flushed out a double agent. Waterman, too."

"Ferrier did that."

Ferrier said, "No. Amanda." And where was she? He had been delaying as long as possible, watching that telephone, hoping it would ring with Al's report that she had just stepped into the lobby. But he had to get over to Tavita's place. He began moving to the door. "Any further instructions—"

"Damn his miserable soul to everlasting hell," O'Connor burst out, rose violently to his feet. "A thousand honest men—doing a job that has to be done, doing it well—risking everything, sometimes their freedom, even their lives—a thousand of them and more. And one Martin comes along to smear them with his filth. One traitor, and a thousand are—" O'Connor broke off, fought for control.

"I always thought the Romans crucified the wrong man. It should have been Judas," Sam said thoughtfully.

O'Connor took a long, deep breath, became aware that Ferrier had stopped halfway to the door, was rooted there by his outburst. "Instructions?" O'Connor asked, picking out the word he had heard distantly in his surge of anger.

"Instructions for Tavita," Ferrier said. And I needn't worry that Martin—or Waterman—is going to get away with it. No, I can stop worrying about that.

O'Connor was back to normal. He said briskly, "Perhaps you should call her first. Tell her to lock up, tight. Not to let anyone enter her house until you arrive. I've got the damnedest feeling that they are all ready to move in."

Because Waterman had come back to the hotel, was probably on his way up here to keep them talking, keep them stuck in this room? Ferrier decided he would rather not face Waterman at all. He didn't trust himself to play it quite so smoothly as O'Connor had suggested. "I'll make the call from my room."

"No need. The security of this place has been shot to hell. Just word your message carefully, that's all. And I'd like to know what she says. If necessary, I'll talk with her, too."

Security shot to hell . . . Yes, thought Ferrier, everything keeps coming back to Waterman. I can't stop thinking about him, wondering what started him on the traitor's road. He made a good haul, here. Max, and Sam, and some of the other agents that Max brought in. And Mike last night in Málaga. Yes, he has learned names and faces, clobbered their security. Good God, I'm talking about Ben Waterman—can I really be talking about Ben? Ben Waterman?

"I'll get that number for you," O'Connor said. "Finish your drink."

It was engaged.

O'Connor's language was getting worse by the second. Sam was grave, Ferrier gaunt with worry. And this was when Ben Waterman arrived.

"Well, well," he said cheerfully, "you look the picture of gloom. I could hear you out in the hall, Bob." He looked at O'Connor enquiringly. He was flushed, perhaps from hurrying, perhaps from the afternoon sun. And if he had been asked, he could have said he had had a very good sleep, thank you. He had changed his suit. He was back to his usual gray. "Who is your target?"

"Everything and everyone and mostly myself," O'Connor said vehemently.

And how do I call Tavita? Ferrier wondered.

"Frustrations," O'Connor went on. "Whoever said this was the simplest way to make a living?"

Waterman walked over to the window, looked out. "Well—you get a view like this one. And all expenses paid. Travel and meet the world." He turned back. "What you needed this afternoon was a good deep sleep. All those late nights and early-morning rising. Why don't you have a nap before dinner? Which reminds me—are we having dinner here, or are we stopping somewhere on the road to Seville?"

"I don't know," O'Connor said, and he was perfectly honest about that. "Possibly we'll be leaving soon—at least I will. No point in hanging around for nothing. Max will probably decide to stay for a day or so. He's pretty mad—"

"Where is that big beef-eater, anyway? I thought we'd have seen him glowering at us from behind a menu at lunchtime. Or has he given up food for the duration, like you, Bob? You'll be in trouble if you don't eat and sleep more. Never pays."

"Max has been seeing his friends," O'Connor said cryptically.

"Some of these mysterious characters who sit over café tables?" Then Waterman became serious as he noted O'Connor's worried frown. He said sympathetically, "Have they been giving him bad news?"

"No news at all," O'Connor snapped. "And that's bad."

"No lead about this Tomás Fuentes?"

O'Connor shook his head. "Just rumors, and all conflicting. The same as in Málaga. The same as in Washington. Who has been feeding us a dish of tripe?"

"Oh, come on, Bob—it can't be as bad as that."

"It can be. A bloody waste of effort and time."

"But this morning when I dropped you off at Tavita's place you seemed pretty cheerful. What has soured you?"

O'Connor seemed to hesitate. "I was following a pretty hopeful lead. It looked good. I thought the whole business was settled. And it wasn't."

"I don't get you. But then, I haven't been told too much."

"No reason why you shouldn't know, now. I thought Fuentes might be there. He wasn't. Not one trace of him. Nothing."

"You searched?"

"All three terraces, every room, talked with the servants."

"And Tavita allowed this?" Waterman enjoyed the picture he was seeing in his mind's eye. "I'd have bet she would have stamped her foot, flashed her eyes, and given you a good old flamenco toss of the head."

"I came as a friend of a friend. And I was diplomatic. Hell, what do you think kept me there so long?"

"Did you actually speak the magic word 'Fuentes'?"

"At the end of the visit. Brought it up unexpectedly. And that was where she stamped her foot, flashed her eyes, and burst into a stream of Spanish, none of it complimentary. She really hates Fuentes' guts."

"Then she knows him. Don't you see, Bob? She is covering up—"

"She knew him some thirty-odd years ago."

"A long memory."

"When you build up that kind of reputation for yourself, you aren't easily forgotten."

"A real bogey man. But he couldn't have been much of a public figure—at least, I never heard his name and I thought I knew some of Spain's history. What is his real importance now? Or is that breaking security?"

"It is. But perhaps it isn't, if what I'm beginning to believe is on the right track. He's another dead myth."

"And all your trip to Spain was based on a rumor?"

"That's how we work, Ben. Just like a newspaperman. We follow a rumor until it peters out. And this one is petering out hard. Tomás Fuentes isn't in Granada. That's the maddening—"

The telephone rang. "Just a minute," O'Connor said. This was either Burt or Al with another report from the lobby. "Yes, go ahead, Max, go ahead." O'Connor listened to Al's slightly astonished voice. But the report was clear enough, even if the phrases were carefully disguised. It was, in effect, a joint report. From Burt came the information that Gene Lucas had returned in the Buick he had been using, parked it in front of the hotel. Three of his friends had already arrived and were staying outside with their cars—a Chrysler and a Mercury, each with a white oval plate clearly marking its origin as the USA.

"Oh, no," O'Connor said in disgust, and then let Al continue his own report. He had seen Lucas talk briefly with someone in the bar and then go to his room after a quick visit to the lounge.

"Beautiful, just beautiful," O'Connor said in even greater disgust. "Not one scrap of confirmation? Come on, Max, your people can do better than that." He listened to Al's brief comment on his remark. Around him, the silence of the room grew solid; there wasn't a movement. "I just can't advise you. Not over the phone. But I'll be pulling out tonight. I've wasted time enough. Sorry about bringing you here . . . I know, I know. What else could we have done? Ignore it? . . . All right. See you next time around." He ended the call, reminded himself to compliment Max on the way he had picked Al (trained, perhaps?), and sat down on the bed. He looked not only beaten but also baffled. "Oh, well," he said, and left his thoughts right there. "Have you a cigarette, Ian?"

Ferrier fished one out from his pack. "Slightly crumpled." *I'm nervous,* he thought. *What the hell do I say next?*

"Anything will do now."

"No go?"

"No go." O'Connor lit the cigarette, took one puff, jammed it down on the ashtray beside the phone. "Oh, yes," he said, remembering, "your phone call. Sorry I held you up for a bit, but I had to keep that line open."

"It's okay now?"

"Sure. Go ahead. Just keep it short."

"I'll try," Ferrier said. "But I'm calling Tavita."

Waterman broke into a broad smile. "Well, trust old Ian to find a new approach. He may get results for you yet, Bob."

"For me," Ferrier said. "Purely for me." He waited for the operator to put him through. "She asked me to dinner. I'm checking on the time."

"I can tell you that. Eleven o'clock. This is Spain."

"I get hungry. Let's see what a slight hint might do." The call went through at last. "Ian Ferrier speaking. Hello, hello—" He stopped in real amazement. "That was a man's voice," he told O'Connor. "Polite but brusque. He has gone to find Tavita. Let's hope."

"Could have been the servant," O'Connor suggested.

"Too much in command for that." Ferrier listened to the background noise. "There's a hell of a din going on." His worry was not faked. "Trouble, I think."

Waterman said, "Spanish households can be noisy at times. Extremely—"

"Oh, shut up, Ben!" Into the receiver, Ferrier said, "Is that you, Tavita? . . . The police?" He covered the mouthpiece, said to O'Connor, "They've been searching the house. She's practically hysterical." Then he listened intently, talked a little, seemed to calm her down slightly, listened some more. "Of course I'll come over," he said at last. "Yes, right away." He ended the call, faced the room.

Waterman pursed his lips. "The police will find what you didn't, Bob. They really are thorough, these boys. And there goes her whole career. A pity. Hysterical? No wonder. She has plenty to fear."

"It didn't sound so much like fear," Ferrier said. "More like indignation and anger. And she had good reason for that. You know what triggered off this visit by the police? An anonymous note. It said she has been harboring a well-known enemy of the state."

"Fuentes?" asked Waterman.

"No name given."

"I don't get it," O'Connor said slowly.

"Are the police still searching?" Waterman asked.

"No, that's over—otherwise she wouldn't have been allowed to talk with me. They found nothing. Nothing and no one."

"You know what?" Sam said, breaking his long silence, looking young and hesitant but terribly sincere. "I think if you find the writer of that note, you'll find the man who started the Fuentes rumor. Or the people who put him up to it. Could have been a skillful ploy to get us all here, out in the open—or almost." Now, he thought, let Waterman digest that.

Ferrier was at the door, ready to leave.

"Do you mind if I come along?" Waterman asked. "Sounds like a good story. And there's no security involved, is there? Nothing to raise its ugly head and say, 'Strictly censored.' Is there, Bob?"

"Not as far as I'm concerned. But I wouldn't write up this story too soon. The police might come questioning you, don't you think? And you'd have to get Tavita's permission—"

"It isn't for instant publication. I'm out of that racket. Just thought it would make an interesting page in my memoirs. Tavita will be flattered, the way I tell it. What about you, Bob? Aren't you coming, too?"

O'Connor hesitated. "No. Better not. Why tangle with the police if it isn't necessary?"

"Oh—a matter of your passport?" Waterman nodded his agreement on that. "Yes, that's right. They'll ask to see it, no doubt. I wouldn't risk showing yours even if it is an expert job. I suppose I'd better take mine along. Dammit, it's in my room! Look, Ian, I'd better meet you at the car. Won't keep you—"

"I'm late as it is. Skip the passport. It probably isn't necessary." Ferrier had the door open, was halfway out.

"It may be useful. Why don't you take your own car? I'll drive mine. I'll be right on your heels." A broad grin. "You'll vouch for me when I arrive?"

Ferrier was gone, leaving the door ajar.

Waterman's parting joke to O'Connor was "You know, Bob, you should be an honest man like me, travel under your own name, and then you wouldn't miss out on the fun." He made a quick exit.

O'Connor and Sam exchanged a long look. "Did you hear that son of a bitch?" O'Connor asked softly.

"And you told *me* not to make any jokes!"

"Now you know why."

Sam nodded. "Revealing." Strange how little things began to add up once you were properly tuned in. "Well, what now?"

"We wait for Al's report from the lobby."

Sam thought briefly. "You don't expect Waterman to go anywhere near his room?"

O'Connor only looked both depressed and worried.

Sam said encouragingly, "You were quite effective with that rumor talk. I'd have believed you—"

"He didn't."

"I thought he was halfway to it."

"Which isn't enough. He needs another nudge."

"The police bore you out. They found no one."

"That's what Ferrier reported. Waterman will check on that. Thoroughly."

"And find that Ferrier told the truth. He did, didn't he? Well, there's your extra nudge. It may do it."

"But what did Tavita tell the police? That's our weak spot, right there. Indignation and anger . . . Yes, I can see her, disclaiming any responsibility for Tomás Fuentes. And by doing that, she is admitting he does exist. And there goes our rumor. And, with it, her one chance of safety. Ironical, isn't it?" O'Connor shook his head, plunged into some unpleasant thoughts.

"But she may not even mention that name."

"Waterman will bring it up. You may be sure of that."

"Well, we made a good try. We might just—" Sam turned to the telephone as it rang, picked up the receiver. O'Connor wasn't even paying attention to it. "It's from Al."

"You take it." It will just be confirmation of what I don't want to believe, O'Connor thought heavily.

And it was. Al's report was concise and damning. Waterman had used the staircase to avoid Ferrier, gone straight into the bar and then into the lounge. At both places, he stopped briefly to speak to a man. The contact was quick, practically unnoticeable, an expert job. Al had recognized the man in the bar; he was one who had arrived that morning from Málaga, along with the Ames girl.

"Any sign of her?" O'Connor asked Sam quickly.

"No mention. What was Waterman doing? Passing the word? Calling off the dogs of war? Or just leashing them until it's safer to pay Tavita a visit?" Then Sam added, suddenly somber, "You know, Waterman must be a key man, carry real clout. Why did he speak with two men?" He thought about that. "One to contact Lucas, the other—Martin? He's giving the orders, that's certain."

O'Connor nodded. Yes, that was the most depressing fact of all: Waterman must have been a long, long time in this kind of work. All these years . . . "Sam, you get downstairs. Make a quiet reconnaissance. Amanda Ames. She's beginning to worry me."

Sam pulled on his jacket, neatened his tie, moved to the connecting door into his own room. "I'll send Al up here," he suggested. "Burt and I can handle the downstairs."

"What? Do you think I need a bodyguard?" He studied Sam with concealed amusement. So I'm one of the old boys, am I?

"It's always better to work in pairs." Sam was all diplomacy.

"No one is going to come in here and hold me up for information at the point of a gun." Not so funny, O'Connor thought as he remembered Fuentes that morning.

Sam grinned. "I wasn't thinking of you so much. I just didn't want anyone bursting in here and finding our attaché case next door. Might put the right ideas into his head. I'd rather we could keep his thoughts snarled."

"All right. Send Al up."

At least, thought Sam as he closed the door behind him, I got a small laugh out of him. He needed it. He worries too much. Amanda Ames . . . Don't we already have enough problems?

22

Tavita's house seemed peaceful. Two small gray cars, properly unobstrusive, blocked the driveway (one had a Málaga plate, Ferrier noted) but the Simca could be edged past them almost up to the garage. Ferrier left it there. He hadn't much time before Ben Waterman would arrive. Quickly, he cut back toward the main entrance. Its door was half open. He stepped into the hall.

Four men stood in close conference, voices in a low murmur. Two in police uniforms, two in civilian clothes. And of those, one was Captain Rodriguez. Ferrier nodded politely, received a return bow. Four pairs of eyes looked at him gravely. But no one stopped him, and so he went into the big room. What the hell was Rodriguez doing here? This wasn't his beat; he was definitely out of orbit unless he had been called in for consultation. But it had looked the other way around: Rodriguez seemed to be listening to the opinion of the other man in civilian clothes. The only cheering thing about that little conference, as far as Ferrier could see, was the paneled wall of the hall, totally in place and undisturbed.

"Tavita."

She had been standing at the opened door to the terrace, looking out at the sky, her head tilted back, her hands clasped. She turned with the usual graceful swing as he spoke, came running toward him. She was a mourning figure, dressed completely in unrelieved black, face pale, magnificent eyes tragic. She took his hand in a grip that was so intense that he looked at her, startled. "You saw Rodriguez?" She was speaking in a half-whisper. "Oh, that fool, that idiot Esteban. Almost ruined everything. Thought he was helping. Oh, Mother of God!" She had almost burst out into loud anger. She controlled it. "He had enough sense to call me, warn me what he had done. At two o'clock. I tried to reach you."

"What did Esteban—"

Quickly, she interrupted him, speaking naturally, as voices sounded more loudly in the hall. "Oh, Ian, I am so glad to see

303

you!" She caught hold of him, reached up to kiss him once on each cheek. Her whisper brushed his ear. "You know nothing of Tomás Fuentes. Nothing!"

Ferrier almost forgot the footsteps coming into the room. He mastered the smile that was beginning to spread across his lips, felt them go unnaturally stiff. But it was outrageously comic to be given the same warning he had come chasing over here to pass on to Tavita.

She saw the amusement in his eyes, drew back angrily. She covered that instinctive action, though, gave it a likely excuse. "An anonymous letter is a serious matter. It is not a pleasant thing to have policemen searching through my house."

"Surely they didn't believe a letter like that. They must get hundreds of them."

"But," said Rodriguez as he joined them, "they must check them all. It is tiresome for everyone concerned."

Tavita said quickly, "If it had not been for Captain Rodriguez—"

"Not at all. This is an unofficial visit, Señorita Vergara. My colleagues in Granada and I had a friendly chat—that was all. I don't even think that my business has any connection with theirs." He smiled tactfully. He looked more like an innocent cherub than ever, strangely clothed in a light-gray suit. "Oh, yes —I have a little business here, too. Some questions. But these can wait." He glanced back with a frown at the hall. "Isn't your friend joining us?" he asked Ferrier.

Startled, Ferrier looked at the hall, too. Ben Waterman had been quietly standing there, admiring the wooden panels. Now, he entered the room. On cue, thought Ferrier bitterly as he recovered. He had expected Waterman to be quick, but not quite as speedy as this. He made the introductions perfunctorily. Waterman was too busy to notice, bending over Tavita's hand, making an extremely adroit explanation-cum-apology for his intrusion: he had always wanted to meet La Tavita, admired her tremendously, and although this was possibly a badly chosen time to visit her, he had been unable to resist the opportunity when his good friend Ian Ferrier had said he was coming here. Would she be gracious enough to forgive his impetuosity, accept his regrets that she should have been put to such stress on this unhappy day? Here, Waterman glanced at the black dress and added that he, too, had been a good friend of Jeff Reid.

Tavita was both touched and pleased; the only thing she didn't quite like—or understand—was the strange look of anger on Ian

Ferrier's face, appearing, disappearing so quickly. So this Waterman was not really the same as the man who had called himself Smith—when he had first entered, she had immediately assumed that he was. Possibly he was just what he stated, an admirer who wanted a few pleasant words and might even end the visit by asking her for a signed photograph. She was accustomed to this, especially with Americans, who must collect more autographs than any other nation on earth. "Yes," she said gravely, "this is a bad day. And now—" She shrugged helplessly, and looked at Rodriguez.

Rodriguez said, "I can wait."

Waterman said genially, "No. I'll wait. May I do that on your terrace, señorita? The view must be magnificent." He was walking toward the glass doors, pulling a heavy-rimmed pair of sunglasses from his pocket. "Coming, Ian? I think Captain Rodriguez will finish his business more quickly without—"

"I would prefer," Rodriguez said, "that Señor Ferrier remain here. There is a small point which he can help clear up for me."

Waterman looked at Ferrier, said, "Now don't tell me, Ian, that you've been getting into trouble again." He was grinning widely as he left for the terrace, putting on his sunglasses before he stepped out into the warm evening light.

Rodriguez watched him standing by the terrace wall, looking down with interest at the roof tops far below him. Then he turned to Ferrier, lowered his voice. "Who is your friend?"

And that, thought Ferrier, is going to give Waterman a sharp jolt. No matter how we lower our voices, he is going to hear every word. That's my guess. I've never seen him wearing these sunglasses before. What kind of listening device is installed in the rim just above his ear? Or am I too suspicious? Yet one thing is sure: Ben Waterman didn't come here to concentrate on any view. "Didn't he show you his passport?" Waterman must have flashed it as well as dropping Ferrier's name to get past the group of policemen so easily.

"It was most impressive."

"Too impressive? Oh, I see. You think he is American Intelligence. No, no. He was a newspaperman at one time—with a good ear for an interesting story. And he still knows where to find one. That's all."

"Here?" asked Rodriguez sharply.

Tavita's eyes widened. She sank down on a couch. "Oh, no—he can't be one of those men who want to interview me. And to find me being asked questions by the police! Oh, no!"

"He didn't come here for an interview," Ferrier said.

"Interview?" Rodriguez had picked up the word, was examining it sharply. "What men?"

"Oh, some journalists or other. They've been pestering me all day," Tavita said angrily. "They are coming this evening at ten. Of course I can't see them now. I know they are important, but I will not see any of them tonight. I'm too tired, too upset. Captain Rodriguez—please finish your questions."

"As quickly as possible," he assured her. "Did you know that Esteban was worried about you? He thought you were alone here, unprotected against—"

"Alone? I am often alone."

"But not when you may be threatened by a man such as Tomás Fuentes."

Ferrier drew a deep, slow breath.

"But Esteban knows very well—" Tavita began.

"Do you know Fuentes?" Rodriguez had quickly switched his attention to Ferrier.

"All I know is that people keep asking questions about him. The first time I ever heard his name was yesterday, around noon."

"Who talked about him?"

"A man called Gene Lucas." Now listen to that, Waterman; are you flinching?

"Lucas?" Rodriguez asked softly.

"Yes. He was looking for Fuentes."

Tavita burst out, "Then this Lucas is a stupid man. Tomás Fuentes is dead. And Esteban knows this," she told Rodriguez. "So why didn't you ask Esteban all your questions and save yourself the journey to Granada?"

Rodriguez said, quite unperturbed, "I did talk with Esteban. He came to see me this morning. He told me a strange story."

"There's nothing strange about it. It happened."

"What happened, Tavita?" Ferrier asked. Better to let her tell this story that Esteban had cooked up—because he thought I had left for America?—than have Rodriguez ask his questions.

"On Friday," she said quickly, "a man came to El Fenicio and asked for me. Esteban talked with him. Esteban always does that with strangers who ask to see me. This man wanted my help— money, shelter. He said he was a refugee from Cuba. Oh, yes, I have given money and shelter to refugees. Often. But they have been friends of my brother, people whose names we knew, people whom we recognized. And *none* of them—" she looked at Rodriguez and shook her head emphatically—"none were ever criminals. Oh, I'm sorry, Ian. I should have told you all this, perhaps, when I asked you to visit me in Granada. Yes, I was a little nervous in case that man did appear again: I thought you would discourage him—as Jeff Reid would have done."

Now this is Tavita embellishing Esteban's story, Ferrier suddenly thought, to let me appear ignorant-innocent of anything that was really going on. A sweet try, but a dangerous one. She'd better stick to the simple outline. Rodriguez is delighted with this little elaboration. "That man?" asked Ferrier. "Tomás Fuentes?"

"*Not* Tomás Fuentes! The man who came asking for my help. He used the name of Tomás Fuentes."

"But why?"

"Because my family had known Tomás Fuentes. That was many years ago. The impostor thought—I suppose—that I would remember that friendship and help him now. But he seems to have known little about the name he had borrowed. Tomás Fuentes is dead. He is buried somewhere outside of Barcelona. He has a sister in Málaga who has visited his grave."

Rodriguez said, "Yes, Esteban told me all this. But a grave does not prove that a man is dead—not a man such as Fuentes."

"But the stranger did not even *look* like Fuentes," Tavita said indignantly. "Oh, I know I was very young when Fuentes walked around Málaga. But this stranger was about your height, Captain Rodriguez. Fuentes was taller. Esteban remembered that, too. He also thought he remembered that Fuentes had brown eyes and dark hair. But this man had gray eyes. And he was too young to be Fuentes. He was *not* a man in his fifties—like Esteban. He seemed to be in his forties. No, no, this man was a pretender. The only thing I could recognize about him was the name he gave. And that is one name I would never help." She shook her head over the man's stupidity. "Of all the names for him to choose!"

"And you refused to help this man? You sent him away?"

"Esteban told him to leave El Fenicio. And Esteban sent me back to Granada. So I drove here yesterday morning. But it seems the man learned I had gone, and he followed me. He telephoned me last night. An extremely short call. I told him he was an impostor, and he hung up—just like that." She cracked her fingers.

"And since then?"

"Nothing. I haven't seen him, I haven't heard his voice." This was the truth, and she spoke with assurance, with a sense of small triumph.

"Why was Esteban so afraid of this man?"

"Afraid for me, perhaps. Esteban is an idiot! There was no need—"

"Was the man a blackmailer?"

She shrugged her shoulders, looked at Rodriguez with large innocent eyes. "He did not have the chance to make any demands. I cut him off. But perhaps he talked more with Esteban."

"And when he followed you to Granada, what did you think he was?"

"A police spy."

Rodriguez stiffened visibly.

"They do exist," she said mildly enough. Then her voice sharpened. "What else is that tinsmith who opened his shop this afternoon, found a letter lying inside the door, and hurried to turn it over to the police?" She was angry now, and getting angrier. "To think they should have even believed that letter might be true! About *me*?"

Rodriguez was not a happy man. But his senses were all working, for he glanced sharply at Ferrier. He asked him, "Do you see some connection between that letter and the man who was refused help by Señorita Vergara?"

Ferrier did. But it was not something he cared to have underlined, not at this moment, with Waterman out there on the terrace interested in every word, every place name. Let's keep the tinsmith, and the courtyard and the museum, out of this. "I doubt—"

Tavita jumped in with her own bright answer. "But of course! It was that man who wrote the note! I turned him down, and this was his way of hurting me—his last word, as it were." She paused, thinking about that, realizing too late that she had come closer to the truth than was safe. She looked at Ferrier, saw the warning in his eyes. Then she rallied. "I am sorry, Ian. I interrupted you. But there isn't much more to say, is there, Captain Rodriguez? We can forget about that man. He will not trouble me any more."

"Why not?"

"Because, if he ever telephones me again, I shall call the police."

"You should have done that right at the beginning," Rodriguez said severely. "And I think it is fortunate that Esteban did come to see me this morning. Or else the police in Granada might have searched your house thoroughly."

"They did search thoroughly," she said indignantly. She rose to her feet. The interview was at an end as far as she was concerned.

"But politely. You will agree that they did treat you politely?"

Tavita nodded. "Except they should never have come here in the first place." She wasn't going to give up that point.

Ferrier was putting up his own small prayer: Quit while you're ahead, Tavita; you've told your story, and it is accepted. It might even be enough to convince Waterman. A doubtful character, a total unknown, had picked on the name of Fuentes, who had known the Vergara family, so that he could blackmail Tavita. Would Waterman believe that?

Rodriguez wasn't going to give up his point, either. "I don't believe you realize what a thorough search means, Señorita Vergara. Your house would not have been left in this orderly condition." His arm swept around. "Every drawer would have been opened; every box, chest, suitcase, trunk."

That shocked her. She looked blankly at Rodriguez. Then she tried to laugh it off. "What? Do they expect a man to be hiding in a drawer or a trunk?"

"He may leave traces—clothes, jewelry, discarded papers. People in flight, Señorita Vergara, often leave something behind them, quite small, but enough to tell a trained eye just what—"

"But there was no man here—in flight or in anything else," she said sharply. "There was no need for any kind of search, polite *or* thorough. Thank you for coming here to make sure I was safe. Good-bye, Captain Rodriguez."

Rodriguez bowed. He was about to turn away. And then, almost as an afterthought, he said, "Do you have property near the Calle de los Mártires, Señorita Vergara? In a courtyard beside the museum?"

Tavita seemed to add three inches to her height. "That was years ago."

"And it is now leased by Esteban?"

"It is his. A business arrangement."

"Oh, yes. About six years ago. Of course. That was when you took control of El Fenicio."

"Yes. As I said, a business arrangement. My property at the Calle de los Mártires was in part payment for my purchase of El Fenicio. But I am sure you know all the details about my private life, Captain Rodriguez." She smiled quite dazzlingly.

Rodriguez bowed again. "I have never known which was to be more admired, your business sense or your dancing." This time, he did leave, and quickly, with only a small nod in Ferrier's direction.

Ferrier watched the neat, dapper figure hurry through the hall. Then he looked at Tavita, shaking his head. "I think he came as a friend," he told her. "Why did you have to—"

"Friend? Ian, he knows. He knows."

God help us, thought Ferrier. "Of course he does," he said as he went over to her. "Did you think Rodriguez wouldn't know about your brother? How long has he been back in this country?"

He pulled her around to face him, laid a finger lightly over her lips, looked into her startled eyes. Would she get his warning?

Partly, at least. She said, "Six years."

"Then Rodriguez knows, but what of that? He has done nothing for six years; why should he make any move against your brother now? It may just be that you worry too much." She was about to talk. He kissed her lips quickly, silenced them. "Were you really being blackmailed on your brother's account?" He glanced at the terrace door, as if he had only become aware that Waterman had stepped inside. The sunglasses were already pocketed.

"Not interrupting anything?" Waterman asked, looking at Ferrier's arm around Tavita.

Ferrier let it drop, eased away from Tavita. "You might have done that earlier and helped us get Rodriguez moving."

Waterman studied his watch. "Yes, he did hang on and on. Cut my time short. I'm afraid I'll have to leave in a few minutes. Now that *is* annoying. What a delightful place you have, Señorita Vergara. I would like to have explored it. But perhaps another time? What is so remarkable is its peace, its feeling of complete privacy. Don't you agree, Ian?"

"Now that the police have gone, yes."

"Well, they didn't disturb too much. Your servants," he said to Tavita with a smile, "will not be able to complain. But probably they aren't the type. My wife would envy you, señorita, for such a well-managed house. We are forever hearing noises from the kitchen—if it isn't laughter, it's scolding, or music or television preaching. We don't have peace like yours. How do you manage it?"

Tavita said, "This is Sunday. The servants are out."

Ferrier looked at her quickly. "But Magdalena is here," he reminded her, mostly for Waterman's benefit. Surely she hadn't left herself alone in this place. Had she sent them all away as soon as Esteban's warning had come to her, so that Rodriguez could ask them no questions?

"I sent her to visit a cousin." Tavita looked at Ferrier curiously, then guessed the wrong reason for his worry. "We will have to cancel my dinner invitation, Ian. No cook. No one to serve. I am sorry. But you understand?"

Waterman broke in tactfully. "I really must go. I'm expecting a call from my wife this evening at the hotel. Señorita Vergara, would you mind if I used your phone to check?"

Tavita had scarcely listened. She shook her head. She seemed suddenly drained of energy, thoughts, words. She sat down on a chair, leaned her head against its high back, closed her eyes.

Waterman looked at her with marked sympathy. He said quietly to Ferrier, drawing him over to the telephone, "What's upsetting her so much?"

"Some character arrived in Málaga, called himself Fuentes, and tried to blackmail her. Or perhaps he was a police spy, an *agent provocateur*. That's what she thinks. She and Esteban have been running a kind of underground travelers' aid society."

"And what do *you* think? Was the man really an impostor? Or is that just a clever story to get rid of Rodriguez?"

"Look—it was Esteban who brought Rodriguez in."

"And what scared Esteban, I wonder?"

"You're a cynic."

"I'm a journalist. You believe all this about an impostor?"

"In a strange way, it fits. That's how the name of Fuentes got whispered around. Actually, he is dead and—"

"Since when?" Then Waterman laughed, noticing Ferrier's quick glance. "That's again the old journalist in me, Ian. Anyway," he added, "this should please O'Connor. We'll be leaving Granada with his judgment confirmed."

"But not as pleased as you think."

"He'd rather be leaving with Fuentes, instead of me? I guess you're right. Well, he can't expect to win them all." He turned toward the phone, and then seemed to have an afterthought. "Ian —you've known me for a long time—off and on, that is, but we do know each other better than O'Connor. Is he playing a little game with us?"

All you could do when you were taken by surprise was to look, quite honestly, surprised. Ferrier made no attempt to disguise it.

"Could be," Waterman said reflectively, "could be. He's a wily bird. Now, what do you find so funny about that remark?"

Ferrier said, "I just had a vision of O'Connor sitting up in his hotel room weaving and unweaving his infernal machinations. Oh, come on, Ben. What game?"

"Put bluntly like that," Waterman said, "it's hard to answer. It's just that I've got a feeling that things aren't what they seem."

That was a pretty rich joke, coming from Waterman. "They rarely are, are they?" Ferrier asked lightly.

"Who's the cynic now?" Waterman began to dial, his back to Ferrier, who moved away politely. But not before he had noticed the first two digits being dialed. Not the hotel's number, that was certain.

Waterman got through with remarkable promptness, didn't even wait for any switchboard to identify itself. "Waterman, of Room 409. I was expecting a call from Madrid. When it comes, tell them I'll be back at the hotel by eight o'clock—no later. I will take the call then. Understood?" He only waited for what must have been a brief reply before he hung up. "I'll give you a lift to the hotel."

"I'll walk. I need some fresh air."

"Aren't you going to telephone O'Connor with the good news?"

Ferrier had been waiting until Waterman left and he could talk more freely. But that might be a mistake, he thought now, as he noticed Waterman's quiet study of his face. "I suppose we ought to. Tavita, do you mind if I too make a call?"

She opened her eyes, shook her head. Then she remembered something important. "But first, would you please phone those people—the interviewers? Tell them—oh, you know what to tell them."

"Where's their number?"

"On a scrap of paper—under the letters on my desk."

He found it, began dialing. The first two digits were identical with those used in Waterman's call. He frowned, stopped speculating, concentrated on giving a terse but definite message: no interview today, quite impossible. Whoever was on the other end of the line had little to say: he had begun with a guarded *Pronto*, ended with a noncommittal *Adios*.

Waterman was now making a warm good-bye that roused Tavita into a real smile. He was filled with regrets that he had ill-timed this visit, but perhaps on another visit to Granada he might have the great pleasure of visiting Señorita Vergara again?

Ferrier watched him, could find no fault with the performance. Performance? There was one part of Ferrier that still kept saying, *Surely not Ben. It can't be. . . .* Then he only had to look down at the telephone number he had just called and he was worrying again, and heartsick; a miserable combination. He began to dial the hotel, and had the usual wait.

Waterman was waiting, too, his good-byes over but with something more to say to Ferrier.

"Just a minute," Ferrier told him, and began speaking with O'Connor. If Waterman had wanted to hear this, he was damn well going to.

It was a strange contrapuntal conversation. O'Connor played the theme straight, asking a series of questions that were too quietly voiced to be audible to anyone else in that silent room. Ferrier countered with short direct answers, followed them with some fancier variations for Waterman's benefit.

Ferrier: Bob? Yes, you were right. The rumors were based on that name you were talking about, but it was an impostor who was using it.

O'Connor: Waterman still with you?

Ferrier: Yes, the man's a fake, no doubt about it. The name was borrowed in order to convince Tavita to help him. He miscalculated, though. She denounced him.

O'Connor: Is Waterman buying that?

Ferrier: I doubt it. Tavita swears the man was a complete phony. So does Esteban. In fact, he brought Rodriguez from Málaga into the case.

O'Connor: So you think there may still be an attempt made to crash her place, question her?

Ferrier: That would be my guess. Rumors feed on rumors, you know.

O'Connor: Then stay with her. Who else is at the house?

Ferrier: Very peaceful, now. The police have gone. So has Rodriguez. They seemed satisfied. Aren't you?

O'Connor: What about servants—aren't they around?

Ferrier: No. Tavita sent them off quite happily. The anonymous note was pure spite. A delayed-action bomb, as it were. Nasty, don't you think? Yes, that guy deserves anything that's coming to him.

O'Connor: I'll send Sam to join you. Perhaps Al, too. They are all I can spare at the moment. There may be others, later. I've got to move out now, keep everything looking absolutely normal. I don't suppose you carry a small equalizer?

Ferrier: Good Lord, no. Just sight-seeing for a couple of days and then on to northern Italy. Time I was getting back into my own life. Sure, I'll tell Waterman you are packing up. By the way, Ben made a definite appointment for eight o'clock. He wants to be back at the hotel then. He's expecting a phone call from Alice.

O'Connor: Eight o'clock? He's rushing it. All right, let's rush him. Tell him I move out by eight o'clock. Tell him I have a plane at Seville waiting. We must leave there by midnight. That should keep him curious—perhaps even make him reconsider his last instructions.

Ferrier: I wouldn't bet on that. I'm usually kept pretty busy when I'm in Washington. And I'd better warn you, my golf game is lousy. Now some mountain climbing or scuba diving—

O'Connor: Good-bye, then. And thanks, Ian. Many thanks. You can depend on Sam. He's in charge now. Promoted in the field.

Ferrier: That sounds a good decision. Good-bye, Bob.

He replaced the receiver slowly, and then turned to face Waterman, who had been absorbed for those last two minutes in tracing the patterns of the Moorish tiles set into a table top. "Well, that's that."

"Surprising."

"What?"

"He needed so much persuading. I thought he had his mind all made up."

"He kept hoping he was wrong, I suppose. Only natural."

"And he's packing up. Definitely?"

Ferrier nodded. "Say, I have a message for you. They must leave by eight. He has a plane waiting at Seville to take them off. If you want to hitch a quick ride back to Madrid, there's your chance."

That had really astonished Waterman. He stared openly at Ferrier.

Ferrier kept a tight grip on his own expression. Waterman must have known about that plane, secretly held for an emergency. He must have linked it with Fuentes' flight. What worried him now, obviously, was the fact that the plane was being put to use, and so quickly. Ferrier could almost see Waterman's mind jumping from possibility to possibility. "But how about your call to Alice?"

"I can always leave word that I'll be home by two this morning. That's all that was really worrying her—what time I'd get back. There's a big party tomorrow at the Embassy. Yes, I guess I'll make that flight." He looked at his watch, called a last good-bye to Tavita, and started for the hall. "Will Max meet us at the plane?" he asked Ferrier.

"I've no idea. Why shouldn't he?"

Waterman opened the door. "He may have a better reason than either you or I imagine, Ian. I told you before—we're the babes in the wood, left to wander." He looked back at Tavita, then at Ferrier. "I wouldn't stay here," he said, and broke into one of his old smiles, broad and genial. "I don't want to interfere with your plans, but what she needs now is a quiet evening in bed and no—"

"Clean up your mind," Ferrier said with real anger. "Cut out the innuendos. Sure, I know bachelors are always fair game, but lay off me, will you? I get pretty goddamned tired of hearing the same old—"

"Touchy, aren't we? Hope you are in a better frame of mind when I see you again."

If, thought Ferrier, if . . . "Have you actually forgotten that Jeff Reid isn't even buried yet?" he asked unbelievingly.

Waterman's amusement faded. He said slowly, "I was as sorry about that as you were." And he left.

23

Ferrier locked the door securely behind Waterman. Not a particularly good lock, either, he noticed. Any two-bit burglar could pry it loose with a hairpin. That was the strange thing about Tavita: she'd bar her windows with decorative iron and leave the keys in her car and the garage open; she'd install some simple-minded contraption to hold fast a modern door like this one, while she'd have elaborate systems for antique hunks of wood. And just then he remembered the ancient lock and its enormous key that belonged to the front door of Tavita's house on the museum courtyard. What had happened to that key? How had O'Connor dealt with it? It was too big, too heavy, too cumbersome to be carried in any pocket. Had he been forced to leave that door unlocked after he had brought Fuentes through it?

Ferrier came back into the room almost at a run. "Tavita—that door to your house on the courtyard—it must be unlocked. Is that safe with all these tourists around?"

She paused in measuring brandy into two glasses. "We need this," she told him. "Of course it wouldn't have been safe. That's why your Mr. Smith locked it when he took Tomás Fuentes out into the courtyard."

"But how do you know he locked it?" Or didn't she know and was just assuming he had?

Her smile belonged to Mona Lisa. "He was so clever about that. I began to like your Mr. Smith very much. Even if he made one mistake—with Tomás Fuentes. He did not see Fuentes slip a note under the door of the tinsmith's shop. But there is no harm done. Fuentes did not destroy me. And he won't!" The smile was gone. "It *was* Fuentes who wrote that note. You agree?"

"Yes." Fuentes bending down to tie a shoelace at the door of the shop. I saw him. I didn't believe what I saw. I can scarcely believe it now. "How could he have taken such a chance? He could have destroyed himself, too."

"Oh, no. He had calculated well. The shop did not open until

317

four o'clock. The police did not come here until almost half past five. So how many hours had he to escape them? He was far away from Granada by then."

Four and a half hours away. Far enough, thought Ferrier.

"And," added Tavita, "he did not sign his name to the note. He knew I would not sign it for him by giving his name to the police. Not to anyone. I will *not* be connected with his name. Ever. He knew that." She handed Ferrier a glass of brandy. "We drink to— to our silence. And to my story. Rodriguez believed it, didn't he?"

"I hope so."

"Well—why not? It could have been true. Couldn't it?"

He had to smile. "Yes," he agreed. The brandy was again too sweet for his taste, but he welcomed it. "About Smith—" he began, puzzled about that door down on the courtyard. "He was clever, you said. How?"

"Oh, that! He simply left one of the windows open, just a little. And after he came out and locked the door behind him, he pushed the key through the opened window back into the room. I found it on the floor and put it on its hook."

"When were you down there?"

"After I got Esteban's call. I wondered if Fuentes was still in the house on the courtyard with your Mr. Smith. Or had they left? You see, you didn't tell me," she said with mild reproof. "And I had to know. So, I went down. They had left. Everything was in good order. I checked thoroughly. I even remembered to bring up the suitcase."

"Fuentes' suitcase?" He stared at her. "Where did you put it?" he asked slowly.

"In the small room where I store all my suitcases and trunks."

"You mean—it was lying there when the police—"

"But it looks like one of mine."

"Until someone opens it. Or did you empty it?"

"His clothes are safer left there until Magdalena can remove all the labels—everything came from Argentina." That amused her. "Then I'll give them to Matéo. My chauffeur. They'll fit him. I know they will." She was delighted with her small secret. For a moment, the exhausted look on her face was replaced by a real smile.

"Of course they will, seeing that Matéo's uniform fitted Fuentes."

The smile drained from her lips. "You saw that?" Now worry and fear flooded back. "Rodriguez was there—you were standing with him outside Jeff's door—did he see, too?"

"He did. Only, he wasn't looking for Fuentes. He didn't even know Fuentes was in Málaga. But don't underestimate Rodriguez. Where's that suitcase?"

She made no more protests, but led him into her bedroom. There, in a windowless box room piled with trunks and bags of all sizes, he found the suitcase. It was unlocked. He checked inside it, found only neatly folded clothes topped by a silver-gray suit. "Where's the key to the tunnel door?"

"You aren't taking it back down to—"

"No arguments, Tavita. The key!"

"I hide it under my handkerchiefs," she said, going into her dressing room. He repressed a laugh as he noticed the bars, highly decorative but definitely iron, across the dressing-room window. The bathroom had them, too. So did the bedroom, although here they were softened by long draperies of red satin. That's right, he thought, everything is tightly secured but you keep an important key in your handkerchief drawer. Tavita, Tavita . . . He shook his head.

"What is so funny?" she asked as she came back into the bedroom, glancing at his face.

"Nothing. Come on, Tavita. Let's get this stowed away." He picked up the suitcase, hurried her out into the living room, swung the bedroom door shut after them. It was a massive antique, its wood hardened by age, heavily studded and banded with iron. Its lock and key looked highly efficient. "Incredible," he said softly.

And tactlessly. She bridled. "Don't you like my room?"

"A study in contrasts." Red curtains, gilded mirrors, lace pillows scattered over a giant bed. And bolts and bars and nails and studs and God knows what. "At least, you sleep in safety."

"Isn't that the most important thing about any house? To be able to sleep in safety?"

Her vehemence surprised him. But this time he was wise enough to say nothing. They reached the hall in silence.

She said tensely, "You have never known what it is to live through a civil war. In Málaga—we did not sleep well. Threats and terror, flames and bombs, midnight executions." For a moment, her eyes brooded on some hideous memory. She turned away quickly, concentrated on opening the panel's hidden door. She stood aside to let him enter, handed him the key. "Are you going all the way down?" She was cool and practical again. "What a waste of time! I have only given you extra work."

"On the contrary. It was a bright idea. And necessary. It saved me a lot of trouble and a long walk. I'll drop the suitcase just inside the second door—it should be safe at the top of the tunnel."

He moved quickly, wasted no time, counted each second. When he got back to the hall, and the panel was securely in place, he had some necessary advice for her. "Let the suitcase stay there for the next three weeks. Don't open the doors. Don't go near it. After that, you can do what you like with it. But I'd burn the clothes, if I were you, keep nothing at all. And I'd drop the suitcase over one of your cliffs on a dark night," he added. "Now where's the fuse box? I'd like to see all the tunnel lights completely out."

Tavita looked at him, but made no comment. And when he had dealt with the fuse box in a coatroom off the studio, she said in wonder, "How could you think of all these things?"

It was his turn to stare. How could anyone not think of these things? They were elementary compared to all the elaborate stratagems that Tavita—and Esteban, too; let's not forget old helpful Esteban—could invent.

"And now you are laughing at me again," she said, and she marched back into the big room.

"I didn't even smile," he protested.

"Your eyes did. Why do you always find me so—so comic?" she asked angrily.

"Not comic," he said quickly. "Often amazing. And sometimes worrying."

That was better. Her voice softened. "Forgive me. I am tired, nervous. And I don't understand why you keep worrying about me. Everything is over." Her words were more bravado than anything, as if she were persuading herself.

"That's just the point. It isn't. Not yet."

"Tomás Fuentes?" she asked quickly, swinging around on him.

"Nothing to worry about him." He watched her relax. "He is dead, remember? Just a name used by an impostor."

She looked hard at him. Then she actually laughed at herself. "Then what do we fear? Let us go out on the terrace, and you can tell me about it."

"I'd like to stay in the room, keep an ear open for someone at that front door. He's a friend. His name is Sam. We thought we'd —well, keep you company for this evening."

"Why?"

"The journalists who wanted to interview you are fakes. All they wanted was an excuse to get in here and search. And question you about Tomás Fuentes."

"Then I will tell them exactly what I told Captain Rodriguez."

"Their questions may be harder than his."

"They would threaten me?" She was angry again, really angry this time.

"They would put their threats into deeds, if necessary. As Fuentes would."

He did not have to explain further. She drew a deep breath. "And how will you and Sam prevent them? For tonight, perhaps yes. But tomorrow, and tomorrow, and tomorrow? Men like Fuentes will not give up."

Yes, he thought bitterly, how do we prevent them—even for tonight?

Tavita said, "I shall call the police."

"No!"

"I shall call them." She went quickly over to one of the small tables—the one with the Moorish tiles inset on its top—and picked up a small piece of paper from under a crystal paperweight. "Here it is," she said triumphantly. "The policeman in civilian clothes left it so that I could get in touch with him if I were pestered by any anonymous notes or threatening phone calls. I didn't pay much attention, frankly, but now it may solve our problems."

"How? What are you going to tell him? You'd better have a good story ready, or else you'll get tangled up with Fuentes." Ferrier looked at the slip of paper. It was authentic, all right. "Was it visible under that paperweight? I mean, was it held only at one corner, or was it—"

"I'll think of something," she said, lost in her own predicament. "I'll keep it absolutely simple and true. Let me see . . . I am very doubtful of an interview that has been arranged. I canceled it. But the journalist insists on appearing."

"He hasn't yet. You'll have to wait until he and his friends arrive before you can make that complaint. And I doubt if you'll be allowed anywhere near that telephone once they do appear."

"We won't let them inside. We'll keep them waiting at the door while I telephone."

"Waiting like me?" a cheerful voice asked, and Sam propped his elbows on the banister of the staircase that led up into the hall from the floors below.

Tavita's reaction was to switch on some lights and then pick up the paperweight again.

"Quick, isn't she?" Sam asked, looking at the paperweight poised and ready. "But we really don't need all these lights. One will do, meanwhile."

"How did you get in?" Ferrier's annoyance with himself turned to anger. "All right, all right, drop the smile. You're the cat that swallowed the bowl along with the cream. Tavita, don't worry—this character is harmless."

"Not a flattering introduction," Sam said, and came up the rest of the staircase. He looked around, nodded appreciatively. Then in quick succession he visited the studio and Tavita's bedroom, crossing the main room silently, flicking on and off lights as he needed them. "These are all the rooms on this floor, Señorita Vergara?" He spoke in Spanish, and fluently.

Tavita nodded, replaced the paperweight. "We are in good hands," she said to Ferrier, half-ironically, half-seriously. So young, she thought, looking back at Sam with growing interest. He was a Spaniard. That was definite. What a relief to be able to pour out her feelings in her own language. "Where do you come from?"

"Just one minute, Tavita," Ferrier said. And to Sam, "How did you get in here?"

"By way of the garage. I put the Simca inside—thought it better be out of sight."

Hell, thought Ferrier, I forgot that damned Simca. "I didn't hear you move it."

"All it needed was a shove." Sam was now standing at the entrance to the terrace, looking around out there. The light was fading rapidly.

"So you found a door in the garage," Ferrier tried.

Sam finished the brief inspection. "Yes. At the back. It opened easily, led down a long flight of open stairs onto a terrace. Another door there, unlocked. Servants' rooms and a kitchen et cetera, et cetera. Stairs up through a dining room and its terrace. More stairs—and then this floor. Simple."

"Too simple," Ferrier said worriedly.

"Yes. I don't like this setup one bit. Doors and windows everywhere."

"Damn all terraces," Ferrier said softly. He didn't insult Sam by asking if he had locked any open doors he had discovered.

"Three terraces by my count. Linked how?" Sam looked over at Tavita and repeated his question in Spanish, taking considerably more wordage.

"By stone steps," she said. "They are short flights, but steep."

"And that," Ferrier decided, "is our weak point." He visualized that flight of open stairs which had brought Sam so easily down from the garage onto the lowest terrace, and didn't like what he was seeing. An intruder wouldn't need to come back into the house to reach this room; all he needed to do was come up by way of terraces to this large wall of window. Ferrier frowned at it as if one of Gene Lucas' men had already appeared out there.

"At least they don't know about it. And I don't expect they'll waste time in scouting around the garage. And if one of them does, then he's going to give us warning: I stuck a watering can and a couple of tin buckets just behind that door at the top of the stairs."

"We may need that warning. Waterman was with O'Connor this morning. They had a good look at this house. With binoculars. Was that long flight of open steps visible, do you think?"

Sam looked at him quickly. So he guessed. He's not easy to fool. "It was," Sam admitted slowly. Then he grinned and said frankly, "Bob told me about it, warned me to check on it." He laughed it off. "I wasn't as bright as I seemed, eh?"

"Or I wasn't as stupid as I felt." Ferrier glanced at his watch. Not long to wait now. "What's the plan of operations? Have we any?"

"Bluff. That's all we have going for us. Bluff, and keeping our lines of communication open. Come on!" Sam pulled out a king-sized cigarette case from his pocket, extended its two small aerials, adjusted them as he moved toward the terrace. "Al?" he asked quietly. "Everything okay? Yes, I'm in place. Here's Ian—get his voice level—just in case." Sam handed his two-way radio to Ferrier. "That's the off switch, this is the on. You speak a couple of inches from there, and listen here." He stopped pointing, "Or do you know all about it?"

"Not this type. Nothing so neat and sophisticated." Like you, thought Ferrier. He spoke to Al. "This is Ian. Coming over it clear?"

"My God—it's Gary Cooper."

Another joker, Ferrier thought. "Okay. Hickory dickory dock. Over to you. And away we go." He handed the radio back to Sam. And at that moment, the telephone rang. Ferrier and Sam looked at each other, then Ferrier stepped indoors. Tavita had picked up the receiver. She was speaking in Spanish, quickly and at some length.

"Anything important?" Sam asked, joining Ferrier.

"Something about a photograph—a private call, I think."

"You take this." Sam gave him the radio that looked once more like a cigarette case. "I want you to stay outside, on the terrace. Keep out of sight—Lucas knows you, doesn't he? I'll be with Tavita. I'm her cousin, spending the night here. At least, we'll see if that will keep them more subdued. Sure, they'll search the place, and we'll let them. And if they threaten Tavita,

I'll threaten them right back." He opened his jacket, showed a revolver tucked into his belt. "That's when you call Al. He will get help here right away. And then you join me, waving this around to back you up. You've used an automatic before, have you?" Sam had produced a very neat model indeed from a trouser pocket. "That's the safety. Then you just point and pull. Tenderly."

Ferrier took the automatic, made sure of the safety catch. "Bluff?" he asked sardonically.

"Until it's called," Sam said grimly. "By the way, Al reports that there's activity around the cars outside the hotel. They are getting ready to leave." He glanced over at Tavita, who was remarkably silent.

Tavita had replaced the receiver. She stood looking at it as if it were a viper coiled on her table. Sam, who had been about to start explaining to her what to expect in the next hour, exchanged a puzzled glance with Ferrier. She said slowly, "They'll never stop. They'll keep after me, after me, after me." She drew a deep breath, raised her eyes to meet theirs. "The police are coming here again. Inspector Cruz is sending two of his men to show me a photograph. I have to examine it, try to identify it. He thinks it may be the man who threatened me—the impostor—the man who wrote the anonymous letter. If so, they will arrest him tonight. It is urgent—most urgent—"

"Cruz telephoned? You recognized his voice?" Sam asked quickly. "Are you sure—"

"It was his assistant who telephoned. And from the right police station. I checked. I am not stupid." Her voice had sharpened. She picked up the paper that Cruz had left her. "And there is its address. Read it for yourself." She held it out tensely to Sam. He took it, glanced at it, handed it to Ferrier. "He was polite, but definite. Either I look at the photograph here or Inspector Cruz will ask me to come down to his office."

"When are they coming?" Sam asked.

"Eight o'clock."

"Eight o'clock?" Sam almost swore, managed to choke the word into silence. He said to Ferrier, "That's the way it goes: you prepare a plan and then you never use it."

"We may need it yet." Ferrier's frown deepened. "There's something I don't like—"

Tavita broke in. "Oh, Ian—why must you always question everything? You give yourself so much worry, so much trouble. And for nothing. The police are coming. So let us think how they

can help us. I'll tell them I've been threatened again, this time
by men who pretend to be journalists and—"

"No," Sam said sharply. "Better not mix the police in this."

"But I will. This is my house. And I will." She stamped her
foot; her eyes flashed. "You are so stupid, both of you. The police
will frighten away these men—"

"No," Sam said. "No police." Stupid, are we? These men
wouldn't be scared away permanently. They'd return, to search
and question. She was only postponing her troubles, even adding
to them. He looked at Ferrier for help.

Ferrier said, "Tavita—Inspector Cruz came to you about the
letter. Right? And Captain Rodriguez came to you about Fuentes.
Isn't that so? Their business was separate. Rodriguez didn't question you until Cruz had left." But Waterman had listened to Rodriguez, Waterman had heard Tavita's answers. He most certainly
had. "So how could Cruz have learned about any impostor?"

"From Rodriguez himself," she answered impatiently. "They
met together and talked afterward. Didn't they?"

"We don't know that," Sam said.

She ignored him. "Couldn't they?" she asked Ferrier.

"They could have, but—"

"Then you frightened me for nothing." She turned abruptly
away. "I shall be in my room until they come," she said coldly,
ending all argument. At its door, she paused with one last question for Sam. "Why are you so afraid of our police?"

"Afraid? You've got me wrong, señorita. I just don't believe
in lying to them—any police, anywhere. Never pays off. Think
that over for the next five minutes, before you come out to
meet—"

She closed the door in his face.

"Four minutes," Ferrier said, "if they are punctual."

Sam calmed down. "Quite an act," he said, giving one last look
at Tavita's door.

"She has been putting on a damned good act. She's scared, far
more than she'll admit. She's exhausted and frightened, and she
has just about had it. Do you blame her?"

Sam looked at Ferrier reflectively. "So that's the reason you
didn't press too hard."

"Well, she may have been right. They could be real cops. I
think they're fakes, but I don't know. There's one sure way of
finding out, though." He moved over to the telephone, looking at
the paper with Cruz's number on it.

Sam reached the telephone first. "No," he said softly. He put his hand down on the receiver, held it in place. His eyes were determined.

"Then I'll try it another way," Ferrier said angrily. Quickly, he crossed to the window, flipping open Sam's cigarette case, and stepped out onto the terrace. Luck was with him. He got Al almost immediately. "Urgent. Get to a telephone. Is that possible?"

"Yes."

"Here's the name and number." Ferrier read them out carefully. He heard Sam's footsteps. "Ask Cruz if he has dispatched two policemen to visit Señorita Vergara's house at eight o'clock tonight. Are they authentic, or fake? Give him my name when he asks for your identification. Got that?"

"Yes," said Al, "but this means the police on top of you. One way or the other. Does Sam want that?"

"He won't have to meet them. He leaves as soon as the real police turn up. Now make that call. Urgent!" He switched off contact, closed the radio. Sam was standing behind him, strangely quiet. At least, thought Ferrier, he didn't try to stop me. That would have been an ugly moment. Good God, thought Ferrier, are my nerves stretched as taut as Tavita's?

Sam said angrily, "I hope you know what you were doing."

"As much as I've known in the last forty-eight hours." Ferrier slipped the radio into his pocket. In the other one, the automatic lay heavily. He shook his head, looked up at the sky. Dusk had come, and the first stars were glimmering.

"What you don't understand," Sam said, "is the fact that the job isn't over yet." He was annoyed, perhaps resentful.

"It is for you," Ferrier said amicably. "Your mission is completed once you get Fuentes out of Spain. And he is out. Isn't he?"

"Yes."

"And still blissfully asleep?"

"Yes."

"Then what's—"

"O'Connor isn't out. And he won't be out until he leaves Madrid around three this morning."

"I don't get you."

"Yes, that's what I told you. You don't get it." Sam allowed himself a patient sigh. The twenty-seven-year-old father explaining the facts of political reality to a thirty-seven-year-old son, thought Ferrier wryly. Sam was saying, "If the opposition picks up one good hint that Fuentes is in our hands and out of their reach, they'll make one desperate move to get him back. In exchange for one of us. Not you, not me—someone really important."

"Bob O'Connor," Ferrier said softly. And he was vulnerable, traveling alone with Waterman. "Surely he has taken some of his own men along," he added worriedly.

"One only. He is leaving the way he arrived. Then he had Mike. Now it's Burt. Couldn't risk more. Had to play it easy and natural. Mustn't give Waterman any reason to wonder—"

"Waterman won't be traveling alone." He would have at least a couple of men following O'Connor's car, ready for any signal they'd receive. Yes, thought Ferrier as he pulled the cigarette case out of his pocket, they'd have gadgets like this one; they'd be geared for any message from Granada. "Take this," he said, handing over the little two-way radio to Sam. "You stay out here, keep your lines of communication open. I'll deal with the police, real or fake. Also with Tavita. I know her better than you do."

That settled any argument before it started. Sam pocketed the radio. "She's the weakness," Sam said. "She's liable to—"

"I'll keep her from embroidering her story." Ferrier was thinking of O'Connor again. Yes, one piece of information pulled out of Tavita could unravel everything. "I suppose Waterman would be snatched along with O'Connor—anything to keep his cover intact—and then turned loose as of little value."

"You learn fast."

"And Burt?"

Sam looked at Ferrier grimly. "Yes, there's a lot at stake, right here in this house." He glanced at his watch. "It's after eight. They're late."

"They'll be here." As Sam had said, there was a lot at stake. And I, thought Ferrier, imagined it was all over except for one last gesture toward Tavita. "Tell me, Sam," he asked, "did Bob talk with Amanda Ames?"

"Now what brought that up?" Sam asked, tried to shrug Ferrier's question away. "If she got back to the hotel before he left, of course he'd—"

"She isn't back yet?" Ferrier's voice had sharpened.

"Look, Ian, I've been busy. She's probably there now." Sam looked at Ferrier's face. Better not tell him we are worried, too, he decided; worried enough to keep a good man, Al, stationed in a car near the hotel, waiting for Amanda instead of being here with us; worried enough to have a couple of local friends scouting around all the taxi drivers who picked up fares from the Generalife toward five o'clock this evening. "I've worked out an idea for getting her away from Martin's tender care. And from Gene Lucas, too. She isn't going back to Málaga, that's for sure. We've got it laid on." And now all we have to do is find her, Sam thought. He kept his voice cheerful, his face impassive. "By the way, how much did you tell her about Fuentes?"

"Nothing." Ferrier glanced quickly at Sam. "Why do you ask?"

"Just curious," Sam said, but there was relief in his eyes.

"You think she's been—"

"I'm thinking nothing."

"If anything has happened to Amanda—" began Ferrier, and then checked himself. Who's to blame? Myself most of all, he thought bitterly.

"Keep your cool, man. One problem at a time. Otherwise none of them is solved. You'll only foul everything up. Let's get this job— Just a moment!" He pulled the cigarette case from his pocket, silenced its sudden buzzing as he opened it, answered Al's call. It lasted only a few seconds, but it left Sam thoughtful. He closed the cigarette case. "Al got through to the police station but couldn't wait for any reaction. Too much happening outside the hotel. O'Connor, Waterman, and Burt have left for Seville. Followed by a Chrysler with American registration and three men—two local talent, one big blond who came from Málaga. Well—" he shrugged his shoulders—"that's three less for us to cope with."

"What about Lucas?"

"He left ten minutes earlier. In his own car, with luggage. That smooth guy, the one with his hair plastered close to his head, came right behind him in Amanda's Buick. And their last car, a Mercury, has just driven off. Two men unknown. They took the road to this house."

Ferrier's thoughts raced. Lucas might seem to be leaving Granada, but he wouldn't—not until he had made sure of Fuentes' whereabouts. But Amanda's Buick? "That smooth guy—if he has thin brown hair, a small round head, a two-button suit, a prissy smile—"

"That's the one."

"Jeff Reid's killer."

Sam's lips compressed. "Department Thirteen? We must look out for that one. He's possibly—"

The doorbell rang.

Sam said hurriedly, "If that's the police, I'll keep well in the background. If it isn't, then we play it by ear, take it as it comes. Can do?"

Ferrier nodded.

"Give me a signal if they're for real. Light a cigarette."

"And if I have never seen them before, but have my doubts?"

"Kick a cushion," Sam suggested with a grin.

Ferrier half smiled. Sam had an answer for everything. Then just as suddenly, Ferrier's smile faded. But no answer for Amanda. He turned away, hurried toward the hall. As he walked, he pulled the automatic from his pocket, where it bulged through the linen too noticeably, and stuck it into his belt. He also remembered to switch on all the hall lights and glanced quickly back at the terrace to make sure. Sam wasn't visible. There was only a band of dark shadows, all the deeper because of the focus of light on the hall.

The bell rang again. Ferrier braced himself, unlocked the door, swung it wide. Two uniformed men stepped inside.

24

The two men were strangers to Ferrier. No weapons visible, he noted. Their khaki-colored uniforms seemed authentic. But then, as he told himself, he wouldn't know what kind of police these were. What he did know was the make of car that stood outside the door. American, big and black. He could only allow himself a quick glimpse and no sign of interest, before he closed the door. "A little late, aren't you? You were lucky to find us at home." That seemed an easy, natural beginning. He wished his voice didn't sound so strained.

The two men stopped staring at him. They were middle-aged, thin, dark-haired, dark-eyed. One of them began talking rapidly in Spanish while the other locked the door and tested it.

Ferrier pretended not to notice. "Sorry," he said to the talkative one, "I don't follow you. Do you speak English?" The man looked at him blankly. "I'll let Señorita Vergara know you've arrived," Ferrier said equably, sticking to English. He led the way into the room. Well within view of the terrace, he kicked a floor cushion aside. One black Mercury plus one locked door added up to a very big doubt indeed. He didn't need to hear the men's quick interchange behind his back.

They were worried. They hadn't expected to find him here. "I have a bad feeling about this," the talkative one was saying. "The woman was to have been alone. That was what we were told. And where is she? Search!"

Better keep them away from the terrace, thought Ferrier, and he wasted no time but walked over to Tavita's door. It opened before he reached it, as if she had been waiting for her cue.

And it was a grand entrance. Even Ferrier, worrying about his automatic—these men might search him, discover it, leave him more helpless than he felt now—was lost in admiration. In the few minutes Tavita had spent inside her bedroom, she had added color to her cheeks and lips, smoothed her gleaming hair, broken the black of her chiffon dress with pearls and elaborate earrings to

331

match. In one hand, she carried long black gloves, a small satin purse. Over her other arm was a heavy silk stole, brightly green, loosely folded. She paused in the doorway, looked at her visitors, said, "Ah, the policemen . . ." Then she moved with easy grace toward the couch, dropped the gloves and purse there. Ferrier followed her, eying the green stole, deciding. "You were late," she told the strangers. "Another five minutes and you would not have found me here." She gave Ferrier a warm smile as he lifted the scarf from her arm. "Thank you, darling. This will not take long." She turned to the two uniforms again, held out one hand imperiously. "Now show me the photograph, and we can all leave."

Quickly, Ferrier slipped his automatic under the heavy folds of green silk, laid the stole beside the purse and gloves. He faced the men again, hoped they wouldn't notice that his jacket was now unbuttoned. They didn't. They were too astounded by Tavita. So this is how she has decided to play it, he thought as he watched her. Gay and charming, slightly *de haut en bas*, definitely beautiful. He glanced at the two middle-aged clods to see what effect this could have on them. Considerable. But then they looked at each other, sobered up dutifully. The silent one made amends for his momentary weakness by scowling angrily. He's working himself up into a good hate, thought Ferrier as he noted the man's eyes traveling around the room with intense bitterness. A strong ideologue, this one: if I can't have all this, you won't, either. A Spanish throwback to less deviationist days; he ought to travel more, see how the other half of his comrades lived. The talkative one was more of the coexistence type: my peace, yes; your peace, no. He began stringing words together in a fine flow of rhetoric that meant little but kept Tavita listening intently while his friend slipped quietly into her room. He was out again, moving quickly to the terrace door—a bad minute for Ferrier—and stepped outside. But he found nothing there to alarm him, and he was back in the room, moving soundlessly to the studio. (Rubber-soled shoes, Ferrier noted. These boys had come prepared.) Again his visit was brief. He ended his lightning tour of inspection by yanking the telephone cord out of its socket.

At that, Tavita's play of sweet innocence ended. "Who are you?" she stormed. "What do you think you are doing?" The man paid no attention at all.

Ferrier said quietly, "They're making sure we are alone here— no surprises waiting for them." He was watching the talkative man draw a revolver from a holster, fit a silencer carefully into place, while his friend came over to Ferrier, gestured to him to open his jacket wide. Quick expert hands slapped his pockets, his arms, his legs.

"Look in her purse," the man with the gun said. And that was done, too, with one glove slipping off onto the floor and Ferrier's heart dropping with it. The purse was closed, thrown back onto the couch with only a contemptuous eyebrow raised by way of comment. Then the silent man glanced at his watch and padded silently toward the front door. "Now you'll see what made us late," the compulsive talker said to Tavita. The delay had irked him, obviously. He and his friend made a capable team.

Tavita's rage had passed through disbelief into a cold, deep anger. If she was afraid, she was hiding it well. But she moved closer to Ferrier.

"Keep apart, you two!" The man gestured with the long-nosed revolver. "Leave it!" And Ferrier, who had picked up the glove, dropped it back on the floor. No chance now to get near the green stole. Any other excuse possible? "No talking!" the man warned them.

Tavita said, "This is my house. I shall talk and I shall do whatever I please." She looked at Ferrier, puzzled, wondering. "Do we have to listen to these—"

"Meanwhile, yes," Ferrier said softly, and hoped she would understand his meaning. At least she had had enough sense not to blurt out Sam's name. He gave her a reassuring nod and went back to watching the front door. It had been opened and closed twice, letting the light shine out briefly in a prearranged signal. Yes, he thought, they were well organized. And all he could do was to stand and wait and worry about retrieving his automatic. When and how? Play it by ear, Sam had said; take it as it comes. That wasn't so easy.

Tavita looked at him, said coldly, "I refuse to wait. And for what?"

"There's no choice at the moment."

"Nonsense. Are you afraid of *this*?" She pointed at the man contemptuously. "He won't dare kill us. He is bluffing." She began walking to the hall.

The man said, "If you take one more step, I put a bullet through your pretty leg. Which do you prefer—the heel or the hip?"

She stopped, faced the man.

"I could," he told her. "And I will. A great pity. No more Tavita." He shook his head sadly. Then his voice hardened, doubled its volume. "Señorita, you heard me. Come back here!"

She didn't come back, but she didn't move toward the hall,

either. She stood exactly where she had stopped and kept her eyes fixed on the stranger's face.

He didn't like it. He transferred his anger to the man who waited at the door. "What the devil's holding them up?" he called out harshly. "Wait, wait, wait. Is that all we have to do?"

"They left the cars on the road. They are walking down the driveway. The old bitch is dragging her feet." It was quite a speech for the silent one. The other added to it considerably. He cursed and complained about foolish delays, dangerous wastes of time, stupid women, complications, unnecessary risks. Tavita stood quite still, her eyes never leaving the man's face. And Ferrier could only hope she'd make no unexpected move. The man was too compulsive a talker to be trusted with a gun in his hand.

Suddenly, there was a crash of metal from somewhere distant, a clatter and rattle that ended as abruptly as it had begun. In the room and hall there was complete silence, a turning of heads. The man at the door drew his revolver, and now two pistols were aimed straight at Ferrier.

"Don't blame me," he said. "Someone must have stumbled on the garage steps. Friends of yours?"

Tavita was beginning to understand. She translated quickly into Spanish, just to keep everything quite clear, and there was a brightness in her eyes as she glanced at Ferrier, sharing Sam's joke with him. We're friends again, he thought, and that's important if we are going to get through the next half hour.

"Hear that, Zacarías?" the talkative one had to call out. "The Americans fell over their own big feet." The idea appealed to him; he went into a fit of silent laughter.

Zacarías only nodded as he pocketed his revolver. He concentrated now on the door, listening carefully as he opened it a couple of inches. Then he swung it wide enough to let three people enter. First, a man, small and dark and somber-faced, who pulled a woman across the threshold. She was old, heavy-set, her head bowed, her feet dragging painfully. Behind her, pushing her forward, was another man, small and dark, round-faced and fat. They dropped her in the middle of the hall. Her legs buckled under her, and she fell on her knees, her bloody hands clenched tightly, arms folded across her breast as if she were holding in her pain. She sank to the floor, a crumpled heap of black clothes.

"Magdalena!" Tavita's voice rose as she called the old woman's name. She ran toward her.

The grim-faced man caught Tavita's arm, swung her round, pointed her back to the room. "In there, señorita. You take a chair, sit down, and answer a few questions. That is all you have to do. Move!" But she tried to pull herself free.

So he's still giving orders, Ferrier thought savagely as he recognized the man and his fat friend, two of the trio who had ransacked Jeff Reid's place last night, roughly handled Concepción, left him with a painful reminder on the back of his head. He paid no attention to them, now, passing them swiftly but keeping out of their reach, and bent over old Magdalena. She was conscious. He tried to raise her. She could give him no help, a dead weight.

"Leave her alone!" the little thin man called out. He was holding Tavita's arm, bending it backward to stop her struggle.

"Lend me a hand," Ferrier said to Zacarías, who had remained by the door. Zacarías only looked away. "That's what I like about you fellows. Your noble ideals." He glanced up at the fat man, who was staring at him in amazement.

"Just look who is here," the fat man said slowly. He wasn't smiling much today; his jaw was swollen, discolored. But his button-round eyes were gleaming with some pleasing prospect that stretched in front of them. A knife slipped out of his cuff.

"Later, later!" his friend warned him. "Start searching!"

Zacarías left the door, went toward the staircase to the lower floors. He kept his eyes averted from the woman on the floor. The fat man replaced his knife, trotted with his short quick steps into the living room, looked around, whistled his approval.

Tavita wrenched her arm free. "If you want any information from me, you will start behaving like real men. What are you? Barbary apes?" She ran over to Magdalena, knelt beside her.

The word "information" had some effect. The thin man watched in silence as Ferrier got a grip on Magdalena's broad waist and managed to raise her to her feet. Magdalena was making an effort now. With Tavita supporting her on one side, Ferrier on the other, she stumbled slowly into the room.

Ferrier said warningly, "Look out for her hands, Tavita." The blood was dried; the fingernails must have been torn off hours ago. But the slightest touch on them, even the drift of Magdalena's long black lace scarf against the raw flesh, made her wince with a deep shudder. No cry, no sob, no moan. He brought her over to the couch.

"Not my room?" Tavita asked quickly.

Not your room, he was thinking. I don't want Magdalena or you in there. What I want are two of these men, somehow, in some way, enticed into that room and its heavy door securely locked. That would lessen the odds. For a short time. But that is what we need: time. He shook his head. "This will do," he said as he set Magdalena down on a white leather cushion. "Get her legs up on the couch, let her lie flat," he told Tavita. He reached for the stole, held it casually in front of him, got a sure grip of the automatic. "We'll cover her with this—she really needs a blanket —shock." He slipped the automatic into his belt, buttoned his jacket, kept on talking in a rush of words. "Yes, that's the way— straighten her legs—gently." Magdalena went rigid with pain. He dropped the stole, looked down at her. The backs of her calves were red-scored, raw.

Ferrier grasped Tavita's wrist, silenced her gasp, pulled her to face him as if to spare her seeing Magdalena's wounds. Quickly, in a whisper, his lips unmoving, he said, "Get the key to your bedroom. Get it." But his hand did not loosen from her wrist. She nodded, wondering, waiting, strangely obedient.

"Keep apart, you two!" came the sharp order from the center of the room, where the small thin man had established his command post. "And let her look at the old woman. An object lesson."

"Why else," put in the fat man, "did we haul the old bitch here?" He had been wandering around, roughly pulling out small drawers, rummaging wildly in large chests, creating the utmost chaos from the simplest actions. His search was more for effect than for any practical purpose: a threat of what he really could do if he set his mind on it. He was over near the studio, now. And the uniformed man, strangely untalkative for these last five minutes, was at the entrance to the hall, where he could keep an eye on the front door and listen for any call from his friend Zacarías downstairs.

Ferrier said to Tavita, his voice at a normal level, "We'd better find something to stop the pain. Where do you keep your medicines? In the bedroom?" He let go of her wrist.

She moved quickly, saying, "I'll get something. Bandages, too."

"You stay here!" The small man had his revolver out. "First, you answer my question. Only one. The old woman told us all the rest."

That stopped Tavita. Her hand dropped away from the bedroom door. She turned slowly, looked at him. Then softly she said, "So it was you who did that to Magdalena. . . ."

Ferrier said quickly, "If you know so much, why did you have to come here? There's nothing—"

"Do you want me to close your mouth for you?" The man's revolver pointed at Ferrier's face, then swerved back to Tavita. "Yes, we know everything. Only one question left. Where is Tomás Fuentes now?"

"Six feet under. Where you should be. Monster!" Tavita was recovering.

"Where is he? He was here yesterday. The old woman—"

"Nonsense!"

"She saw him."

"She saw a man. A stranger."

"Tomás Fuentes."

"You put a name in her mouth. She did not know any Tomás Fuentes."

Ferrier was listening tensely. Tavita believed what she was saying, he was sure of that. Yet the man seemed so confident. Bluffing?

"She saw him," the man said. "Here. Yesterday."

"Not Fuentes," Tavita insisted. "A stranger. I threatened to call the police. And he left. Magdalena neither heard nor saw any of this—she was downstairs."

"We watched this house from the moment you arrived here yesterday afternoon. We were watching. No man left."

Ferrier felt a surge of relief. A definite lie, he thought. They did not start watching this house until they became suspicious of it, and that was only after they had knocked me cold on Jeff Reid's living-room floor and filched Tavita's address out of my wallet. No one was watching this house yesterday afternoon—not until eight or nine o'clock in the evening, if that. He tried to signal Tavita with his eyes, but she kept looking at the man. She had known what Magdalena could actually tell these men. She had known they were lying when they talked about the naming of Tomás Fuentes. But now her confidence was gone. She was believing this new assertion. Had they seen Fuentes arriving? Her face was blank with worry. Ferrier said clearly, "I'll get the medicine." He crossed rapidly to the bedroom door. "He's bluffing," he said quietly as he reached Tavita. "One big bluff."

"You stay here!" the man was yelling at him. "Or I'll put a bullet in your spine."

Tavita's eyes widened, narrowed. She pushed the bedroom door violently open, smashed it shut behind her.

The fat man dropped the large vase he had been examining, let it splinter around his feet as he ran toward the bedroom. "What has she got in there? Who?" He flung the door wide and entered.

"No one is there," said the uniformed man, finding his tongue again. He had come out from the hall, but no more than a few feet. "Zacarías searched. We made sure."

The thin man wasn't impressed. "Stand aside!" he told Ferrier, who was partly blocking his view of the bedroom. He began fitting a silencer onto his revolver.

He won't threaten any more, thought Ferrier. Now he will act. So Ferrier drew to one side of the door, stood there with a shoulder against the wall, his arms folded. He could feel his automatic hard against his side, waiting for his hand to reach it. But the man was watching him. Ferrier kept absolutely still, while his mind raced: one in that room—one here—one hovering near the hall— one, Zacarías, somewhere on a lower floor—two Americans now being very quiet indeed after their stumble on the garage stairs, but where? Helping Zacarías search below? Or investigating the terraces? Well, that would be Sam's problem. "Tavita?" Ferrier called, turning his head toward the bedroom, listening. He had hoped to divert the man's attention from him, just for a split second. And there was plenty to hear: a short, sharp argument, voices distant, as if they were coming from either the dressing room or the bathroom.

But the man's eyes never left Ferrier. He did take a step forward, almost reached the threshold of the bedroom. "What's she doing?" he called out angrily. "Tell her to drop everything. Come back here." He had a command for Ferrier, too. "And you get back over by the couch. Move!" To the uniformed man near the hall, he tossed another order: "Keep an eye on this one. Shoot him if he tries anything." His eyes narrowed as he looked at Ferrier, who had taken only one step away, and that slowly. "I give you two seconds to—"

A high-pitched scream jerked their attention back to the bathroom. It ended in a strange cry, abrupt, cut short.

"Bernardo?" called the man near Ferrier. His pistol instinctively pointed at the bathroom door, his eyes questioning.

Ferrier shot him in the right shoulder. His second shot was for the uniformed man. It caught him in the chest, so that he fell backward even as he fired silently and his bullet ripped upward into the ceiling above Ferrier's head. The revolver fell out of his hand, skidded over the tile floor. The man with the shoulder wound stood with his right arm sagging, his long-nosed revolver drooping helplessly by his side. There was a look of utter astonishment on his face, then pain, then rage. His other hand reached for the gun. Ferrier shot him in the left wrist.

Three seconds all told. Ferrier moved quickly. He pocketed his small .22 and picked up the powerful .38 complete with silencer. The other .38 had slid under the edge of the couch, and he left it there. Neither man was likely to use it, he thought grimly, as he ran lightly through the bedroom, skirting its walls, keeping out of

direct range from the half-open bathroom door. When he reached
it, he paused, drew close to one side, looked cautiously. It was
Bernardo who lay on the floor just beyond the door.

"Tavita?"

She stepped into view, a knife in her hand. There was blood on
it. She let it drop beside the red gash in Bernardo's chest. "His,"
she said. She raised her other hand, holding an empty glass. "I
threw this in his face. He dropped the knife. I picked it up." She
looked down at the dead man. His hands were up at his eyes, as if
he were tearing out that searing pain.

Ferrier took the glass, smelled it. Disinfectant of some kind,
strong. Tavita was already finding another glass, filling it with
water, searching for a box of pills, some fresh linen towels, a tube
of sulfa ointment. "There are others," he warned her, and handed
her his small automatic before he turned to go back to the living
room.

She didn't take it. "Guns make me afraid," she said. She
reached into the low neck of her dress, produced a key. "You see,
I did not forget," she told him. She stepped carefully over the
pool of blood, followed him quickly. He had halted at the doorway to the main room. He put up a warning hand for silence.

On the couch, old Magdalena had begun to cry softly. The man
on the floor was stirring restlessly, groaning. But the thin one had
gone. He might not have been able to hold a revolver or throw a
knife or shout an order, but he had used his legs. They had taken
him, in a weaving pattern of trailing bloodstains, toward the
terrace. Perhaps he expected help there. But of Zacarías, who
ought to have reached the head of the staircase by this time, there
was no sign. No sign, either, of Gene Lucas. No sign of Reid's
killer. Perhaps they were all out on the terrace.

Ferrier looked at the stretch of windows, treacherous, dangerous, tried to calculate the remaining odds. Suddenly, he felt his
exhaustion. He was unable to think, to guess ahead, to plan. He
could only stare at that window wall.

Tavita pushed past him, hurried over to the couch, spilling the
water in her haste, swearing at her clumsiness. The flow of words
seemed to comfort Magdalena. She stopped crying. She began to
speak in a long, low murmur, explaining, explaining, explaining.

And then Ferrier's senses came alive. Across the room from
him was the studio door. It had been closed when he had left here.
Now it was ajar, a slit widening as he watched. "Keep down,
Tavita!" he yelled, watched her fall to her knees beside Magdalena as he flattened out against the bedroom door and raised the
heavy revolver.

"Just me," Sam's voice said from the window, and he stepped into the light of the room with his revolver prodding the wounded man ahead of him. "So keep your itching finger off that trigger, Ian. You really took care of this character, didn't you?" He urged the man forward.

"Studio!" Ferrier shouted as its door swung open. He fired as a shot hit the wall beside him.

So did Sam, going into an automatic crouch, swerving, all in one quick movement. Then he was circling the room at a run to reach the studio, drew to one side and fired again. "Drop the gun, hands high, come out," he said in rapid Spanish.

There was a brief hesitation. Ferrier kept his eyes fixed on that black gap of studio door. A strange battle, he thought; nothing but an interchange of mild plops from three silencers. Comic, in a way; but deceptive, too. These bullets were twice as lethal as those of his small automatic. So he kept watching the studio, didn't relax until a revolver was tossed out and Zacarías followed with his hands at least halfway raised.

No one else. Just Zacarías.

"I'll have that knife, too," Sam told him, and picked it neatly out of the man's cuff. "Face the wall, legs apart, and lean!" The search was professional, speedy, and thorough. It uncovered a second knife, strapped above the ankle. "Just a bundle of tricks," Sam said, and herded Zacarías well away from the other two. "Keep an eye on this fellow, Ian." Sam turned to the little man with the wounded shoulder and wrist, searched cautiously, discovered a sheathed knife in a hip pocket. "Lucky you spoiled his reach." He studied the man critically; he was suffering considerable pain, now, but he was still rebellious, ready for any despairing move. "Kneel!" Sam told him. The man looked at him angrily, drew himself more erect. "Kneel, or you'll get a bullet in the leg." The man knelt.

"I'll keep an eye on that one, too," Ferrier said, and Sam moved over to search the uniformed man sprawled on the floor.

The man groaned, but offered no resistance. He had brass knuckle-dusters in one pocket, a switchblade and a coil of thin metal chain in the other. "Glad this wasn't the one I met on a dark terrace," said Sam.

So he had got one of the two men who had made their entry by way of the garage, Ferrier guessed. Which one? And where was the other? Gone? Sam would not be here if there was one left prowling around. "Let's stash these people in the bedroom," Ferrier said, "and then we can talk." There were several answers he wanted out of Sam. "Tavita—you'll find a spare revolver at the corner of the couch. Keep that man saying his prayers while I tie up Zacarías."

Tavita found the pistol, picked it up with distaste, saw the kneeling man was watching her. She stood quite still. Her face hardened as slowly she pointed the revolver at his mouth. "I will end his prayers forever," she said.

"No! No firing," Sam said quickly. He had finished his search, and was holding the last two finds in his hand. He rose to his feet, frowning down at them. The lighter he recognized as one of the neatest little cameras that had been so far developed for long-distance work. One of ours, he thought, but how the hell did this crude type get his hands on it? The other small object, very small this one, was a thin little silver pencil with elaborate decorations. Puzzling. Sam slipped them into his pocket. Zacarías, he noted, had seen them. Zacarías was showing his first sign of fear.

Tavita said angrily, "Why not? He deserves to die, this one. More than any of them. He is a monster." She didn't fire, but she was supporting her right wrist with her left hand.

"No, Tavita," Ferrier said quietly. He gestured angrily to Zacarías. "Over here, you. Into the bedroom! Come on, hurry it up."

"Monster!" Tavita repeated. Her voice changed to bitterness. "Who started all this, anyway?"

And that was a damned good point, thought Ferrier grimly, as Zacarías came obediently forward. Strangely obedient. What had scared him? But that moment passed. Zacarías looked at him contemptuously and spat. "You should listen to the lady," Ferrier told him. "That's the question that is going to defeat all you guys once people start asking it. Or would you rather hear it according to Lenin?"

Zacarías stared at him. He may not have known much English, but the word "Lenin" got through.

"Who, whom?" Ferrier quoted. Then he hit Zacarías smartly on the back of his neck and made sure he would be totally harmless for the next ten minutes. "Ready for packaging," he called to Sam, who was pulling the other uniformed man by the heels into the bedroom. "Hey there—aren't you a bit rough on him?"

"Not rough enough." Sam was thinking of a miniature camera and a small silver pencil. He let the man drop far away from Zacarías. "We'll keep them well separated."

"There's one in the bathroom."

Sam looked inside quickly, came out with both eyebrows raised. "And you called me rough," he said, shaking his head. "Or was it our avenging angel? My God—" He rushed back into the living room, grabbed the kneeling man by his collar, and yanked him to his feet. "You don't know how close you were to getting your brain blown into mush," Sam told him as he hauled the man into the bedroom. "Or perhaps you do," Sam added, noticing the man's frozen fear.

Ferrier was pulling off the heavy curtain cords, testing them for strength. "Do we really need these? The police will be here any minute."

Sam said nothing, just began tying Zacarías securely. "I trust this one least of all. Know what I found down on the first floor? Right in the middle of the kitchen? A delayed-action bomb. Timed for midnight. They thought they'd be well away by then, business completed, corpses obliterated. Nice people." He made an extra loop around Zacarías' wrists, with an additional tug on the tight knot. "Don't worry. We'll have our bomb expert around here long before midnight. He'll take care of it." He looked up at Ferrier. "Don't worry, I said!"

They finished tying up the three men in silence.

25

They came back into the big room without speaking, Sam avoiding Ferrier's eyes. Tavita was sitting on the floor, one hand on Magdalena's shoulder, the other dropping down toward the efficient pistol lying beside her knees. Her head was bent. She was utterly exhausted. There was no sound at all except the quiet, steady breathing of Magdalena.

Sam walked to the terrace, pulling out his cigarette case. Ferrier followed him, suspicion now a certainty. "So," he said sharply, "Al didn't send my message."

"About the police?" Sam was conciliatory. "He tried. The inspector was off duty."

"Like hell he was."

"Al tried," Sam repeated, and started making contact with his radio.

"Not hard enough."

"And do you want the police here now?" Sam turned his back. "Would it have been a good idea?"

"Not particularly," Ferrier admitted slowly. As things had turned out—not particularly, he repeated to himself. "But I don't like being lied—"

"Look—would you have preferred being told that there was no outside help coming? That you and I and Tavita were on our own?"

Put that way—no. "Where was Al?" Ferrier asked angrily.

"Busy," Sam said, made contact, began talking quickly and quietly.

Ferrier went back into the room.

He walked around for a couple of minutes.

"Where is Sam?" Tavita asked.

"Getting help," said Ferrier bitterly. But he remembered the time-bomb in the kitchen waiting for an expert's loving care and he calmed down. Sam's help might be on the late side, but it was

343

welcome. "I'll drive you and Magdalena to a hospital. Some quiet little place—do you know one?"

She nodded. Then she looked at him in horror. "Dressed like this? Bloodstains all over my skirt?"

She's getting back to normal, thought Ferrier.

"And what could I tell them? I have thought and thought and I do not know what I can say. Not even if I explained exactly what happened would they believe me. It just couldn't sound true." She glanced at the locked door of her bedroom, perhaps saw beyond to the bathroom floor.

"These men attacked you inside your own home," he reminded her. "They used—"

"I know, I know." She kept staring at the bedroom door, now seeing the weeks, the months of enquiries and testimony and the whole smothering octopus arms of the law courts. "Ian—what do I tell them—the police?"

"No police. Sam's advice."

"But how do we—" She gestured to the bedroom hopelessly.

"That's Sam's problem. He says he can solve it."

She drew a long breath. "Thank God," she said fervently, "thank God for that."

Ferrier watched the relief spread over her face. He nodded. Then he walked out onto the terrace and joined Sam. The dark sky was bright with stars and a clear moon. From somewhere far below came the intermittent drift of guitars. The night-flowering shrubs around him were heavy with scent. "What now?" he asked as Sam closed the cigarette case.

"Al will be here in a couple of minutes. He and three friends—Max sent them in from Córdoba just in case we needed some support—are up on the road above the house."

And I still don't know what made them drag their bloody feet, thought Ferrier, but he said nothing.

"They saw Gene Lucas get into his car and drive off."

"Al let him go—just like that?" It was hard for Ferrier to keep criticism out of his voice in spite of all his good resolutions.

"We want Lucas in Málaga. That's where he will be heading, right now. We want him to feel safe and undiscovered." Sam laughed softly. "He kept well out of sight tonight, didn't he? But that's his line; he's the boy in the background, pulls the wires, watches the puppets jump. And we'll watch his puppets, too, see just how far and deep they reach back into America."

"When did he start running out of here?"

"As soon as your toy pistol started shooting. He had come

partway up through the terraces, just to check—from the background, of course—what was going on. I kept in the shadows. I had hidden—well, come on and see. We'd better carry it upstairs, anyway, help Al and his Spanish friends clean up the mess." He was hurrying along the narrow terrace, Ferrier following quickly. "There wasn't much cover for me up here, so I went down onto the second tier." He descended a short flight of steep stone steps, high and narrow. "I chose this one, right here." He pointed to the apricot tree, planted close against the wall that backed up to the terrace overhead.

"More comfortable than those," Ferrier said, and looked at a neighboring clump of stiff saw-toothed leaves. "Spanish bayonets." But the Spaniards wouldn't call them that. Perhaps French bayonets? Napoleon's legacy.

"Then this figure came drifting up from the third terrace. A careful type. Melted into the shadows. Moved soundlessly. Except I was expecting someone to come up and guard these windows upstairs. If you and Tavita were the kind who'd leave old Magdalena on the couch and make a dash for the terrace—well, you'd never have made it." Sam shook his head. He said nothing more. He led the way down onto the lowest terrace. Here, there were more bushes and shrubs planted against its back wall. "And this is where he landed." He pointed to the paving stones underfoot.

"You threw him from the second terrace?"

"After I jumped him." Sam chopped his hand sharply, karate-style.

"And where—"

"Behind here. Small problem. Give me a hand." Sam reached behind a high flowering shrub, avoided the jagged blades of Spanish bayonets which grew nearby. "I had to hide him in a hurry when I heard Lucas' footsteps coming this way."

They got the man out from his shroud of sweet-smelling petals, laid him on the terrace flagstones. Ferrier struck a match, shielded it, looked down at the dead man's face. He looked peaceful. He was the man who had killed Jeff Reid, and then walked so calmly out of the hospital.

"Did I get the right one?" Sam asked, showing his first sign of anxiety.

"Yes."

"Heave him over my shoulders."

"Why not over the wall?"

"And let him scare the daylights out of some poor guy who's strumming his guitar in his own back yard? No. We'll give him a taste of his own brew. He was going to drive the Buick. It's up on the road waiting for him." Sam's lips were tight. "Let's get him upstairs."

Amanda's car. Ferrier looked at Sam's strangely grim face, felt his own heart flinch. "I'll give you a hand. Quicker, that way. Tell me—is there any news of—"

"Wiser, too. If Al doesn't wait for someone to answer the doorbell, Tavita may start using that .38 on him. She isn't much in the mood for any more invasions." That silenced any questions from Ferrier. Both their energies went into getting the limp body up the steep climb to the main terrace. There, they dropped it just outside the wall of windows. "That's far enough." Sam was watching Tavita. She had recovered a little, and was working off her restlessness by walking around the room, closing drawers, pushing back silks and satins into the chests. On the couch, Magdalena was deep in an untroubled sleep.

Ferrier caught Sam's arm as he was about to enter. "Did Al have any news of Amanda?"

"He has been searching for her. That was the delay—"

"News?" Ferrier insisted.

How do I tell him? Sam wondered. He brought two small objects out of his pocket, opened his palm to let Ferrier see them. "I found these on the man with the chest wound."

Ferrier picked up the pencil. "This is Amanda's. I don't know about the lighter."

"It's a camera, actually. That son of a bitch who stole it didn't know its value, either."

Ferrier said slowly, "She wanted to take a photograph. I talked her out of it." He handed the little silver pencil back to Sam. "But perhaps I didn't," he said very quietly. "Did she go back up there?" And then, "But I saw her get into a cab. I saw her. And drove away."

"We found the driver. She got into his taxi, changed her mind, joined a busload of people walking up to the Generalife. But they were too slow for her. She hurried ahead of them. Then the taxi driver got another fare."

Ferrier said nothing.

"Al started an intensive search, once we had placed her at the Generalife. We knew the exact area where she was heading, so we concentrated on that. But no results."

She is dead, Ferrier thought, and Sam is wondering how to tell me. "And where did you find her?"

"In her car."

"Up there on that road? When?"

"Five minutes ago. Just before I spoke with Al." Sam waited. There were no further questions. So he tried to explain. "First, they must have taken her to the house where they put the old girl." He looked over at Magdalena. "But nothing like that," he added quickly. "No marks on her. A broken neck. What you might expect if her car crashed into a tree on her way back to Málaga. Yes, I think that was their plan for her."

Ferrier turned away, started indoors.

"Look—I'm just telling you why Al was late in getting here." Sam had been more resentful about that than he had allowed himself to appear. "When the Lucas car and the Buick left the hotel early, Al had a couple of men tail them. That's how we discovered the house. They saw Magdalena being taken out; then Amanda—"

"I don't need the details," Ferrier said harshly. "And there's the doorbell."

Tavita stood in the middle of her peaceful room. She looked around her with wonder. The strange young men had left, and Sam was out in the garage. The two bodies had been removed, a thin carpet was rolled around one of them, while the other— brought in from the terrace without a wound on him—was being taken to some Buick up on the road. The prisoners had gone, too, jammed into the big American car that had stood for all that hideous hour outside her front door. There were still scars and stains, her quick eyes noted, but rugs had been pulled over the worst ones. And tomorrow, she thought, I will have my own people scour and polish. Now all she had to do was to close the door behind her and go to the garage, where Sam had already placed Magdalena inside the big car. He was going to drive them. Ferrier, Sam had explained to her privately, had to get back to the hotel, and she wasn't to question him or talk much, and least of all was she to let him know that Sam had told her so.

"I'm ready," she told Ian Ferrier now. Together they walked out of the house. Ferrier locked the door, gave her the key. "Don't worry," she told him, "I shall be safe. I am taking Magdalena to friends—a doctor who is devoted to me—he runs a very good clinic. She will get well. And I am no longer afraid. Thank you, Ian."

"I'll be leaving Granada tomorrow."

I guessed that, she thought. "Then we will meet when you come back." She reached up, kissed him. "To some happier time," she said, with tears suddenly filling the large beautiful dark eyes. She left him before he could say anything, got into the car.

Sam waved as they passed Ferrier, felt better when he saw Ferrier nod and wave back.

"Did he really want to walk to the hotel?" Tavita asked. "We could easily have given him a lift."

"He wanted to walk."

"And not talk?" she asked shrewdly.

"Well—he's had a pretty rough day."

She was silent for a few moments. "Tell me, was there really a bomb? In my house?"

"You have quick ears."

"The men were speaking in Spanish. It was easy to have quick ears. A bomb . . . Esteban will never believe it."

"Don't mention it to Esteban or anyone else."

"But why shouldn't I—"

"It would be one way of saying thank you to all of us."

"You come from Madrid. I knew it. Your accent. Your manner—so self-contained, so independent."

"No, my mother came from Madrid. My father from Barcelona. I am strictly Toledo. Toledo, Ohio." He broke into a wide grin.

She looked at him, incredulous. And then she thought how pleasant it was to be startled only by something as simple as a joke. "Very well," she said. "I shall tell no one—not Esteban, not anyone—about the bomb. I shall put everything out of my mind. Except—when I dance and the music is angry. Then I shall think of these men."

Sam glanced in the rear-view window before he turned off this stretch of quiet dark road with gardens walling it on either side. Ian Ferrier had come out of the driveway. He was walking slowly, hands in his pockets, head bent.

"You see him?" Tavita asked quickly. She turned to look, but the car had swung to the left.

"Yes. He's all right. The walk is just what he needed." What I need, too, thought Sam. A rough day for all and everyone, and I have a couple of hours ahead of me before I can relax and take a deep breath and have a little time to feel and think. Then as the car passed under an avenue of trees, broken moonlight dappling the road ahead of them, he heard the murmur of little fountains, flowing water, sad and plaintive. "Do you know Machado's poem?" he asked. She didn't, of course, but he quoted a line from it, anyway. *"Granada, agua oculta que llora."*

She shook her head. "That is too sad. There is another Granada. A hundred other Granadas. When you come back—you will come back?"

He laughed and nodded a half-promise, which was all he could ever guarantee. Here today, and tomorrow where? "I'll see you dance in Málaga." That was one promise he would like to keep.

Ferrier went out onto his small balcony, leaned his arms on the railing, looked down over the steep drop to a cluster of lighted streets far below. The noises were distant, rising in muted waves to reach him up here on these heights. Pleasant to hear: faraway laughter, a child's high voice calling, a surge of guitars. There was a little square strung with bright-colored bulbs, crowded with strolling couples. And beside it, the old church, with its small tower illuminated and its bells silenced, stood guard.

"Come in. The door's open," he called over his shoulder. He wasn't the least surprised to see Sam. "Everything under control?" he asked briskly. Sam looked relieved, came out to join him on the balcony. "Just getting a bird's-eye view," Ferrier said, and pointed down. "Odd, isn't it? Every Sunday night that little square will be lighted, the same people will walk there, new children will appear and the older ones will start strolling with their girls instead of throwing a ball around. Every Sunday night . . ."

"Not for me," Sam decided. "Not for you, either."

"I guess not. But it's kind of nice to watch."

"Have you eaten?"

"I didn't feel too hungry. Thought I'd get to bed early. But I don't feel much in the need of sleep, either."

"What about dinner with me?"

"It's after midnight."

"The kitchen is still cooking its head off."

"No. You go. I'll just unwind here for another half hour."

Sam relaxed completely. Ferrier's voice was easy, his manner natural. He had taken off his tie, opened the neck of his shirt, and now he sat down on the sill of the French windows and stretched his legs comfortably. "That walk did you good."

"Yes. It cleared my head. Got the old brains working again. And I came to a decision."

"Oh?" Sam lit himself a cigarette.

"I'm giving you all six months, Sam."

Sam took the cigarette out of his mouth, stared at Ferrier. "What's that?"

"Six months to watch Gene Lucas, learn everything you can about him and his contacts, find out just how much danger he is to the country. And then I'm coming back. To Málaga. And I'll deal with him myself."

"What?" repeated Sam.

"I'll take care of him," Ferrier's calm, quiet voice said.

There was a pause. "We may take care of him ourselves before that."

"Then good and well. But if some of the higher-ups start stalling, want more time, keep thinking up new notions—well, they are going to be disappointed. You'll know all you need to know in six months."

"You're crazy."

"Now that," said Ferrier with some amusement, "is just a little below your normal level of thought. On the contrary, Sam, I'm being very sane when I say that Gene Lucas has already done too much damage. And you are crazy if you let him run around loose. Are you?"

"Not that crazy."

"So you agree with me?"

"I see your point."

"That's that," said Ferrier. He rose to his feet. "I'll be moving off early tomorrow." For Madrid. And a meeting, if that was possible, with Adam Reid. What shall I get? A sullen look, a smartaleck snub? Or some human questions, a willingness to listen even a little to another side of an unhappy story, perhaps a show —just one small show—of compassion? Useless, Rodriguez had said yesterday; but he had kept his promise and delivered Adam's address, a small scrap of paper slipped quietly under Ferrier's door this evening. Useless? All I can do is try, thought Ferrier. That is all that Jeff Reid would ask for. A try.

Sam was watching him. "You know, you might do better to take it easy for the next day or so. What's the rush?"

Yes, thought Ferrier, take it easy for a day and then find Adam Reid had gone before I reached Madrid. He smiled and said, "I'm tougher than I look." He held out his hand, added, "You did a good job, Sam. All of you. Glad you are on our side."

They shook hands firmly. "See you around," Sam said.

"Sometime," Ferrier completed. They both laughed.

"Oh, by the way—" Sam signed to Ferrier to come indoors. He dropped his voice back to the old conspiratorial level. "I've just had word from Bob O'Connor. They got to Seville without incident. He's now aboard the plane, en route for Madrid."

"And Waterman?"

"Churning out all his oldest jokes. Just a little ray of sunshine."

"How many men does O'Connor have with him on that flight?"

"Five. Enough to please you?" Then he turned serious. "We owe you a lot, Ian. That's what Bob said. Special thanks to you."

"I'll pass it on to Jeff Reid. And Amanda."

Sam hesitated. "There was a film in that camera. Two clear pictures, a third blurred. Waterman is cooked. She got the proof."

There was a long silence.

Sam spoke again. "She would say it was worth it, Ian. If she did not believe that, she would never have been in this job." He paused, asked with real sympathy, "Did you know her well?"

Ferrier thought about that. "No. And yes." Then he said in that quiet, cool voice, "I only met her twice." But she will be hard to forget. "Good night, Sam."

And when he was alone, Ferrier went back to the window, sat down on the sill again. From here, he had a wide view of the dark-blue canopy overhead, soft and rich, like a throw of velvet. A solitary guitar was playing, its slow unhappy music rising to him from a distant street, losing itself as it tried to reach the stars. This, thought Ferrier, was how it all began. A guitar in a court-yard, the night sky above . . . Jeff, and Tavita. And Amanda.

Yes, she would be hard to forget.

The guitar died away. He rose and went back into his room Tomorrow was an early start.